Perfume
GIRL

USA TODAY BESTSELLING AUTHOR
VANESSA FEWINGS

Cover design by Najla Qamber
(NajlaQamberDesigns)

Cover photo from Depositphotos: Martyna1802
Formatted by: Champagne Book Design
Book edited by Debbie Kuhn

ISBN: 9781725976511

Perfume is the art that makes memory speak.

—Francis Kurkdjian

For Margaret

Chapter
ONE

Raquel

Before

THE LOVING FINGERS THAT SWEPT OVER THE PETALS OF THE SWEET-smelling rose were the same ones that cut through its thorny stem with shears.

I'll give you another life, I thought, dropping the shears to the ground.

I raised my gaze to the bay window to see if Mummy had stirred. She usually slept in, allowing my nine-year-old mischievous self to take advantage of her absence.

I continued exploring the garden's gems, finding a sprig of mint. I plucked it from the ground for the sole purpose of turning it into perfume.

The roses wither and fall, but not you. I've chosen you and surely that means something, surely that alone soothes the bitterness.

Inhaling its delicate perfume, I carried my little treasure across the garden all the way to the bottom of our property and opened the door to the corner shed, hurrying in and finding my usual place on the tarpaulin to protect my dress's hem. On my knees, surrounded by tools that hung where my father had left them weeks before he left, I plucked each velvety petal from the blossom and dropped them into the base of my marble mortar. Reaching for the round-ended pestle reserved for grinding herbs from this very garden, I began crushing them with a twist of my wrist.

Although I knew stealing a flower from our garden was wrong, I couldn't deny myself the poetic pleasure of smelling the sweet licorice scent that filled the air.

Yet nature is selfish.

I batted off a wayward bee, lured by the aroma of my precious elixir, too enticing for an insect driven by its obsession with nectar to resist. When the black and yellow insect persisted, I waved my pestle in the air until it rushed to escape, blurring from sight.

My focus returned to creating a perfume unlike any other. This is what I imagined glamour to be…the pathway to a happy ever after, a pampering self-love in liquid form. I'd surprise my mum with this later and make her smile.

Yesterday, when she'd braved leaving the house and we took the bus into Truro to visit the elegant perfumery near the cathedral, I had watched her sniff scents from the prettiest glass bottles. Her worry lines softened as she forgot herself in that sweet-smelling room, choosing a favorite scent and rubbing her wrists together—a perfume she never bought.

"It's not quite in our budget," she told me. "Maybe I'll get it for Christmas."

I had wondered who would buy it for her. After all, Daddy was gone and she never spoke to Grandma…and I was far from being able to afford it.

I watched her sadness return as she led me toward the cathedral to speak to a God that never answered her, no matter how much she bruised her knees in prayer. Or so it seemed.

I would find another way—create my own for her.

The petals within my mortar were giving up their perfume and waiting patiently for me to add other ingredients to balance out the bouquet—like a dash of lavender or ginger, or even the spice I would hunt down later.

A beetle crawled up my forearm to take a closer look at all this activity in his usually quiet sanctuary. I brushed him off with care and watched him scurry across the uneven ground back to his hideout.

A minute later I heard a familiar buzzing sound. Though this time the bee sounded angry—

Suddenly I felt a sting and an all-consuming pain in my forearm. I panicked as my throat swelled and dizziness overtook me.

I had a vague sense of being carried out in someone's arms.

I never did return to the garden or that house. Not even the street.

And though it had been flowers that had ruined my life, I'd remained under their spell. This, after all, was how I held on to the memory of my old life.

The one with Mummy.

My brush with death in that idyllic English countryside changed everything. Three days later, after being released from the hospital, I stepped over the threshold of my first foster home.

I stood at Mrs. Clark's living room window and peered out at her well-tended garden.

And I began again.

Grinding petals into the base of a pestle, sure if I got the formula right and created a pretty scent, I'd get it to Mummy and somehow, some way, we would go home.

Chapter
TWO

Raquel

FROM WHERE I SAT ON THE WHITE LEATHER SOFA IN DAZZLE AND Bazaar's waiting room, staring through the impressive window overlooking Plaza Street, I could see the downpour had lifted and the sun had broken through the clouds. Unlike England, Orlando's climate would be warm despite the rain.

Even now, after living on the other side of the pond for years, I marveled at the sunny weather. The invigorating rays brightened my Monday morning.

"It'll be a few more minutes, Ms. Wren." The receptionist's voice drew my gaze away from the window. "They're just finishing up."

The pretty blonde had spent the last twenty minutes unabashedly looking at her iPhone from behind the desk. Her pale blue eyes were now focused on me.

I feigned a grateful smile. "Thank you."

She returned her attention to the phone.

Don't do this.

Don't give away your finest work.

I pretended this was easy for me. That being here and doing this was just fine.

"How much longer do you think it will be?"

"Five minutes."

Perfect. Enough time to check my hair and make-up. I pushed myself up and walked the few short steps to the restroom.

Even in here I found a classic elegance—pristine gold taps and marble sinks. In minutes, I'd be sitting opposite the infamous Anna Rosenthal and I was determined to wow her. She could be cold—I'd read that about her—and impatient. Each second in her presence counted.

I stood in front of the mirror and fluffed my long brunette hair, which shone with amber highlights. The same sun that had tinted my locks had brought out freckles that kissed my nose and cheeks. After softening the eyeliner beneath my turquoise eyes, I retouched my lipstick.

This morning I'd gone for dynamic and now I just saw severity looking back. I changed my mind and decided the "girl next door" look offered a less competitive edge and I needed this to be all about my product instead of about me. Anna hated self-importance, too, apparently.

I faked a smile—a convincing one that said all was well in my life and I was a shining example of success. Anna didn't need to know my world was falling apart.

Not once had I considered the possibility that I would be divorced at thirty, a recent separation after what had felt like a happy marriage. But as I straightened my pencil skirt and smoothed my gold satin blouse, I felt my self-respect returning.

I recognized that brightness in my gaze, that sense of aliveness.

I was back.

The drive from Dunedin had been pleasant—fun even—in my open-top Alfa Romeo. No matter how much Damien wanted it I was keeping the car. It was my ex-husband's fault I was here.

Still, if I managed to license my new scent I would be able to save Perfume Girl—my beloved store nestled on Broadway in Dunedin. My heart and soul was invested in that place and I wasn't going to let it go without a fight. It was either this plan or I would have to sell my perfumery and give him half the money. The bastard didn't deserve anything. Not after leaving me for *her.*

I'd found a way out of this nightmare and licensing my new scent was it. Even if it broke my heart to let it go.

His greed left me no choice but to offer my new fragrance to one of the industry's prominent companies. A formula so alluring it would take the industry by storm with its unique properties. It needed one more ingredient to elevate it to a new level, but that would only be shared with Anna after a contract was signed.

It was my finest work.

Licensing it would enable me to take my life back. If I kept this special scent for my business, it would sell well but I would be challenged to market it to a wider audience on my modest budget.

Time I didn't have.

Raising my head high and exuding a sense of calm, I left the restroom and made my way back to the waiting area, reaching into my handbag for the bottle of perfume. I would present this to Anna Rosenthal within seconds of entering that meeting.

Start out strong.

Hell, yes.

This was my moment to shine.

I jolted to a stop, my hand continuing to rummage in my handbag, not feeling the small Lalique bottle.

The receptionist raised her gaze. "They're ready for you, Ms. Wren." She pointed to her right. "Through that door."

Kneeling on the carpet, I tipped my bag and spilled the contents, searching for the precious object.

"It's gone," I said, my voice cracking.

"You forgot something?"

"I double checked before I left."

She got up and rounded her desk. "They're waiting."

"It doesn't make any sense." I mentally replayed every step I had taken this morning. "I...don't know what happened."

"Wanna reschedule?"

She was right, of course. You didn't keep an executive like Anna Rosenthal waiting. Her status was far-reaching. She was to perfume what Coco Chanel was to fashion. A legend in her own right—and I'd been moments away from meeting her. A *yes* from her would have breathed new life into my career.

Vaguely, I realized the receptionist had walked back behind her desk.

Her gaze met mine above her computer screen. "Three weeks okay?"

"It will be too late."

This was my last chance to save my life's work.

"I'll let them know you're cancelling."

Stunned, I returned the items to my bag and pushed unsteadily to my feet. *This is my walk of shame*, I thought, making my way back along the hallway decorated with colorful photos of my competitors' products—scents welcomed in the highest echelons of Dazzle and Bazaar.

I took the elevator down.

With my heart racing I headed out to the parking lot. Desperation had me searching every inch of my car for the finely cut glass bottle that held my future.

Finally I gave up and slumped in exasperation in the driver's seat. Taking a moment, I sat there gripping the steering wheel unable to drive.

I blew it.

Solemnly, and half in a daze, I drove those terrible hours back to Dunedin. Not even the journey over the bridge with its sweeping ocean views on either side could soothe the ache of failure.

You left it on the countertop, I said reassuringly to myself as I parked my car outside the store. I managed to get the key in the door's lock at last, my hands shaking in anticipation.

Once inside, I scanned the countertops for my bottle, inhaling the heavenly aromas that melded together from a generous collection of both vintage bottles and modern pieces meant for the younger crowd and their flair for fun.

The same fun I had given up to make this place a reality. I couldn't fathom losing my beloved store. Couldn't understand how my usual pedantic methods had fallen short. I was a chemist, for goodness sake. Nothing I did was spontaneous or without conscious effort.

Usually, I would be pleasantly distracted by the sunlight flooding in through the front bay window, reflecting off the rows of perfume samples and throwing colorful rainbow patterns around the room—but not now.

Now I was frantic.

The bottle wasn't here.

I couldn't understand how it had slipped away from me. I had left the store at ten this morning after placing the bottle in my handbag. After locking up, I had raced off to fight the traffic so I could make good time for my meeting with Anna.

Where the hell was it?

I hurried down the hallway and shoved open the door to the work-room, ready to scour the countertops. I stopped short when I saw my set of scales on the floor, smashed to pieces. Where my iMac had once sat was a fine square of dust.

Breathe.

Heart racing, I glanced toward the stairs that led to my private space, listening for any noise that might hint the thief was still here. The alarm had failed…though I remembered setting it right before I left.

How could so much go wrong so quickly?

In a daze, I walked toward the storeroom cupboard that was ajar and cautiously stepped inside. My Orris root oil was gone, my most expensive ingredient flown in from abroad. I backed out and spun around, realizing all my formulas were gone.

I still had my notes.

Right?

As long as my ledger was untouched I could replicate my cre-ations—including the one that was two years in the making. Each minuscule drop carefully documented in that ledger, each tincture extracted, each combination of bourbon vanilla, rare spices from Tibet, roses from Penzance.

Every day of the last two years dedicated to not only running this place but crafting a wondrous fragrance. I had perfected its top notes and painstakingly tweaked its base notes until I'd captured a scent with all its complex mysteries. More than this, I had invoked an ethereal experience, a profound sense of being.

Hurrying over to the cabinet where I kept my ledger, I reached out and grasped the drawer handle, knuckles taut with tension. I stole a few seconds to stir my courage. The formula was so elaborate it had been impossible to memorize.

That ledger had to be in here.

As this truth burned through me, I inhaled a desperate breath and pulled open the drawer.

Chapter
THREE

THERE WAS ONLY ONE WOMAN I WOULD ALLOW TO DERAIL MY MONDAY.
Though, admittedly, The Artisan Cafe was a decent choice for
lunch, so this spontaneous meeting with Penelope would at least
be bearable.

Dealing with my sister was at times entertaining and other times
strained. Our personal visions for our company clashed with the same
fervor as the Cuban blood surging through our veins, albeit third gener-
ation. Penelope's volatile temperament and my more reasoned outbursts
saw us flashing hot and cold and everything in between. Of course, running a multi-million dollar business meant that passion was the bedrock
of our success.

Here, in the outside seating area, I waited for the concierge to tell
me which table would be ours. Beyond, upon still waters, a yacht sailed
by and I took a deep, envious breath of fresh air, wishing it was me out
there on that never-ending blue expanse.

The serenity here wouldn't last.

The tables would fill with diners and all of them would be vying
for the best view overlooking Bel Harbor with its stretch of Atlantic.

"Sir, your table's ready," said the young waitress, ending my daydreams.

Turning, I threw the petite blonde a warm smile and she froze for a beat. This wasn't an uncommon response. My heritage had awarded me a light golden complexion, and my raven locks contrasted appealingly with my hazel eyes. Today I was wearing a bespoke suit tailored with extraordinary skill and cut to highlight my physique. I took more amusement than I should have from towering over her, reveling in her soft blush when I flashed a wicked grin.

"I have a great table for you with the best view." She licked her lips seductively.

Okay. That was an interesting development; her tongue was pierced and that shiny bauble promised no end of pleasure. I gave her another heart-stopping smile.

She spun around and led the way.

I strolled the short distance across the patio wondering why my unpredictable sister had chosen to meet here rather than our South Beach office.

"Thank you," I said graciously as I sat. "Someone is joining me."

"That's fine." Her gaze flitted to the empty seat. "Can I start you off with a drink?"

Start me off?

Those years at Eton in England had garnered me with an unquestionable arrogance when it came to the use of language—after my highbrow education where I'd sat in classrooms beside future kings, sons of presidents, and the men who would become Dubai's finest leaders. I'd returned to South Beach bearing unrealistic expectations that no mortal could live up to. British aristocracy had threaded its way beneath my skin and I still hadn't shaken it.

While there, I had been taught to favor luxury over austerity, pleasure over pain, and had been exposed to an addictive level of power. It left me with expensive tastes in all things, including sex. I liked my pussy gold-plated—a woman who could match my intellectual sparring. But not a relationship...not even close. I preferred the "fuck me hard and call me if you want" kind of lover. The non-clingy, no commitment necessary type.

"Start me off" girl may have tempted my diabolical side but she was too sweet to ravage. And although my imagination ran wild with how I could bring this flirty bud to blossom, my demands would no doubt leave her weak, needy, and addicted to a level of passion she hadn't earned. Wallflowers needn't apply.

Though that blush on her cheeks was alluring, and I couldn't deny the soft scent of vanilla gave off the impression of pure innocence. What followed were the rakish notes of bubblegum—fucking bubblegum. She was wearing *Play With Me,* a scent that made me die inside each time I caught a waft.

"Water. Still." And as it was Penelope's habit to be late I reached for the menu and considered an appetizer. "Sparkling water, too, please." My sister would be out of breath and thirsty, or at least she'd feign she was for keeping me waiting.

I set about conducting business on my iPhone, as time was too valuable to burn.

The waitress returned with our drinks and casually slid a coaster toward me. It had a phone number on it. Hers, I assumed.

There was no regret in her fresh-faced expression. "I know I shouldn't," she admitted.

"What's your name?"

"Skye."

"You want me to call you later, Skye?" I flipped the coaster between my thumb and forefinger. "After your shift?"

She batted her eyelids flirtatiously. "If you like."

"And then take you out on a date?" I leaned back, intrigued by her forwardness.

"Sure." She pressed a tray to her chest as though it were a shield.

"And then?" I coaxed.

"Then?"

"I would take you to a luxurious setting where a bed would be waiting and then bring you so much pleasure I would ruin you for all other men." I shrugged. "Doesn't seem fair."

"Maybe there'd be more?"

"More?"

"Maybe we'd get along and things would become serious?"

"And then boredom would set in. A kind of slow death."

She chewed her lip, seemingly annoyed by the way I'd rounded out our tedious future.

I leaned forward. "Can I let you in on a secret?"

"Yes," she answered quickly, her tone breathy.

"Before you commit to any time spent with me go read *Dante's Inferno*, it's a reasonable preview." Noting her frown, I added, "It's a fourteenth century poem—"

"I know what it is."

"Good. I desire nothing more than to take you through Purgatory—and if you pass that level, Heaven—"

She looked shocked. "The next one's Hell."

"So it is."

Her confliction turned to consideration.

"Welcome to Purgatory," I said matter-of-factly. "How's it looking from the cheap seats?"

She reached for the coaster and snatched it back. She hurried away, turning her head to glance over her shoulder at me with a seductive smile to hide her embarrassment.

I wasn't in the habit of seducing spring-breakers and then decimating their hearts. No, I preferred a different kind of woman altogether. Someone older, more confident—a woman with verve who would not be threatened by my desire to ravish her into oblivion.

I'd been kind to Skye. Maybe it was the ocean air that had brought out my congenial side and my decision not to ruin her.

A slender woman hurried toward me in an inspiring flurry of frenetic energy. Penelope's stride grew faster when she saw me. "Am I late?"

I tucked my phone into my jacket and gave her my usual look of disapproval, which she dutifully earned on a daily basis.

I'd made the best use of my time by answering emails, sending off texts to my staff at The House of Beauregard, and had even gone over our sales numbers. Our business was thriving and we were fast becoming a front-runner. However, the competition was always hot on our heels. There were too many perfumers out there with vintage scents that had garnered loyal customers. The same customers I was going to steal away from them with my superior products.

I threw my sister an unimpressed smile.

And then it wafted over me…

She was wearing a scent so devastating it took me a few seconds to gather my thoughts. The notes stilled my mind and elicited an easy escape from the present—a masterstroke that was truly humbling.

Penelope's smirk revealed her mischievous side. She knew I'd picked up on her new perfume and the fact she was wearing a competitor's scent was maddening. Irked, I perused the menu pretending to read it as I quietly seethed.

Skye reappeared and took our order, all the while avoiding my gaze. That deranged whiff of bubblegum came back around to assault me and I coughed to clear my airway. She caught the intensity of my disapproving glare and spun around and hurried briskly toward the kitchen.

"What happened?" Penelope reached for her serviette and laid it over her lap.

"In what regard?"

"Astor?" Penelope said, her tone amused. "What did you say to her?"

"The waitress?" I recalled our last interaction. "Something like, 'I'll have the lobster salad. Light on the dressing.'"

"You scared her."

"Me?" I reached for my glass.

Penelope blew out an exasperated sigh.

"So has the time come for you to leave the business?" I asked flatly.

"Why would I?"

"That's not why we're here? So you can tell me privately?"

"No, it's not." She sat back. "Why would you say that?"

"You're never in the office. You hate the lab. You're reluctant to attend PR meetings. And I'm using the word 'reluctant' as a courtesy. Though you do enjoy wearing the profits." That strike was aimed at her Chanel suit. "What's going on?"

She waved her hand in annoyance. "I work from home. You should try it. You work too hard. You've grown boring."

"In what way?"

Skye reappeared with two plates of imaginatively displayed salads and placed one in front of each of us.

She focused on Penelope. "Will there be anything else, ma'am?"

My sister gave a gesture of dismissal and turned back to me. "How's Vedado?"

"My horses are fine. All of them."

"He's your favorite."

"I don't have a favorite." My spine straightened. She was wearing a fragrance I didn't recognize. It was remarkable. "What perfume are you wearing?"

"I've been working on something unique for us."

I sat back stunned at her admission.

Her face brightened. "It's exciting and arousing and—"

"You created this?"

Penelope lifted her Hermes bag and rested it on her lap, rummaging around in it for an annoyingly long time.

Forcing a courteous smile I said, "You have it on you?"

With a triumphant flip of her wrist she presented a small Lalique bottle containing a clear liquid. Shards of light reflected off the crystal in a hypnotic prelude to the fragrance.

"It's not finished though, right?"

She looked impressed. "I'm almost there. Thought I'd get your input as you're the expert at refinement."

"Is that Oud I'm picking up?"

Penelope removed the stopper and raised the bottle with pride. She rose a little out of her seat, leaned over the table and sprayed. I waved the mist away from my face.

"Well?" She tucked her tongue in her cheek.

I pushed to my feet and my chair scraped loudly. It drew unwanted attention. "I have a meeting."

"You don't like it?"

It was the fact that this masterpiece had been showcased in a damn restaurant. This wasn't proper etiquette, it was classless, and she knew this setting would throw me off and give her the advantage. A place she loved to reign.

Snatching the bottle out of her hand, I clutched it in my palm possessively. "I'll take a look."

"Hey!"

"I'll see you back at the office." I pulled out my wallet and tossed cash on the table to cover lunch as well as a new perfume.

"You haven't finished your meal!" Penelope called after me.

The scent she'd spritzed me with soaked into my senses and a shiver ran up my spine. I spun around and faced her.

She looked amused. "It's good, right?"

"It's worth a closer look."

Yes, there was genius here, but it needed something more…

I made a beeline for the door and entered the inside seating area, weaving my way through the tables.

In the corner, Skye was chatting with the barman who was placing drinks on her tray. She saw me and hurried over.

"My sister will take care of the check," I reassured her.

Skye's scent was a cacophony of noisy notes, reminding me of a crazy night out doing shots and other unscrupulous acts of rebellion. Conduct that would end up being recorded on a phone and streamed online, tarnishing an already shaky future.

I gave her a warm smile. "Skye, may I offer you some life-changing advice?"

She looked intrigued.

"Don't wear *Play With Me*. Go with something like *Espíritu de Amor* or *La Vida es un Angel's Quest*. The House of Beauregard has an exceptional line. "

She rested her hands on her hips. "Like I can afford that."

"I left you a generous tip, Skye. May I suggest you use it for the sole purpose of not smelling like a call girl?"

"And you'd know how a call girl smells."

"Only the high-end ones." I headed for the door.

"What are you wearing?" she asked.

Turning, I studied her awed expression.

"I like that one," she said as she studied the delicate bottle in my hand. "It's different, it's…"

"It's not finished. I need more time with it."

"What?"

"This is too sophisticated for you," I shot back. "You've not gotten to the age where you can appreciate the profoundness of being."

Because that's exactly what this scent elicited…a profound aliveness.

She hurried after me and rose on her toes to whisper, "There's a name for men like you."

I smiled. "Yes, and it probably describes me perfectly."

I walked away from her.

"Sure you don't want my number?" she called after me.

The fresh sea air hit me when I stepped outside and my *Jesus, take the wheel* moment was answered as Skye's bubblegum scent released its claws.

Yet this one…

The same one kissing my skin, the same one Penelope had a hand in was absorbed into my being. This scent was a goddamned miracle. My mind reeled over the fact that it had been my sister who had developed this masterpiece.

Climbing into my Mercedes, I drew in a luxurious, serene breath, reluctant to let this experience dissipate.

I could finish this…refine its chemistry and take it all the way to perfection.

Chapter
FOUR

Raquel

DESPITE FEELINGS OF HUMILIATION, I HELD MY HEAD HIGH AS I navigated the tables of Dunedin's La Traviata, all the while ignoring the glances from staff who knew I was the ex of their head chef.

Standing in the doorway, staring across the sleek kitchen, my gaze fell on the man who I had once found mesmerizing. Even now—after the carnage of our divorce—I still understood why I had fallen so hard.

Though that love had been shattered the moment I saw Damien with *her*.

The memories flashed real and raw as I watched him preparing a signature dish…

"Happy Birthday!" The masseuse's forceful fingertips found all the right places, forcing the tension out of my tired limbs.

"Thank you," I replied, grateful for it all.

"What a terrific husband."

"He is," I managed to say, despite the pressure of her elbow between my shoulder blades. "He's spoiling me."

Everything about this spa was heavenly, from the classical music to the hypnotic massage oil that had me nearly drifting off.

Afterward, I showered and prepared for my next treatment. A manicure and pedicure that I needed after spending the last three weeks tackling Christmas season in Dunedin. Though it had been hard work, I had seen my sales soar and my brands becoming more popular.

The interview published in Vogue had made a big difference to my online sales too, and this had been my best year yet.

Waiting in the private spa to be called for my next treatment, I was met by an associate.

"Mrs. Silver," she greeted me. "I'm sorry. Kristen was supposed to do your nails, but she had to leave. Everyone else is booked up. I understand it's your birthday, and we want to bring you back to make up for this."

I'd been looking forward to this treat—my nails were almost badger-esk.

I let out a sigh. "That's fine. I hope everything works out with Kristen."

She handed me a piece of paper. "Here's a coupon for any two services, not including the one you didn't get today. Happy birthday."

Yes, another year down and feeling just as fabulous.

After the heavenly massage, the drive home was even more relaxing. I peered out my window at the lush beauty of green trees, exotic wildlife and endless ocean. We'd be heading out on the water this afternoon with a picnic hamper and a heart full of happiness.

Though I did think it strange my husband had booked me a spa day so far away from home. There and back was an hour's drive. As usual, he probably had been in a hurry due to running a busy restaurant.

I pulled into the driveway of our home, noticing a red Mazda parked to the side. Wondering who it belonged to, I peered through the driver's window looking for clues, but didn't see anything that gave the owner's identity away. Perhaps his mother had gotten a new car.

I let myself into the house and came to an abrupt stop when I saw a handbag on the kitchen counter—a Burberry. With my heart thundering in my chest, I closed the gap between me and the island and opened the purse.

I wasn't meant to be back yet.

Feeling numb, I walked into the foyer. I paused at the bottom of the staircase, and then slowly began the ascent to the upper floor. I didn't want this to *be true…didn't want to believe Damien would betray me.*

How could I possibly survive the pain?

I told myself there had to be a good explanation, though my throat still tightened in trepidation as I made my way down the hallway to our bedroom.

The two of them were on our bed, their clothes strewn on the floor right next to my dignity.

The naked blonde was on all fours with her butt in the air. Damien was pounding her from behind, his grunts matching her loud moans thrust for thrust.

Five months after our divorce, the ache in my chest still hadn't lifted…nor would it ever.

La Traviata's kitchen was hot as hell and I wondered how the staff could stand it.

Damien's blonde locks were damp and ruffled. The deep blue eyes that were capable of so much kindness were focused on his work as he stood at the central island.

He sliced through the bloody slab of meat with the same indifferent precision he'd used to slice through my life.

That tattooed hunk had once been my everything.

His gaze rose to meet mine and for a moment, just a moment, he looked happy to see me. That lazy smile reached his eyes, crinkling into warmth.

Feeling wary, I took a deep breath and bravely stepped toward him. "Hey."

The smile faded. "Raquel, you need to call first." There was tension in the way he held his knife.

I glanced over at his colleague. "Can you give us a moment, please?"

"We're kind of busy, babe." Damien threw an apologetic glance at his friend.

I stared at him. "I'm not selling the store."

"Not here," he scolded.

"You don't return my calls."

"I've been busy."

With *her*. He'd been busy with her.

"I had a break-in at the store."

He laid his knife down and leaned forward on the countertop, his forearms flexing. "You're okay though, right?"

"Did you know about it?"

"The insurance company called me."

"And you didn't think to check on me?"

"They told me no one was hurt."

God, what an asshole. "I refuse to sell the store, Damien."

"Then write me a check and we're even."

"They took my formulas—"

"Why don't we do this later?"

"Do what?"

"Talk about why you should sell the store." His eyes narrowed and his expression looked like condemnation.

"I'm not ready to do that."

"What did the police say, babe?"

"Don't call me that."

He shrugged. "Any leads?"

"No." I glanced at his co-worker self-consciously, and then looked back at him. "They stole my Orris oil."

"That's expensive, right?" He lowered his gaze. "Well, how was the trip to Orlando?"

"It didn't work out."

Damien glared at his sous-chef. The man headed for the door, leaving us alone at last.

"So you didn't get the money from licensing?"

I let out a shaky breath. "I had to reschedule the meeting with Anna Rosenthal."

"You went all that way for nothing?"

I refused to tell him I'd lost my perfume. I was already feeling vulnerable because this was the man who had always made everything better—right up until he made everything worse.

"What are you cooking?" I asked.

"Beef Wellington...your favorite." He gave me a sympathetic smile. "You doing okay?"

"Not really." I squeezed back tears.

He rounded the counter and got closer to me...too close...and that familiar waft of his soft cologne clouded me in memories.

He was wearing one of mine.

"It'll be okay." His touch turned into a caress on my upper arm.

"I need it to be."

He dragged me into a hug and I felt the crush of his chest against mine—that familiar scent of home.

I peered up at him. "We were good together once, weren't we?"

His gaze roamed over me. "We were."

"Where did we go wrong?" I whispered.

"Don't."

"It's all a blur."

One minute we were the kind of couple our friends envied, the type who took romantic boat trips out on the bay, enjoyed candle-lit dinners we cooked together, and had the kind of PDA that made our friends blush. It all ended too soon.

Damien leaned down. "You smell amazing," he whispered.

"It's not finished. I'm wearing it to inspire myself."

And you've lost the formula.

"God, what I wouldn't do to taste you one more time," he said huskily.

I glared up at him.

"Yeah, don't give me that look. You love it when I talk dirty."

He was so right. My flesh tingled, nipples tightening, my core responding to the way he pressed his chest to mine.

The ache in my heart suddenly returned, and I stepped away from him. "I want..."

"Yes?"

"I want to forget seeing you with Embry. There's no erasing it." I blinked back tears.

He frowned. "Wanna know why we didn't work out?"

"I've met her," I snapped. "Mid-fuck, so I can guess it has a lot to do with her body."

"What I have with Embry isn't superficial. She's smart and funny—"

"Great at guessing when there's a storm coming!"

Quite literally, because Damien had fallen for Miami's TV Weather Girl—excuse me—meteorologist. With her tight dresses and suggestive smiles, the bombshell had a knack for flirting and had stolen my man with a wave of her manicured hand.

Why no one had named a hurricane after her was beyond me.

"You were never spontaneous," he replied tersely. "You always needed advance warning to do anything fun."

"Sometimes it's good to be cautious," I reasoned.

"You can't live like that."

"And what you did to me proved I was right to be wary. You betrayed me in the worst kind of way."

"May I make a suggestion?"

"No."

"Hit the gym."

"Fuck off."

"This is my kitchen. You fuck off."

Inhaling sharply, I forced myself to calm down. "I need more time to come up with the funds so I can keep my store."

"We're buying a house," he bit out. "I want the money I put in."

"You never did anything for the store."

"Did more than enough." He strolled back behind the counter.

"You hung a few pictures." I gestured in frustration.

"I built those shelves."

"That's right, but you weren't there for the opening. And now I know why."

"Next time go through my lawyer."

I wanted to spew insults and accusations, but no words came out. I was too full of heartache to convey what I wanted to say.

I headed for the door.

"Babe," Damien called after me.

I turned and glared back at him. "What?"

"'When a storm's coming?'" he quoted me.

"Karma," I replied with a nod. "It always finds you."

He gave me a smug little smile. "You've lost everything, Raquel. So how did being cautious work out for you?"

"I was going to surprise you for your birthday. I was taking salsa classes." So I could wow him...match the bastard move for move when he partied hard.

You left it too late.

He smirked. "You'd have surprised me all right."

I bit my cheek in frustration. "You know what your problem is? You underestimate me. Always have."

"You think so?"

"Just reminding you that I'm a fighter. I always bounce back and I always find a way."

"Good, because I wanna see that two hundred and fifty K in my bank by the end of the month. That store was a waste of time." He reached for the knife and began slicing.

His words cut deeper.

I turned and made my way back through the restaurant with my heart racing and my mouth dry with panic, realizing that the storm had already made landfall.

Damien was right...I had lost everything.

All I had left was *me.*

Chapter
FIVE

"**W**HAT THE HELL ARE THESE?" I STARED INTO THE BOX AT THE pair of shoes and cringed.

"Crocodile." Taylor held out my tie. "Jasper thought they'd give you a millennial edge."

I accepted the tie from her and wove it around my neck while staring at the monstrosities that were meant to pass as footwear. "I can't wear these, Taylor."

"They're y."

I gave her an incredulous look.

"Maybe try them on."

"Maybe I'll fire everyone."

She looked unfazed.

Taylor had been my personal assistant for over a year and I appreciated her professionalism. She'd followed my instructions flawlessly, booking a suite in The Setai, Miami Beach Hotel, and inviting Katy Kittredge over, the award-winning journalist from *TIME* magazine.

I didn't want this interview conducted at my home.

Earlier today, Katy had toured The House of Beauregard and then requested a more in-depth interview with me. I'd relented to her request but on my terms. I wanted a place I could walk out of if I had to—though I was determined to sit through this one. The coverage was good for business, and good for my image.

I'd come straight from Bridgestone ready to discard my jodhpurs and riding boots and take a shower. Getting ready here had been a stellar idea—or so I'd thought.

"Well, at least the suit fits," I said.

She looked at her phone. "Penelope can't make it."

I fastened my jacket. "Does she say why?"

"She has a meeting that clashes."

Relief washed over me. "We need to do something about these shoes. Take the elevator to the top floor and throw them off the roof."

"They might fall on someone's head."

"Hopefully Jasper's."

Taylor whispered something under her breath and it sounded a lot like Tagalog, her first language. Though born in the Philippines, she had come to the States as a child with her family. Her studies in Florida had landed her with a degree in communication, and for that I was eternally grateful. Right up until the point she'd presented me with these Crocodile Dundee shoes.

I narrowed my gaze. "What did you just say?"

"Just thinking how handsome you look." She gave me a mischievous grin.

I looked down at the shoes again. "Do we have time?"

"I would need to delay the meeting."

"Fine."

"I'll call Katy and push it back an hour."

"Otherwise I'll look like a gangster! What the fuck, Taylor."

She suppressed a chuckle. "They definitely make a Mafioso statement."

The last thing I needed was to be immortalized on a magazine cover wearing these ridiculous shoes. "Make it happen."

I spent an hour alone lounging in the suite and flipping through TV channels as I waited for Taylor to drive the short distance to my home and back with my stylish leather shoes. I snacked on peanuts and M&M's and downed a bottle of Perrier.

By the time Katy Kittredge arrived, I was ready to get this interview behind me, feeling confident in my bespoke suit and black leather Armani dress shoes. Taylor guided Katy into the luxury sitting room and the tall, slender journalist took the seat opposite mine.

I stood to shake her hand and guessed her age at around fifty. Katy had an enduring beauty and an easy elegance with a warm smile that lit up her face. Her deep blue eyes reflected kindness, an attribute that usually got her "victims" to open up, I assumed.

She set a recorder on the table between us.

"I would've loved to have visited your home, Astor," she said, flipping open her notebook.

"Maybe next time."

"I'm wondering how such a private man feels about being interviewed?"

I crossed one long leg over another and leaned back. "It's a pleasure to talk with you, Katy."

She glanced at her notes. "The House of Beauregard is close to becoming a goliath in the industry. What secret strategy will you use to take your company to the next level?"

"Perfume is our passion. It's where we begin and end. What we do is not for the accolades, of which there are many, or for financial gain, for which we are deeply grateful. Our main focus remains on creating accents that inspire, soothe, and transcend what others create. We will never lose sight of that goal."

"What makes The House of Beauregard stand out as a front runner?"

"We don't test our products on animals. We use a scientific approach that keeps our customers safe and guilt free. We are constantly placing high quality products on the market that have longer shelf lives, thanks to our patented formulas—some of which take years to perfect. The process can't be rushed."

"Like a fine wine?"

"Very much so."

Katy revealed an impressive understanding of my company and the industry at large. She asked intelligent questions, including where we saw ourselves a few years from now and how much input I offered for the invention of our dazzling scents.

"How involved are you?"

"I'm a chemist, Katy, so very."

She gave me a quizzical look, tilting her head. "Are you dating?"

"How did we go from science to that subject?" I quipped.

"No personal questions," Taylor piped up.

Katy gave a nod of acknowledgment. "Revealing more of yourself to our readers will provide a personal connection."

I leaned forward. "What you see is what you get."

She gave me a thin smile. "The world wants to know more about you."

"I'm flattered."

"You use your mother's maiden name, Beauregard, for the business. Not your father's. Why?"

"It suited the company."

"You adopted it as your surname as well. Sure there's not a compelling story behind the reason?"

"You want to know more about me?" I paused briefly. "I'm involved with several charities. I'm a passionate polo player—"

"Vedado is your favorite horse?" Katy glanced at her notes.

"I rescued him as a foal. He was mistreated."

"That's nice, but I'm more interested in you."

I glanced at Taylor; this interview had landed a PR touchdown for our company, but the message about keeping my personal life private had fallen through the cracks.

"What is your usual routine?" Katy asked.

"I work out, read the news, ride in the late afternoon—"

"Horses?" she said, smirking.

I ignored her innuendo. "We have plenty of land at Bridgestone to exercise my horses. I head back to the office after having a break in the afternoon and work late into the night—"

"No dating?"

"That again? Why don't you ask me something else?"

"What are you reading right now?"

"*Sophie's World* by Jostein Gaarder."

"So you consider yourself a philosopher, Mr. Beauregard?"

"Are we not all philosophers?"

"We are not all elusive." She sat back. "Tell us a little about your childhood."

"A happy one."

"You went to live in Cuba at thirteen and yet your sister remained behind?"

I drew in a wary breath. "It was a decision my mother made after my father's death. I respected it."

"Your father's death…how did it affect you?"

I leaned forward and pressed STOP on the recorder.

"Sorry." She looked apologetic. "I forgot."

"I remembered for you."

She didn't seem deterred. "How did you cope with being so young when you were sent away? Separated from your family…no time to grieve."

"Admirably."

"Was it because your mother was grieving? Or something else?"

"My heritage was important to my family. It still is. I visit Havana often."

"What about Penelope?"

"I'll let her answer her own questions."

"She's not here."

I forced a smile. "I was allowed to experience and appreciate my heritage at a very young age and, as such, it shapes my work and influences my creations."

"Were you lonely?" she asked softly.

I glanced at the window, feeling suffocated. "Turn the air conditioning up, please, Taylor."

She rose and headed across the room. "I'll take care of it."

I looked over at Katy. "Where were we?"

"We were talking about the Cuban monastery where you lived as a boy?"

"Sir," Taylor got my attention and raised her phone. "Sorry, this email just came in and it says it's urgent." She threw Katy an annoyed look.

Katy's skeptical expression let me know she saw through our ruse.

I stood and walked over to Taylor, taking the phone from her.

"Will you excuse me, Katy? I have to deal with this." Not waiting for her reply, I strolled into the bedroom and shut the door, then turned and leaned against it.

With my breathing finally under control, I continued into the bathroom and sat on the edge of the bathtub. After loosening my tie, I rested my face in my palms.

I just needed to take a moment.

A trickle of sweat snaked down my back as the heat of a Cuban sun scorched into my consciousness. The brunt of a punishment I hadn't earned.

Vaguely, I became aware that Taylor stood in the doorway.

She came in and knelt beside me. "It was the crocodile shoes that started you off on the wrong foot, wasn't it?"

I chuckled.

"You okay, Boss?"

"I'm fine." *Or I would be eventually.*

Taylor rose and gave my shoulder a squeeze. "Want me to cut this short?"

"Let's get the photo shoot over with." I pushed myself up. "Katy will no doubt offer to continue the interview over dinner. Make sure that meeting never happens."

"Got it."

I followed Taylor back into the sitting room.

Chapter
SIX

Raquel

T HE BLUE LIQUID WHOOSHED WITHIN ITS GLASS BOTTLE...AND I DIDN'T
have the heart to tell the young woman that what she was
holding would set her back hundreds. It was by *Rene Rue,* a
high-end, renowned product.

She put the bottle down, picked up another, and then sprayed
some of the scent on her wrist.

I froze when I saw what she was holding—a Lalique bottle containing my most treasured creation. The same bottle I had mislaid for
that Ann Rosenthal meeting. What the hell was it doing amongst the
others?

I hurried over to her. "That one's not for sale."

She placed the bottle in my hand. "I've been looking for this one."

"It's never been on the market."

"Are you sure?" She looked surprised.

Yes, I was, because what she was holding had never been out of
my store. And it wasn't unusual for the untrained nose to confuse a
scent. The art was a gift few possessed.

"What do you have that's like that one?" She pointed to the bottle
in my hand.

"This is one of a kind." I set it on the countertop.

She looked thoughtful. "Do you have *Angel's Quest?*"

"La Vida es un Angel's Quest?"

"I was told that's a nice one."

"We don't carry it." It'd probably cost her a week's salary. "I'm Raquel."

"Skye." She looked sheepish. "Someone told me my perfume's nasty. So I saw your store and thought I'd treat myself."

"Good for you. We'll find you something special."

"This one's pretty." She reached for a square bottle.

"Lilies & Freesia, it has soft summer notes. It's youthful and yet sophisticated." And it was one of mine. I took the sample and squirted it onto a paper stick and offered it to her.

Skye sniffed. "How much?"

"I want you to have it."

"For free?"

"Yes." I reached for a paper bag stamped with the shop's logo. "I'm closing my store."

"Early?"

"For good."

"Oh."

I couldn't believe I'd even spoken those words. "We have plenty more over here."

She pointed to the small Lalique bottle on the countertop. "Sure I can't have that one?"

I curled my fingers around my beloved scent. "Actually, it's not even finished."

"That's what he told me."

"What? Who?"

"This guy I met back in South Beach. He smelled like that."

She's wrong.

I humored her. "Do you remember his name?"

She shrugged. "I can find out. We have a reservation system at The Artisan Café. I'm training to be a manager there. The man was sitting in my area."

"This was in South Beach?"

She nodded.

"You're a long way from home."

"I'm visiting my mom." She pointed in the direction of Monroe Street. "She works at the House of Beer."

Skye fished her phone out of her purse.

"I can access the reservations on here," she said. "It was last Monday."

"You don't need to do that." I raised my hand to stop her.

"I got it." Her gaze rose to meet mine. "Penelope Beauregard booked the table."

"Beauregard?" I was stunned.

A perfumer...? It was too much of a coincidence.

"He had that exact bottle." Skye looked sincere. "I remember the way it makes the perfume glint like a potion."

"This one?" I pointed to mine, which was one of two Lalique bottles I'd purchased from an antique store in Paris.

The same trip that now had an entirely new meaning. At the last minute, Damien had pulled out so I'd been forced to tour the city alone. I'd mixed business with pleasure and had thoroughly enjoyed my visit to one of the most beautiful cities in the world. Of course, now I knew why Damien had bailed and those otherwise happy memories were now tainted.

"That scent is unmistakable." She looked around the store, not catching my incredulous expression.

I struggled out of my melancholy. "Was it Penelope who recommended *Angel's Quest*?" It was one of their scents.

"No, the guy with her did."

I grabbed my phone from behind the countertop and with a swipe and a quick search brought up a photo of Penelope. According to the names listed beneath the photo, that striking man beside her was her brother, Astor. I was surprised by his age; he was around thirty, maybe a bit older. Their last name, Beauregard, sounded haughty and I had imagined a much older man helping his sister run the business.

I turned my phone towards Skye. "Was this him?"

"That's the asshole." She grinned. "Though he smelled amazing."

I flipped the screen back around and stared at his handsome face. Had he really been wearing my scent?

It was a long shot…and it was impossible to prove. Yet who else would be interested in a startling new scent other than perfumers? Only they would realize what they had.

I removed the bottle's cap and had her sniff again. "Are you sure?"

"I asked him what it was and he got all defensive."

"Really?" I mulled that over. "Let me get a bag for your *Lilies & Freesia*."

After Skye left I locked up the store in a daze.

Within minutes, I had researched where Penelope lived and was heading toward South Beach, the other side of Florida. I had a long drive ahead but I needed answers. I couldn't rest until I knew the truth. With a heart full of hope and a head full of ideas, I navigated across the state.

This is madness.

Then again I had nothing left to lose.

As I neared Penelope's property, the same one mentioned in the year old *Vanity Fair* interview I'd read online during my search, I clutched the steering wheel and replayed the plan.

Okay, there is no plan.

There was just me hunting down Penelope and asking her where the hell she'd gotten my new fragrance. Though, in her defense, she probably had no idea it was stolen. Somehow, it had found its way onto the black market and right into the heart of her company.

This trip into the unknown was me taking back my power.

See, you can be spontaneous.

The long driveway reminded me I was heading toward a wealthy estate—the kind that would probably have a security guard somewhere on the property.

A flash of black suddenly appeared before me and I yanked the wheel sharply to the left to avoid the horse and rider. My car fishtailed and sprayed up dust and gravel, sliding toward a brick wall.

I slammed on the brakes and was jolted forward and then slung back by my seatbelt, stopping only inches from the wall.

Jesus, the horse!

I unbuckled my seatbelt and shoved open the door, heading toward the man who was trying to calm the panicked stallion. The rider raised his hand in the air to warn me to keep my distance.

"I'm sorry," I called out.

The stallion reared up. The rider's strong arms grappled with the reins, trying to calm the animal and keep the impressive beast from bolting. The horse was obviously a thoroughbred. With its curved spine and arched neck, it had a height of at least fifteen hands.

When the stallion settled down, the rider directed the animal to walk toward me.

I took in the man's leather boots and his tight jodhpurs, outlining his taut thighs, and then my gaze landed on the extraordinary features of Astor Beauregard. The strong line of his jaw was remarkable—and those piercing hazel eyes were fixed on me with a judgmental expression.

He directed his skittish horse around my car, all the while throwing me condescending glances.

"That's a good idea," I offered. "Let him see the car is harmless now."

Astor tugged on the reins and maneuvered the horse toward me, coming so close I could literally reach out and touch his mane.

I took a step back and my heel caught in the gravel. I fell, landing on my bum.

"Now we're even," Astor said darkly. He leaned down, offering me his hand, and with an impressive athletic ability quickly pulled me to my feet.

I brushed gravel off my skirt. "I'd like to talk with you about a—"

"Get back in your car and leave."

No way, not after driving all this way.

Something told me his sister would be more reasonable. "I'm here to see Penelope Beauregard."

"She's not here."

I walked over to my car and gently closed the door. "I'll wait inside the house."

"You'd have to be invited in to do that."

"Then I'll wait here." I folded my arms across my chest and leaned back against the car.

"You're trespassing."

"I don't appreciate being threatened with a horse."

"I was decent enough to stop."

I narrowed my gaze, disapproving of his arrogance.

He squeezed his heels against the stallion's ribs and headed off in the opposite direction.

I called after him, "Mix the scent of your conceit with the aroma of your boots and you'll have a winner for the fuck-boys."

He tugged on the reins and forced his horse to turn sideways. "You know who I am, then?"

"I do."

Even if I hated him, I couldn't deny how impressive—and hot—he looked while he was getting his frisky steed under control.

He loosened his chinstrap. "And who do I have the displeasure of meeting—on my land, I might add?"

"*Your* property?"

"Yes."

"Isn't this your sister's home?"

"So you got your info from *Town and Country*?"

"*Vanity Fair*." I swallowed my doubt. "What time will she be back?"

"She rarely visits."

"Where does she live?"

"Who are you?"

"I'm a perfumer." I gave him an accusatory glare. "And a good one at that."

"Are you here to be interviewed for a job?" A muscle in his jaw twitched. "We only hire superior chemists."

"Obviously not," I said. "Because I'm standing here and not in your lab."

"You really think you're that good?"

"Yes."

"Spice or Oud?"

"Both, if muted with jasmine."

His mouth curled into an amused smile. "Lime basil and mandarin…"

"Goes well with English pear and freesia."

His gaze narrowed. "Iris, jasmine and…"

"Lily."

He gave me a smoldering look. "Proves nothing."

"I'm open to learning new techniques," I replied, fluttering my eyelashes.

Fuck it. I was all in.

"You want me to teach you?" He stared down at me with burning intensity. "It takes a certain discipline to come under my tutelage."

A feeling of rivalry came over me and I drew in a deep breath.

He nudged his horse and headed back toward me. "I'm in charge of hiring. You go through me for the privilege of working at The House of Beauregard."

"Then I was misinformed." That would rub his ego the wrong way.

"Come." He gestured for me to follow and I walked behind his horse, wondering if he was going to berate me some more.

When we reached the stables he said, "Hold his bit."

"Why?"

"I'm going to dismount, and he still might be a tad skittish." He caressed the horse's mane. "I'm just climbing off, boy."

Wrapping one hand around the bit, I held the horse still and caressed his muzzle. I felt calmer, too, as I breathed in the earthy scent of stallion and leather and fresh air, and gazed off at a dazzling sunset.

The stables went on forever and I wondered how many horses he owned, and how much help he'd hired to care for them. To the left was an area covered by a large white dome, which looked like a place where horses were trained.

Astor's heels landed on the dirt. He moved over to me and took back the reins, his hand brushing over mine, sending an electric shock through my fingers.

"You can make it up to him," he said.

"What?"

"Help me groom him. We'll talk."

"About?"

"Coming to work for me."

I didn't want to work for him. *Arrogant bastard.*

"Is that your usual expression?" He flashed an amused glance my way and then led his horse into the stables.

"I'm just trying to figure you out, Mr. Beauregard."

He looked over his shoulder at me and flashed a wry smile. "I run a multi-million dollar business and like horses. There you go…mystery solved."

Hooves clipped along stone and I smiled when his horse glanced back as though checking to see if I was following. Astor patted his neck with affection and led him into a large stall.

I stood near the doorway and watched Astor shove the stirrup aside from the leather flap and unhook the saddle. He eased it off and perched it on a dividing wall, then grabbed a brush.

The air was filled with the scent of straw and horse. Mingled with his soft cologne, it created an earthy combination.

"What's his name?" I moved in closer.

"Vedado." He ran the brush slowly over the horse's rump and down his hind leg.

"He's beautiful."

"He's a stallion so let's not offend his pride."

"Like a stud?"

Astor's mouth twitched with amusement. "Let's keep the

conversation strictly on the horse."

"Funny."

"Do you think you could make it? If I hired you?"

"Make what?"

He paused and turned to face me. "A scent for fuck-boys?"

"From leather and arrogance?" I mused at his brashness.

"Yes."

"So you'd be the one wearing it?"

"I'm serious."

"In the right environment I can make anything."

"Come here."

"Why?"

"The only reason you're in here is because of my horse." He offered me the brush. "Let's not waste his time."

I walked over and took the brush out of his hand. Moving past him, I faced Vedado and began running the brush over his long neck. His flesh shivered as I swept it beneath his mane.

"Slower." Astor stepped up behind me.

That commanding deep tone of his had me wondering what he was like in the bedroom. Masterful? Bossy? Dangerous? My flesh tingled, betraying me with the distraction of these thoughts. Beauregard looked like the kind of man who would throw you onto a bed and then move you around beneath him until you passed out from pleasure. A playboy. The love you and leave you kind.

There, less than five minutes with him and I knew his type.

My body stiffened when Astor cupped his left hand over mine to direct the brush over Vedado just so. His touch was firm and demanding, and I allowed him this control, at least, to lead each stroke, each lift of the brush as it began its downward glide over pure muscle.

He stepped back and watched me intently, his gaze studying my every move, causing the fine hairs on my forearms to prickle. This was obviously the point of his charade, to seduce me or, at the very least, to weaken my resolve.

He gave a nod of approval. "You never told me your name."

I looked back to observe his reaction. "Raquel."

"Raquel." He ran his tongue along his lower lip. "I'm Astor."

"I know."

He broke into a smile that looked adorable.

I was here to fight with him and his family, not swoon like a victim of his superior masculinity. An important fact I forced into my frontal lobe.

"Astor's an unusual name," I said.

"It means Thunder God."

"Aren't we the lucky ones?" I continued to rub the brush over Vedado.

Astor moved closer and though he wasn't touching me, I could feel the heat of his body behind mine. It made my toes curl and my core tighten. "Any more questions, Mr. Beauregard?"

He leaned down and whispered, "Are you sure you want to work for me?"

A shiver ran through me and I was sure he'd sensed my reaction.

"Where did you come from, Raquel?"

"Clearwater." It was a small fib.

"Ah, where the ocean is blue and the sand is like silk." His tone had become hypnotic.

"It's true."

"What are you wearing?"

"My perfume?"

He leaned closer and breathed me in. "Yes."

"Nothing."

He went silent.

I spun around and stared up at his ridiculously gorgeous face. I could understand why he was used to eliciting a female's submission with little to no effort.

"So, why this profession, Raquel?"

"It's my calling." I refused to look away. "And you?"

He paused. "Me too."

"You're obviously good at what you do."

"Oh, I'm very good."

"Scent is important," I blurted out. "It makes more decisions for us than we dare to admit. It decides who we are intimate with, it helps process memories, stirs our emotions and—"

"Alerts us to danger." Speckles of gold glinted in his hazel irises.

"And…it affects our taste."

"In every respect." He lowered his gaze to my lips. "Taste is everything."

My clit panged with pleasure. "Is it true you would go to any lengths to get ahead, Astor?"

He leaned forward and pressed his body against mine so I was trapped between him and his horse. "My critics regard me as ruthless, yes."

"You don't mind being thought of in that way?" My nipples were taut and my body tense. I didn't hate the pressure of him against me. In fact, I reveled in the sensations it caused. I would never have imagined I'd be flirting and sparring with the enemy.

"I want to know all about you."

"In what way?" My voice sounded breathy.

He oozed danger and passion—a cocktail of combustible substances that shouldn't interact.

Astor leaned in to kiss my neck and I closed my eyes, tilting my head to the side.

He pulled back. "What happened to your ring?"

Glancing down at my left ring finger, I saw the impression that the gold band I'd once worn had left behind. I could tell him about my divorce, but I didn't trust myself to believe I had any good instincts left when it came to men.

When I didn't reply, he leaned in closer, his lips almost touching mine.

"I am many things to many people, but to you, Raquel, I will always be the gentleman who walked you to your car."

The air stilled. Astor stepped away from me and the spell was broken.

I let out a shaky breath. For a second I had thought he was going to kiss me—and I would have let him.

He reached for my hand and led me out of the stables.

To hide my embarrassment over our near intimacy, I turned my attention to the house. It was a regal-looking property with white walls and tall pillars. I could see it was right on the water.

"Who lives with you?" I had to ask.

"I don't live there."

"Who does?"

"I want to sell it." He turned to face me. "What's your last name?"

"Wren." I gave him my maiden name.

"Mrs. Wren, it's been a pleasure." He lifted my hand and kissed it. "This is how a playboy says goodbye."

Astor dazzled me with a smile that made me blush.

"Call my office," he said, opening my car door. "They'll send you an application."

Feeling self-conscious, I tucked an unruly strand of hair behind my ear. "I want you to know that—"

"Yes?"

"I'm usually more cautious."

He leaned forward and answered huskily, "I know."

I drew in a sharp breath at his flirty goodbye. A way to keep me thinking of him long after we'd parted, no doubt.

I knew this man's work, or at least his colognes. Each scent lured a woman in with the promise of forbidden love infused with danger.

That was Astor's brand.

This wasn't the time to ask him about my perfume. Here, he clearly had the upper hand and I wasn't willing to have him send me away forever.

I needed more time to strategize. Take what I had learned and methodically weave a plan that would see my formula returned to me. Everything in my being told me he had it.

I turned to thank him for his time but no words came; I was too struck by the knowing look of confidence on his face—and that dazzling grin. I thought I might drown in the alpha pheromones he was giving off.

"I'll personally review your application," he said.

Work for him? Hell, no. Never going to happen.

I climbed into my Alpha Romeo and Astor shut my door like the gentleman he'd promised to be. He stepped away as I started the engine.

I backed my car slowly away from the brick wall, a reminder to both of us of my dramatic arrival.

Easing down the gravel driveway, I glanced in my rearview mirror to see him standing where I'd left him—tall and dashing and dangerously addictive.

Something told me the intensity of Astor's aura would stay with me long after we'd parted.

Chapter SEVEN

Raquel

I T HAD BEEN A WEEK SINCE I'D SEEN ASTOR AT BRIDGESTONE, AND HE WAS still haunting my every conscious thought. It was his cologne, I reasoned. A spell like that can last for days.

It had nothing to do with true feelings at all—it was all chemistry and pure science. Somehow I'd let myself get caught in the crosshairs of an East Coast playboy. Time…that's what was needed here, along with a good deal of distraction.

Moroccan rose and passion fruit bath salts would lift my spirits— and this tall glass of sparkling Perrier with a dash of lemon would help take my mind off *him*.

I slipped into the warm bath water trying to clear my mind. The heat soaked into my bones and brought on a wave of relaxation. This kind of self-care had been missing from my life for quite a while, and it was such an easy gift to give myself.

I glanced out the window and noticed the rain had ceased, which meant the sun would be out soon and brightening up the place again. I slipped farther down in the tub and welcomed a rush of luxurious contentment.

This upper floor wasn't strictly home. When Damien and I had parted ways we'd left our cozy home in Dunedin. He'd flown into the loving arms of Embry and I had ended up in this cold loft with no heat. Luckily, the climate was favorable most of the time and when it wasn't I had a portable heater.

It was a decent-sized loft that sat conveniently above my store, and though I'd never planned on living up here, it had all the amenities I needed to get by. My store was one of a row of shops that had once been terraces. This room had been scheduled to be gutted with the next wave of improvements, which never came. And though I had searched for a new place to live, I'd resigned myself to saving every last cent I could manage so this had become my temporary home.

A far cry from Astor's place on the waterfront. No doubt my loft would be the equivalent of a cupboard in that vast manor. I wondered who else lived there.

I'll probably never know.

I needed to retrieve my perfume from The House of Beauregard as soon as possible. Then, I would return to the offices of Dazzle and Bazaar and hopefully get at least thirty thousand dollars for my creation. Not a lot, but enough to get me into a new store that was more affordable.

I couldn't keep myself from thinking about Bridgestone again, and the stables where Astor had pressed his body against mine.

I wouldn't have kissed him—at all.

I cupped one of my breasts, letting the feeling of just how much I hated that man wash over me as my fingers languidly played with my clit. Pleasure saturated my senses and my back arched, shudders wracking my body as a delicious climax surged through me.

My thoughts returned to Astor's jodhpurs…

I yanked my hand out of the water and reached for my glass of Perrier, taking a cold gulp of reality. Settling back and closing my eyes, I tried to think of something mundane and pleasant.

He really did have a lovely horse.

Fuck Astor Beauregard and those muscular thighs that no doubt squeezed you through an everlasting orgasm.

This wasn't going to work.

Lying still just meant my thoughts could find me…Astor could find me.

I got out of the tub and dried off, then spritzed myself with white datura flowers; a subtle scent that always soothed my nerves.

Rummaging through my makeshift wardrobe, I grabbed my jeans and found the T-shirt given to me by my friend Hazel, who had also served as my divorce lawyer.

"Ditch Damien and upgrade, darling," Hazel had joked in her southern accent.

Facing the mirror, I read the backward words on the T-shirt she'd given me on the day I had signed the divorce papers she'd prepared.

SECOND HUSBAND VACANCY
No FUCKWITS need apply *this time*

I needed to do my laundry, but this would do for now. I wasn't going to see anyone, so I skipped the make-up as well, grabbing my sunhat, sunglasses, and slipping on flat sandals.

Within minutes I had packed a picnic basket with olives, cheese, biscuits, chips and salsa. I threw a bottle of mineral water in there, too.

This was a *me* day.

Sundays were traditionally dedicated to going out on the boat—for me, anyway. I'd taken Florida's required boating safety courses and was more than capable of heading out alone.

Leaving through the front door was becoming more difficult. I drew in a sharp breath of courage and walked ten more steps into the store.

My beloved glass cabinet was full of designer bottles of all colors and shapes. To my right was a long shelf showcasing my personal collection alongside the other brands. I had earned the right for my scents to sit beside them. Even now the way the light refracted off the glass mesmerized me. It was very often this display that drew customers in from the street.

Then I saw it…

Savage King, a cologne from The House of Beauregard for the customer who liked to burn money. I reached for the box and opened it, pulling off the bottle's cap. The aroma reminded me of dirty, forbidden sex.

This place needed a touch of air freshener. I squirted Beauregard's cologne around the room. Three more ten dollar squirts and I was breathing in *him.*

Damn it.

I threw the bottle back onto the shelf and it clinked against the others, sending one rolling toward the edge.

Gawping in horror, I watched my precious Lalique bottle fall and bounce on the floor before disappearing beneath the counter. I fell to my knees, cursing, and realized I'd need help to move the hefty cabinet to get to it.

Astor's *Savage King* had played a part in this mayhem. I needed to get out of here and onto the ocean where my problems would feel more manageable.

I rose, dusted off my knees, and grabbed my beach bag.

Within twenty minutes I'd made it to Ybor City Harbor and was boarding *My Fair Lady,* our small Sundancer yacht. I applied copious amounts of sunscreen and put on my sunhat. I couldn't wait to take the boat out as I ran through the pre-launch checklist.

When I saw the low fuel indicator, I groaned in frustration. Damien had used the boat during the week and hadn't refueled.

I took in a deep breath of salty sea air and resolved to be patient. It wouldn't take too much longer to get her ready to launch.

Staring out at the ocean, I always felt a sense of peace. It was the way the light sparkled off the surface of the water, the endless blue bringing on feelings of tranquility as pelicans soared on the breeze and seagulls demanded attention.

I was so ready to answer the call of freedom.

"Hey!" That voice was familiar.

My head snapped around toward the dock and I saw Damien holding a picnic basket. My heart wrenched.

I shoved my sunglasses onto my forehead and squinted at him. "You had the same idea?"

A hopeful tingle whirled in my chest at the flurry of possibilities. Maybe, just maybe, I could have him join me and bring the conversation around to Perfume Girl. I might even persuade him to hold off on forcing me to sell the store. Maybe he'd let me repay what I owed him in manageable installments.

He grinned, holding up his picnic basket. "Perfect day for it."

"Come aboard." I waved him on.

A part of me wanted to believe that what we'd had was too special to be thrown away so easily. Perhaps today life would turn around for me.

And then I saw Embry hurrying down the boardwalk, her blonde locks flying. She had on a skimpy dress and high-heeled sandals, all ready to take on summer in a pair of designer sunglasses. As she caught up with Damien, she plopped a straw hat on her head and held it down as it billowed, looking windswept and happy.

In her other hand she carried an oversized beach bag similar to mine. No doubt she'd packed her sunscreen, and perhaps even a bottle of wine.

"Sorry, babe." Damien turned to look at me. "We've been planning this all week."

I needed to go out on the water, needed to escape. I really needed to forget these people. "I'm about to kick off."

"You mean launch."

"Launch, then."

Damien glared at me. "Don't be like this."

"Like what?"

"There are two of *us*," Embry piped up.

Her logic wasn't welcome here and neither was she because this boat had always been *ours*.

My heart sank as I realized I was bound to lose this argument.

"Whoa!" Embry's gaze widened as she took in something behind me.

Turning to follow her gaze, I winced into the sun and saw an enormous yacht gliding through the water toward us. Its size caused a large swell, and I had to hold on to my boat's railing to keep my balance. Shielding my eyes from the glare reflecting off its sleek sides, I realized it was about to dock not far from me.

When I turned to look back at them, Damien was frowning at my chest. "Is that shirt meant to be funny?"

I gave him a sheepish smile. "A friend gave it to me."

A wall of white loomed high on my right and drew my attention back to the titanic vessel anchoring beside me. Written elegantly along the side was the name *Riveting*.

When my gaze returned to the unfriendly couple, Embry had weaved her arm through Damien's. It felt so wrong I had to bite the inside of my cheek to stop my chin from trembling.

The unsteadiness I felt beneath my feet was a metaphor for my life.

An ebullient crowd disembarked from the yacht. The well-dressed men and women hurried off toward the restaurants, their laughter carrying on the breeze.

Defeated, I scooped up my beach bag and jumped over onto the dock.

"You forgot your picnic basket," said Damien.

I'd lost my appetite. "Keep it."

"Great minds think alike," said Embry, raising her bag.

I rolled my eyes and sucked in my annoyance.

"Raquel?" A luscious deep voice drew my attention away from them.

Astor Beauregard was standing on the dock beneath the high stern of his yacht, looking ridiculously gorgeous in his crisp white shirt and tailored pants. The designer sunglasses he was wearing hid the expression in his eyes.

"Sorry for the squall." He offered a wave of apology.

"It was nice," I blurted out. "I mean, fine."

"Fantastic yacht," said Damien. "What kind?"

"One of a kind," replied Astor. "I had it commissioned because I couldn't find one that suited all my needs."

"It's really big." I could feel my cheeks burning.

Astor suppressed a smile. "I'm flattered."

"Is that like a garage on the side?" asked Damien, sounding impressed.

Astor followed his gaze. "I keep my speedboat in there."

"Two boats for the price of one." I cringed at my joke.

"Hardly, babe," said Damien.

Astor didn't seem to notice my embarrassment. "We forgot the champagne so we're stopping off to nab some."

"What an amazing coincidence," I muttered.

Astor turned to look up at his yacht. "Perfect weather for an outing."

"Partly cloudy," said Embry. She couldn't help herself. "Ten percent precipitation and winds up to nine miles per hour."

"Humidity forty-nine percent." Astor seemed to hold her gaze.

Damien swapped a wary glance with me.

Don't look at me, buddy—I know! This is Beauregard's thing. All he has to do is stand there and women fall at his feet.

They could take their precipitation and shove it up their—

"Thank you for this, Raquel," said Damien, pointing to our boat, which looked ridiculous compared to Astor's. "You always were reasonable," he added.

"Well, it's been lovely." I gave myself kudos for feigned politeness and raised my hand to let them know I was outta here. "Have fun."

"Really, you're leaving?" gushed Embry.

My teeth clamped down on my lip in frustration.

"We double-booked with her," she explained to Astor, tucking a golden lock behind her ear.

Astor was lording over the marina with a sultry stance that reminded me of a young sea captain or a sun-kissed god. I couldn't stop looking at him, and then I realized he was staring at my T-shirt with a puzzled frown.

SECOND HUSBAND VACANCY
No FUCKWITS need apply *this time*

"It was a gift," I told him.

He grinned. It was that same cute smile that had convinced me walking into his stables alone with him was a good idea.

"Raquel has very kindly given us the boat because it's our day." Embry followed that up with a grateful smile my way.

Somewhere in the divorce papers it had been mentioned that *My Fair Lady* would be going to Damien. Maybe today had been my last chance to enjoy her.

I pulled my sunglasses down over my eyes.

"Join us," Astor said, his tone enticing.

"That's very generous of you!" Embry burst out.

"Actually, I was asking Raquel," he said blandly.

I stood there stunned at his invitation.

"I was expecting your call, Raquel." Astor threw in a smile. "We have a job vacancy for a chemist at the House of Beauregard."

"What job?" asked Damien.

"The one I offered her," replied Astor.

"That's great, babe." Damien looked conflicted. "She'll really need one after closing the—"

"I am interested in hearing more," I interrupted.

Astor started to respond, but Damien cut him off.

"I'm her ex, by the way." Damien reached out to shake Astor's hand.

Astor shook it, his gaze darting back to my shirt.

"Yeah." Damien rolled his eyes. "You see what I had to contend with."

"I do," said Astor. "I had the pleasure of meeting Raquel in South Beach. It was truly inspiring."

Damien looked at me. "When did you go there?"

"A week ago," I replied, not that it was any of his business.

"I'm Astor Beauregard." He reached out to shake Embry's hand, too.

"Mr. Beauregard, you invited me in for an interview," I clarified. "There was no official offer."

"Let's continue this on *Riveting*." Astor pointed to the yacht.

I felt tempted. It was the way he'd spoken those words, the way he'd invited me onto his "pleasure palace," seemingly the center of his world where answers awaited and hope lived on.

The same happy crowd who had disembarked now made their way back on the yacht. A member of the staff followed them carrying a crate of champagne.

I recognized Penelope Beauregard, the elusive woman I'd been trying to hunt down. She was dressed in a white trouser suit and I could see a bikini top showing through her open blouse. She glanced my way and then quickly boarded following the others.

"Raquel," Astor said, "since you've lost access to your boat for the day, please take advantage of mine."

I had to remind myself that this man was my enemy. He swaggered around with a wealthy bad boy attitude that riled me up. The way he smiled—oh, so innocently—and most of all the way he loomed over everyone with his intimidating height.

I didn't trust myself to be close to his sister either. Being trapped on a yacht in the middle of the ocean after confronting either of them would be a nightmare scenario.

Maybe Astor was playing with me. Maybe he knew who I was. That strange glance back from Penelope had intrigued me. It could have been guilt, but then again my T-shirt was a close contender for her disapproval.

How long had I waited for the chance to get close to her and ask the kind of questions that would bring about a resolution to my dilemma? Still, being spontaneous brought with it the kind of risks I didn't take.

"If you change your mind," Astor said, heading toward the ramp, "we leave in ten."

My gaze followed him and I couldn't look away. He strolled onto his boat with confidence, keeping his hands in his pockets as he boarded without looking back.

"I'd jump at the chance to work for him," admitted Embry, her tone incredulous that I'd passed on his offer. "What?" she said, responding to the disapproving look from Damien. "Look how rich he is. He'd pay well."

"He'd take advantage of Raquel and then toss her away when he's done." Damien fixed an accusatory glare on Astor's back.

My ex was an idiot. He and Embry deserved each other.

Years of hard work and endless crafting of perfection in a laboratory had been lost because of that theft, and right there on that love ship were clues to help me get my perfume back and secure my future. All I had to do was follow Astor up those steps.

All I had to do was be fearless.

Chapter EIGHT

AFTER BOARDING THE *RIVETING*, RAQUEL STOOD JUST BEYOND THE ramp wearing her Wayfarer sunglasses and sporting that crazy T-shirt.

I would have drawn more amusement from the situation if I hadn't done the unthinkable to strategize getting her on here—though I felt no guilt. I had a billion-dollar empire to protect, staff to pay, and I was willing to go to any lengths to preserve it all.

That didn't mean I couldn't have a little fun with her.

Raquel's long brunette locks were being ruffled by the wind, and the freckles sprinkled across her nose made her look like an all American girl; though remnants of her English heritage lingered in her porcelain complexion, her cheeks made rosy by the brisk breeze. The unassuming way she assessed the guests was endearing, but she knew she was beautiful.

I strolled toward her. "Good timing. We're about to launch."

"I'm not staying."

"Well, that's disappointing." I smiled anyway.

The yacht suddenly rocked beneath us and she slammed into me, clinging to my chest as she regained her balance. She fit too well against me, and I let her rest there for a moment.

Wrapping my hands around her waist, I eased her back. "Steady, Mrs. Wren."

She blushed wildly as she stepped back. "Sorry."

"You're forgiven." I fought the temptation to steal a kiss and draw the truth from her.

"It's Miss, now. Wren's my maiden name."

I raised my sunglasses, wanting her to see the steeliness in my gaze and heed the warning. I wasn't about to fall for her ruse.

"Tell them not to leave yet." She sounded breathless.

"I'm the one taking us out."

"Oh, okay." She looked around, her expression uncomfortable.

I detected that maddening scent of hers, the same one that'd had me thinking about her since she'd left my property. Something else lingered too; I tried to place the flowers.

She glanced up at me. "Do you have a few minutes?"

"Sure." I glanced toward the marina. "That was your ex?"

"Unfortunately." Regret flashed across Raquel's face.

The same man in the happy photos she'd once posted on Facebook, but something—or someone—had caused their relationship to come to an abrupt end. I had to assume that "someone" was the woman with him on the dock. Embry's face was familiar and I tried to recall where I'd seen her before.

"It was nice of you to invite me."

I took her arm and led her toward the balustrade. "Are you here to say yes?"

"To what?"

"The job offer."

"You haven't even seen my résumé," she said. "Sure you don't want to take a look at it first?"

"When we met you assured me that you are the best."

She was doing that thing with her mouth again, that pout, and it had been what had weakened my resolve last time and prevented me from seeing through her game.

"Let's be honest," she said, as she leaned against the railing, "you don't know much about me."

I shoved my hands in my pockets. "I know you own Perfume Girl."

She blinked in surprise and looked as though she was searching for something to say.

"I had to wonder why you would be at my place for an interview, if that's the case," I added.

"I'm thinking... of closing it."

"You're having financial issues?" And then I realized her predicament. "Your husband owns half the store?"

She broke my gaze, realizing I knew more about her than I'd initially let on. *These are the consequences of you coming to my home uninvited, Raquel.*

And there would be more...though I wasn't in the habit of seducing corporate spies. I let myself imagine the way her body would react to mine, the way she'd resist her desires at first, fight against my control, but then she'd have no choice but to surrender.

I wondered how much Raquel had been offered by Dazzle and Bazaar to infiltrate my lab. They had no doubt offered her the kind of money that would save her store. Right there was her motivation. My contact at D&B had informed me that Ms. Wren had attended a meeting with Anna Rosenthal. That phone call had ruined my day.

"How come you're here?" she asked. "In this harbor?"

"Champagne run."

She stared at me, and I held her gaze.

With a nod, she looked away. "This is a nice yacht. Why do you need another boat? I mean the one inside it?"

"For speed, of course." I leaned toward her. "Thirsty?"

"Excuse me?"

I smiled. "Champagne?"

"Well, as you went to all this trouble."

"No trouble." I fought this irrational desire to pin her against the wall and press my body against hers. "Wait here, please."

"Yes, sir, Captain," she replied, smirking.

I rounded the boat until I was out of sight and rested my back against the dome, trying to get a handle on my feelings and fight off the effects of her sultriness. No one had gotten under my skin like this before. I desired nothing more than to turn back and demand the truth from her…

Raquel was flirting into my consciousness and my cock was quick to alert me to the danger of her seductive prowess. I was usually immune to this kind of attack. I shifted myself in my pants so the pull wasn't obvious. I knew how to curb this ache—all I had to do was lead her off to one of my private cabins, bury myself deep inside her and bang her into blinding pleasure until she confessed.

My counterattack would leave her spent and moaning. Within an hour I'd have cracked her secret wide open. I was willing to go that far if necessary.

Ignoring all of my other guests, I headed off to fetch our drinks with that idea burning up my brain with its ingenuity—and with my dick in full agreement.

As I was carrying two flutes of champagne back to Raquel, I heard Penelope's voice coming from around the corner, and I paused for a second. When I joined them they looked like they were having a strained conversation.

"I see you've met my sister?" I handed Raquel a glass of Veuve Clicquot.

She immediately took a long sip as though needing more courage. Penelope's voice rose. "Did you invite her?"

I smiled. "Why, yes, as a matter of fact. Allow me to introduce Raquel Wren."

Penelope's eyes widened as she realized this was the woman I'd told her about—the same one who had lied about having an appointment with her.

I took a sip of ice-cold champagne. "This is the chemist I was telling you about," I threw in for my own amusement.

I wondered how well Raquel would cope with being trapped in

the same space as my sibling. Leaving them alone to talk would be cruel, but I craved the entertainment of throwing this pretty woman at Penelope.

I walked away.

"Mr. Beauregard," Raquel blurted out. "I'll take the job."

When I turned around, I saw a fissure of doubt shudder through her.

Penelope had gone pale. "What?"

My sister ought to know I could handle this; she needn't worry.

"When would you like me to start?" asked Raquel, with a stone-faced expression.

Penelope's eyes blazed with anger.

Raquel was going for the *in* and I wasn't sure whether to praise or punish her for such an obvious play. It wasn't so much as a trap as it was an invitation from me to step into a place where I could get to know more about her and keep tabs on her. Then I would find the source of this betrayal.

"Leave us," I snapped the order at Penelope.

"Why?"

My patience had run out ten minutes ago. I moved swiftly and grabbed Raquel's wrist, pulling her away from my sister until we reached a private cabin door. I opened it and gestured her inside before following.

"You looked like you needed saving," I said.

"I can hold my own."

"Still." I set my drink on a side table.

"Maybe Penelope's right to be concerned, Mr. Beauregard."

My interest piqued and my cock responded in kind. "Why is that?"

"Maybe she sees me as competition." She drew in a steady breath. "There's only one reason I came aboard and you know what it is."

"Actually, I find you somewhat of an enigma."

She studied me for what seemed like an eternity and then said, "I will shine at your house."

"I believe you will."

"I can deliver anything your heart desires," she said, smiling. "Just say what it is you want and I will create a scent that will astound you. I will bring you nectar from the gods."

"Is that all, then?" I teased. Then my expression became serious. "Why are you accepting my offer now?"

"How do you mean?"

"You still own your business."

She set her drink next to mine. "I have to close by the end of the month."

"Perhaps a generous salary would keep it afloat?"

"That wouldn't cover it."

"I see. I'm sorry it didn't work out. Many businesses don't. And perfumery is a tough one."

She ran her hands through her tousled hair, as though reflecting on what she could have done differently.

"Raquel, I need to know this is something you really want."

"Everything fell apart—" Her gaze locked on mine. "But now it seems to have come together."

"Are you certain?"

Her gaze lowered and then found mine again. "Your colognes are profound, Mr. Beauregard. I've always thought that." She stepped back and turned toward the oval window, her form becoming an erotic silhouette as sunlight flittered over her.

Her flattery wasn't needed here. We were a leader in this field and everyone knew it. And that was why people like her had to be stopped before they did any damage.

Rays caught the highlights in her windswept hair and she looked as bewitching as Guinevere—the woman from that Arthurian legend. She was beautiful, but she undermined a king's efforts to thrive...to rule.

But the way she owned her personal wreckage without bitterness, the way she seemed unscathed by life...something told me Damien would realize the mistake he'd made. The moment he'd gotten the other woman out of his system, he'd beg Raquel to take him back.

She flashed me a warm smile. "I'm open to learning new skills."

This was what made dealing with her so perilous; she knew her worth.

I had run a background check on her and it had turned up some interesting facts on the woman who had gate-crashed my Bridgestone estate. Raquel Wren had studied chemistry at Cambridge. Later, she'd been headhunted by the team over at Parfums De Royale to head up their lab on the East Coast, which was where she'd met Damien, I assumed. She'd thrived there for five years before breaking out on her own.

What Raquel may not suspect was that I had visited her social media pages. On a few sites she had posted selfies while at this harbor—every single Sunday.

She may hate spontaneity but that didn't dampen her bravery. She had built her business from the ground up. Under any other circumstances, I would have been elated by this potential new employee and her verve.

Raquel stared out the window, appearing distracted. Perhaps she needed a few more seconds to think this through. She was diving into the deep end and something told me she was assessing the risks.

"It's a great view," she finally said, turning around to face me again.

"Even better out on the ocean."

"It was nice of you to invite me. It's just that…"

"I understand," I said softly. "You need some alone time."

She looked surprised and then broke into a grateful smile. Raquel's complexity made me want to pry further. She was a lost island waiting to be explored and God how I wanted to explore her—which was all the more reason to keep her where I could control her.

"You would have the run of a state-of-the-art lab," I said, hoping to seal the deal. "The freedom to create."

"Sounds ideal."

I wasn't usually the one dealing with potential spies, but I was involved now and that made her my problem. "I have no doubt you'll be an asset."

Her breath caught. "Thank you."

"You will have two weeks to live up to my expectations. After that, I will reevaluate."

"Only two weeks?"

Then I'm out of this contract, Wren.

And so are you.

I straightened. "Problem?"

"No, that's fine. I appreciate the opportunity."

Her pleased expression caused a flurry of sensations to run through me. It reminded me of when we'd spent time alone in the stables, the way she'd looked at me then with the same curiosity, her interest piqued as she seemed to peer beyond my physical appearance.

I had to put those thoughts out of my mind.

"I look forward to joining The House of Beauregard, Astor." She went coy. "May I call you that?"

"In private, yes."

Destroying this woman and her threat to my business was going to be a delicious pleasure.

"Welcome aboard, Ms. Wren. I can't wait to see what you come up with." *Right before I crush you.* "How does this Thursday sound? That gives you enough time to find a place closer to work."

"That's great. Thank you."

"One more thing." I stepped forward and peered down at her. "I'll even go so far as to personally mentor you."

"I'd better go now," she whispered.

"I'll escort you."

"No need." She hurried out the door without looking back.

I stood there riveted by the exotic scent of daturas. It had taken me a while to figure out what she was wearing, but that poisonous, beautiful flower was unmistakable. Raquel had thought that it alone could lower my defenses. If I knew the cause of this sudden arousal, then I could fight it. It was my strength.

She'd met her match.

Yet Raquel was a dichotomy. Her presence had filled the room with light, and now there was a void where she'd been standing—so much so that I re-imagined her there. A shudder of pleasure ran up my spine.

She could use that voluptuous body of hers with devastating effect, her sensual curves enthralling a man to forget all reason. Her personal scent offered a promise of so much more, and I had to lean against the wall to prevent myself from going after her.

I needed to cleanse myself of her and there was one quick way to do just that. Moving swiftly through the cabin, I stripped naked when I hit the bathroom and then stepped inside the small cubicle, standing beneath the showerhead.

I squeezed my eyes shut as a gush of freezing cold water drenched me. I desperately tried to wash off her aura.

But my mind soon betrayed me with its wild imagining of Raquel's mouth opening to take mine, willingly accepting my tongue as it ravished hers, me conquering her entirely, me entering her and burying myself deep inside her…Raquel arching her back and screaming my name.

I rested my forehead against the glass door, my jaw tight with frustration and my breathing ragged. I dared Raquel to risk it all by challenging me. *Me.*

My senses were still being ravaged by her exotic datura scent. It had found me again, even in here.

She was bewitching.

I had to quell my addiction to this stranger.

And fast.

Chapter
NINE

Raquel

I HAD QUICKLY FOUND A LOCAL HOTEL SUITABLE FOR A TEMPORARY STAY IN South Beach. And I was learning how to navigate around this grandiose structure where I was now employed.

The lab was my safe place, and even with its sterility and high-tech equipment it was cozy enough to help me forget that it wasn't really mine, it was *his*.

Soon I would rescue my formula and get back to the life I loved.

I tried not to think about Astor Beauregard, whose office was above me on the top floor. And I tried not to think about how easily he could seduce a female with that arrogant smirk of his and those deep hazel eyes.

There were probably a slew of women hanging off his arm when he partied late into the night at those high-end clubs this town was famed for. I wondered what type of companion he preferred. Not that I cared…his private business had nothing to do with me.

I just wished Astor wouldn't look at me with that all-seeing gaze. His glare went right through me—*inside me*—as though he were searching my soul for answers to an unspoken question.

He was the kind of man no woman in her right mind would go

near. Yet my body rebelled at this logic whenever I was in the same room with him, and it was obviously because he smelled so damn good. His brand of sin was a terrible distraction.

My focus returned to the marble mortar before me. The Sonata lily petals I'd ground to liquid in the bottom had released the softest hint of lemon; this was innocence captured on the ray of the morning sun.

Lifting the mortar to my nose, I became lost in the essence of the flower that ancient Greeks had placed upon the heads of innocent brides as a symbol of their hope for a fruitful life. Its allure was purity.

This lily was free from pollen and kind on those with sensitive skin. It offered a light feminine touch, and with this watery droplet of bluebell oil I added with a squeeze of a pipette, I'd brought a hint of coolness to this sweet distraction.

I'd create concoctions only in my imagination if I had to…spend my days dreaming up twists on nature that were just as compelling. Stored inside my mind was a haven of gathered memories of the scents I'd collected over the years.

My happiness faded as I looked around the lab. Here, the pressure to deliver was on everyone's mind, it seemed. The other ten chemists made little conversation. Although they always sneaked off at ten for their coffee break.

I'd not yet gotten invited into this clique. Even my supervisor, Arabella, with her turned up nose and pristine attitude, seemed to want to get to know me better before inviting me to join them.

Like clockwork, everyone headed to the break room except for Arabella, who was finishing up on a call in her corner office. In this sterile environment the people were colder. I couldn't wait to get back to Perfume Girl where I belonged. For now, my beloved shop had a CLOSED sign on its doors and just the thought of it broke my heart. Still, I was doing all of this for a good reason and in the end it would be worth it.

Everything screamed superiority in this place, from the vast open-plan foyer that invited in light to chase away the shadows to the monitored entry points. My initial guided tour had included a brief visit to the upper level, but there'd been no sign of him.

Thank goodness.

Glass sculptures from famed designer Dale Chihuly were strategically positioned throughout to catch the sunlight flooding in from the tall windows; these brightly colored pieces of glass-blown flowers were easy to fall in love with.

Astor was hailed as cologne royalty, and if it wasn't for the fact I believed he—or his sister—may have stolen from me I may have been proud to work here. This luxurious place with its flashy light fixtures and dark furniture was a reminder of his exquisite taste, which was clearly Astor's only redeeming feature.

I was getting used to my quiet corner; though it was impossible to forget I'd once been my own boss with all the perks of independence. At least I could still create freely, but anything I came up with would be owned by The House.

From my comfy barstool I could see straight into Arabella's office. She rose out of her seat and shuffled a few papers on her desk. As predicted, she headed out to join the others without looking my way. The hiss of the air-controlled door signaled she'd left for the east corridor.

I rushed over to her office.

Inside, I rounded the desk and grabbed the mouse to her iMac, moving it back and forth to prevent her screen from locking. With my heart hammering, I searched the desktop for the link to their database.

A thrill ran up my spine when I found the icon for The House of Beauregard's formulas. With a click I had the file open. As I scanned the document titles I realized I would need more time. There were hundreds of combinations and all of them were listed under codes.

This will never work. I'll have to find another way.

My gaze shifted to the left side of the desk where a stack of envelopes lay waiting to be opened. On top was a gold-embossed card sticking half-way out of its cream envelope. I pulled it out and read the personalized invitation. Arabella had been invited to join Astor at the Key West Yacht Club for a party aboard the *Riveting*.

I slid the invitation back inside its envelope. Anyone working here was a suspect as far as I was concerned. On the chance that I might find my ledgers, I yanked open Arabella's top drawer and looked inside, but I was disappointed.

What they might have discovered by now was that the final ingredient hadn't been added—the formula was incomplete. I had been days away from adding the final touch when the bottle was stolen. This meant I was working against the clock. If they completed the formula it would be officially stamped as theirs.

The elevator pinged to announce someone had arrived on my floor. The air-controlled door slid open. I rushed to leave Arabella's office and froze in the doorway.

Astor Beauregard was standing beside my workstation. His gaze locked on mine and I strolled towards him nonchalantly, feigning business as usual.

"Hello, Raquel," he said darkly.

The tone of his voice sent a shiver up my spine as I moved around him to sit on my barstool.

He looked around. "Everyone at break?"

"Yes."

"You didn't join them?"

I looked down at my mortar. "I've had a breakthrough with something special." I swiveled so my back was to him again. "I'm going to keep going."

It meant I didn't have to look into those intense hazel eyes or be distracted by his chiseled features, though I still felt the heat of his gaze.

There was a kick to the rung of my barstool and I felt myself being spun around to face him.

Astor removed his foot. "Elaborate?"

His scent reached me and it was like the aura of an Arabian night, the full glare of a midday sun, a forbidden spice that made my clit tingle.

Damn him.

"Everything okay?" he asked.

"Yes." I folded my arms to hide my beading nipples.

"What are you working on?"

I crooked my neck to look back at the counter. "An instant classic."

Taking a step forward, he lifted the mortar to his nose and flinched. "Jesus."

My cheeks flushed as I watched him set the bowl down with annoyance.

I raised my chin with pride. "I've yet to add the Madagascar ylang-ylang—"

"Please don't."

"But—"

"Ms. Wren, you vowed to create a product I could market to distinguished gentlemen. Gentlemen of good taste. Something I could wear." He pointed. "What the hell is this?"

"It's for women."

"I'm aware of that."

"I was going for innocence."

"Well, you're halfway there. This *is* for a nubile—one too timid to attend her own prom." He waved his hand through the air. "She's scared to admit what she wants. She remains unfulfilled. Frustrated…"

Was that a bloody accusation?

He tutted. "This isn't worth my time."

I slid off my barstool and rested my hands on my hips.

"So you were serious when you asked if I could create a scent for fuck-boys, then?"

"Leather and sex." He didn't blink. "That is what you promised me."

"I would need—"

"This lab contains all the ingredients you would require. Now deliver."

"Where's the leather?"

"You have a memory don't you?"

"I need reminding." *Asshole.*

His expression turned provocative. My gaze shot to his shoes as though he was hinting for me to kneel and whiff his Brogues. This man was incorrigible.

He unclipped his belt buckle.

Oh, no.

I stared as he began weaving the belt out through the loops of his pants and tugged it free.

"Leather," he said, offering it to me.

My fingers tingled when they brushed against his as I took it from him. I lifted the leather strip to my nose and breathed in raw earthiness. A stirring of erotic pleasure surged through me.

"Raquel?"

"I would need to keep this for a while."

"I have others. I keep a spare suit in my office just in case."

"Oh, an extra belt in your office?" I winked.

"Let's keep this professional, Ms. Wren."

I suppressed a smile and thought it was cute the way he tried to hide his amusement. I'd gotten to him, made a crack in his steely armor and it felt good to see his human side. Thank God no one was around to watch us flirt.

He stepped closer. "What reaction does the scent of leather evoke in you, Raquel?"

"A primal need. Carnal, even."

"In what way?"

"It awakens the senses." I went for it. "Causes a delicious arousal."

"I see." He looked intrigued.

"Though I have a cold coming," I said, sniffing. "I'm probably way off."

"Ah."

"I'll grab some vitamin C on the way home."

His gaze locked on mine. "I'm interested in collaborating with you on this."

"I usually work alone."

"So do I, but I'd like your help in creating a sensation of craving."

A shudder ran through me and reached my core. The husky way

he'd spoken those last few words made my breasts ache for his touch.

"In a bottle," he added. "I have a feeling you know how that feels."

"I can do that."

"What inspires you, Ms. Wren?"

"Um…a place, a person, a memory…"

"Let's start by you imagining the perfect man, Raquel. Someone loyal, distinguished, wealthy, well-traveled and intelligent, of course. And above all…honest." His gaze darted to Arabella's office.

I didn't flinch. "Are you describing yourself, Mr. Beauregard?"

"I haven't finished."

My throat tightened.

He stared at me. "I want to create a cologne that gives fuck-boys the advantage."

What about the women?

"You already have it," I blurted out. "I mean, they do. Not that you're like them."

The warmth of his smile threw me for a second.

I sighed. "Okay. How would it work?"

"Us working together?" He stepped back. "We both come up with the desired effect we want to arouse and reverse engineer our outcome as we merge…a product we can be proud of."

"I'm not used to collaborating."

"You work for me. So the answer is clearly, 'Yes, Mr. Beauregard'."

He tucked his hands into his pockets and turned and walked away with that usual swagger.

The hiss of the air-tight door came and went.

I sat on my barstool and watched him ascend in the glass-walled elevator. His intense gaze stayed on me until he disappeared from view.

Arrogant bastard.

I took another whiff of his leather belt, thinking this wouldn't be a punishing assignment. I was willing to believe I could learn more about the cologne industry from him. It would also give me an excuse to visit his office, and maybe I would find myself alone in there so I could search for my ledger.

Running my nose along the strip of leather, I absorbed his scent which spoke of haughtiness and danger. A jolt of inspiration hit me...

I'd flip his desired outcome and create a twist of chemistry that would have the fuck-boys on their knees and begging for it.

Challenge accepted, Mr. Beauregard.

Chapter
TEN

"**I**T'S HAPPENING."

The call came in around 10:00 p.m. I closed down my iMac, changed into jeans and a sweater, grabbed a bottle of water and headed out. This was going to be a long night—there would be no sleep.

I drove across town and soon arrived at the beach. After parking, I saw the conservation team at our checkpoint and headed toward them.

My concern rose as I approached Lawrence, a student and assistant to Dr. Garcia Rena, our senior marine biologist who was heading up this project. Lawrence looked panicked, which was a change from his usual cheerful demeanor. Sierra, his girlfriend, stood beside him, looking just as worried.

"Hey, Astor," said Lawrence, coming over to shake my hand. "Thank you for being here."

"Wouldn't miss it." I smiled at them. "Where is everyone?"

Sierra sniffed. "They're doing a garbage sweep before the hatching starts."

"I'll join them." I scanned the beach. "Where's Garcia?"

"He's at Romero's across the street," said Lawrence. "The

restaurant owner is refusing to turn off his lights."

My attention snapped to the stores and restaurants lining the street opposite. Romero's was lit up like a Christmas tree.

Shit.

Things were about to turn deadly. Thousands of sea turtle eggs were about to hatch and the babies would be making their way toward the ocean in droves. The moon and stars would lead them to the brightest horizon, but right now the lights of the restaurant would confuse and disorientate them.

I gave a nod. "I'll handle it."

"The owner won't budge," said Lawrence. "We've all tried to reason with him."

"I can be pretty persuasive when I want to be." It didn't take me long to jog across the street and enter Romero's. It was a decent-looking place, clean and buzzing with guests, the kind of place I might even have joined friends for a cold beer. Rounding the tables, I made my way toward the back.

A waitress hurried over when she saw me heading toward the kitchen. "Can I help you?"

"I'm looking for the owner."

"He's talking with someone right now. Why don't you grab a drink at the bar—"

"I believe he's talking with a friend of mine, Garcia Rena? He's the head biologist over at South Beach Marine Center."

"Oh, okay. They're chatting in Hank's office."

"Where's that?"

She pointed me in the right direction. "What's this about?"

"Time is of the essence."

She led me down a short hallway and I followed the raised voices. Garcia Rena was going at it with the restaurateur. This was not like him—Garcia was a quiet spoken man who had dedicated his life to his work. He led the conservation volunteers with integrity and a sense of fun. I was proud to call him a good friend.

For years, I had joined his team on their quest to save the turtles, clean the beaches, and offer both financial support and time. It was a great distraction from business and a worthwhile course that had me feeling like I was giving back.

I hated seeing him like this. "Hey, Garcia," I let him know I was here.

The office was small and dank and the man on the other side of the shabby desk had a red face and a bad attitude. Both of them looked riled up and equally backed into a corner.

Garcia's kind eyes were full of worry as he held my gaze. "Hey, Astor. He refuses to cooperate. He's keeping his lights on no matter what."

"May I?" I stepped into the office. "Garcia, why don't you go join the others? The turtles have started hatching."

He glared at the man behind the desk. "This is the law. You know that."

The man's jowls wobbled. "Fine me."

"Garcia." My tone was insistent. "I've got this."

He gave a nod of acknowledgment and I watched him leave, right before he gave me a look that told me he needed this done.

I faced the man, resting my fists on his desk. "Thousands of sea turtles are about to hatch. They will crawl toward the brightest horizon which happens to be this place, which means they won't survive. Turn off your lights."

"I've been over this with Garcia."

"It's Dr. Rena, to you. Why won't you be reasonable?"

He reached out to shake my hand. "Sorry, didn't catch your name?"

I stood straight, not falling for the attempted distraction. "My name doesn't matter. What matters is that you're using a long wavelength light for the front of your restaurant. The law says your walkways need to be shielded. What the hell is the problem here?"

"Speak to my lawyer."

I pointed toward the beach. "This place is about to cause a massacre."

"So what if a few sea turtles get turned around."

"We can't afford to lose even one."

"Birds are picking them off all the time."

"You do realize sea turtles take care of the grass bed that millions of fish, crustaceans, and shellfish depend on to survive. No sea turtles, no fish."

He leaned back. "I'll serve steak."

I relaxed my hands so they didn't form fists. "We can call the press to cover this. How about they feature this place and match it with photos of hundreds of dead turtles outside. Imagine the headline...customers having to step over the bodies of baby turtles when they arrive. That will dull their appetites." I folded my arms across my chest. "Alternatively, and by far the best offer I have, is having the press cover the story of how every restaurant complied with the law and saved the lives of thousands of turtles. We can feature Romero's and bring you more customers. Choice is yours."

"Are you threatening me with slander?"

"Only the truth. I can have the news team down here with their cameras focused on your clientele, asking if their lobster dinner was worth the burden of knowing what it really cost them. Cut to a dozen dead baby turtles and you have your story."

He pushed to his feet. "Who the fuck are you?"

"Astor Beauregard. And I'm leaving. We have a long night ahead. We don't have time for this. When I reach the other side of the beach your lights will be off. Am I clear?"

"Who's going to cover my lost profits?"

"Visit every table and explain to your customers why you've turned out the lights. Be the hero here. That will have them showing their loyalty and coming back." I turned and stormed out.

When I made it to the other side of the street, I turned and waited, counting the seconds as I reached into my pocket for my phone. Calling the news station wasn't an idle threat. I brought my iPhone to my ear, ready to make the call.

I'd shut that place down in a heartbeat.

Romero's lights went out

I turned to face the others and we raised our fists in triumphant cheers.

Sierra came over and wrapped her arms around my waist. "What did you say to him?"

"I told him I was going to send you in to deal with him." I smiled at that.

She smiled too. "I'd have burned the place down, only that would've just lit the place up worse."

"Defeats the objective really." I gave her back a pat. "Let's follow Garcia's lead and proceed as peaceful warriors."

"That's a better idea." Sierra took my hand and led me across the sand. "Come see. They're so cute."

With the moon lighting our way, Garcia and Lawrence joined us and we stood a little way back from a mound of golden sand and watched a hatchling wriggle to the surface. Soon he was joined by his siblings rising out into the evening air with their shells soft and their eyes bright.

They waggled their way down the beach toward the ocean and we stood guard, all of us ready to redirect the ones that were drawn to car headlights or other distractions of light or noise.

I kneeled next to a baby turtle that had rolled onto his shell and was struggling to right himself, his legs waving in the air.

"I know it's tempting," said Garcia from behind me.

I wanted to give the edge of his shell a nudge to turn him right side up. "Hardest part of the job," I admitted.

The turtle flipped himself over and we watched him scurrying to catch up with the others.

"Thank you for being here, Astor." Garcia knelt and we shared a smile. "I don't think you quite realize how many lives you saved tonight."

I shot him a look. "You've saved far more, Garcia."

"We're a team." He tapped my back with affection.

"It's because of you we're here."

And here was where I was meant to be.

Chapter
ELEVEN

Raquel

I HAD DRIVEN TO KEY WEST ALL THE WHILE REASSURING MYSELF I COULD back out of gate-crashing this work party at any second. I was close to blowing everything up and my plan to remain beneath the radar at The House of Beauregard was in jeopardy.

That terrifying thought stayed with me as I strolled along the wharf. When I recognized the *Riveting* moored to the docks, I was again reminded of the Beauregards' impressive wealth. It's not like they needed the money—though the rich always wanted more. And Astor struck me as a man who loved to wallow in luxury.

Still, up there on that yacht was a possible resolution to all of this. And this time I'd be staying aboard no matter what.

I was wearing my floral print dress and gold sandals, and I felt sure I could easily hide in the crowd. I made my way along the bridge and was met with loud club music and people talking over it. Some guests wore bikinis…this didn't look like a professional soiree *at all*.

So this was how the Beauregard family threw a big reveal—they served champagne and appetizers on silver trays carried by staff in white uniforms. They played rock music and gave the party a relaxed feel to woo the staff into thinking they were a fun company to work for.

I didn't recognize anyone as I hurried to find a secluded area to hide out in until we left the harbor. We'd be halfway out on the ocean by the time I made an appearance. I sought out a cabin where I could avoid the guests and lock myself inside. If they were showcasing my work tonight, I would get the chance to get close to it. Then I'd confront Astor and his sister in front of everyone.

The engine thrummed to life and we headed out to sea.

Pacing back and forth in the small space, I ran through all the events that had led me here. I should have gone with a different security company. Not the local firm that was the least expensive and the most likely to fail to keep my precious place safe. I'd been so obsessed with my work I'd not raised my head long enough to see the threat from my competitors. Knowing my carelessness had caused the loss of my most unique scent left a bitter taste in my mouth.

It was easy to restock the store, but the theft of my beloved fragrance, the one I had worked so hard to perfect, left me feeling violated. After my divorce it felt like the final blow. I wasn't sure I'd ever get over this string of betrayals. The dull ache in my heart was a constant anguish I couldn't shake.

There's no other way.

My chances of getting that scent back were slim to none, but I clung to the hope. Being on this boat was like stepping out onto a high wire knowing that a fall was imminent.

Time dissolved as I finally settled into a comfortable chair and waited while going over all the things I was going to say if I got caught before I pounced on them.

Someone rapped on the cabin door.

I sprung up out of my seat and waited to see if they knocked again.

"Ms. Wren." A woman's voice.

Oh, God.

With a twist of the lock I had the door open and peered out at a waitress holding a tray carrying a glass of champagne and a plate of chocolate-covered strawberries.

She gave me a polite smile. "Mr. Beauregard wanted to offer you some refreshments."

Almost cringing, I opened the door wider to see if he was with her.

"Can I come in?" she asked.

I stepped back and she walked into the cabin, placing the tray on a side-table.

"Mr. Beauregard wanted to make sure you're comfortable."

"I'm fine."

She turned to leave.

"Do you know where Mr. Beauregard is right now?"

"He just left."

"What do you mean he left?" *We're out on the ocean!*

She glanced at her watch. "You might catch him."

I recalled Astor mentioning he had a garage for his speedboat on the *Riveting.* "Is he getting on his boat? Can you take me there?"

"Sure."

I hurried along the starboard side of the ship close behind her, stealing a glance at the vast ocean. We were definitely in the middle of nowhere.

When we reached a narrow staircase, the girl pointed down to the deck below.

"He's down there."

She left to return to her duties and I descended the winding steps into what looked like a hub.

I stopped halfway down when I saw Astor.

He was dressed in black slacks and a white shirt and was tieless, looking all kinds of suave as he lowered a speedboat into the water. His gaze rose to meet mine.

"How's the party?"

I suddenly felt tongue-tied, and cringed through the awkward silence that followed.

He grinned and it was one of those heart-stopping smiles. "I'm making a getaway before anyone notices."

I smiled, trying not to look guilty. "I thought this was a work event."

"Private party." He gestured toward the upper deck.

"You're not revealing something new?"

"No." Astor watched me carefully. "But now that you're here you're welcome to stay."

I didn't want to be left alone with Penelope.

The speedboat swayed as it met the water and then floated into the center of the hub.

Astor held out his hand to me. "Wanna escape?"

I flew down the remaining steps and accepted his outstretched hand. As I climbed into the speedboat, it wobbled slightly beneath me. I made myself comfortable in the passenger seat and then watched Astor climb in beside me.

When he leaned toward me super close I froze, and then realized he was securing my seatbelt by tugging it across my chest before clipping it in. His cologne wafted over me and a shudder ran up my spine.

He gave the belt an extra tug before moving away. "We can never be too careful, Raquel." He faced the control panel without clipping his own belt in.

I made a mental note to mention it to him once my breathing returned to normal and my heart stopped hammering. This man's charisma was off the charts. He probably knew I was on the boat the moment I boarded, and me not mixing with the other guests had to have looked suspicious.

The engine roared to life. We were forced back in our seats as we zoomed out from beneath the *Riveting*, skimming along the water. I turned slightly to see the yacht getting smaller behind us. At this speed we'd be back to Key West in no time.

"How was your first week?" Astor raised his voice above the engine.

Locks of hair whipped around my face and I tried to get them under control.

"Great," I yelled.

"Settling in?"

"Yes, thank you."

Astor drew back on the throttle, reducing our speed so we could talk more easily.

"So tell me more about you, Raquel."

"I grew up in England." I reached out and gripped the side of the boat as it bounced along. "I was hired by Parfum De Royal to head up their lab. Stayed there for five years until I opened my own place." I felt a stab of regret for bringing it up.

"That was how you came to America?"

"Yes."

"How about before then?"

"I studied at Cambridge."

"And before that?"

"I grew up in Penzance."

"Are your parents still living there?"

"No, not anymore." On his glance my way I added, "I was in foster care for a while."

"May I ask why?"

"My mother wasn't well enough to take care of me." I drew in a sharp breath and prepared to tell the tried and tested tale. "She had leukemia. She died soon after I arrived in my first foster home." I gave a shrug. "My memories of her are happy ones. Trips to the beach... building sandcastles, eating Cornish ice cream. Visiting her favorite perfume store in Truro. She made Christmas and birthdays special."

"I'm sorry." He seemed genuinely sincere. "There weren't any other relatives who could take you in?"

"No."

He caught and held my gaze. "You've done well, Raquel. Your mom would be proud of you."

I bit the inside of my cheek, not wanting to disagree and ruin the moment. I was a divorcée who was in the process of losing all I had built up over the years so I felt more of a failure than I ever had. "I was offered a job in New York and things took off from there."

He flashed a smile. "Your résumé is impressive. I'm flattered you want to work for me."

I gripped my seat when we hit a wave. "You're the best there is, Mr. Beauregard." Then quickly added, "I mean...your company is the best."

The sunset was glorious and even though I'd failed to get the answers I needed there was still a possibility I would find a moment to talk with Astor later. I was sure he'd be reasonable. He was certainly being accommodating right now.

I laid my head back and savored the sunny view, the rush of the wind cooling my face. I found myself relaxing and then realized I was actually having fun.

"Can I ask you something personal?" he said.

"Sure."

"Are you in debt?"

"Not if I sell my store. Why?"

"Just trying to work out your motivation."

"For working for you?" I turned to look at him. "I'm grateful for my job."

"I have this feeling, Raquel, that you're not telling me the truth."

"About what?"

He stared at me, his smile seductive.

"Does this have anything to do with the quality of my work?" I asked.

"I'm sure your work is exceptional."

Ahead, I could see what looked like the mirage of a harbor. I squinted to try and locate a landmark, but nothing looked familiar. I was going to have to find my way back to Key West. Maybe Astor would consider giving me a lift.

"Where are we?" My frown deepened as I took in the whitewashed homes and colorful stores beyond the marina. I still saw nothing recognizable as he directed the boat toward the dock.

"This is your moment to confess, Raquel."

"Excuse me?"

"I don't like secrets—especially when they affect me."

"I don't have any," I said, glaring at him. "Why would you say that?"

"The evidence."

"What evidence?"

"You turned up at my home unannounced and apparently my sister had no appointment with you."

"A misunderstanding."

"Ah, so that explains it."

A feeling of dread stole over me, giving me goose flesh. "Where are we?"

He held my gaze. "Havana."

I blinked at him, trying to process the information, and hoping I would soon hear the punch-line of his joke.

Pushing himself up, he threw the rope to a young man who secured our boat to a wooden post as he chatted with Astor—in Spanish.

"This isn't possible," I muttered.

I stared at the foreigners milling about...*no, I was the foreigner*. I tried to calm my panicked thoughts, my chest tight with disbelief. "Are you getting off here?"

"I've arrived at my destination." He leaped onto the marina. "So apparently I am, yes."

"I didn't bring my passport!"

He faced me. "They don't take kindly to illegal entry." Reaching into his jacket, he removed his wallet and pulled out several banknotes, handing them to the young man. "Watch my boat, please, Samuel. Eres bueno con eso?"

"Sí, señor." The Cuban gave him a wave.

Astor strolled off down the wharf.

I climbed onto the wooden dock and called after him. "You're not seriously going to leave me here?"

He turned around with a grin, ambling backwards.

"Good luck, Ms. Wren."

Chapter
TWELVE

I NEEDED TO BREATHE...REMAIN CALM AND NOT PANIC.

Under normal circumstances I'd have been happy to be here. I adored traveling and seeing new sights, meeting new people, and exploring richly layered cultures.

But at the moment I was about to hyperventilate. I'd probably pass out and fall into the ocean and be swept away, cursing Astor with my last thoughts.

I hurried after him with unsteady legs, pulling at the back of my dress which was stuck to my skin with sweat. I had no intention of spending the night in a Cuban jail.

Charging round the corner, I skidded to a stop and peered into the crowd. I couldn't see him. A car sped by and I leaped onto the sidewalk to avoid being hit.

I felt a jolt of relief when I saw Astor entering an impressive building with spiraling white pillars.

I sprinted after him.

Bursting into the foyer of the Hotel Inglaterra, I watched Astor heading towards the east wing. On the way he gave a nod to a man who looked like the concierge, who handed him something, though I couldn't see what.

My heels clipped on the blue and green tiles as I tried to keep up with him, shuddering at the sudden chill of air-conditioning. Lush palms and towering plants lined the corridor and the impressive décor surrounding me was a pleasant distraction from my sense of impending doom.

At a casual pace, I followed Astor into a well-lit room. He was at the bar casually ordering what I assumed was an alcoholic drink.

Cheeky bastard.

Breathless, I caught up with him. "Why are you doing this?"

"Ordering a drink?"

"This is highly inappropriate."

"I'm rather fond of this place." He accepted the shot glass from the barman. "A rum for the lady, too, please." He turned his gaze on me. "Looks like you need it."

"You've lost your mind."

"And yet you're the stowaway." He raised his drink to look at it. "I'm tempted to leave you here."

The bartender slid my drink over to me and I threw it back, tasting caramel and brown sugar. I made an O with my mouth to cool the burn of rum.

"Do you treat all your employees like this, Mr. Beauregard?"

"Just you." He threw his drink back and clenched his teeth as though it had scorched his throat. "Another." He slammed down his glass and slid it toward the barman.

"I'm the honest one here," I said, seething. "You're the one who needs to take a long hard look at yourself."

"I'm done playing games, Raquel. Why were you snooping around Arabella's office?"

"I was looking for a pen."

"Seriously?"

I made a rude noise. "You smuggled me into a foreign country. I don't have to wonder anymore what kind of man you are."

He lifted another shot of rum and held it in front of my face. "Drink."

"I'm not drinking anything else."

"Finish it. Then I'll take you home."

I took the glass and held his stare, trying to figure out if he was telling the truth.

"Promise?"

"Yes."

I threw it back.

"First, we talk." He threw pesos on the bar and then grabbed my wrist, leading me back down the hallway.

We stopped at an elevator. He punched the UP button.

I glared at him. "Where are we going?"

The elevator doors slid open and Astor stepped inside. I had no choice but to follow. He leaned back casually against the wall, looking hot as hell with his windswept hair and casually open shirt.

A rush of warmth and lightheadedness hit me—the rum was making me heady.

I was going to turn this situation around and have Astor confessing what he'd done. We got off the elevator and hurried along a red carpeted hallway. He suddenly stopped at one of the doors and with a wave of his keycard, it unlocked with a click.

"How come you have that?" I pointed to the key.

Then I remembered the concierge had handed him something.

Astor went on ahead into the room and I followed. My addled brain made out the luxury furniture of a hotel suite, and I guessed the bedroom was through one of the doors on our right. As my eyes adjusted to the dimness I straightened my back in defense.

Astor stopped in the center of the room and pivoted to face me.

"Start talking." His dark tone burned through me.

"I don't know what you mean."

His gaze narrowed. "Are you working alone?"

"I work for you, Mr. Beauregard."

"This won't be the first time one has infiltrated my lab."

"One what?"

"Spy."

I sat on the arm of a chair. "I'm not a spy. Why would you think such a thing?"

"I'm giving you a chance to explain yourself, Raquel. Which is decent of me under the circumstances."

"I create and sell perfumes. That's what I do."

"And I read people. Trust me, I'm good at it."

"Has someone said something?" I asked calmly.

"There's no point in denying it anymore. You're hiding something."

"Yes, I am. Humiliation." I pushed to my feet and closed the gap between us. "My marriage fell apart because my husband ran off with a younger woman and now he's pulling his share out of the business so he can buy a fuck-pad with an ocean view. I've lost my store, and along with it my job. I'm a woman who no longer trusts anyone. Maybe that's what you're picking up."

His frown deepened.

I added, "What you see is a woman fighting back and refusing to drown."

"Raquel, swear you're being honest with me."

"Have you been honest with me in every respect?"

"Yes."

I looked around at the décor of his hotel room and let that serve as my accusation against his integrity.

He gave a cursory nod. "I don't usually bring women here—"

"And then abandon them?"

"Pablo was watching over you."

"Who?"

"The Chief of Police."

"Oh, well that's fine, then," I said bitterly. "Notify the authorities, why don't you."

"You're so careful all the time…this gave you the jolt of adrenaline your mind and body has been craving. Enjoy it while it lasts."

My hand twitched with a desire to slap him, but instead I balled it into a fist of frustration. He was still my boss, after all. "What happened to you, Astor?"

"How do you mean?"

"You don't trust anyone, either."

He waved that off. "Those who cross me regret it for the rest of their lives."

A shiver of uncertainty scurried up my spine.

He towered over me. "Do you want to know the kind of man I am?"

"It's obvious."

"Ah, but what you have observed is merely the surface." He shoved his hands into his pockets. "I could revel in the slow burn of torturing you."

"Quite the confession." This man didn't scare me. "Is this how you chase away the competition?"

"You are the competition."

"My store is about to close. I'm hardly a threat."

"And yet…"

Outside the window came a burst of laughter from a crowd passing by, but it didn't ease the tension between us. Outside another world awaited, but I wasn't meant to see it.

"You're a cautious businessman," I said. "I respect that."

"I think you underestimate me, Raquel."

These were the same words I'd used on Damien back at his restaurant, and it made me flinch. "You want to test me? Observe my resolve?"

He stepped closer. "Beg for mercy."

"I really don't think I will."

"You crash into my world flaunting your beauty, using it as a weapon, and I intend to find out your motives one way or another."

A swoon hit me hard. The scent of rum on his breath was sweet and enticing.

"You think you can scare me off?" I said softly.

"The rum has given you false courage." He reached up and curled a finger around a lock of my hair. A moment later, he seemed to realize what he'd done and let go.

"You're the most conceited man I've ever met."

My gaze slid to his lips. His mouth was full and parted and seductive.

"Raquel, you are maddening."

My breath caught in my throat, and I was close to blurting out an accusation…but something stopped me. Maybe it was the way he seemed to be covering up something himself. Maybe it was because I knew he would deny it and I would lose my chance to find my perfume.

Or maybe it was because he was so close to me I couldn't think straight, and I no longer cared about the danger he posed. My mouth parted and I wondered what his kiss would be like, the one I never got to experience back at Bridgestone. A rush of arousal sparked deep inside me, causing me to shudder.

He saw my reaction. "Tempted?"

"By what?"

"The promise of blinding pleasure."

"I'm not like that."

"Perhaps you should be."

Caution hadn't served me well in the past. All those times I'd held back had led to missed opportunities and eventually heartache. What if I acted on the passion rising within me and leapt into this moment with abandon. "I'm not the threat here, Astor."

There was something predatory in the way he stared at me. I sensed he was waiting for me to surrender so he'd have the upper hand. He was the enemy yet my body yearned for his touch.

"This is not why I brought you here," he said through clenched teeth.

"Why did you?" My nipples beaded and the sensation felt divine; my body trembled with the realization that he, too, was feeling the chemistry between us.

"I only want the truth," he whispered.

"All that I am is true."

"I want to believe that."

"Are you as bad as you say?"

"I brought you to Cuba." He opened his palms to make his point. "I consider that tame."

"What else would you do to me?"

"Sure you want me to answer that question?"

I gave a wary nod.

"Each enemy is dealt with differently."

"I'm not the enemy."

His seductive gaze turned dark. "Your punishment would be me taking you to the edge of pleasure and then plunging you over into an abyss. If you consent to it."

"Doesn't sound so bad."

He gave me a cruel smile. "So…you wish to be ravished entirely? And then destroyed? Ruined?" He stepped back and started to walk away.

"Yes."

He turned around to face me with a curious expression.

"I want that," I said huskily.

Astor moved closer, looming over me. "Do you believe you deserve such treatment?"

"I want…" *To feel something, anything. I want to be free of this numbness…*

Astor tipped up my chin. "You're already broken."

I rose on my toes and bit down on his lower lip. He groaned and yanked me against his chest in a full kiss, reaching up to cup my face as his mouth ravaged me. I felt his hardness against me as our tongues lashed—his battling mine as he fought for control, fought to conquer me.

I forgot both time and place, knowing only the divine sensation of being held against him, sinking deeper into my need, this yearning to be desired so fervently.

He nipped my earlobe, and then pulled back, looking conflicted. "Raquel, you had two shots. I need to know you want this before you let me do more."

I let out an impatient sigh. "I'm a scientist, Mr. Beauregard, which means I take my time and carefully explore all the details before making a decision."

"Of course." He stepped away, frowning. "Forgive me."

"My answer's yes." I raised my chin proudly. "However, it will be the last kiss I allow you."

He leaned forward and whispered, "Then I'll make it count."

My jaw dropped in surprise as he knelt and lifted the hem of my dress. His palm slid up my inner thigh and then he reached for my thong, sliding it to the side to expose me.

I'd not been intimate with a man for what felt like an eternity. I couldn't think clearly, couldn't work out how we'd gotten here...but I wanted this more than oxygen.

His seductive gaze rose to meet mine, his sharp, gorgeous features mesmerizing.

His tongue darted.

Okay, wow.

It felt amazing, this tingly pleasure owning me as he ran his tongue along my clit. I shuddered at the sensation, stunned I was letting the enemy do this to me.

This was more than flirting, this was reckless—and I was wildly abandoning all sense of control. I savored the feel of his tongue spiraling against my clit, causing it to throb deliciously.

His mouth widened and he possessed me entirely, rhythmically sucking my clitoris and then pounding it with the tip of his tongue, a delectable, daring gesture that caused waves of never-ending bliss to rush through me. My nipples ached and my body began to tremble. "I'm going to..."

He reached around with both hands and dug his fingers into my butt, holding me firmly against him so there was no escape. My head fell back and my pelvis rocked against his face as wave after wave of ecstasy rushed through me, taking me into the stratosphere.

This was different to anything I'd ever experienced. This was a man who knew how to devour a woman and wasn't afraid to do it at her feet.

I shuddered through an endless climax, gripping his head to make sure he didn't deny me the last drop of pleasure possessing me. My legs went weak and I whimpered as he lashed me with his tongue for the final time.

He rose with the same masculine grace with which he'd knelt. "I want more of you."

With a shaky nod I permitted him to lean forward and press his mouth against mine, only it was a tender kiss this time, sharing my sweet taste with his passion to possess me. Instinctively, I fought against his ownership, nipping at his lip—and he groaned, his tongue warring with mine more fervently as he pressed me to him in a tight embrace.

Finally, we broke apart and held each other's gaze. I was certain he was questioning our actions, too.

Astor laced his fingers through mine and led me into the bedroom.

The room offered simple luxury. A burgundy quilt covered a large four-poster with tall, swirling carved posts. On either side were matching bedside tables. A white vanity sat near windows covered with closed red curtains.

"Tonight you are mine to please, Raquel," Astor said. His hand caressed my arm and electricity shot along my skin. "Turn around."

I did as he asked and my thighs weakened at the sensation of his fingers working the catch at my nape. He lifted my arms and eased the dress over my head, tossing it across the room.

Self consciously, I covered myself with my arms. "I haven't...for a while." I hated confessing it.

I felt the gentle touch of his lips against my left shoulder, and then he proceeded to rain kisses along my back and over to my right ear. I was in a foreign place feeling foreign sensations and I found it all so hard to believe.

Just breathe...

Astor rested a hand on my lower back, coaxing me toward the bed. His hands moved down the curve of my spine and over my butt, which he squeezed, causing a jolt of pleasure to rush through me. He wrapped his arm around my waist and pulled me back against his chest, burying his face in my hair.

The warmth of his body left mine and I felt him working the catch of my bra strap, unclipping it and setting my breasts free. I crossed my arms over my chest and stared across the room, embarrassed by my vulnerability.

He quickly pulled down my panties and I stepped out of them.

"Don't be shy with me, Raquel."

I spun round in his arms. "Maybe this time we can just do the ravishing part. Leave the destroying bit until next time...if there is a next time. Not that I expect there to be—"

He placed a fingertip on my lips. "Shhh," he said, smiling. "I'm taking the lead."

Closing my eyes, I pressed my cheek against his chest and breathed in his masculine scent, feeling my fears dissipate.

"I ravaged your pussy," he said softly, then nipped my shoulder. "So everything that comes afterwards will be easier for you, surely?"

My body shuddered as his words resonated through me.

"That doesn't mean..." He paused, lifting me and throwing me back onto the bed. "That I won't be thorough."

I bounced on the mattress, laughing, as he began to undress.

He unbuttoned his shirt and pulled it off, revealing chiseled abs and a toned athletic form. As he stripped out of his pants, my gaze ran over his long, firm legs and muscled thighs. He showed no shame in his nakedness—unlike me, who had reached for a gold-braided throw and was using it to cover myself.

He stood at the end of the bed and whispered, "I didn't intend..."

I stared at his face, trying to understand his concern.

"I don't have a condom," he said.

"Ahhh. I do." I felt his gaze on me as I rose from the bed and hurried out to grab my purse.

The fact I had a condom was a miracle. Hazel had thrown it to me over drinks one night and had told me getting laid was a good way to get over my ex. I'd popped it into my handbag, assuming it would expire before I needed it.

Now I was feeling stunned that I had seriously considered going bareback because I wanted him so badly...his kiss, his body crushed against mine, his cock buried deep inside me.

This was the biggest risk I'd taken in my life—or so it felt. It was wild and spontaneous and delicious.

I handed Astor the condom packet and he studied it, his gaze rising to meet mine.

"Only one?"

"Yes."

He grinned. "We'll just have to be imaginative then, won't we?"

I climbed onto the bed, my gaze riveted on Astor as he rolled the condom onto his hefty erection, its length and girth impressive. The promise of pleasure had me licking my lips in anticipation. In a daze, I pulled the throw over me once more.

Astor leaned forward and tugged the throw out of my grip. "I want to look at you." He crawled slowly onto the bed as though stalking me.

In a flash of raw power he grabbed my wrists and pinned them above my head, using his knees to spread my legs. It felt rough and primal and sent my senses reeling. This was the kind of raw passion I'd never imagined I'd experience again.

I opened my thighs wider and raised my hips against his weight to coax him inside me. His mouth captured my right nipple and he suckled firmly, sending sharp pangs of delight radiating straight down.

He let go of my wrists, moving his mouth over to my other breast to play with my pert nipple. His languid gaze found mine and in that moment I forgot everything else. It was the way he looked at me, the authority he wielded, the passion he exuded...it was easing away my sadness.

I turned my face away to hide my emotions.

"You have a beautiful body, Raquel." He ran his palm up my waist and along my arm. "You are a living poem," he cooed. "Perfect in every way." His warm hand ran over my belly. "Your curves are that of a real woman." He kissed my stomach and then lowered his head between my thighs, pressing his lips to me. "You're ready for me."

"Yes." I sighed. "So ready."

He pushed himself up until his body lay along mine and then pressed his cock against my tautness, easing himself in as he stared down at me, watching my reaction at his deep thrust. A dull ache of pleasure enveloped me as he circled his hips slowly to heighten the sensation. Then he leisurely withdrew, only to plunge all the way in filling me completely. I squeezed myself tightly around him, milking his hard shaft as waves of ecstasy wracked my body.

My breathing became ragged as I wrapped my legs around him possessively, needing him more than I'd realized before, but then letting go as he took the lead, my pelvis rocking perfectly in sync with his.

In his expression I suddenly saw a flash of vulnerability appear, and he buried his face against my neck as though to hide it. Maybe this man was more sensitive than he wanted me to see.

"Look at me, please," I whispered.

He lifted his head and held my gaze, and I saw his façade fall away and kindness fill his eyes. It felt like we were the only two people in the world as we moved in perfect rhythm with each other.

"Astor," I said softly.

"You okay?" He slowed for a moment.

"More than okay."

"Tell me what you need."

"I only need this."

He rose a little and rubbed his pelvis hard against mine. It felt divine.

"Do that again," I begged.

"This?"

"Yes, I like it."

"Then I think you'll like this, too," he said, grabbing me and flipping us over.

I lay on top of him with my back against this chest. With a fierce shove he was inside me again, his right hand reaching low to strum my clit as he pounded into me. My body burned with desire at his masterful touch, the dexterous blend of speed and rhythm bringing me blinding pleasure, as though his fingertip and that small bud were one.

His left arm wrapped around me possessively to bar any escape. I was his entirely.

This wasn't me...I'd never moaned wantonly like this before. I didn't remember ever making any noise. I'd stayed silent and endured what was offered.

But this...this was so much more. This was me running into the flames and burning up entirely. With thighs splayed, breasts bobbing, my body and soul completely exposed, I was groaning loudly, not even caring that the headboard was banging the wall.

I had surrendered completely...

When his left hand squeezed my nipple, the fierce jolt of arousal sent me over the edge and I lost all sense of time and place. My mind clung to the exquisite sensations, never wanting the orgasm to end.

I lay in his arms, perspiring and panting, still shuddering from the blinding pleasure. When he brushed a stray lock of hair out of my face, it felt so tender, so caring, that I yearned to stay here in this room and hold on to this feeling forever.

Be strong. Let this become the happy memory you deserve. Let it push out all those thoughts that are no longer welcome...

I rolled off him and onto my side.

Astor lifted the covers. "In."

We shoveled beneath the sheets and he pulled me against him, guiding my head to rest on his shoulder. I lay there fighting sleep for as long as possible.

Once the afterglow faded, we'd be enemies again. Or maybe, just maybe, I'd be ready to tell him the truth.

Tiredness tugged at me and I could no longer resist falling asleep.

I awoke to blackness, my head achy and my body tender and that deep pang below had me searching my memory for the reason.

Crazy, brilliant sex with Astor Beauregard. And then there was the rum. I'd downed two shots and this was why my mouth was so dry.

I threw my arm out, reaching for Astor.

He wasn't there.

I listened for him, adrenaline surging through my veins, but only heard silence.

In a panic, I leaped out of bed and hurried into the living room, dragging the throw with me and wrapping it around myself as I went in search of him. Blood pounded in my ears and my temples throbbed.

When I didn't see him, I ran back into the bedroom and searched for my dress as a dreadful realization hit me.

Astor had left me here.

Chapter
THIRTEEN

T HE NIGHT BROUGHT COOLER AIR, MAKING IT EASIER TO WALK HAVANA'S streets without the oppressive humidity bearing down on me.

I adored this city…even though it tried to destroy me as a child and very nearly did. The painful memories felt like a knife in my heart as my gaze swept over the familiar colonial architecture with its Moorish influence. The breeze carried all the rich, flavorful scents of Cuban cuisine.

This city still owned a part of me. Time after time I'd been seduced into coming back for the art and music of the island.

The eclectic culture made me feel at home and took me back to a simpler time.

A crueler time.

With an easy stride, I made my way back to where it all happened, all the way down to Plaza de San Francisco to the abandoned basilica and the monastery of San Francisco. Peering up at the one hundred thirty foot tall bell tower, I easily recalled how it had wakened us every morning…the orphans, the reprobates, and all the other boys of ill-repute who had been sent here as a last resort.

I had been the only American. Sent here alone at thirteen, and then forgotten.

My fingers wrapped around the windows and I rose on my toes to do what I always did when I visited Havana, peer into that deserted classroom and let the memories envelope me. The only way to hold onto my power was to remember what I had survived and how far I had come.

There, through the barred window I saw an upturned school desk...

Cuban summers brought stifling temperatures. My fellow students had grown used to the heat and rarely complained. As instructed, we remained quiet as we sat through our science exam, which I flew through with ease. My education back in America had been top-notch, and thanks to my nanny back in the States, I was fluent in Spanish. Looking around at my classmates, I saw that I was the first one to finish the test paper.

My motivation for speeding through the questions was Sister Mary's promise that she would get a letter to my mother, so I stole a few precious minutes to write, tearing off paper from my notebook and beginning:

"Dearest Mommy,
Father Patrick says that you have decided not to visit."

I had started it wrong.

I balled up the paper, lifted the lid of my desk and hid the evidence. Then I began again.

"Dearest Mommy,
I am being good and studying and Father Renaldo has given me a book of poetry that he thinks I'll enjoy. I like the way the words sound. We play sports most afternoons though the other boys are rough. They like to win. My favorite class is chemistry. Father Renaldo says I will make a good scientist one day if I keep my studies up.

I miss you. Do you think it might be time to tell them what happened? I believe this would help. I want to come home."

Raising my gaze, I saw Father Emesto stomping toward my desk. The short, fat monk, whose eyebrows met in the middle, didn't seem to like teaching—or us, for that matter.

"What is that?" he demanded, looming over me.

The once quiet room was now swirling with the whispers of the other students.

"Silence!" Emesto ordered.

Staring up at him, I tried to gauge his anger. "I finished my exam, sir."

He frowned. "Already?" He spotted my letter and lifted it off the desk to read it.

"It's for my mom. I had some time left."

He scanned the letter, scrunched it up and stepped back. "Pick up your test paper and come with me."

Panic rushed through my soul. "Have I done something wrong, sir?"

Emesto reached for the scruff of my collar, dragging me out of my chair and down between the rows of students who were pretending to ignore us.

"Report to the Dean's office," snapped Emesto, as he pushed into the hall. "Tell him you were caught cheating." He slammed the classroom door in my face.

With my paper in hand, I headed off to see the Dean, who I knew would be reasonable. He would see that my answers were honest.

Sitting in his stuffy old office, I waited on the other side of his desk as he reviewed my exam paper.

His gaze rose to meet mine. "This is one hundred percent correct." He turned the paper for me to see.

"I studied a long time, sir," I replied meekly.

He slammed his hand on the desk. "Don't lie."

"I'm not, I swear."

He pushed to his feet and rounded the desk, looming over me. "You are right-handed as far as I can remember?"

"Yes, sir."

"Put your left hand on the desk."

I did as he asked and watched in horror as he reached for the ruler and raised it high.

The ruler snapped down on my flesh and pain shot through my fingers. I jerked my hand back and hugged it to my chest.

"Hand down," he ordered. "No one cheats in this school."

"But I didn't, sir."

"One more lie and you'll be back in solitary confinement. Do you understand?"

No, not that…anything but that small, dark room where my thoughts consumed me and I was forced to replay every second of my life…

All the way back to that night at Bridgestone.

"Hand on the desk," he repeated.

My gaze broke away from his fierce stare as a bell rang out. The other students were free to play outside, free to roam the library, or the playground, they were free to hide from the monks and be free of pain.

A rapping pulled our attention to the door, and Father Renaldo stepped in to the Dean's office. He gave me a comforting smile and then turned his attention to the Dean.

"I heard what happened," he said, his concerned gaze roaming over me.

"He's refusing to admit it," the Dean said tersely.

"Let's give the boy a chance, Ari."

"A chance to do what?"

"I have another test paper here. Let's see how he does on this one?" He handed it over to the Dean, who studied it with an intrigued expression.

"This is for boys a year above his level."

Father Renaldo nodded. "It will prove he has a gift for science."

They set me up in the corner of the Dean's office, at a desk that was too high for me. I barely reached it. My hand felt like it was on fire, but I tried to ignore the pain as I read the questions and answered each one.

This exam was harder than the test I'd just finished, and I cursed the letter I'd written for my mother. That bad decision had caused this. Had I merely sat there quietly going over my answers, I wouldn't have a bruised and swollen hand now. Or the threat of going into that room, alone, for days.

Within an hour, I had completed the exam. I sat patiently and watched Father Renaldo and the Dean read over my answers.

Father Renaldo's gaze rose to meet mine, and he said to the Dean, "I have a friend at Eton. He's the right age."

"Would his mother approve?" asked the Dean.

"His mother gave us full authority," said Renaldo. "Let me see what strings I can pull. Astor would do well at such a prestigious school. He's advanced."

The Dean turned his fiery glare back on me. "How's your hand?"

"Fine, sir, thank you, sir," I replied, lying for the first time.

"No more writing letters home," he said. "Your mother has been through enough. Am I clear on this subject, young Beauregard?"

Father Renaldo's eyes glinted with kindness as he conveyed to me that the right answer was "yes."

I did not return to America for many years. And when I did, time had wedged its way between me and my family. Though there had been a benefit in that grand education. So, all in all, this shell of a place no longer mattered. Soon this property would be mine, and I would tear down these walls.

And maybe, just maybe, quiet these inner ghosts.

With that comforting thought, I strolled down the cobbled street glancing at the new storefronts that had sprung up and the bright smiles of the locals who valued life and love and all that flowed between.

A flower shop caught my attention and I went inside.

I made my way back through the revolving door of the Hotel Inglaterra and paused to chat with Sergio, the concierge, and asked him to arrange dinner for two to be sent to my room. He told me the chef's special was the snapper, but I was in too much of a hurry to decide.

Raquel was a rare treat I would allow myself for now, and though there remained suspicion surrounding her, I couldn't deny myself the pleasure of her company. Her demeanor was refreshing and I could sense her vulnerability. I knew firsthand what it was like to fight my way through the chaos.

Once Raquel admitted what she was doing at my company, I might even forgive her.

Inside the elevator, I lifted the bouquet of flowers I'd bought for her and breathed in the scent of bougainvillea, perfect for the woman whose layers were seemingly endless.

The elevator doors opened.

Raquel stood there looking disheveled and full of confusion, clutching her handbag to her chest.

"What's wrong?" I stepped out and faced her.

"I thought…"

Realizing what she meant, I pulled her against me. "Raquel, I would never have done that to you."

She trembled and I hugged her tighter. I deserved her doubt after I'd walked away from her at the harbor, but surely all we had shared since had given her some comfort. Our intimacy had been astounding and our chemistry was unquestionable.

I stepped back and offered her the flowers. "For you."

She accepted the bouquet and brought them to her nose, breathing in the heavenly scent. "They're beautiful." Her hands were shaking.

"Come inside." I reached into my pocket for the keycard and waved it before the lock. Giving the door a push, I ushered her inside the room.

Her questioning stare told me she still wasn't convinced. I was incapable of giving her what she had needed above all else… a sense of trust. I shouldn't have left her alone in the room, but those haunting memories had found me and I hadn't been able to sleep. A late night meandering stroll usually cleared my thoughts and inspired me, though this time the loneliness had clung heavily.

She inspired me, and seeing her affected by my actions brought on a wave of doubt that I would ever be what she needed.

"I've ordered room service," I told her. "Hungry?"

"Not really." She lowered the flowers to her side. "Can we go back?"

"If you wish."

"You have a shower on your yacht?"

"Of course." I looked around to make sure we didn't leave

anything behind. "Want to talk first?" I offered.

"No, people are expecting me."

"Who?"

"Friends."

I stepped back, realizing she was frightened. "Back to the boat, then."

Cuba faded into the distance as we headed out to sea on the speedboat. She sat clutching the flowers while I held the wheel in a white-knuckled grip, tight-lipped and feeling uncertain.

We made it back to the *Riveting* just after 2:00 A.M.

It wasn't just Raquel's beauty that captivated me; it was her serenity, her enduring calmness.

And I'd scared her.

Back on the yacht, I offered her my private cabin so she could freshen up. After thirty minutes I went to check on her, needing to know I hadn't caused her too much distress. The room was empty and I heard her moving around in the bathroom.

Raquel appeared in the doorway with a towel wrapped around her body and her hair wet and dripping over her shoulders.

I stepped forward. "What do you need?"

"My dress." She pointed to where it lay on the bed.

I reached for it and handed it to her.

She seemed to read my expression. "I had fun, Astor."

It was the way she spoke my name… "Are you sure?"

"Of course. We're both adults."

Raquel gave me an endearing smile. She moved closer and rose up on her toes, giving me a sweet, gentle kiss.

The friend kiss.

"I may have pushed you too far," I admitted.

She winked. "You're forgiven."

"Was there any of it you enjoyed?"

"You're right," she said, her eyes twinkling. "I need to be more spontaneous. No one was hurt and I got to see a bit of Havana."

She looked beautiful standing there, trying to behave as though she needed no reassurance that we could be more after the mind-blowing sex we'd had.

She raised her dress. "I just need a few minutes."

I turned to head out. "We'll be docking soon. Are you okay to drive?"

I looked back at her and saw a smile flit across her face at my obvious concern. I cringed inwardly at the thought that this woman had me caring about what happened to her after she left my presence.

I hesitated before leaving. "May I ask for your discretion?"

She looked worried. "Oh, no. I've already posted the details on Instagram about how we got it on in Cuba. And your dick pic is setting off a Twitter storm."

Damn her for making me chuckle.

"This never happened," she whispered.

"Right."

I left the cabin to let her get dressed. One more second in that cabin and I would've been tempted to take her again.

I had made the wrong moves at the wrong time—and now there was no going back to salvage what could have been between us. Anyway, we were oceans apart.

It was over.

The harbor's lights reflected off the water, welcoming us back to the mainland. I exhaled a shaky breath, realizing how much last night had affected me. Raquel had breached my defenses and all I could think about was burying my face between her thighs and tasting her again, having her arch her back and scream my name.

Like she had last night…

This never happened.

For some reason those words stung more than they should.

Chapter
FOURTEEN

ANOTHER CASUALTY OF DIVORCE, OTHER THAN HAVING YOUR HEART shattered into a trillion pieces, is the loss of your friends. I reasoned they felt they had to choose between me and Damien, and as he was the master chef who wowed during our late night dinner parties, he'd effortlessly stolen the show and them along with it. Throw in a celebrity girlfriend and I didn't stand a chance as the ex who has a thing for smells.

So when Taylor Lee, my new friend from The House of Beauregard, invited me to a weekend market with the promise of open stalls, live music, and the flow of Caribbean coffees, I took her up on the invite to Clearwater.

The Sunday drive to the country club was pleasant and the weather a perfect blend of sunny and breezy. I could never drive past one of the many lakes and not wonder if an alligator was lurking beneath the surface, but most of the wildlife wasn't as scary. Seeing pelicans do a fly-by over my car gave me a rush of happiness.

Today would be fun and it was good to get out.

Taylor was the first person at work to befriend me, and as Mr. Beauregard's executive assistant I figured she'd be an asset. When the time was right I'd casually lead the conversation around to Astor.

She didn't need to know about Havana.

That would remain my deepest, darkest secret, which I replayed when I was alone with nothing but time during the quiet hours of the night.

Nothing had changed with my plan, even after that passionate rendezvous. Astor had avoided me since…or maybe it was me avoiding him. I'd not searched him out at work to ask about the mutual project he wanted us to work on. It was better this way. It meant I could take the time I needed to research the lab and snoop at will.

I was destined to hate him, and that amazing, mind-blowing sex had merely been a detour on my way back to my old life. Though very little of my old life had survived.

Astor had been kind of fun, actually, with his dimpled smile and that intense stare that made me tingle. It had been his alluring cologne that had seeped into my consciousness and forced me to let my guard down. He'd been a scent trap I'd fallen for.

Never, ever, again.

Yes, the passion had been the most incredible I'd experienced, but when you were dealing with a playboy who'd had plenty of opportunities to practice his talents beneath the sheets it was a given he'd be great in bed.

Memories flooded in and made me blush.

I'd been so quick to leave Cuba and so willing to deny myself any more pleasure—but in my defense I wasn't meant to be there. It was clearly the intimacy I'd been craving, and now that it was quenched I could move on and forget *him*.

Chewing my lip, I wondered if Astor liked to dance. Not that I cared, not really. Had we liked each other differently I may have brought it up in conversation. Not sure why I was even thinking about it now.

Still, thoughts of him made it easier to cope with my divorce.

Perhaps I should move away. Colorado Springs was my first choice, with its romantic setting at the eastern foot of the Rocky Mountains.

I loved the snow in winter and the beautiful way the leaves changed in the fall. Though Florida had the warm, sunny days covered and this state had been my home for years. If I did leave I'd miss the ocean views, palm trees, and my beloved wildlife. I mean, where else could you watch fish jump out of the water at sunset, or see curious dolphins trailing alongside your boat?

I'd have to make sure I stayed away from the places that brought the kind of memories I wished would fade. Damien and been my first, and with those edgy tattoos he had intrigued me enough to say *yes* to a date when my gut had screamed *no*. And all that followed was me not listening to that small inner voice.

As I drove through the country club's crowded lot looking for a place to park, I realized the knot in my stomach had eased. I was being brave enough now to analyze where we'd begun so I could better understand how we had ended, and for some reason it felt less painful. That gut-wrenching ache was easing.

I parked and strolled toward the market with a bounce in my step.

The hustle and bustle of locals and tourists gave this place a family atmosphere. Crossing the street, I headed toward The Breakfast Club Café.

Taylor was sitting in a corner booth. She rose to wave and then pointed to the coffee she'd bought for me on the table. Her bobbed hair and soft make-up made her look pretty. She was thirty, maybe, and had swapped out her snazzy business suit for ripped jeans and a leather jacket.

When I saw her helmet I gave her an impressed grin. "Where is it?"

She pointed through the glass window at the red Ducati. She was always full of surprises, like that time I learned she loved anything British. I suppose that's how we bonded in the first place—me bringing in English candies for her to try and us chatting about which British TV show was our favorite.

I'd decided to wear a spring dress and sandals so there was no way I'd be hopping on the back of her motorbike anytime soon. "Go,

Taylor," I said.

"It's exhilarating."

"I bet." I glanced at the coffee she'd bought me. "Thank you. Am I late?"

"No, I'm unfashionably early."

"Well, on that thing you probably arrived before you left."

She laughed.

I blew on my hot coffee. "Did you ride the bike all the way from South Beach?"

"Uh-huh. Took me about five hours. I visit my mom on the weekends."

She went on to tell me a little history of the market and how she loved to visit each Sunday. Her mom lived round the corner so this was an easy trip for her.

"So glad you could make it," she said.

I sipped my drink and savored the creamy coffee. "It's good to get out."

It was even better to be out of what was my temporary home surrounded by all those memories.

"How are you settling in at the lab?" she asked.

"Great." I sat back. "I've gotten to know where everything is so that's half the battle."

And since she worked for Astor I'd have to be cautious in case she reported our conversation back to him. I knew Taylor's loyalty would rest with him.

"How long have you worked at The House of Beauregard?" I asked.

"Five years."

"So you like it?"

"Yes. Astor's a great boss…generous and fun. He puts on this stern demeanor but that's only because he's got a big business to run. He's nice to me, anyway."

"I'm glad, especially as you see him so much."

"I know, right? I've worked for some real assholes."

"I worked for myself for years before getting hired there."

"What made you come back to the corporate side?"

"Got divorced—" I bit my lip, considering where to take this. "And when Astor offered me the job I saw it as a great place to grow. There's less stress when you don't have to worry about managing a store."

She removed her coffee lid to dip a finger into the frothy layer and taste the cream. "Astor really cares about his employees."

"That's good to know."

"When Arabella's son became sick he rushed off to join her at the hospital."

My heart skipped a beat, and I leaned forward. "Are they in a relationship?"

"No, she's married. About a year ago she called him from the hospital in a panic because her little boy was covered in bruises and she was being questioned by social services."

"Oh, no, really?" And then the scientist in me kicked in. "Bruises?"

"It was leukemia." She gave a nod. "Astor was right there and ended up paying their medical bills."

"That was kind of him." A lump of guilt wedged in my throat when I thought about how I'd been snooping around Arabella's office.

"Astor's been through a lot himself, too," added Taylor.

"How?" My breath stilted as I waited for her to continue.

She stared down at her coffee. "Why do they make it so tepid?"

"I think someone sued a fast food restaurant once," I said. "You were talking about Astor?"

She looked around as though checking to see if anyone was listening. "When he was thirteen, he was sent away to live in Cuba."

"Why?"

She shrugged. "He never talks about it."

"What do you think happened?"

"I think it's connected to his dad but I'm not sure."

My heart flinched for him. "I was expecting someone older when I met him."

She agreed with a nod. "His last name, right?"

"Yes, Beauregard is so…"

"Grand." Her smile faded as she leaned forward and whispered, "Something happened in that house when he was a boy. It was so bad he was sent to live in Cuba in a monastery."

"Not with a relative?"

"No." She shook her head. "His sister stayed behind."

"Penelope? Maybe his mom couldn't cope with two children?"

"They had a nanny."

"What do you think happened?"

"Don't know, but his dad died and then the next day he was gone." She raised her hand in defense. "Before I accepted his job offer, I thought it was a good idea to do some research on him."

I hadn't read anything about these details, and assumed it had happened so long ago I'd not dug deep enough. "What did you find?"

"I shouldn't gossip."

"You never asked him what had happened?"

She looked horrified. "No."

"And his sister?"

"Penelope's stuck up. I hardly talk to her." Taylor took a sip of coffee. "I think she's afraid of him."

"Astor? Do you know why?"

"She once warned me that Astor's willing to go to any lengths to protect what he loves. It was during my annual report. I think she was trying to scare me."

"Why?"

She shrugged. "I was getting on great with him."

"How great?"

"You know, we respect each other. Strictly professional. " She lowered her voice. "He's certainly not the marrying kind."

"I got that impression."

Taylor leaned forward. "Penelope was in the house, too, when the thing went down."

"What thing?"

"The reason Astor was sent away. She would have been eleven."

I wondered just what it was that had changed their lives so irrevocably.

"Don't tell Astor we talked," she said nervously. "He's deeply private."

Something happened in that house. Taylor's words hung in the air

What probably happened was Astor's mother was so wracked with grief she couldn't cope with a strong-willed son. My heart ached for him, losing a father and then being sent to a monastery at such an impressionable age.

Still, why Havana? Why so far away?

Taylor gestured to the door. "Wanna take our drinks and go for a walk?"

"I'd love that."

We strolled through the center of the market, perusing the stalls on either side as we sipped our coffee. There were so many things to capture our attention, from the local painters who were selling their art, to jewelry makers and carpenters showcasing their skills. There seemed to be something for everyone.

From somewhere came the sound of cheering and clapping and it reminded me of those lazy Sundays back in England when I'd watched my dad play cricket. I tried to cling to those happy memories of him instead of remembering how he'd walked out on us. I'd forgiven him, but that didn't mean he was welcome in my life.

Taylor had stopped and was conversing with a middle-aged woman behind a stall. She paid for a small picture frame and the lady put her purchase in a paper bag.

"What's that cheering?" I asked as we strolled away.

Taylor flashed a smile. "How are you with horses?"

"Love them."

"There's a match."

"Match?"

"Polo."

Vaguely, I recalled Astor mentioning something about his fondness for the sport. I wondered if Vedado was a polo horse—his thoroughbred stature certainly qualified him and he was agile enough. Not that I knew very much about it…though somewhere I'd read that the horses needed to be able to turn on a dime.

"I wanted to surprise you," she said.

We made our way around the corner and beyond us lay a wide-open green. Eight horses were galloping around each other, all ridden by men who were driving them hard. I marveled at their tenacity to navigate so fast around each other, all of them wearing helmets and kneepads over their jodhpurs.

Cheers rose from the spectators as one of the polo players made a mad dash for the other end of the green. The other riders galloped after him.

We continued toward an impressively large white tent and after five minutes of trudging down a path made it to what was clearly a private event. A few hundred people mingled about, all of them sipping from flutes of champagne and making lively conversation. It was a contrast to the family atmosphere we'd just left.

But I wasn't in the mood to make small talk with obviously affluent strangers showing off their glitzy clothes while I was wearing a sundress from Target.

I reached for Taylor's arm. "Are you sure it's okay?"

"Of course. Want some bubbly?" She swept two flutes off a passing waiter's tray.

I glanced around nervously. "Where do we pay for it?"

"It's complimentary. This is a charity event."

I followed her gaze toward the noise of hooves striking the turf and drew in a sharp breath at the speed and tussle of men and animals all fighting over a small white ball.

This wasn't a bad afternoon…spending time watching those masterful men on their well-bred horses. They were literally halfway off their saddles leaning down with their long-handled mallets as they swept low to strike a ball that they then catapulted in front of them—a bit like hockey, but way more dangerous.

I knew that polo was considered the sport of kings and reserved only for the ranks of the privileged who had an appetite for peril and a desire for glamour. It was invigorating to watch.

I was mesmerized. "How did you know there would be a match?"

"The boss is playing." She frowned toward the green. "Crazy."

I spotted Astor riding one of the horses and my breath caught in my throat.

He was galloping toward two goal posts and beside him another horseman was right up against him—both of them making a run for the other end of the pitch.

Taylor gestured towards them. "They gallop up to thirty-five miles an hour."

"Is it safe?" Because it didn't look it.

"They fall off the horses, break things, and worse, sometimes."

"What's worse?"

"Astor got knocked out once." She tucked her arm through mine. "Let's get closer."

Astor wouldn't notice me amongst all these people, so I could enjoy watching him from a safe distance. He looked fearless and was clearly a competitive player.

Taylor's words from the café found me again and I wondered how all those experiences had shaped this man. There was so much more to him than I'd imagined.

I wasn't the only one riveted; many of the guests had lined the far side of the tent to watch the controlled chaos of horses and men all striving for the win.

When the match ended I didn't expect Taylor to wave aggressively at Astor to get his attention. I cringed when he looked our way from atop his stallion.

Oh, no.

He nudged his chestnut horse in our direction, unclipping his helmet as he neared the edge of the tent where we stood. I tried to hide my embarrassment.

Astor pulled on the reins and peered down at me with a curious expression. His high-spirited stallion didn't want to stop, but Astor masterfully controlled him with a squeeze of his heels and a tug of the bit. The earthy scent of horse and leather wafted over me.

"Hey, boss." Taylor shielded her eyes from the sun as she looked up at him.

"You two friends now?" he asked.

Taylor swapped a glance with me. "Well, hello to you, too, Mr. Beauregard."

Astor stared at me. "How are you, Raquel?"

"Fine, thank you." I avoided his gaze.

He dismounted and I couldn't help but ogle his tight butt in the dusty jodhpurs. He looked even more ruggedly handsome.

Astor brought the reins over his horse's head and led him closer. "I wasn't expecting to see you." He directed the comment at me.

"Wasn't expecting to be here," I countered.

"I invited her to the market," Taylor said. "Doing a bit of shopping."

Astor looked down at Taylor's bag. "What sort of crap did you end up buying?"

"A photo frame," she answered, looking sheepish. "Was considering putting your photo in it and then I remembered I see more than enough of your smug face at work."

He smiled. "So...having fun so far?"

Taylor looked over at the other players. "Just got here."

"You want me to take you up on that offer?" he asked huskily.

"I have no idea what you're talking about." She grinned.

"Come on, then." Astor smiled at her fondly and gestured for her to follow.

She turned to me. "Will you be okay for a few minutes?"

"I'll be fine."

She smirked, giving me a mischievous look.

They ambled off down the green and Astor's gorgeous horse walked beside him, its hind legs impressively tall as it swaggered along beside him. They both looked magnificent—two thoroughbreds out for a stroll. From the way the other guests followed them with their admiring gazes, I wasn't the only one who thought so.

Let's not make the same mistake twice.

Fuck-boys are a no-no.

Astor got the attention of another player, a handsome man who looked just as striking in his polo get-up. I watched as he introduced Taylor to him. The man was a little older than Astor, though from the way Taylor swooned before him, he was just as charismatic. It was fun to see her enamored, and I had to give credit to Astor for being kind, since this looked prearranged between them. I hoped he wasn't introducing her to an asshole.

I turned and went back into the tent, making a beeline for the long table decadently displayed with an assortment of food laden on silver trays. My mouth watered at the thought of the chocolate-covered strawberries that I'd glimpsed from a thousand feet away. They were just like the ones I'd not gotten to tuck into on Astor's boat. No way was I denying myself this time.

I halted abruptly, my heart sinking and my heels snagging on the grass as I saw *them* through the crowd. I cringed as I watched Damien wrap his arm around Embry. They were both dressed to the nines to fit in with the crowd. It looked like life was treating them well—not kicking the shit out of them like it was me.

My breath stuttered at seeing the man I'd once been intimate with during years of marriage now being affectionate with another woman. A range of emotions swept over me, from disgust to jealousy, and then that deep-seated heartache returned and I feared it would never lift.

Rubbing my chest didn't help.

I had to get out of here…

Yet all I could do was stand still and watch them as though I deserved this slow torture. They looked at each other like they were the only two people in the world and all they needed was their love.

Don't punish yourself with the memory of it…

The night I'd learned that everything about my marriage had been a lie. The first clue had been an expensive Burberry handbag on my kitchen counter. Embry's perfume had hung in the air as though she'd marked her territory...and it was one of my creations that Damien had given her. The realization still hurt, though the pain of that was not as bad as recalling them in bed together.

I set my glass down on a linen draped table and stepped back, hoping not to be seen as I turned to go. I was weaving my way through the crowd when I heard a shrill voice.

"Raquel! What are you doing here?"

Shit.

Embry had recognized me.

I turned and forced a polite smile. "I came for the market," I called back.

Embry navigated through the crowd toward me, as tall and striking as a model, pulling Damien behind her and drawing the attention of the onlookers.

I glanced in the direction of the stalls. "There's some great art for sale around the corner. You should check it out."

"Not here for the polo, then?" Embry looked amused. "You gotta admit it's kind of hot."

Damien glared at her and then focused on me. "You look good."

"You too." My lips failed at a smile; this was hell and I glanced around trying to look for a way out.

"I did the catering," explained Damien, pointing toward the lavish display.

Jesus. I'd nearly scarfed down *his* chocolate-covered strawberries. That would have been the equivalent of siding with the enemy.

"Want to join us?" asked Embry.

Or preferably, I could run into the center of the polo match when it started up again and have those horses trample me. The outcome would be the same.

"Hey, beautiful!" Astor called out. He was walking through the crowd carrying two champagne flutes and wearing a smile I didn't recognize.

I searched the faces around us for the lucky girl who'd won his heart, feeling a spark of jealousy that she'd made him beam with that level of happiness. My gaze snapped back to Damien, not wanting to see Astor's type. Embry's stunned gaze seemed to be following him, too.

Astor sidled up to us and offered me one of the tall flutes. "There you are."

I took it from him and vaguely noticed Embry's mouth twitch uncomfortably when Astor wrapped his arm around my waist.

"We won." Astor grinned. "Though having the best horses helps, obviously."

"Obviously," said Damien. "Well done."

Astor pulled me against his side and raised his drink to take a sip. "You're as stunning as always, Raquel. So glad you made it."

"Thank you?" It came out as a question.

"If you'll excuse us," he said to Damien, "I want to introduce her to my friends. They're curious to meet you, sweetheart."

I was feeling both relief and confusion as I was led away from Damien and Embry. Astor guided me all the way to the other end of the tent.

"That was impressive horsemanship." I wasn't sure what else to talk about.

He smirked. "Thank you."

"Must have strong thighs for that."

"Well, you know I do."

I clenched my teeth. "Fancy seeing you here."

"You are delightful when you're thrown."

"I'm merely enjoying a Sunday off." I grimaced. "Well, I was until I saw them."

"You didn't know they'd be here?"

"No. Damien did the catering. This is a charity event?"

"For a children's hospital in Palm Harbor."

"That makes up for the pomp and ceremony." I flinched. "Sorry, didn't mean—"

"It's fine. On the surface polo is a spoiled man's sport and the wealthy pay well to watch as they enjoy their hors d'oeuvres. But out

there..." He turned to look back at the field. "...it's the most dangerous sport in the world. It's war. There is nothing that rivals the adrenaline of winning against such remarkable competition."

"You seem to have that level of passion for everything you do,
Astor."

"If I find a subject that interests me, I'm all in."

"That's commendable."

Astor licked his bottom lip as he studied me. "You look pretty in
that dress."

"Targay," I twisted the name of the store. "Target," I added on his
confusion.

"Green suits you." He turned to peer back at Damien. "Was he
polite?"

"Yes. The rudest thing he's ever done is fuck the weather girl."

"Ah."

"Apparently, the best revenge in circumstances like this is to double down on the yoga and get skinny." I let out a sigh. "Only I like
cheese and olives."

"Looks good on you."

"Please."

He glanced over his shoulder at the couple. "Rescuing you from
them is me making it up to you."

"You mean for what we did in that hotel room?"

His gaze shot to mine. "I was referring to the unexpected boat trip
to Cuba, which got us there."

"Well, we both know you have perfect timing. Thank you for saving me." I turned to leave.

"Have dinner with me."

I took a moment to study him. "Why?"

He shrugged. "We can discuss our mutual project. That's all.
Nothing more complicated than that."

I handed him my drink. "You have my number."

"Raquel." He came closer. "I appreciate your discretion about the
other night."

"And I yours."

"Of course."

"Are you feeling better now?" He nodded toward Damien.

"Not really."

"What can I do to change that?"

I mulled his question over for a few seconds. "Kiss my cheek."

"You want to make him jealous?"

I rested my fingertip on my cheekbone and gave him a cute smile. "Let's do it."

Astor lowered his gaze. "And here I was assuming you'd fallen hard for me."

"I'm far too sensible for that, Mr. Beauregard."

He shook his head. "Take your drink."

"Why?"

"Go on, take it. Now."

I accepted the glass and he reached out and placed his hand on the back of my head, pulling me toward him. His mouth dragged across my lips leisurely, his tongue darting into my mouth for a lust-fueled kiss.

"That wasn't my cheek," I stuttered out as soon as he stepped back.

"Let me try that again." He leaned in and pressed his mouth to mine, giving me another intimate kiss...the kind of kiss that lovers share when they care deeply for one another. It had me swooning and forgetting where I was.

As he pulled away, my bubbly sloshed all over my hand, but I didn't care. "I can't stop thinking of you either," I confessed in a rush.

Astor stared at me as though my confession had stunned him into silence.

"Sorry to interrupt," Damien said from behind me.

I looked at my ex, realizing I had just confessed my feelings to Astor. My cheeks burned with embarrassment.

Damien glared at Astor and then turned his gaze on me. "I need the spare keys to the boat." He gave me a thin smile. "We're ready to take the next step and divide up the rest of the property."

"We?" I said.

"You know what I mean."

"We'll get them to you," said Astor.

"I love that boat." I hated to let it go.

Astor grinned. "I'll buy you another."

He'd taken our role-playing to the extreme. Still, it seemed to have Damien rattled and his jealousy made this day a little more bearable.

"How long have you two been together?" Damien asked.

I ignored the question to lick champagne off my hand, pausing midway when I felt their eyes locked on me.

"I love it when you do that," said Astor huskily.

Damien turned around and walked away from us.

I faced Astor. "When I said 'I can't stop thinking of you' I knew he was behind us."

A slow smile slid across Astor's face.

"I mean it. I haven't given one thought to Havana." *Other than to replay it moment by moment.*

"Not even the boat trip?" he asked.

I dragged my teeth across my lip.

He stepped forward. "How about us having drinks in the hotel bar?"

"Where we argued?"

"*You* argued. I listened."

"Well, let's not bring up what happened next."

"What happened next?" His eyebrows arched seductively.

"I do remember warning you there'd be no more kissing," I said firmly.

"I did what you asked of me." He lifted the strap of my dress, which had fallen halfway down my arm.

His touch sent tingles along my shoulder. "Damien probably doesn't even think of me."

"Yet he's looking this way."

"Is he?"

"Damien must realize he let the most beautiful woman in the world slip through his fingers."

I laughed at that.

"I have even more devilry up my sleeve." He winked playfully.

"Really?"

"Ultimate revenge. It's taking it to genius level."

"Are you suggesting I flirt with a hot guy in jodhpurs?"

He suppressed a smile. "I'm sure I know someone who would cooperate."

Astor nudged me backwards and my butt hit the table. He set down his glass and then took mine and placed it beside his.

He put his hands on my waist and lifted me onto the edge of the table. "We're working on your adventurous spirit, Raquel. This should help."

"I think people might be looking."

"What people?"

My breath stuttered.

"I was thinking of something like this," he said silkily. He stepped between my thighs and pressed against me.

A rush of pleasure hit me. "This seems like it might work."

"It will undoubtedly prove you've moved on." He kissed my neck.

"I'm even jealous of me," I quipped, feeling breathless. I was ready for anything.

He brushed a strand of hair out of my eyes, and then gently pressed his lips to mine. His tongue darted inside my mouth and I tasted champagne. The sensation caused me to moan, and I felt Astor respond. He embraced me tightly, his groin rubbing against me, which felt divinely forbidden.

His kiss became more savage, and our tongues battled, both of us drawing as much from this moment as time would allow.

Our chemistry felt exquisite. It was impossible to deny that our bodies melded perfectly.

We broke away, breathless and panting, with me still wanting more.

Astor reached up and rubbed his thumb along my bottom lip. "I smudged your lipstick."

His touch enraptured me. I loved the way his eyes glistened with emotion when they looked into mine.

I didn't care whether Damien was watching or not.

"Raquel?" He tipped my chin up.

"You've gone above and beyond," I said.

"Pleasure's all mine."

I let out a sigh and it betrayed me with its wistfulness. Astor may be the enemy but he was so damn dreamy.

He stepped back a little. "You have to let him go, Raquel."

"I have."

"I was watching you watching them. "

I broke his gaze. "I was remembering how I found them together."

"You caught them…"

"Yes." I slid off the table, his spell broken.

He blew out a breath of concern. "They don't deserve to be part of your life."

"Right."

"It gets easier."

"Have you ever had your heart broken?"

"No, but I have broken quite a few."

"So you're the expert, then?" I said sarcastically.

"Oh, yes. Damien doesn't want you, but he still wants you to want him."

"Thank you for the insight."

"I'm here for you. Just ask. Any matters pertaining to the breaking of hearts, I'm your man."

"You're nothing like Damien." I gestured. "I mean, look at you."

Astor was front cover material for *Horse & Hound* magazine—and when naked he'd be right at home in *GQ*.

"You're a gentleman," I muttered.

This man was in an entirely different league.

"And I would never hurt you." He seemed surprised by his own words.

"Yet I thought you savored going in for the kill?"

He blinked at me and his expression became taut...offended, even. "Why do you say that?"

"Back in Havana," I clarified. "You warned me how—"

"I have to go, Raquel. I have to take care of my horses."

"Of course. Thank you for saving me."

"Be ready at seven."

"Okay."

"What's your address?"

I hesitated. "Pick me up at the store."

"What about your home?"

"The store is fine."

His gaze narrowed on me. "Tonight will be strictly business, Raquel. You would do well to remember that."

I fluttered my eyelashes at him. "Yes, sir."

"Tease me at your peril, Wren," he whispered. His hand trailed up my forearm, causing a shiver along my skin.

I feigned disapproval at his teasing, and as he walked away I couldn't help but stare. Even from behind he was a striking specimen of a man. It was his confident, regal stance...the broad shoulders and that perfectly firm bum.

What the hell was happening?

All I wanted to do was bury my teeth into his alluring pert cheeks and then kiss him all over. Pleasure rippled through me at the thought of my tongue running along his—

Astor spun round to look at me and a grin slid across his face.

I swore under my breath at getting caught admiring his assets. My breath hitched when he walked back toward me, and I said breathlessly, "Yes, Mr. Beauregard?"

"Why did you call your store Perfume Girl?"

"It's what my mom used to call me. She'd say, 'Here comes my perfume girl.'"

"That's sweet…and a perfect name."

"I think so."

He gave me a nod and strolled away. "See you tonight, perfume girl."

My heart raced. I watched him leave, my bruised lips still tingling from his delicious kiss.

Chapter
FIFTEEN

I TOOK IN THE DISTINCTIVE BLUE AND WHITE PERFUME GIRL SIGN AND THEN lowered my gaze to admire the shop's stained-glass front window. This was all so *her*.

A perfect fit for downtown Dunedin's classic style and a remarkable achievement for any chemist. This proved Raquel was talented in both business and chemistry, and if it wasn't for her husband letting her down she'd continue to thrive. If I hadn't planned this visit in order to spy on her, I'd have been stoked to be meeting with such a gifted entrepreneur.

Her location was great for foot traffic and was situated next to a bakery. That "spoil yourself" mentality probably spilled over to the shop. Many customers saw perfume as a luxury item, which meant marketing was tailored toward the impulse buy.

The House of Beauregard's clientele were repeat customers because they couldn't find that level of quality anywhere else. Their loyalty was rewarded with compelling formulas that satisfied even our most discerning customer. We sold a profound experience to the sophisticated elite, whereas Raquel offered the public a more affordable line. I was looking forward to sampling her scents.

The CLOSING DOWN SALE sign stuck on the front window nagged at my conscience. I could save this place. *If* I chose to. Instead, I would get what I needed from tonight's interrogation and then fire her.

Raquel would be out of my life and my business would have survived another threat. She'd be okay. From the brief time I'd spent with her, I'd come to realize that she was a survivor.

The doorbell rang as I stepped inside and I felt the chill of air-conditioning. I paused for a moment on the tiled floor, picking up the aroma of *Savage King*, a Beauregard cologne with dark notes and dusky ripples.

"I'll be right there," Raquel called from the back of the store.

Moving farther in, I looked around at what had probably once been a thriving store. Large black and white prints hung on the walls, one a picture of a white tulip and another had captured a white rose in mid-bloom. A gold-framed mirror covered the entire length of the far wall.

The shelves were stripped of their bottles—other than one long glass shelf on my left that still had a few on display...as though Raquel had not been ready to remove them all. A stack of boxes sat in one corner of the room, and a chaise lounge in another.

A feeling of sadness hung in the air as thick as my cologne. Passion had been very much alive here once, with Raquel placing her personal touch on everything from the decorative light fixtures to the glass-fronted counter, creating an eclectic atmosphere for her customers to enjoy.

I imagined this place had been popular amongst locals as well as tourists. I was sure the other shop owners would be sorry to see her go, too. If Raquel couldn't save this place she'd lose money as well as her dream. I suddenly understood her motivation for doing whatever it took to salvage her flailing business, and it caused the hairs on my nape to prickle.

How far was she willing to go?

I supposed it all depended on how much she was willing to fight for this place. There was still a chance for her store's survival, but at what cost?

On the floor in the far corner lay a red ribbon, the kind used to wrap gift boxes, and resting next to it glinted something that could have been a perfume bottle.

"How do I look?" Raquel appeared beneath the arch of a doorway, looking stunning in a red chiffon dress. She hurried past me toward the corner and swept up the bottle, cupping it in her hands as though hiding it from me.

"You look beautiful, Raquel."

She spun around playfully and hid the bottle behind her back. I was distracted by her halter-neck dress, complimented by strappy heels which almost made her as tall as me. Shiny auburn locks spiraled over her shoulders and her make-up looked natural.

I admired this sultry version of her. No doubt she was trying to use the power of her beauty to fracture the ground beneath my feet.

I smiled. "What are you hiding in your hand?"

Raquel carried the bottle across the room, and then opened a drawer and placed it inside before closing it.

She turned to face me. "You look very handsome, Mr. Beauregard."

"I'm a little dressed down for you." I'd gone for Levi's and a white shirt.

"You look good in anything," she said.

My memory betrayed me with flashes of our kiss this afternoon in Clearwater, the way she'd looked so bohemian in that sundress at the polo match, such a natural style compared to all those other guests. Her easygoing nature had provided a welcome freshness to the stuffy atmosphere. Her lips had tasted like sunshine and sugar—devastatingly erotic, reminding me of how she'd moved beneath me in that bed, and God, her beauty…

For the love of all things holy…get your head back in the game.

"Everything okay?" she asked.

"Of course." I looked around the front room. "This is a great place."

My gaze drifted to a familiar bottle.

"Something wrong?" she asked, following my stare.

"*Savage King?*"

"I was testing it. Your colognes are popular. I sell about five a week."

"Only five?"

She smirked. "I encourage them to buy mine."

"Ah."

"Well, I did once." She looked vulnerable in that moment.

This time I'd be wary of her easy seduction. There'd be no more flirting on my part, no more reckless decisions that involved intimacy. This morning's connection hadn't thrown me at all—in fact it had made me more resolved to end this façade. We had nothing in common other than our mutual passion. Yes, this woman radiated a compelling blend of sensuality and serenity but that was probably just an act.

"How does it feel having to shut this place down?" I asked, a little cruelly.

She shrugged. "I never saw it coming...but I'm happy in my new job."

"Show me around."

"There's nothing much here." She used her thumb to point behind her. "I have a small laboratory in the back."

"I'm interested in seeing it." Stepping closer, I savored us almost being the same height. She'd probably worn those heels so she could feel more like my equal. But it would take more than that for her to gain control of this evening.

She stared at my mouth as she ran her tongue over her lips. I could handle a flirty woman. Hell, I was a goddamned expert at emotionally jousting with enticing sirens.

She swallowed hard. "There's nothing to see back there."

"Still."

Raquel gave me a relenting look and strolled elegantly through a small hallway that led to another room. Her curves were deadly and her ass ridiculously squeezable.

She's out of bounds.

I followed her through another doorway and we stepped into a clinical setting. The chrome countertops were covered with small glass bottles and half-heartedly packed boxes. A desk had papers scattered across it.

I leaned back against the central island. "So this is where the magic happens?"

"Happened."

"You're ready to let it go?"

She held my gaze. "There's always a silver lining."

"What happened to your scale?"

"I'm sorry?"

I pointed to the broken scale on the floor. "You probably could have sold it."

Her gaze locked on mine. "It's all part of the dismantling."

I gestured toward the stairs. "Where does that lead?"

An expression of panic crossed her face. "Storage."

I sprang forward and headed up the stairs.

"Wait!" she called after me.

Pausing, I glanced back at her.

"Can we just go?" Her hand tightened around the banister. "I'm starving."

"I've booked us a table at Oceana on the Water. It's worth the wait." My grin widened and I sprinted upstairs.

I felt around for a switch and flicked on the light, seeing the stark, open floor plan of the room. My smile faded.

Raquel caught up to me, slamming against my back.

I spun around. "Tell me you're not living here?"

But I already knew the answer. A mattress lay on the floor in the corner covered by a blue duvet. It was a devastating view, and from the way she cowered at the top of the stairs she hadn't planned on me seeing it.

"Don't I pay you enough?" I muttered.

"Pinching pennies," she stuttered out. "I can't afford rent on an apartment as well as here. It's temporary…obviously."

I eased away from her and strolled toward the small fridge in the far corner. I knelt and opened the door, peering in at a carton of skimmed milk, a bottle of Pepsi, and some leftover sushi. I stared at her questioningly.

"I can survive roughing it for awhile." She made it sound like a joke.

"Why are you saving your money if you're letting this place go?" I pushed to my feet.

"I just made the decision."

Maybe she was in denial.

"Where are you staying in South Beach?" I asked.

The driving distance between South Beach and Dunedin was at least five or six hours and from the way her clothes were scattered on the floor, including the dress she'd worn this afternoon at the polo match, I surmised she must be staying here on the weekends.

"During the week I'm at a hotel," she explained.

"Which one?" I dared to ask.

"It's nice. Cozy."

"Which one, Raquel?"

"Fairweather Inn Hotel."

I didn't bother trying to hide my horrified expression. "I have a place. It's close to work and comfortable. You will stay there."

"I'm fine, really."

"Do I look like I'm negotiating?" I scanned the room one final time. "Pack your bags. We'll leave for your new place after dinner."

"What's the rent going to be?"

I smiled. "How about a month rent free? That'll give you enough time to close the store and find a decent place."

She lowered her gaze. "I don't want your charity."

"I'm your employer. I need you focused. You're probably not getting any sleep in that *motel*." I corrected its name.

"This is a lot to take in."

"Time to pack, Ms. Wren." I waved my hand in the air. "Living here isn't even legal."

"That's none of your business."

"It just became my business. Gather your things."

"This is so embarrassing," she mumbled.

"Hey—" I walked over and brought her in for a hug, feeling her tremble against me. "There's no strings attached. I won't bother you. You'll have a safe and comfortable home that is a big improvement on this or any hotel."

She stared up at me. "I'm more independent than you realize."

"That sounds like a *no*," I said darkly. "It's a word I'm not used to hearing."

"How will I repay you?"

"You and I are friends," I said, trying to soothe her. "And this is what friends do." I hugged her tighter, cursing myself for making everything more complicated than it already was.

This level of empathy wasn't usually in me.

There was just something so authentic about Raquel—and I knew pain when I saw it. If all of this was indeed an elaborate trap to bewitch me, I would turn it around and set my own. I could handle this. Handle *her*.

As long as I kept the promise to myself that there'd be no more intimacy between us, everything would work out fine and we'd find a resolution. The thought crossed my mind that I could tap the phone in my beachfront property, and the surveillance I had in place would ensure I could watch her coming and going more closely. Though there were no cameras in the bedroom. I wasn't a complete psycho.

There was something to be said for keeping one's enemy close.

I leaned against the wall and watched her pack. She'd asked me to wait downstairs but I didn't want to take my eyes off her.

Raquel brought out a large suitcase. Soon, I was carrying it down the stairs for her and then rolling it through the front of the store. I loaded it into the back of my Mercedes while she locked up the store. When she hurried over to me, I could see a flurry of emotions crossing her face. Raquel exuded strength, but there was an underlying current of confliction running through her and it was this sentiment that stirred my sympathy.

We arrived at the marina within minutes.

I threw the keys to the valet and Raquel and I headed along the boardwalk toward the restaurant. Halfway there, Raquel suddenly fell behind. I paused and followed her gaze down to her shoe, which was stuck between the wooden slats. When she pulled her foot up the heel was hanging off.

She snapped it the rest of the way off and her gaze rose to meet mine. "Bit of an incident, but nothing I can't handle."

I threw a polite smile at a passing couple who glanced our way. Raquel was trying to snap off her other heel.

"Were they expensive?" I asked.

"Kind off." She gave the other shoe's heel a tug. "I'll have to even them out. Can you snap this one off, too, please?" She handed it to me.

I went to break off the heel. "Are you sure?"

"Yes. I packed another pair in the suitcase. I'm too hungry to go back. Break it off."

I applied enough pressure to snap off the heel and then handed the shoe back to her, slipping the broken heel into my jacket pocket.

"How is it?" I watched her walk, admiring her no fuss attitude.

"Like it never happened." She grinned up at me.

"Back down to fun-size." I nudged her arm. "Just how I like you."

"I aim to please."

"I'll remember that." I winked at her.

Her blush was endearing. "Look…" She raised her foot for me to see "I've invented a new style," she said, giggling. "If all else fails I'll go into the shoe business."

"Quite the scientist, Ms. Wren." I wrapped my arm around her.

I wanted her relaxed with a large glass of wine in her so I could explore who this woman really was. No one could keep up such a good girl façade for long with booze inside them. The truth would slip through the cracks.

Oceana on the Water had honored our reservation despite us being late. I expressed my gratitude for their courtesy considering the place was extra busy for a Sunday night. We followed the concierge through the restaurant and I reached back for Raquel's hand. She wrapped her fingers around mine and it felt right, although it was hard to define why.

We stopped off at our respective restrooms to wash our hands after the shoe escapade, and were quickly reunited and led to the outside seating area. The warm breeze shook off the chill from the air-conditioning as we strolled toward the best table they had to offer. I slid out Raquel's chair for her and then took the seat opposite.

The delicious scents of garlic and flowing wine stirred my appetite and I asked our waitress to bring us bread while we waited for our meal. I ordered steak and Raquel chose salmon.

"What a wonderful view." Raquel pushed to her feet and leaned on the balustrade, staring out at the ocean.

The sun was setting on the horizon, its bold reds, oranges and golden yellows reflecting off the water. The scene never failed to inspire me.

Raquel looked like a windswept miracle, her hair flowing about her delicate features, seemingly unaware of her sensuality as her chiffon hem lifted in the breeze, just enough to flaunt her thighs.

"It's so beautiful." She looked back at me, her face lit up with joy. "I'm so grateful, Astor." She took her seat and reached across the table for my hand, holding it in hers. "Thank you for this."

"This is the easiest thing I've done all year."

Her gaze broke away from mine, as though she felt overwhelmed for a second, and I saw she looked conflicted.

"Everything okay?"

Raquel stared out at the nightscape and I heard her let out a wistful sigh. "You're being very kind."

"I'll be glad to see you eat. When was your last good meal?"

"I eat well enough." She rolled her eyes. "You probably think I'm a mess. That shoe incident didn't exactly inspire confidence."

"I admire you."

She gave me a rueful smile. "Why?"

"There's no pity party being thrown. I see a woman who will find a way to get back on her feet in no time." I lowered my gaze. "You provided a demonstration minutes ago."

She glanced at her feet. "Sorry if I embarrassed you."

"Grace under pressure. I think you could handle anything. Or anyone, Raquel. I'm looking forward to revealing more of your skill set."

"Oh?"

"Anything you want to share?" I waited for her to answer.

"Not really, no. Why?"

"You just seem a little unsettled."

"I really liked those shoes."

I remembered the uncomfortable expression on her face as she'd looked around her old laboratory. That scale on the floor was out of place. She didn't strike me as someone who'd treat her equipment with disrespect. Or maybe she'd snapped from the pressure and beneath that serene demeanor was someone on the edge.

I leaned back. "What I'm interested in knowing is what lengths you'll go to."

"For my store?" she whispered. "I'm doing okay."

Pulling out my phone, I opened up the browser and typed in Perfume Girl, searching the recent headlines all the while pretending to read a text. "I'll only be a second," I reassured her.

"Of course." She buttered her bread roll. "You probably don't get a day off."

The news article was on the second page of the Google search, and I selected the header that took me to an online article in the Dunedin Weekly. Apparently, her store had sustained a break-in a week ago.

Someone had thrown that scale to the ground. Someone had tipped their hand, and this was as much about greed as it was an emotional strike. Even more startling was the fact that Raquel had not mentioned it.

My gaze rose to meet hers. "Red or white wine?"

Chapter
SIXTEEN

"I'D LOVE A CHARDONNAY." I COULDN'T LOOK AT HIM.

I was afraid he'd see how conflicted I was because I was enjoying his company, and yet I'd inserted myself into his lab for one purpose only.

If it wasn't for that ultimate goal, this would be the date of my dreams—though Astor had made it quite clear this evening was strictly business.

I was still inwardly cringing over the fact he'd discovered I was living at my shop. It was considerate of him to rescue me, but it made my situation more complicated. If Astor was innocent, he'd remember this evening and end up feeling betrayed on the deepest level. Either way, all of this was temporary and as wonderful as it was to spend time with him it wouldn't last.

We wouldn't last. Even losing him as a friend would hurt more than it should.

The waitress interrupted my dark musing when she turned up with a glass of wine. Astor declined to drink as he was driving. I took a large sip of chardonnay, and when I saw him watching me I took a calming breath and quickly thanked him for bringing me here.

Astor had chosen a lovely restaurant with a spectacular view of the harbor and its row upon row of yachts, their tall masts reflected dreamily in the water. A cool breeze blew in from the ocean and the dark clouds in the distance told me a storm was brewing. At some point it would rain tonight.

"What are your thoughts?" he asked softly.

"I know we won't be going back to Havana together," I admitted. "But I had a lovely time."

"When we made love?"

My gaze broke away from his and I stuttered out some answer about how I remembered it all fondly. Why did he have to use the word "love" as though there'd been that sort of endearing emotion between us?

I inhaled sharply. "I need you to know those hours at the hotel..."

"Say it."

"It was good for me."

He hesitated as though mulling over his answer. "I haven't given it any thought."

Grabbing my napkin, I laid it over my lap and took a few seconds to smooth it out, preferring to sweep my gaze over the other guests who were chatting away and seemingly enjoying their meals.

I forced a smile. "I've been thinking about our special project."

He lifted his glass of water and took a sip, and it was easy to be mesmerized by the way he wiped the condensation off the base. Those same fingers had swept over my body, giving me so much pleasure...

"I'm listening," he said, his tone seductive.

"We can use olibanum—"

"Frankincense."

"Yes, and add black suede."

"You don't think I've done that before?"

"I haven't finished, Mr. Beauregard. If you add Rose Synactif it will provide those luxurious qualities you're looking for."

"I've used that combination—"

"But have you added liquid gold?"

He leaned forward. "Oud's doable."

"And musk."

"I hope you're referring to the synthetic version?"

"Yes, because that species of deer is endangered and you don't strike me as a man willing to go to those lengths to leap ahead of the competition."

"Never. Though I'm perfectly willing to destroy the competition if need be." He held my gaze.

"Surely you're not threatened by my little store?"

"The one that's closed?"

I sat back. "Working on anything new?"

"I'm actually working on something very special." He studied my face.

I refused to take the bait and smiled sweetly. "Do tell."

"What are your thoughts on Orris?"

And why would he say that unless he knew my Orris oil had been stolen. I could be sitting with the man who had ordered the strike on Perfume Girl. Maybe he was letting me know he was on to me, too.

I was spiraling toward danger.

"Something wrong, Raquel?"

"What do you think of my suggestion?"

"Give me your foot."

"What?"

"I can see your feet are hurting."

"Turns out I'm not such a genius in shoe design after all." I eased off my shoe and lifted my leg toward him.

Astor pulled my foot up onto his knee and caressed my arch, soothing the tension and soreness with a deep press of his fingertips. His touch felt amazing.

"I'm getting to know your brave face," he teased.

The way he was caressing me sent mixed signals to my body, arousing me and making me heady.

"You've never married?" I burst out.

"No."

I glanced around to see if anyone was witnessing this intimate scene.

"You never came close?" I tried to pull my foot away.

Astor's grip tightened. "Never met someone willing to put up with me."

"Maybe your standards are too high?"

His thumb dug into my arch. "I don't want to end up divorced."

I squirmed at the pressure. "No one does."

"It strikes me as strange that two people who set out so in love could turn around and hurt each other."

"I didn't hurt him," I said in my defense.

Astor's eyes narrowed and I suspected he was wondering if that was the first time Damien had cheated on me.

"Still, you seem to have it all," I said.

"Do I?"

"A successful business. A loving family."

He went to speak and then seemed to think better of it.

"I suppose you have to make sure the woman you are pursuing has pure motives."

"Are yours pure, Raquel?"

I hesitated only for a moment. "They are," I whispered.

The waitress appeared and I managed to pull my foot out of his grip as our meals were placed before us. I needed a few seconds to gather myself and bury the memory of his touch.

The food looked delicious.

"I'm fascinated by your talent," he said, slicing through his steak.

I lifted my knife and fork. "I can say the same about you, Astor."

"Your choices of ingredients are unusual." He tilted his head. "But I think they'd work."

"I had Orris oil once." I said it without thinking and on his frown, added, "You mentioned you have a new fragrance made from Orris?"

He rose and then came around to my side of the table to place his jacket on my shoulders. "Want the heater on?"

I glanced at the patio heater above us. "I'm fine."

His cologne was masterful. I stilled to savor the waves of pleasure it brought, appreciate the elegance of it. Those possessive properties told me it was one of his.

Astor took his seat. "Eat. Then I'll take you home."

"Your guest house?"

He lifted his fork and held my gaze. "It will be your home for now."

"Not sure I should take advantage of your kindness."

"Finish your wine, Raquel. It'll make for a more relaxing drive to South Beach."

He was right—we had a long drive ahead.

Was I really willing to go as far as necessary to carry out my plan? The risks were becoming greater every day, and Astor had been different around me tonight, leading me to believe he might know more about me than he was letting on.

"Those who cross me regret it for the rest of their lives." Astor's words came back to haunt me, causing me to shiver.

His steely gaze swept over me. "I'll have them turn that heater on."

Chapter
SEVENTEEN

"I WASN'T EXPECTING..." RAQUEL'S WORDS TRAILED OFF AS SHE LOOKED around the luxurious living room.

"What were you expecting?" I asked.

"Not sure, really." She slipped off her shoes and walked barefoot on the polished wooden floorboards, a respectful gesture.

A plush white couch sat in the center of the room surrounded by armchairs, with Persian rugs strewn here and there. The modern art had been personally chosen by me to avoid unnecessary pretentiousness. Most of it was created by local artists, bohemians who'd fled to Florida to escape the rat race of other cities. Like Raquel, I was drawn to the earthy types.

The color scheme and furniture style were meant to have a calming effect. This simplistic theme was continued on the other side of the glass wall to include the infinity pool, where one could appreciate the ocean view.

Bridgestone belonged to my mother, and so many times I had asked her to let me sell it for her. I guessed those lonely hallways served as a form of punishment, though she didn't deserve it, not really. She apparently drew some comfort knowing I kept my stables there, which meant I could be found on the estate most weekends, feeding and grooming the horses.

But this place was easily my most precious sanctuary.

Perhaps it would have been wiser to take Raquel to a hotel and not fill my home with memories of her. Yet, inexplicably, I felt compelled to have her here. Maybe she'd see the benefit of our friendship and learn to trust me. Maybe she'd open up and tell me all her secrets.

Raquel rubbed the sleepiness from her eyes as she walked around the living room. She picked up a photo of my mother and sister and studied it.

She turned the frame around. "Your mom?"

"Yes."

She grinned at me. "I can see where you get your looks from."

She put the picture frame down and glanced around the room. My smile faded when I realized she was looking for photos of my dad. She didn't find any, but was polite enough not to mention it.

A worried frown appeared on her face. "You live here, don't you?"

"Yes.

"Then I'm putting you out."

"No, I have somewhere else I can stay."

"I didn't expect to be a guest in your home."

I smiled at her. "I think you'll like it."

"I feel you here," she whispered. "It's got your touch."

"In what way?"

"There's nothing complicated about it. The room is serene."

Her words sent a shiver through me because that was how I thought of her.

I countered with, "So, we agreed upon a month, right?"

"How will I repay you?"

"No need. Let me show you around."

We took a tour of the rest of the home and Raquel looked adorably overwhelmed. It was the way she flitted a nervous glance my way when I explained that the tile in the kitchen had been imported from Italy, and the way she ran her hand over the carved wooden banister, showing her appreciation for the craftsmanship.

I had never minded living alone. I'd gotten used to it, but I felt some inner peace knowing she would breathe new life into this place just by being here.

We strolled down the upper floor's hallway and she stopped to admire the small painting by Sandro Botticelli.

"Is that real?" She looked at me, wide-eyed.

"Yes." I hid my amusement, and pointed down the hall. "My room's at the end."

I led her to another door, and opened it. "This is the guest bedroom." I gestured for her to go in.

Raquel stepped into the room, her gaze sweeping over the generous bed with its white duvet and stacked pillows, and the antique nightstands on either side.

"Are you sure you don't want to stay here?" she asked softly.

"My other place is fine." Even as I spoke those words I knew it wasn't an option. Not if I wanted to sleep. There'd be no chance of avoiding the relentless nightmares if I was under the roof of the place that triggered them. Too many shadows filled the dark hallways.

I'd check into a hotel. Throw money at the problem.

I reached into my jacket. "Here are the keys for the Mercedes. Now you have no excuse not to get to work on Monday." I waggled my eyebrows.

"What about you?"

"I have a Range Rover in the garage."

"Thank you." She blinked at me. "You are being incredibly kind."

"Give me your phone. I'll enter my number."

"You can write it down," she said warily.

I held out my hand. "I promise not to peek at your latest Google search."

She rummaged in her handbag and fished out her phone, unlocking it for me.

I took it from her and entered my number. "There," I said, handing it back.

"Thank you."

I led her back into the kitchen. "Eat anything you like. Down there is the wine cellar. Choose a vintage."

"From your priceless collection?" she asked, with a smirk.

"Help yourself. But if I see you tucking into my imported Spanish sausage, we'll have an issue."

With a snort, she burst out laughing. It made me laugh, too.

The kitchen was one of my favorite rooms and I loved to entertain in here. The long table could seat eight people whenever I had friends over for a home-cooked meal, and the cellar stocked enough wine to keep the conversation flowing.

"Let me show you the other pool."

She blinked in disbelief. "You have *another* one?"

"For when it rains."

I led her down the winding staircase to the subterranean level.

We continued along a hallway and then stepped into the vast chamber that housed the indoor swimming pool. Lights glimmered off the water, and the blue and green tiles and low lighting enhanced its relaxing mood. I'd come up with some of my best ideas swimming laps in here.

I knelt and dipped my hand into the water. "I heated it for you in case you want to have a swim before you head into work."

She looked suspicious. "How did you know I'd be staying here?"

"I didn't."

"But you heated it just in case?"

"I have an app." I pulled out my phone and showed it to her. "Everything in here can also be controlled by remote. I turned it on before we left the restaurant."

"Oh, wow."

"I think you have everything you need, right?"

"Yes, only I feel terrible about throwing you out of your home."

"You're not. I'm spoiled for choice when it comes to places I can stay." I leaned forward and kissed her cheek. "Sleep well, Raquel."

In her presence, the ghosts from my past retreated and the

loneliness eased. I'd grown used to a solitary life, but whenever we parted the feeling of isolation grew more intense. It was as though she filled spaces I didn't know existed within me.

With confidence that Raquel would enjoy her stay, I left her to get comfortable and headed out.

I double-checked the front door to make sure it was locked and then strolled toward the garage. Off in the distance came a rumble of thunder. A storm was headed this way. I'd be caught in the imminent downpour if I didn't hurry.

I actually loved storms, but I didn't enjoy driving in them. They cleansed the air and inspired me with their frenetic energy.

An unfamiliar wave of happiness rushed through me.

I'd never allowed myself to get close to any one woman before, but my heart was whispering that there was something special about Raquel. Maybe I was wrong about her.

Love…this wasn't a sport I pursued or would ever come to know—it just wasn't in my DNA. Yet with Raquel I was driven to protect her as though that sentiment moved between us with all its flux and mutability.

My fondness for her was my weakness.

My subconscious was warning me I was playing chess with a master, and when she chose to make her move, I couldn't afford to be distracted by my emotions.

Raquel Wren was an addiction I didn't need in my life.

I raised my gaze skyward in frustration, realizing that I'd left the keys to the Range Rover sitting on the hallway table. Turning, I walked back to the house and pressed my palm against the panel to unlock the door.

Forgive her, whatever she is doing in there. Walk away and don't let your reaction control your destiny.

I went back inside.

Chapter
EIGHTEEN

Raquel

I COULDN'T BE WOOED BY THE MAN WHO WAS THE BIGGEST THREAT TO MY future—I'd come too far and risked too much.

God, how did I end up here?

Astor's home was the most opulent place I'd ever stayed in. To be honest, I wasn't going to miss sleeping on the floor, either. And damn...seeing his kinder side tugged at my heartstrings, causing me more than a twinge of guilt.

I couldn't get over that view—an infinity pool that led your gaze out onto an endless blue ocean. I strolled closer to the wall of glass to better see the pool bathed in a soft blue florescence. If I had been invited here under different circumstances, I could have savored every second of this luxury. My gut wrenched at my deceit.

Still, this was an advantage I had to make the most of. I was going to find his bathroom and check out Astor's colognes to see if there was anything in there resembling mine.

My thoughts turned back to him and I wondered how he felt about me being here. I'd sensed he really wanted to do this and that made me feel a little better.

Off on the horizon dark clouds rolled closer. Soon the sky would open up and a downpour would cleanse the air.

To the left of the pool was a row of sun loungers, and I imagined Astor barbequing and entertaining friends. No doubt he was an amazing host. He'd certainly gone above and beyond to heat the pool downstairs, and I wondered if the one out there was heated, too. A swim would dissolve this post-wine haze.

I located a panel on the wall. With a punch of a button the glass door slid open and a burst of warm air blew in. The heat from the tiled patio soaked into my soles as I padded toward the water.

I knelt and dipped my fingers into the blueness, just as Astor had done downstairs. Goodness, how rich did you have to be to own two of these?

I whooshed my hand through the warmth and it felt good against my skin. With the high wall on either side of the vast property, and the dim lighting, the neighbors wouldn't see if I took a dip.

I grabbed one of the plush towels from the corner stack and lay it on a nearby lounger for when I got out, then stripped off my dress and underwear.

Naked, I threw another wary glance around and then waded in until I was fully immersed, my body quickly acclimating to the heat. Pushing myself off to swim toward the other side, I wondered if spies ever felt a tingle of remorse for deceiving those around them. Here I was enjoying Astor's place and yet my ulterior motives were complicated.

I made it to the other side of the pool and kicked off, continuing with sweeping breaststrokes, doing laps while admiring the two-story property that was worth millions. If I lived here I'd never want to leave. I loved the way Astor had decorated his home. There was stillness within the walls, a Zen-like atmosphere that reminded me of him.

Don't let your guard down and be seduced by all this luxury.

Turning to swim in the direction of the seacoast, I marveled at the infinity pool that concealed the boundary between here and the ocean. I let out a sigh of happiness.

A crack of thunder came from a mile away and I cursed the

weather for turning so quickly. I'd get out soon. Swimming during a storm was a bad idea, but I had another lap in me before I'd have to climb out.

Lightning zigzagged across the night sky.

I heard a crack and a hiss...

A loud splash came from behind me. Turning, I saw the blurred shape of a man cutting through the water fast toward me.

My scream was muffled as he grabbed me, my head going under the water for a few seconds before he lifted me up and shoved me unceremoniously out of the pool onto the terrace, bruising my arms and knees. Panting, my heart pounding in my ears, I pushed myself up ready to sprint away—I had to make it to the house and lock him out.

I froze, throat tight with panic, realizing it was Astor.

He climbed out of the pool and leaped toward me, scooping me up in his arms and hurriedly carrying me into the house. I gasped as a blast of cold air hit my wet skin. He put me down and I staggered backward, falling onto the couch.

"You okay?" He was out of breath.

Thunder rolled and a bolt of lightning lit up the sky.

The worry that I'd stained his sofa with chlorine was followed by the realization that Astor was behaving like a madman. The embarrassment of being naked was overruled by my anger.

I pushed to my feet. "The chance of being struck by lightning is a million to one!"

"Tell me you're okay?" He stood there dripping water onto the rug.

I looked around for a throw. "Your couch is ruined."

Astor stepped closer. "Fuck the couch." Still looking panicked, he ran his fingers through his hair, probably realizing how much he'd scared me.

Outside a flash of glittering sparks caught my attention and I side-stepped him to take a better look. I stared wide-eyed at the neighbor's downed power line that had been snapped by a lightning strike. The thing was snaking violently near the pool, looking like a wild anaconda.

Astor followed my gaze and winced at the sight of sparks shooting in every direction. With another whip the cable jolted high and then bounced into the center of the pool, thrashing jolts of electricity in every direction.

The garden lit up.

"Oh, my God." I was unable to turn away, or breathe, or think. My body trembled uncontrollably. If Astor hadn't come back...

In a daze, I felt him lift me in his arms. He carried me up the staircase and then kicked a door open. It was his room, but I couldn't see properly, my vision blurred from the adrenaline coursing through my veins, causing me to shake.

"You're in shock." He put me down. "I have to warm you up."

He grabbed my wrist and pulled me into the bathroom, guiding me into a marble-tiled shower. Falling water tumbled over me and I blinked through the downpour as I watched him strip off his shirt and throw it on the floor.

He joined me beneath the chrome faucet. "Body heat." He pulled me against his firm body and rubbed my arms.

Pressing my cheek against his chest, I exhaled in relief. "It could've gotten you."

"Takes more than that." He gave me an amused smile.

He'd saved my life and risked his own for me. The thought of all I'd done to him these last few weeks...all the lies, all the deceit, screeched guiltily across my conscience.

"I'm sorry."

"Nothing to be sorry about," he soothed. "It was a freak accident."

"I was about to get out of the pool..."

"Don't give it another thought." He pressed his lips to my forehead. "You're safe now."

"Astor..." *I have to tell you something.*

Have to confess why I'm in your life.

"Shush." He rested his thumb against my lips to quiet me.

Opening my lips wider, my tongue darted out to taste his skin. I drew his thumb into my mouth and suckled it, the sensation as comforting as it was sensual. I let go, crushing my cheek once more against his firm chest, his provocative scent filling my senses.

I want this.

I wanted him.

It felt like fireflies would burst out of my solar plexus. I licked his chest, causing him to groan. In a flash of power he gripped either side of my head and went to kiss me.

His mouth so close…

"Raquel," he whispered. "I have to make a call."

"What?"

"I have to warn my neighbors about the cable. Have them turn off the electricity. Make the area safe."

"Of course." I stepped back.

Hiding my embarrassment, I watched him grab a towel and wrap it around himself before strolling out. I spun round and raised my face to the streaming faucet, squeezing my eyes shut in shame. He'd wanted to warm me up and I'd come on to him like a hussy. I covered my face with my hands as though it might help hide my humiliation.

My joy from earlier came crashing down.

When I heard the bathroom door open behind me, I summoned my courage, turned, and forced a smile. "Everything okay?"

A towel was wrapped tightly around Astor's waist, his body sprinkled with droplets of water. His abs were chiseled and his dark complexion mesmerizing. His masculine beauty made me more self-conscious of my nakedness.

Astor stepped forward and rested his forehead against the glass. "Their power's off. A technician's on the way."

"Good."

"Raquel…"

"Yes?"

"I'm sorry." He tipped his head toward the shower. "It was impulsive of me to get in there with you."

"I liked it."

"I brought you here to feel safe. I broke your trust. After everything you've been through that was wrong of me."

"Everything I've been through?"

"Your divorce. Losing your business. Your home."

My eyes stung with the tears I was holding back.

"And you work for me," he added. "I have a responsibility and I shouldn't take advantage."

"It's fine." I didn't trust myself to say anything more.

He gave me a kind smile. "It's not that I don't want to open this door and walk in there…that would be easy."

"Right."

"And to taste your lips again." He squeezed his eyes closed.

To feel his mouth on mine was everything I wanted. All the pain, all the heartache, all the deceit, all the hope I'd once chased after no longer mattered in this moment. He was all man standing there with a sheen of water shimmering off him, his hair as black as night, framing that perfect face, his features softening as he smiled my way with those endearing dimples, his hazel eyes filled with empathy.

Perhaps he was waiting for me to speak, but I had nothing to say, not really. All I could do was find a way to cope with the ache I felt below that had me trembling with need. I reached down to cup myself to soothe this yearning.

His gaze followed my hand as I covered myself and then rose to meet mine. My face burning with embarrassment, I snapped my hand away and covered my breasts with my arms.

"Raquel." He shook his head.

I pressed my fingers to my mouth, longing for his kiss.

His voice was deep and penetrating. "If I come back in…"

Leaning forward, I nudged the door open for him.

Slowly and deliberately, his fingers wrapped around the top of his towel and he pulled it away, letting it slip to the floor, exposing him. The ridges running along the shaft's wide girth, its enormity, and the way he caressed its length with a firm hand left me mesmerized. A sigh escaped my lips as I studied the purple head, watching his masterful strokes and yearning to feel its power.

I licked my lips…

"We take it slow," he said softly.

My gaze rose to meet his. "Yes, kisses…foreplay."

He shook his head. "Us. I meant us."

Us.

That was more than I could have hoped for, dared to wish for, and as he opened the door farther and came toward me, I raised my mouth to his and let out a soft moan as he captured me in his arms. His kiss was gentle and soothing, so different from the way he'd kissed me before, loving and yet possessive.

He reached down and gripped my wrists, walking me backwards until my back met the tile. Then he raised my arms above my head and pressed his body to mine, his kiss pressing into the curve of my neck and sending shivers through me.

He nipped my bottom lip, his tongue darting into my mouth as his warm body trapped me deliciously.

"It's not enough," I whispered.

"Want me inside you?" His voice was husky.

"More than anything."

Astor let go of my wrists and with a gentle motion ran a fingertip along me, circling my clit. I shuddered in response as tingles of bliss shot through me.

His gaze blazed with passion as he lifted me up.

I flung my thighs around his waist, crying out, needing him in me more than my next breath. When I felt the first thrust I buried my face in the crook of his neck, ready to take all of him and bracing for the discomfort.

Astor gave a fierce shove and slid all the way in, filling me completely. I felt myself stretch painfully, accommodating his maddeningly large girth. As his hips shoved forward again he let out a moan and then withdrew slowly, only to push farther inside until I felt him so deep that a burst of pleasure flooded through me and my toes curled.

"Ready?" he said huskily.

It was going to be the passion we needed.

Cupping my buttocks to hold me in place, his fingertips digging into my flesh, Astor pressed me against the tile in a long, deep thrust and then eased out slightly, lifting the pressure momentarily. Then he became wild, fucking me furiously like a brilliant piston and sending wave after wave of pleasure though my body so intense all I could do was dig my fingernails into his back and hold on, never wanting these sensations to cease.

This position felt incredible, with my pelvis tipped upward to meet each strike so he grazed my clit. I became lost in this moment, lost in him, pleading with whimpers for what he was already giving me.

My thoughts obliterated into nothingness as I shuddered through a raging orgasm.

"You feel perfect," he muttered. "So real."

He raced toward his own climax, shuddering as he spilled his heat with such intensity that it sent me over the edge again, my cries drowned out by his groans.

Stillness came, and the only noise was that of the falling water and our breathing. This was the serenity in life I'd craved but until now had failed to find.

He pulled away to look at me and his warm smile made me feel cherished. It nudged out all that had gone on before between us, all the tension, all the confusion, all the doubt. When he eased me off him I moaned with need and it made him smile.

"Let's continue this in the bedroom," he said.

In a flurry of movement, he tugged me from the shower and grabbed two towels, drying us both off. Then he took my hand, interlocking our fingers, and led me out of the bathroom toward the bed. *His* bed.

A trickle leaked down my inner thigh, but I didn't care because he'd marked me with his essence and the thought of it made me swoon. This was evidence of us as a couple and that made my heart soar. This was the passionate lovemaking I had craved but never found.

Astor pushed me gently onto the bed, on my back, and then stood between my legs. He saw the white trail on my thigh and ran his hand over it, his lust-filled gaze finding mine.

"Sometimes words are not enough," he said affectionately. "So we find other ways."

I didn't feel self-conscious about my nakedness and I wasn't pre-occupied with the change in our relationship...all I cared about was enjoying this intimacy. I refused to think too much or explore those dark recesses of my mind that were filled with doubt.

Astor kissed the arch of my foot and then slowly moved up to my ankle. He pressed his full lips all along my shin and then his mouth found my inner thigh, causing me to squirm with pleasure.

Before I could protest, his tongue began flicking my clit, his two fingers slipping inside me and working me back into a writhing frenzy. It felt wild and messy and out of control and I sucked in deep breaths, trying to endure the rising fragility of my heart at this level of surrender—what had once felt like a forbidden intimacy.

Finally, I wasn't sad for all that had gone before...all the heartache and betrayal that had led me to him. It felt glorious in its exquisiteness.

Astor rose and flipped me over, facedown, and his right hand came down hard on bum. I yelled my delight at the shock of the sting as he gripped my hips on either side and entered me once more, owning my pussy with each fierce blow. His right hand reached around to strum my clit, sending jolts of pleasure to my very core. He brought us both to that place of forgetting once more, and we tumbled into a seeming abyss.

An earth-shattering orgasm snatched my breath away, and all I could do was curl my fingers into the sheet, gasping for air.

This passion between us was all-consuming.

He was all-consuming. He had me on my knees, continuing to ride out his pleasure behind me, his hand sliding up and down my spine. He didn't seem to want our love-making to end either, and was as determined as me to stay locked together as one.

My arms and legs were shaking from enduring all he'd unleashed and I could no longer hold myself up. I collapsed onto the bed.

"Not yet," he teased, and rolled us over.

With my back against his chest and my thighs splayed over his, clenching him tightly, I felt him reach low and squeeze my clit beneath his palm. My breathing became ragged again, my body yearning for more of this endless pleasure.

But then the sensitivity became too much and I rested my hand on his to pause him.

"Take your hand away," he whispered huskily.

"I'm not sure—"

"I'll know when you're ready again."

I trembled through his titillation.

"This is where we begin to trust each other, Raquel. Do you think you can do that with me?"

"Yes." *I'll try.*

My hand slipped from his and I brought it up to ease my beaded nipples, soothing the ache.

He pressed firmly against me and the pressure made me throb deliciously as my thoughts drifted, the call of sleep seducing me. In that moment it felt as though he knew my soul and with him teasing my clit just so, bringing on waves of pleasure, *he did.*

This level of devotion I was feeling was more than I imagined possible. Still, I wasn't ready to fall so quickly. I'd not let myself be *that* vulnerable.

I could enjoy this, though. Revel in this enticing man and use these intimate moments to heal that part of me that had been hurt.

The rest of me…my heart and my thoughts, were walled up safe from anyone who might try to get close.

A shiver ran up my spine when I felt his fingertip begin massaging my clit. He was insatiable…the way he played with me felt incredible and with him inside me still, his cock growing harder by the second, I surrendered to the heat burning inside me once more.

When his left hand reached up and squeezed my nipple, he sent me hurtling toward another orgasm and I shuddered violently in his arms. My head crashed back onto his chest as I caught my breath, panting as my heartbeat slowed to normal.

Finally, he lay alongside me, his body's heat seeping into mine as he kissed the nape of my neck, still deep inside me and throbbing deliciously.

"I didn't know it could be like this," I admitted.

"Even more than this, Raquel." His lips pressed against my shoulder with affection.

Astor had restored my ability to feel…but with the opening of my heart came the greatest risk—I was afraid I was already falling for him. I rolled away from his warmth and buried my face in a pillow.

All this intimacy was forcing my vulnerability to the surface and I couldn't let him see it. Though from the way his fingers trailed through my hair, I sensed he was weakening, too.

Chapter
NINETEEN

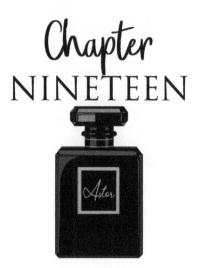

I AWOKE TO FIND MYSELF ALONE IN BED.

Rolling onto my side, I reached for my Chopard and after a quick glance, tossed it back onto the bedside table. We'd slept all night. Or at least I had and it had been one of those deep sleeps that I rarely experienced. Having Raquel here was making a difference.

I ran my hand along the sheets where she'd lain next to me, feeling bothered by her absence. In the past, seeing her gone would have brought me relief, since there'd be no need for small talk as I schemed a way to get her out. But now, with Raquel, I hated thinking that she'd changed her mind about staying and left.

Lifting the sheet, I stared down at my erection.

Last night…

Jesus, last night…the memory of us rolling around and going at it like two crazed lovers came flooding back. I savored the way she'd reacted to me, the way she'd stared into my eyes in awe as I thrust deeper, wanting to send over the edge again and again. It had been all I'd wanted—her writhing in pleasure, her screaming through another climax, her reaction to the way my cock owned her—the need was becoming addictive.

Unfamiliar emotions were stirring deep inside me, and I knew it was the way she responded to every kiss I gave her, every caress, every thrust that made her come in my arms.

Spending time with her was all I wanted to do today.

I could still smell her on me, that erotic scent that sent shivers up my spine. And her taste, *God*, her taste was exquisite. I could see myself becoming obsessed with this woman.

Both my mind and cock responded with a *yes* when I heard Raquel moving around in the bathroom.

I climbed out of bed and strolled over to the closed door.

"Everything okay?" I asked, with a quick knock.

Code for let me in so I can see you.

"I'll be out in a second," she called back.

Rubbing a hand over my stubble, I walked over to the closet and found a robe, pulling it on and marveling at my level of introspection. I cared what she thought about me. Usually, I'd be proud to show what was on the agenda before breakfast, but with her, I sensed I'd have to traverse all matters of the heart mindfully.

My questions could wait for now. This…this was what we both needed and business could wait.

The bathroom door opened and I stared at Raquel—the breathtaking morning version of her. She'd used my comb on her shiny locks, and now lush tendrils fell neatly around her face. Her mascara had been wiped away, giving her a fresh, natural appearance. She'd wrapped herself in a towel to hide her curves.

I stepped closer. "How are you feeling?"

"Fine," she said, peering up at me. "How are you?"

"Never better. Come back to bed."

"Did I wake you?"

I shook my head and gestured toward the bed. As she walked past me, I reached out and grabbed her towel, whipping it off her. She laughed and hurried to get back under the duvet.

Letting my robe slip open, I caught her gaze roaming over my body as she dragged her teeth across her lip seductively.

"Move over," I said, climbing into bed.

I pulled her close and she rested her head on my chest. This snuggling was what I'd missed earlier when I'd first awoken. It wasn't something I'd ever allowed myself to enjoy in the past, but she was impossibly huggable and I pressed my lips to her forehead to let her know how I was feeling.

She reached up and traced her fingers along my jaw. "How come you look this good in the morning?"

"I was thinking the same thing about you."

Her tenderness was something I'd craved without even knowing it. Her affection seemed pure and, even after all my threats, she still looked at me as though she saw a decent man.

"Can I get you anything?" I asked.

"I have everything I need right here." She wrapped her arms around me and let out a contented sigh.

I traced a fingertip up and down her arm. "Last night…"

Her concerned gaze snapped to mine.

"How do you feel about it?" I asked.

"You mean the part where you saved my life?"

I shook my head, recalling that near disaster. I'd pushed the memory out of my mind because the consequences were too devastating to contemplate. "I meant me fucking you hard, Raquel."

She giggled. "That's what I meant."

"Ah."

"I know, you're the big bad wolf and I'd be wise to remember you don't do relationships."

"Who told you that?"

"You did." She held my gaze. "I don't blame you. Certainly not after all I've been through. Life can be…"

"Don't let the world break you."

She frowned, as though she wanted to ask me if I spoke from experience.

"This place is lovely." She studied my face. "Why do you have two homes in South Beach?"

"This is my fuck pad."

Her gaze narrowed.

"I'm kidding, I'm kidding, seriously." I grinned down at her.

"You better be."

"Usually the falling power line stuns my lovers and leaves them powerless against my advances. Last night it missed you…a technical glitch."

She dug her fingertips into my ribs and tickled me.

"I'm joking!" I grabbed her wrists and held them together. "Actually, my neighbor better sell that property to me or they'll face a lawsuit."

"Don't be hard on them." She eased her wrists out of my grip. "It was an accident."

"Andrew's a musician. He's stoned most of the time so he's letting the place go. I don't need him bringing down the value of this area."

"Still, you'd never sell? It's paradise here." She exhaled slowly. "Now I really feel bad you weren't going to stay."

"I'd have been fine."

"Would you have stayed at Bridgestone?"

Hell to the no.

"Haven't stayed there since I was a boy." I raised my head to look at her. "I use the stables there because of convenience." *I don't go in the house.*

"Your parents live there?" she asked.

"My mother does."

"Isn't that where you grew up?"

I looked at her suspiciously. "I went to live in Cuba for a few years."

"Why did you leave America?"

Of course, I'd led Raquel into this formidable conversation where my past could be exposed. I chose to breathe through the rising tension and remain silent.

She stared at me. "Astor?"

"I was sent to Havana to round out my education." I rolled onto my chest and rose up, using my elbows to keep my weight off of her.

"Tell me about you, Raquel. I want to know more."

"You already seem to know so much about me."

"I want to savor exploring you." I dipped my head and drew her nipple into my mouth.

She let out a soft moan.

"And?" I coaxed, planting kisses on her chest and slowly moving lower over her abdomen. I trailed my tongue down over her pelvis, lingering there with more kisses. "I'm curious to hear how you ended up in Dunedin." I watched her carefully as I spread apart her thighs.

"Um...well...I visited the town and fell in love with the ocean views and the small community and it was the perfect place to...oh, that's amazing..."

I lapped at her clit, circling it with my tongue, teasing her until her panting was short and sharp.

Pulling back, I rose up to grab her wrists and pin them over her head. "I have a question for you."

"Ask."

"Sure?" I used my knees to spread her thighs wider and maneuvered my pelvis so that the tip of my cock slid against her, nudging in a little. The sensation was as much a tease for me as it was for her.

Raquel's hips rocked against me insistently.

"You want my cock, Raquel?" I cooed into her ear.

"Yes."

"First, answer this," I began, my tone dark. "Why didn't you tell me your store was broken into?" I shoved my cock deep inside her and she arched her back, letting out a long groan that was a mixture of want and panic.

I went balls deep and held her down. "I want to know why you kept that from me."

Chapter
TWENTY

Raquel

HOW DARE ASTOR ASK ME SUCH A QUESTION WHEN HE WAS DEEP inside me...

And yet his forceful thrusts had my inner muscles clenching around his girth as a pang of discomfort morphed into pleasure. My wrists stung as he pressed them into the mattress above my head.

The expression on his face was primal. "I want to know why you kept that from me."

He knows...

I met his fierce gaze, my body going rigid. "Are you spying on me?"

His quick withdrawal was followed by another thrust as he buried himself all the way in and then remained still, not releasing his iron-clad hold on my wrists. The sensual pressure from the way he'd captured me caused me to tip my pelvis in response to the erotic sensations surging through me.

"Want me to stop?" He circled his hips.

I gasped in response.

Astor's scent consumed me. This was sex and sin and danger and it was making me heady and I tried to understand why I wanted more of this, my body yearning for his harshness, his domination. "Fuck me, then. Go on."

"First, answer my question."

"This is not you."

"Clearly it is."

His sudden change was overwhelming and yet it was turning me on, taking me to a place I'd never explored. I was so aroused I was on the precipice of coming.

He nipped my chin. "Don't let my hospitality fool you."

"What did I say to trigger this?"

His expression became sincere. "Tell me what's going on."

"You're asking me…like this?"

He smiled seductively. "I like having a captive audience."

I tried to wriggle my wrists out of his grip but he was too strong, too insistent. His erection buried deeper…impaling me.

"I was embarrassed to tell you," I bit out.

"What did they steal?"

"Everything."

He pulled out of me. I rolled onto my side and went to get out but he grabbed me from behind and pulled me back, hugging me against his chest.

"I'm sorry," he said softly.

Even now in the heat of this battle I was turned on, and I wanted to hate him for it, wanted to scream that he had no right to make me feel this confused, this needy, longing for his touch even now.

I turned my head to look back at him. "They stole my handwritten files."

His grip tightened around my waist. "Did you make copies?"

"No. Why?"

"It's a logical question." He let out a frustrated huff. "What else?"

"The perfume I was working on." I turned completely and stared at him. "The one I tried to sell to save my store, but it never made it to its destination."

"What destination?"

"Dazzle and Bazaar."

He mulled that over. "What happened?"

I broke his gaze. "My meeting was sabotaged."

"How?"

I shrugged, letting him know I was done discussing the subject.

His hand smoothed my hair. "Tell me."

"Are you sure, Astor?"

He pressed his erection into my back. "What do you think?"

I leaned back against him. "You're sending mixed signals."

"This level of compassion is unusual for me."

"Care to elaborate?"

"I don't do cuddling in the morning."

"Then I'm honored."

He kissed the back of my neck. "Why didn't the meeting at Dazzle and Bazaar work out?"

I let out a sigh. "When I arrived at their office my perfume was missing from my handbag. The one I was going to license to them." I squeezed my eyes shut, reliving the humiliation.

"Did you find it?"

"Yes."

"Where?"

"On a shelf where it didn't belong—where I would never have put it."

"Did you meet with Anna Rosenthal?"

"No, I had to cancel."

"Have you ever met with her?"

Snapping my head around to look at him again I said, "No. Why?"

"Just curious."

I tried to pull away. "I'm curious about you, too, Mr. Beauregard."

He crushed me back against his chest. "Why would you say that?"

I was destroyed all the way to my core and this wasn't me feeling sorry for myself, this was me hurrying up the inevitable.

"I want you to trust me, Raquel."

"Really, after this?"

Our uncomfortable silence filled the room as an annoying trickle of perspiration snaked down my spine.

"What did the police say?" he asked softly.

"The thief left no trace."

"Who threw your scale on the floor?"

"The thief, I'm assuming."

"A personal strike."

Whether or not the person knew me, I felt violated by their actions. I buried my face in my hands at the thought of a stranger being in my beloved store.

Astor's strong arms wrapped around me. "Share that thought, Raquel."

I didn't speak. My mind and body reeled with confusion. Last night had been one of those too good to be true moments and I wasn't falling for his charm anymore—or the dashing way he'd saved my life.

"Let me take you again," his voice was barely a whisper.

"Why?" I asked, staring up at him.

He arched a brow. "Because it's what my cock wants."

"Not what you want?"

"It's attached, so we agree on most things." He reached low and his fingers trailed along my clit. "Let me apologize for the way I behaved. I've upset you."

I managed a nod and tipped my hips back. He eased into me and as he filled me completely, we rocked as one as though no harsh words had been spoken between us.

I hated that it felt so good.

As though reading my mind he said, "I see you, Raquel. I remember everything you say. I remember every encounter. And I'm getting to know your body, too."

With his left arm wrapped around my chest to hold me still, his right hand reached low over my belly to play with me. I let out a desperate sigh as he flicked my clit, sending me hurtling toward the edge.

"And I want in on your mind, too." Astor's hand left my pussy and he raised it to my mouth, sliding his fingers between my lips. The erotic sweetness sent a shock of arousal through me and I moaned into his palm, suckling his fingertips. He yanked his fingers out of my mouth and grabbed my throat, and I melted against him, swooning at his show of power.

"I want this," I stuttered.

"So do I."

But I could never be his lover after this. I would never allow myself to be used for another's carnal pleasure only to be discarded later. "Why did you say it?"

"Say what?"

"That there could be an *us*."

"I'm not ruling it out. Just don't cross me, Wren. Understand?"

"You've made yourself quite clear."

He caught my glare and added, "I really like you, Raquel. Maybe more than I should."

"I thought you didn't do feelings, Astor."

"That was before I met you." He reached low, using two fingers to strum my clit fast with a heady beat.

I rose into a blinding climax that had my toes curling and my thoughts scattering into the ether but all I could manage was, "Don't hurt me."

"I would never hurt you on purpose, Raquel." His lips pressed against my shoulder.

Yet I was too far gone to gauge the sincerity of his words. I felt like I was caught up in perilous waters with the deadly undercurrent being Astor Beauregard himself.

He used a firm hand to turn my chin so he could look into my eyes, and then he gave me a heart-stopping grin. "Don't mind me."

"What are you going to do now?"

Astor moved lower and then nestled between my thighs. "I'm

having breakfast."

I stared down at him, stunned by how insatiable he was as he lavished affection with his mouth, working his tongue along my inner folds, my body shuddering with unbearable pleasure.

Time was running out, and as this orgasm snatched me away into oblivion, I knew that soon all I would have left of Astor was the memory of him.

Chapter
TWENTY-ONE

DAYS BEFORE I KNEW RAQUEL NEVER STARTED LIKE THIS...
Before today I would have spent the morning reading, swimming, and maybe even catching a movie...alone. It wasn't that I didn't have any friends—I had plenty, I just preferred to kick off the day with my own thoughts and in my own way.

Having Raquel here was easy. I liked everything about her...other than her possibly being a corporate spy. But the more I got to know her, the more I doubted the possibility of her betrayal.

Usually the women I'd bring back here never stayed past 9:00 A.M. and—*hell to the no*—never ate breakfast with me. I would make up some excuse to get rid of them, yet here I was sitting at the central island in the kitchen with Raquel, both of us sipping coffee and eating cereal and swapping the occasional smile.

She stared up at the walled TV watching CNN spewing its doom and gloom. I reached for the remote control on the counter and changed the channel to a documentary about Africa. When Raquel knitted her brows together in the way of an inquisitive reaction I gave her a friendly smirk.

"Can I get you anything else?" I asked.

"I'm fine."

I carried our bowls and mugs over to the sink, rinsed them off and then slid them into the dishwasher.

When I turned to face her, sunlight was kissing her hair and she looked ethereal, her expression one of peace. She was threatening me with happiness and I refused to trust it.

"Excuse me." I strolled out and headed toward the lounge.

I walked up to the glass wall and stared out at the scene of last night's near disaster, taking in the empty pool that was now drained of water and the sunlight glinting off the blue and white tiles. The downed power line was gone. Over the wall, on my neighbor's property, a technician was at the top of the pole fixing the line.

Outside the sun burst its brightness over the garden—a contrast to the unrelenting tension that resided inside.

What if she asks about your past? What if she digs around for the truth?

My life had been dedicated to protecting my family, and when a woman got too close there was only one way to deal with their curiosity. This secret was my burden to bear.

And besides, I hardly knew Raquel and no doubt I'd have to come to terms with ending this self-indulgent urge to spend time with her. Though in the world of perfumery she was clearly my equal in chemistry and there was something intriguing about that.

But I didn't want her to know about my past.

The haunting words spoken by Father Fernando all those years ago had not been meant for my ears.

"If that's what a boy can do imagine what the man will be capable of. We must save him from himself."

Ignoring these macabre thoughts, I opened the sliding door to gaze out at the ocean. I breathed in the fresh, warm air and admired the seascape beyond.

When I turned around, Raquel was standing behind me.

She didn't look like someone who was pleased with themselves for infiltrating my space, if that was indeed why she was here. She merely appeared intrigued with the man who had invited her on a whim to stay with him, no strings attached. Yet last night…

I gestured for her to join me. "Come here."

She walked over and stood beside me. "Astor, thank you for breakfast."

"Of course. Make yourself at home."

"I'm very low maintenance, usually," she said softly.

"You should never admit that." I broke into a smile. "Let them think you're worth every second of their time."

She turned her attention to the garden. "I meant…if you have somewhere to be today."

"I can see I'm going to have to build up your self-esteem."

"My self-esteem is fine."

I arched a brow, and she added, "Please don't ever again ask me a personal question while your dick is inside me." Her eyes flashed with passion.

"I'm a cautious man."

"Take your arrogance down a notch, okay?"

I found her sudden feistiness arousing. "I will do my best—"

"I'm not done."

"Let's have it then, Ms. Wren."

She pointed in the direction of the kitchen. "Don't ever change the channel on the TV when I'm watching it. You can ask me if I'm done watching it first." She raised her hand in her defense. "I know I'm a guest and I'm grateful but I'm nipping that in the bud right now."

I gave her an amused smile. "Okay."

"You hate me now don't you?"

I stared at her for the longest time. "So no changing the TV while my dick is in you. Got it."

She slapped my arm playfully and gave me a warm smile.

Taking her hand, I brought it up to my mouth and kissed her wrist. "There's a risk we won't leave the house all day."

Her puzzled frown turned into a smile.

"I want to make today memorable for you," I said.

"It already is." Her focus returned to the pool and her expression became thoughtful. Was she thinking of our night together?

"Do you like sea creatures?"

She looked surprised. "You mean for lunch? I like salmon. And shrimp."

I smirked. "No, I mean would you like to go visit some living sea creatures, ones that are protected. If you're going to leap into the water and start gnawing on them…" I burst out laughing.

She looked a little embarrassed. "I'd love to. Where is it?"

"A surprise. Let's leave in twenty minutes."

"I'm not taking you away from anything important am I?"

I cupped her face in my hands and leaned in to kiss her, my tongue leisurely lashing hers. "You are my something important."

The sweetness in her gaze made her look so young.

"Go get dressed."

She smiled broadly as she turned to head upstairs.

"Raquel," I called after her.

She smiled back at me.

"I'm glad you're here."

"Me too."

I watched as she ascended the winding staircase and moved out of sight. No one had talked to me like that before and gotten away with it, and yet with her it felt so damn arousing. If there was a match in this world for me, Raquel Wren was close.

I found myself following her up and around the twisting stairs. A faint trace of her perfume hung in the air, the scent of lilies. For a second it reminded me of Penelope's new product, with the base notes reminiscent of her masterpiece.

It's a coincidence. Yet my back stiffened with the realization that I'd detected underlying notes of Orris.

When I entered the bedroom I found Raquel stripped down to her bra and panties, bending over and rummaging through her suitcase.

"What perfume are you wearing?" I asked.

She rose and turned to look at me. "Have you seen my jeans?"

I dragged my fingers through my hair. "Sorry about the

interrogation earlier." My gaze flashed to the scene of the crime that was my king-sized bed.

"Apology accepted." She strolled toward me, staring up at my face as though reading my sincerity. "Every time you do the right thing, Astor, you'll be rewarded."

My jaw slackened in surprise when she knelt before me, her gaze holding mine as she fiddled with my belt buckle. She unzipped my pants, reached in and withdrew my cock, which immediately became firm in her grasp.

She ran her tongue around my head, lapping along the length of my cock to tease it until I was rock hard and my balls were tight. When she dipped her head to draw them into her mouth all I could do was stare at the ceiling as my thoughts scattered and my heart thrummed in my ears.

I was enraptured by her.

This...this was my all-time favorite morning activity and I was amused that Raquel had sensed it, too. She stroked me up and down and with her other hand she cupped my balls, her mouth opening wide and welcoming all of me. When the back of her throat closed around my tip, the pressure to my head forced my body to shudder and I covered my eyes, moaning.

"Do you like your reward, Astor?" she cooed, before taking me in so deep and fast it made me forget everything.

"I'm gonna... "

In these unfolding moments, Raquel's control over me was maddeningly enslaving. Her touch aroused and yet soothed, provoked and teased, proving she was enamored with me.

Her groans thrummed through me and I could no longer hold back. My hips rocked, bursting heat into her mouth. Silently exalting the way she swallowed and lapped at what spilled over, I let her bring me down with tender kisses, hearing her soft sighs of appreciation.

I reached out and gripped the doorframe, resting my weight against it as I slowed my breathing.

"Well done," said Raquel as she pushed herself to her knees.

"Now, where did I put those jeans?"

With every cell still buzzing from my orgasm, I shoved my dick back into my pants and zipped up my jeans. "Raquel…"

"Yes." She turned and smiled, knowing she had just delivered a mind-bending orgasm.

"So it's gonna be like this, is it?"

"Oh, yes, Mr. Beauregard. Steel yourself for a lot more of that if you please me."

Her smug smile told me she was feeling proud of herself for having me so vulnerable before her. Her scent lingered on me like an erotic curse.

"And if you please me," I countered, "I will leave you sore for days."

"I look forward to it."

"You definitely should," I said darkly.

She bit the end of her tongue seductively. "You taste amazing, Astor."

My gaze lowered to her panties, where a wet patch of her arousal dampened her lace. She followed my gaze and a momentary flash of embarrassment crossed her face.

I strolled forward and knelt before her. She looked down at me and narrowed her eyes as though daring me to go further, holding on to that look of pure defiance.

She'd done well holding onto the power for all of *ten* minutes.

Reaching up, I tugged her panties so they slid down over her thighs, exposing her completely, her pussy only inches from my face.

Her aroma was dazzling.

If I could bottle this scent I'd own the industry.

"Let me see." I held her gaze to taunt her.

Raquel's jaw flexed with frustration that her little game was up. This evidence proved she had been as equally aroused as me. With gentle fingers I eased apart her folds, examining her swollen clit. "Remain still, Ms. Wren."

She shivered and let out a long breath.

"Arms by your side," I demanded.

She dropped her hands to her side and haughtily raised her chin.

"Ah." I brushed a fingertip along her folds and then held my fingers out for her to see that they were soaked from her pussy. "Evidence of just how much you enjoyed my cock."

She shot me a proud look.

Again, I trailed my fingertips along her and eased her apart to fully reveal her. "Steel yourself, Ms. Wren. If you continue to be a good girl there'll be plenty more of this happening to your pussy in the future."

She looked straight ahead as though trying to hide her mortification at being so wet for me.

I let her go and pushed myself to my feet. "Change your underwear. Then get dressed. Meet me downstairs."

Turning away from her, suppressing a smile, I headed out and down the hallway, relishing how I'd felt a crackle of electricity in the air between us. Playing with Raquel was becoming my new favorite sport. Bringing my fingers to my mouth to taste her sweetness, I savored her all over again.

For twenty minutes, I sat on the couch with my gaze locked on the winding staircase in anticipation of Raquel walking down it.

Soon, she appeared wearing her skinny jeans, a white shirt and flat shoes. Her hair hung loose and lovely around her shoulders and delicate bracelets dangled from her wrists. She descended the staircase slowly as though needing time to gauge my reaction, and then stood in the middle of the lounge with her expression full of anticipation.

I gave her a triumphant smile to warn her I was still in charge.

"Is this okay?" She glanced down at herself.

"You'll need a sweater."

"Where are we going?" she asked breathlessly.

I stood and walked over to join her. "On an adventure."

Chapter
TWENTY-TWO

Raquel

As Astor drove us up the coast in his Range Rover, I constantly stole glances at his gorgeous profile.

I had been destined to spend another night alone sleeping on the floor of my shop, and this was so far from what I imagined my Sunday was going to look like. I had not expected to be whisked off to South Beach and spoiled by this man who kept throwing me dazzling grins.

I soaked up the sunshine while the fresh ocean breeze blasted my face. The astounding views of wide open spaces never failed to inspire me.

Gripping the armrest, I sat forward with excitement when we passed a sign: MARINE SANCTUARY OF SOUTH BEACH.

Astor parked the car and killed the engine. "Ready?"

"Can we go in?"

"That's why we're here."

A rush of excitement made me squeal with happiness.

He reached out and twirled a strand of my hair between his thumb and forefinger. "Already having fun?"

I grinned. "Yes, thank you."

It was easy to admire the beauty of him, the masculine yet elegant way he climbed out of the Range Rover and rounded the front. He opened my door and offered me his hand. I didn't want to break this spell, didn't want to think of why or how our circumstances had brought us together...or how they may rip our friendship apart. I just wanted to appreciate the here and now and savor this day.

He helped me out of the car, his chest almost brushing mine as I slid down, my feet finding the gravel, my head tilting up to look into his kind hazel eyes.

Astor leaned in. "This is a very special place."

"I feel it."

I closed my eyes as his lips touched mine. I could have been anywhere in that moment, all I knew was him...the confidence of a man who made me feel truly alive.

"I haven't taken a day off in months," he admitted. "You're good for me, Raquel Wren." He slipped his sunglasses over his eyes.

We walked the short distance across the gravel to a dome-shaped building that rested on the water's edge.

Astor pointed to the vastness of the structure. "This is a hospital for sick and injured marine life. It's a great place for students to visit and learn about their environment. Many of the animals are released back into the wild, but some wouldn't make it on their own so they house them here." He opened the door and gestured for me to go ahead. "They don't let tourists back here but my friend Garcia Rena is the senior marine biologist so we get access."

The chill from a blast of air-conditioning hit my skin. "How did you meet him?"

"Charity gala. He's a great guy."

We made our way down a long hallway and the air became even chillier. The air-conditioning was apparently turned up to the max. I realized this was probably why Astor had told me to bring a sweater as I pulled it on.

No, way...

Up ahead the cutest penguin hopped toward us and I stood back to make way for him as he passed. I threw a big smile at the young woman in khakis following him closely, her grin as big as ours. Astor knelt to greet the little guy and the penguin hopped up close to him and then waddled off.

"How's he doing?" asked Astor.

"Great," she told him. "Are you looking for Garcia?"

On Astor's nod she pointed. "In the tank. Ruben goes home today!"

"Good to hear," Astor said. "I'm glad we got to say goodbye."

Once we made it through another door, the pungent scent of fresh fish hit me. Beyond I saw a gigantic tank filled with water. Leaning over the tank was a thirty-something man wearing a wetsuit who was feeding an exuberant dolphin one fish at a time from a bucket.

He turned and looked down at us from his elevated height. "Hey, Astor."

"Hey, Garcia," he called up. "This is Raquel. She has a thing for dolphins."

"Well, you've come to the right place." Garcia beamed at me.

With my chest tingling with happiness, I approached the tank and rested my palms on the glass. The dolphin circled the entire space with what looked like glee. Being so close to this creature made my heart soar. "What's his story?" I asked.

"A few weeks ago he was rescued by our team," Garcia explained. "Ruben suffered some tail damage but we managed to save his fluke."

"Thank goodness." I was mesmerized by the breathtaking dolphin, which paused to peer through the glass at me, seemingly just as fascinated.

"We were feeding him every two hours for a while there," said Garcia. "We nursed him back with nutrition and attention."

"Will he be released?" I asked.

"Actually, today's the day," said Garcia. "His pod's been spotted off the coast and we are prepping to take him out now."

"How do you know it's his pod?" I asked.

"We track the other dolphins in his family," Garcia explained.

"Several are tagged so we can monitor where they go."

"You saved his life," I said, amazed at this place and the good they were doing.

"These creatures are saving us," said Garcia. "Without them we can't survive. The eco system will be unbalanced."

"Want to feed him?" asked Astor.

I flashed Garcia a look of hope. "Am I allowed?"

He laughed. "He might splash you."

"I don't care."

Astor directed me where to wash my hands and within minutes I was standing on a ramp and leaning over the tank. The cutest dolphin was making clicking noises as though asking for fish.

"Will he be okay when you set him free?" I turned to ask.

Wiping his hands on a cloth, Garcia smiled. "We'll track him. Ruben's pretty resilient."

"His future is bright because of this place," said Astor.

I reached into the bucket and threw Ruben another fish. He swallowed it whole and made noises that sounded like chuckles.

"Do you think he knows he's leaving?" I asked.

"Maybe. They're very perceptive," said Garcia. "He's probably picking up on our anticipation."

I climbed down and rejoined them.

Astor was staring at me. I sidled up to him and whispered, "What?"

"Nothing," he replied. "I was just enjoying watching you."

"Feeding the fish?"

He shrugged and then whispered, "Being you."

"I'm always me." I headed over to the sink and washed my hands with soap and water.

Astor washed his hands beside me. "Usually you're a lot more guarded."

"I don't think I am." I threw the paper towel in the trash and then pressed a fingertip to Astor's chest. "You're guarded. Bit of projection going on there."

Astor wrapped his hand around my finger and gave it a shake.

"Point at me again and see what happens."

"What will happen?"

"I'll throw you into the shark tank."

I glanced over at Garcia and called out, "Do you have sharks here?"

He looked surprised. "Not right now. Why?"

"Just wondering." I narrowed my gaze on Astor, who smirked.

"I'll throw you in with the penguins, then," he said. "Let them peck you to death."

"I'll throw you in with the octopus," I said, amused. "Let him sucker you to death."

"I've already been sucked enough." He shook his head. "In so very many ways."

I slapped his arm.

Astor dodged me and we caught Garcia smiling our way.

We toured the state-of-the-art facility with Garcia escorting us, visiting a sea turtle rescued after it had been found in the harbor with a straw embedded in its nose, now removed. We also checked in with an incredibly cute wild otter that had been abandoned by its mother. Another highlight was seeing a manatee up close that had gotten tangled in some fishing net and ended up dehydrated. He'd be going home soon, too.

I loved watching the way Astor responded to the animals with compassion and patience, and the way he chatted with Garcia, asking smart questions about their care and progress.

Garcia left us to walk over and speak with the other staff members. Through the glass window we watched a marine assistant feeding fifty or so penguins that were hopping around.

"What?" Astor had sensed me staring.

It was hard not to admire that gorgeous face when he was distracted, and it had been nice to get an insight into the person he really was. When I had first met Astor he'd seemed unapproachable—yet now I was seeing the real him.

"You're full of surprises," I said.

"Well, you can always trust animals."

I stepped back.

He turned to look at me. "I meant generally."

Those words had thrown us headfirst back into reality, reminding me we were potential enemies. I hid the hurt by focusing on the penguins.

Astor's hand rubbed my back as he intuitively sensed my tension. "Small steps, Wren, small steps."

"For you?" I said quietly so the others wouldn't hear.

"For both of us."

A penguin hopped up to the glass, breaking the tension as he peered up at us.

"I have no fish," Astor called to him, and opened his palms to prove it.

"Maybe the penguin likes you for who you are and not what you have," I said.

"That would be a first." He waggled his eyebrows playfully at the penguin.

"Why did you invite me to stay with you?" I asked. "You know I would have been fine."

"Honestly, Raquel, I don't know."

Watching him carefully, I looked for any sign he regretted what he'd just admitted.

Astor's attention was now focused across the room on Garcia, but after a few moments he turned to look at me. "You and I love similar things, but other than that we are opposites."

Though usually opposites were meant to attract. I was a newly divorced woman with the residue of heartache, and Astor was a multi-millionaire with expensive tastes who had the reputation of being a playboy. Maybe I had read him all wrong.

"I can leave when we get back," I said.

Astor looked distracted. "I'm sorry, what?"

"When we get back to your place."

Astor's brow furrowed. "You're not my prisoner, Raquel. Leave anytime you like."

He threw me a reassuring smile and headed over to Garcia who was deep in conversation with the others.

Embarrassed, I turned to stare through the glass window at the fake cold climate setting that the penguins lived in. They ate the fish they were fed and then demanded more with their adorable trumpeting sounds.

I wrapped my arms around myself to ward off the chill. When I looked back at Astor he was deep in conversation with a young woman dressed in khakis. They looked like they knew each other well. More staff appeared and huddled to talk with each other in the corner. Whatever was going on seemed tense and I hoped Ruben was okay.

Astor's gaze held mine and then he seemed to change his mind on a thought and turned his back on me. I watched from afar, trying to read what was going on and not wanting to get in the way.

After ten minutes, Garcia headed over to me and gestured for me to follow him. "Something's come up. Why don't you wait in my office?"

I looked over his shoulder and watched Astor disappear through a door. "You're doing great work here."

"We have great sponsors like Astor," he said. "He's pretty generous when it comes to donations, and with his time, too."

"Where did he go?" I kept my tone calm.

"He's going to help us with a situation."

I threw Garcia a warm smile, trying to hide me nervousness. "Can I help?"

"We're on it."

When we reached his office he entered first and then gestured to a corner seating area. "Make yourself at home." He reached for a remote control on his desk and turned on the walled TV. "Astor's going to be a while."

"How long?" I'd pushed all his buttons and he'd pushed mine and now we were at an impasse, apparently, with him ignoring me for the rest of our visit. "Not sure I can sit still."

"Oh, I forgot." Garcia rummaged in his pocket and pulled out a set of keys. "Astor told me to give these to you if you would rather make your way back to South Beach. We'll drive him home later."

I stared at him, stunned and confused. "Garcia, what happened? I mean, how did Astor seem to you?"

Garcia looked surprised. "He looked good to go."

"Go where?"

"He didn't tell you?"

"Tell me what?"

"The coastguard just got a distress signal. A tourist reported her friend is drifting out to sea in a canoe. She needs rescuing."

"And they can't go?"

"The coastguard's dealing with an upturned yacht a few miles out. So we've answered the call. We're sending out the *Allure*, she's the fastest boat out there. Our team's about to head in the opposite direction. We could bail on returning Ruben, but Astor has stepped up to go get the girl."

"Alone?"

"It's all hands on deck with Ruben." Garcia gestured for me to follow him. "Wanna go with him?"

"With Astor?"

"Yeah, why not?"

Chapter
TWENTY-THREE

I SECURED THE ANCHOR INSIDE THE BOAT AND TURNED ON THE ENGINE. IT thrummed to life, hiding its horsepower beneath its purr. Now this…this was a speedboat. It would be like being behind the wheel of a racecar.

The alert had gone out for any free boats in the area to answer a rescue call. Since we were located closest to where the young lady had last been seen canoeing, our team was the most logical choice for finding her.

A local would know about the tides, so this tourist was facing double the danger. Apparently, she and her friends had hired canoes for the day and then crossed the safety zone. Throw in the impending storm and the threat was raised, along with the risk of hypothermia. With my concern growing for her, I readied to head out to sea.

Then I saw them…

Raquel and Garcia were on the dock, walking quickly toward me. It made me wonder if the girl had been found.

"Everything okay?" I called over.

"Raquel's coming with you," said Garcia.

I straightened my back and gave him a look that told him this was a bad idea.

Raquel went to climb aboard. "I'll help you."

"I'm handling this," I shot back.

"Astor," she replied firmly, "you need to steer and I need to help the canoeist."

"It's choppy out there," said Garcia. "She has a point…two is better."

"Where's the first-aid kit and blanket?" She climbed in. "I'm a boater. I'm more than capable."

Garcia looked amused and I shot him an annoyed glare. "I'm the captain, you do what I say."

"Yes, sir." Raquel threw off a salute.

"All the best with our dolphin," I said to Garcia, waving goodbye.

With Raquel seated beside me we navigated out of the harbor, and then I opened up the throttle taking us fast out to sea.

With the dashboard lit up with our coordinates and a map of the shoreline, I pointed at it and said, "This is where she was last seen. I've tracked the currents. She's possibly around this region."

"That's a lot of water to cover," she said.

"It's not an exact science."

"Binoculars?"

I pointed at the glove compartment in front of her.

"You know this boat well?" She turned to face me. "How long have you volunteered here?"

"About ten years."

She looked impressed. "So you've rescued someone before?"

"As part of a team. Never alone. It's just us this time."

Raquel found the binoculars and peered through them. "It's pretty choppy out there."

"So says the forecast." I threw her a wary glance.

"This boat is—" Her gaze roamed over the dashboard. "It's gorgeous."

"I like to think so."

"Did you buy it for them?"

"What does it matter?"

She shrugged as though hinting she was merely making conversation, but I could see she was impressed. I didn't want accolades. I wanted that young woman safe on land again and her family and friends free of the worry they'd be going through.

We flew across the water at two hundred twenty-eight knots. I checked in with the coastguard for any updates and to share our location.

"I want you to stay." I glanced at Raquel. "At my place."

She looked away.

"I made you feel uncomfortable earlier," I said. "You're only my prisoner in the bedroom."

She laughed. "Say that and you may never get rid of me."

"Maybe I want that." I surprised myself as much as her, apparently.

Raquel blushed and I found it disarming. "It's a big thing you're doing, Astor. Letting me stay at your home."

I waved that off. "I just wanted to put that out there. That I like having you."

"Thank you, I appreciate it."

"It's cheaper than a maid," I joked.

"Very funny. Though I'm not averse to playing a topless maid if that floats your boat."

"Is there such a thing?"

"You know there is."

"I've never given it any thought."

She shook her head, amused, and then changed the subject. "I hope Ruben makes it."

I shifted gears as we hit the waves. "He's in great hands."

"So you've met Ruben before today?" she asked. "You're at the center a lot?"

"As much as I can be, yes."

"My man of mystery is opening up."

Reaching out, I rested my hand on her inner thigh and she placed her palm on my hand. The connection felt good. I *was* opening up and now all I needed was for her to do so, too. She was still so guarded.

Our gazes scanned the ocean and now and again Raquel raised the binoculars to take a better look.

"Over there!" She pointed east.

Turning sharply, I directed the boat toward what looked like an orange canoe and at the same time called our location in to the coastguard.

"Oh, God," Raquel was seeing what I saw.

A rush of dread hit me when we neared and I realized the canoe was upside down. "Hold the wheel," I shouted.

"Are you going in?" Raquel sounded panicked. "You need a life vest."

"I need to get under there." I leaped up onto the edge of the boat and dove into the ocean. When I hit the water the chill felt like knives stabbing my flesh. I swam swiftly towards the canoe.

The sea rose and fell with a dangerous swell. No wonder she couldn't get back, the tide was fierce out here and those dark clouds were ominous.

After grabbing the side of the canoe I drew in several deep breaths and sank below the water, bracing myself for possibly finding a drowned girl as I swept my hand along for where a body could be.

Surfacing, I sucked in air. "She's not here." I flipped the canoe right side up. "She'll have a life vest on."

Raquel pointed urgently. "Over there!"

A freak wave rolled me upward and then lowered me and I saw the girl floating with her life jacket on...and she looked unconscious. The engine thrummed behind me letting me know Raquel was close behind.

"Astor," she called out. "I saw a fin."

I spun round to look at her. "Shark or dolphin?"

"Get in," she was panicked. "Get in the boat."

"What kind? It makes a difference."

"I don't know." She looked freaked. "I think it's a shark."

I tried to follow her line of sight but the swell prevented me seeing pretty much anything other than a bob of orange. "I can reach her."

"Oh, my God, there's another one."

"You know that thing we're working on with you?" I called up.

"What thing?" she yelled.

"That sense of adventure." I wiped water out of my eyes. "Now's a good time for it kick in."

She called after me, something about a life vest but it was hard to hear. With broad breaststrokes I closed in on the woman who was pale and still. As I got closer I noticed she was Japanese, and she looked like a teenager. Relieved we'd found her, I allowed myself to glance around for any sharks. I sent out a prayer they'd not dived beneath us.

A trickle of blood flowed down her brow. Maybe she'd hit her head on the canoe. Maybe fatigue had caused her to drop her paddle and she fell in trying to grab it.

Whatever the reason, we had to get out of the water *now.*

Sharks picked up the scent of blood, one part per million.

"We've got you," I told her. "Hang on."

Raquel moved the *Allure* up beside us. She leaned over, reaching for the girl's shoulders. She pulled her up as I pushed the young woman until she rolled onto the boat.

I hoisted myself onto the deck and scrambled to make sure our patient was in the recovery position. She was already stirring, about to regain consciousness.

I tried to stay focused. "Call the coastguard. Tell them we need medics ready."

Raquel made the call. I wrapped a silver heat blanket around her as Raquel hurried into the driver's seat. She steered back to shore as I checked our girl for any more serious injuries.

Though Raquel was pushing the speedboat to its limits, the ride back felt excruciatingly long. I hated each second we were losing. Our patient was slipping in and out of consciousness.

Emergency services were waiting when we pulled up to the dock, immediately taking over the girl's care. Raquel and I stood side by side, watching them wheel her into an ambulance.

We watched it pull away and for several minutes neither of us spoke a word.

Staff at the center let me shower in Garcia's office bathroom. It took me half an hour to feel warm again as I blasted hot water over me. The shower was pretty shabby and I made a mental note to do something about it. Although it was a renovation Garcia would probably decline because he wanted all the money going to the animals.

I borrowed some of the spare clothes that he kept here, but his shoes didn't fit and mine were still drenched. Not that I cared...I was still too concerned for that girl and her recovery.

Luckily, I recalled that I had a pair of shoes in the car, thrown in the back after a hike I'd taken a few weeks ago.

"How's my superhero?" Raquel said, walking into Garcia's office.

"I needed you out there, Raquel. You did great."

"You did better." She came over and wrapped her arms around me. "I'm only doing this so you'll have body warmth."

I kissed her forehead. "And that's just me thanking you for saving a life today."

"Do you think she'll be okay?"

"We'll call later. They're taking her to Miami Beach Medical Center."

"Not sure I like your brand of excitement, Astor."

"You'll get used to it if you stick around."

"Thank you for today," she said softly.

"We had a detour but we're fine, right?"

"You're the best friend a girl could have."

Whether it was me coming down from the adrenaline rush or her comment describing us as only friends, I suddenly crashed with exhaustion. I stepped away from her and sank into a seat, taking a few deep breaths to center myself.

"You okay?" she said.

"Yeah, the threat of you diving in and gnawing on a shark was all too real."

She tapped my arm. "You were brave out there, Astor."

"Let's get home." I pushed to my feet. "Garcia's jeans are so tight I feel like a 1980s rock star."

Raquel's laughter rippled over me, and as I laughed too, I felt intensely happy that we were going home together.

Then reason and reality caught up with me, crushing my post adventure high as I remembered who she was. "Raquel," I said, getting her attention.

"Hmm?" She looked windswept and as pretty as ever.

"I have a new formula that needs perfecting. It's missing an ingredient. Is that a project you'd like to help me with? I think it could be a stellar creation."

She turned her back on me and said softly, "Of course, Astor. I'd be happy to help you with that."

Chapter
TWENTY-FOUR

O N THE WORKBENCH IN FRONT OF ME SAT A MARBLE BOWL, READY for me to begin creating something new. Though after yesterday's adventure on the high seas it was hard to concentrate—I couldn't stop thinking of the young woman and the danger she'd been in.

Astor had risked his life for her and he'd not given it a second thought. He'd not even panicked when I'd warned him about the sharks. What kind of man did that?

A good man, surely. Certainly a man who was brave and decent. So far, everything I had seen about him highlighted his integrity.

Yet at the same time I sensed I was getting close to the razor's edge of truth. Astor wanted me to help complete a formula…*my formula*. And if I did one second of work on Astor's project all I'd risked would be lost to the House of Beauregard.

I had already implicated myself in some kind of corporate espionage, and what had started out as me searching for clues had turned all the more complicated because of our intimacy. The confusion I'd come here with was front and center in my every thought and emotion.

I had to act fast and think my way to a quick resolution. There could be no more intimacy. No more evenings cuddled up on the couch watching TV in his beachfront home as though we were a normal couple. Because if this hurt me any worse I'd be forced to walk away from everything.

I could do that, right?

Too restless to sit still, I slid off my barstool and reached for a couple of ingredients I had planned on playing with.

My phone lit up and I answered. "Hello?"

"Ms. Wren, you have a visitor." It was Sarah, the receptionist.

"Who?" I asked.

"He didn't give his name," she said. "I have another call coming in. Can you come up to reception, please?"

She left me staring at my phone, wondering who it could be as I headed to the elevator and pushed the button.

I checked my watch. Astor wanted to meet just before noon and that time was looming closer.

When the elevator doors opened onto the foyer, I saw Damien sitting in the waiting room, leafing through a magazine.

When he saw me he shot to his feet. "How are you?"

"Fine." I threw a reassuring glance at the receptionist. "What are you doing here?"

"I was in town and thought I'd swing by."

"Is Embry with you?" I looked through the window toward the parking lot.

"No, she's out in the field. There's a hurricane in the Caribbean and it looks like it's going to head toward Dunedin."

I mused darkly that maybe the hurricane would suck her into the eye of its storm and do us all a favor. "So…why the visit?"

"I have something I need to talk with you about." He gestured towards the door. "We can talk in the Beamer, if you like."

"Here is fine."

"Um…it's best if we talk privately."

"I don't have long," I said.

"Bit of a change from when you were your own boss."

Yes, Damien, you asshole. I held my tongue.

"Anyway," he said, "I won't take much of your time."

I followed him out and wasn't surprised when he didn't hold the front door of the building open for me. He merely went on ahead and climbed into his silver BMW. I rounded the car and joined him in the passenger seat. Astor opened doors for me all the time and it was something I never took for granted.

My gaze roamed over what had once been our car, looking for Embry's things. The lemon and lime scented air freshener that was clipped to the rearview mirror assaulted my senses.

"You ready for the hurricane?" asked Damien.

"Yes," I lied.

"Good, that's good."

"Is this about the shop?" I snapped. "I know you want it sold. I'm doing everything I can to work with the realtor." It was a bit of a lie. I was helping as much as delaying.

"Don't get upset." Damien looked uncomfortable.

"I have to go."

He reached out and gripped my wrist. "This is important."

I let out a frustrated sigh.

"Are you in a relationship with Astor Beauregard?"

Those kisses he'd witnessed at the polo match had hit the mark, apparently.

"We're good friends."

"Friends who fuck?" He held my gaze.

"That's kind of private."

"Look, I know what this sounds like but we have a history and it's my job to watch out for you."

Are you kidding me?

I didn't say anything, though, just bit the inside of my cheek to hide my annoyance. I didn't want to get into an argument. We'd already shared every bitter word we could think of and there was nothing left to say. More than anything I needed to stay focused because my own disaster was unfolding within those walls. I didn't need Damien to complicate things more than they already were.

"I'm just gonna come out and say it." He turned in his seat to face me. "Astor Beauregard's a dangerous man."

"You can't be jealous," I snapped.

"Of course, seeing you with someone else isn't easy."

My expression turned incredulous.

"This is coming out wrong."

"It's coming out just how you intended. Look, I have to go—"

"Embry's dad was on the police force."

I shot him an angry look. "What? Astor got a speeding ticket?"

"No, listen, we were talking about our store—"

"*Our* store?"

"I put up half the money."

"Our money." I wanted to get out of the car, but his hint that he knew something about Astor made me stay.

"A few days ago we were at Embry's parents' place. They have a house overlooking the water in South Beach. Her dad's a big boater—"

"Sounds perfect."

"It really is. We're going to buy a home down the road from there."

"A house overlooking the water?"

"We've already found something we like."

"I'm *so* happy for you," I said, glaring at him. "Get to the point."

He rolled his eyes.

"I happened to mention you were now working for Beauregard, and her dad told us he knew him." He lowered his voice. "Astor was sent to Havana when he was thirteen."

I studied Damien's face to see if he was enjoying this situation. Ironically, it had been Astor who'd warned me that Damien might not want me anymore, but he didn't want anyone else to have me either.

"This is very personal—"

"I know."

"Not sure what it has to do with you."

"Well, if you're considering a relationship with him."

"You didn't see me poking around Embry's past."

He let out a frustrated sigh. "Can I speak, please?"

I clenched my teeth, amazed at Damien's arrogance.

He continued. "I'm sure there were extenuating circumstances, but according to Embry's dad—"

"You know I hate gossip."

"This is based on his personal account. He was one of the responding officers called to that big manor in South Beach—"

"Bridgestone? Well, isn't that convenient," I bit out.

"Astor shot his dad." Damien dragged out a silent pause for emphasis. "He killed him, Raquel. Shot him in cold blood."

My lungs struggled to inhale. "I don't believe you."

"Well, Astor probably looked like a good catch for a second there."

"Don't you even dare—"

"I didn't have to say anything to you." He turned his gaze toward the building. "But then I saw you kissing the guy at the polo match."

"I'm allowed to date."

"Sure. Just not murderers."

"Did he go to prison?" I tried to fathom why I was even asking such a question.

"Nope, which was kind of strange don't you think? Turns out his mom knew the judge. Some weird family connection. I mean, he should have ended up in Juvi."

"I want proof."

"He was a minor so the records are protected."

"That's too convenient."

"You can't share this with anyone…especially not Astor. The last thing I need is for him to come after me. Things have changed between us, Raquel, but that doesn't mean I don't care about you."

"You're lying."

"About caring for you?"

"About Astor."

"Yeah, thought you wouldn't believe me at first. Just don't shoot the messenger, okay?"

Astor had never once shown any leanings toward violence. He was domineering, yes, but there was a kindness to him that I'd unraveled layer by layer.

Taylor's words screamed back into my thoughts, *"Something terrible happened in that house."*

"Damien, why would a boy do what you described?"

"I don't know. But it was obviously intentional."

"How do you mean?"

"The police were called to the house in response to a disruption *before* the gun went off. That's all I know. Sounds like his parents were scared of him."

I didn't want to believe any of this. Damien didn't have any real evidence.

He leaned forward. "How well do you know this guy?"

I shook my head. "I bet you couldn't wait to deliver this news?"

"I should have taken Embry's advice. She said you wouldn't listen."

"No, really, thank you for telling me," I said dryly, my gaze returning to the building that hid so many secrets within.

"I think you should leave this place," he said. "Open a new store. Nothing is stopping you."

"Other than the money."

"Take out a loan."

"I have to go." I opened the car door and swung my feet out. When I stood my legs shook from the strain of his words.

"Raquel," Damien called after me. He had gotten out of the Beamer.

I spun on my heels and glared at him.

"Do you want me to help you with your stuff?" He took a step closer. "Help you clear out your desk?"

"I'm perfectly capable," I told him, and headed toward the entrance.

When I made it to the door, I turned to see Damien driving off and then froze with my hand clutching the handle. In my peripheral vision I saw a man getting out of a Range Rover.

Refusing to look Astor's way, I pretended not to see him and pulled the door open, hurrying inside and letting the door close behind me. With my heart jack-hammering, I counted the seconds it would take for Astor to reach the building.

Hurrying into the elevator, I faced the foyer, reeling with what I had just been told. The man I'd been sleeping with had been sent to Cuba because he was dangerous.

Dear God, don't let it be true.

Astor marched across the foyer to join me.

When our eyes locked, the doors shut. I held his gaze through the glass. Was I really staring at a man who'd murdered his father?

He stared back, bewildered by my state.

My glass tomb descended with a jolt.

When the elevator opened, I hurried into the basement, racing through its temperature controlled entrance. A burst of cold air hit me. I scurried toward my workstation, realizing the place was empty. Everyone had gone on their break, leaving me alone in here.

Perhaps Astor had been playing with a gun and it had gone off. I wondered what had caused the disruption that the police had been called for. All the scenarios were too terrible to contemplate.

I'd experienced so many different emotions since meeting Astor, but until now fear had not been one of them. Trepidation, yes, but not apprehension for what this man might be capable of. The bond between a son and his father affected a childhood in so many ways and this kind of devastation would have damaged him beyond repair.

Was it in his nature to kill? Had he killed anyone since?

Why him? While I was falling hard and fast and my heart broke for what he had to carry each day…guilt, self-hatred, a distrust of the world…all I ever felt from him was kindness.

My chest tightened when the elevator rose out of its glass structure and headed back up to the first floor. The mechanism stilled and then came the familiar twisting and rolling of cables that meant it was descending once more.

I focused on my workstation and dragged a notepad toward me, pretending to be busy. I turned to look in the direction of the elevator to convey a natural curiosity, not a terror-drenched panic.

Astor's dark stare was on me as he waited for the doors to slide open. He stepped out and strolled toward me with his right hand casually tucked into his pocket. He glanced around at the empty workstations.

"Ms. Wren." He closed the gap between us.

"Astor." I licked my lips nervously.

"Everything okay?" He cupped my cheek with his palm. "You left before we had time to talk."

"I'm fine."

"Sure?"

I nodded, closing my eyes. I couldn't get the terrible vision out of my head...Astor pointing a gun at his father.

The ping of the elevator as it began to ascend startled me and I opened my eyes.

Astor ran his thumb over my mouth.

"What did Damien want?"

"To talk."

"About?"

I lowered my gaze.

Chapter
TWENTY-FIVE

"DAMIEN WANTS ME TO HURRY AND SELL THE SHOP."

"Nothing new there."

"He's going to buy a home on the water." I bit the inside of my cheek. "They found a place."

"In South Beach?"

"Yes, he's in town for business. He might be checking into getting a job transfer. I forgot to ask."

"What else did he say?"

"Something about a hurricane."

"A category three has hit Jamaica. Did you see that?"

"Yes, it might head our way, right?"

He shrugged as though he didn't care. "It could. I'm going to let the staff leave early."

"That's a good idea." I gave him a kind look.

"Just visited the horses. With the weather turning I wanted to make sure they'll be okay and my staff has everything they need."

"Any news on the tourist from yesterday?"

"She's going to be fine."

"Thank goodness. And Ruben made it?"

"Back with his pod."

"Great news all around, then."

"I was so proud of you yesterday."

"You were the real hero, Astor."

He smiled. "If you ever want me to talk with Damien, I'll tell him to back off."

"I appreciate that."

"He upset you." Astor ran his fingers through my hair, grabbing a lock at my nape and forcing me toward him. He pressed his mouth to mine, forcing my lips open and ravaging my tongue, his moan of want reverberating through me.

This man's affection felt like the brightest star shielding the truth, and despite everything he still set my body alight.

And yet there was a new threat looming...

I broke away. "Someone might see."

"Don't care."

"I do."

Astor intertwined his fingers with mine and led me toward the supply room. He opened the door and motioned for me to go on ahead.

Did he know that I'd found out about the incident at Bridgestone? Had I given myself away?

I walked in and headed all the way to the end of the small room, grateful we'd talk in private. My gaze swept over the neatly stacked supplies and then settled on the bottles of Orris bulb oils on the top shelf...those overly expensive flowers caught in liquid form before blooming.

I'd never know if one of them was once mine. That was the problem—I was clouded in doubt constantly and the strain was taking its toll. I needed relief from the stress and for some reason it was this man who always brought calmness my way.

Astor directed me to turn my back on him and place my hands on the shelf in front of me.

"Hold on," he ordered.

I glanced over my shoulder. "Why?"

He leaned forward and buried his face in my hair, breathing me in. "All I could think of was getting back to you. You're my sanctuary, Raquel."

In a flurry of movement he hoisted the hem of my skirt above my hips and tucked it into my waistband, completely exposing my butt. Then he knelt behind me and tugged my panties down my thighs.

In a daze, I stepped out of them and watched him shove them into his pocket. "I better get those back."

"It's unlikely."

Shuddering at his touch as his hand eased my hair over my shoulder, I refused to deny myself the pleasure he brought, wanting this intimacy more than my next breath. He'd awakened my adventurous side. Astor's domination was arousing and formidable and all I could do was rock my hips back against his erection. He pressed his hardness into the arch of my lower spine.

A rush of adrenaline sent me reeling. I was drawn to him like a moth to a flame.

Minutes ago, I could have made my getaway from this place. I could have gotten into that elevator and hurried out of the building. Yet I was so close to the truth I couldn't back out now. Fighting my conscience, I tried to snap out of this trance of desire, this magnetic pull towards a man who could be my greatest enemy.

My greatest threat.

"Bend over." He put his hands on my hips.

"No."

He spanked my butt, sending a shock of desire through my body. The rush of pleasure from his touch sent a shiver of want up my spine as I leaned forward, reveling in this forbidden lust that had my skin tingling and my heart racing.

"Do you want my cock inside you?" he said darkly.

"Yes." I clenched my teeth, frustrated at how fiercely I tried to resist him and always failed.

"Hold tight," he warned. "I'm going to fuck you very hard."

"I want this."

"I know. I'm going to give you what you need."

I tightened my grip on the shelf, knowing he was right. Astor was always able to soothe me.

His hand came round and cupped me, his fingertip sliding along my clit. Ripples of pleasure made me gasp. I felt him part my folds and then his first thrust jolted me forward. I pushed back and braced myself to accommodate his enormity as he slid in deep and I tightened around him.

His pounding was immediate and demanding, his hands clutching my hips as he pummeled me possessively. His erection filled me completely, his balls striking hard and sending ripples of need through me.

This was pure fire and light...the meaning to everything I'd been searching for but had never found until now. It was both beautiful and cruel with its fragility.

He stilled and reached around again to play with my clit, flicking it so fast I had to close my eyes to endure the blinding pressure.

"Say you're mine, Raquel."

"I'm yours." I squeezed him inside me insistently.

"Even if Damien falls to his knees and begs you to return, you are mine. Remember that."

"Don't." I shook my head. "I want this to be about us."

This was wild and daring and reckless, and yet my body felt alight with pulses of electricity. I had to grit my teeth to bare the euphoria of being fucked by him.

This is wrong.

But it felt so right as I welcomed each smack of his pelvis and each thrust of his cock, a hammering that went on and on. I didn't want it to end.

He tried to pull all the way out, and my muscles seized him, causing him to sigh.

"This is our time," he whispered. "I'm going to enjoy you."

"Fuck me like you mean that." I let go of the shelf and pressed my palm against his hand as it cupped me. "Show me how much you want me."

He rammed himself inside me again, though this time harder, his hot breath on my neck, his fingers resuming their play on my clit, making it throb with pulses of bliss. These delicious sensations held me suspended in a rapturous state.

I want this to go on forever.

He pumped his hips savagely while I milked his cock, and suddenly my breath was snatched away by my climax.

"Let me come in your mouth," he demanded as he pulled out.

I spun around and sank to my knees, staring up at him as I unbuttoned my blouse, silently counting the minutes we had left.

I yanked my bra down beneath my breasts, my fingers tweaking and caressing them as my gaze fell on his glistening shaft, being pumped vigorously by his strong hand as he directed the tip toward my lips.

Awed by his lust-fueled aggression and his spontaneous change from master to wanton man, I leaned over and suckled his balls, unable to resist tasting my own sweetness and savoring their plumpness as they tightened in my mouth.

"Jesus." His gaze rose to the ceiling before returning to me once more.

I raised my chin and opened my mouth, ready for him.

"Pull your blouse wider," he insisted.

Hurrying, I unbuttoned it further and eased the material apart so I was completely exposed, showing my beaded areolas. A gasp escaped my lips as he tapped my bottom lip with the head of his penis, and with precision sent a spurt of heat to the back of my throat.

I swallowed all of him, gulping his heat and licking the tip of his shaft as I raised my gaze to look at him.

Astor was panting like a man possessed, and then his mouth curled up in a ghost of a smile. "You're a goddamned miracle, Raquel." He reached low to wipe a trickle of cum from the corner of my mouth and ease it between my lips.

I lapped at his fingertip gratefully.

"Up," he ordered, as he tucked his cock back into his pants and zipped them up.

Pushing myself to my feet, I stood facing him.

This man had again bewitched me completely and I'd lost track of time. "We need to go back," I said huskily.

"Soon." He knelt and then made sure my hem was securely tucked inside the front of my waistband. His face moved closer to my sex, and my clit tingled with anticipation. It was maddeningly erotic.

"Play with your tits," he ordered.

I pinched my nipples until they were hard, and then kneaded my breasts.

He rested a hand on my leg. "Open your thighs wider."

I obeyed, needing more lust-filled seconds promised by this man's strokes and pats to my pussy.

Astor's gaze held mine as he ran his tongue along my clit, up and down and around, slowly at first and then more fervently, sucking and lapping and brilliantly nudging me toward another orgasm. He reached up, easing my hands away from my breasts and taking hold of them, pinching and twisting my nipples so firmly it became hypnotically seductive. I forced my pelvis toward his face, reaching back to hold on to the shelving to steady myself. With my trembling thighs splayed to expose myself, my blouse open with my swollen breasts on show, I was gone completely, enraptured entirely by his relentless possession of me.

Astor continued devouring me, consuming me like this act of intimacy could save him, his twisting fingers pinching in rhythm and casting an incantation that held me over the precipice of nirvana for what felt like a lifetime.

My limbs were trembling violently from the strain of my pose and yet I remained in position, my focus mesmerized by the way he owned me, wanting to please him so that he'd not stop his brilliant mastery.

I shook violently through another climax, too euphoric to care that I must have looked like a wanton siren rocking my hips against his chin as his tongue lashed me.

Panting, my skin flushed from another orgasm, I watched him rise to his feet and find a paper towel. He dabbed me gently down there, patting me with such a sensuous touch that I feared it might send me over the edge again.

Astor smiled as he shoved the paper towel into his pocket. "I'm hiding the evidence." He tucked his shirt into his pants and gave me a roguish smile.

I pulled my hem down and straightened my skirt, still trembling.

He stepped forward and cupped my cheek with his palm. "Report to my office in fifteen minutes."

"Report?" I mirrored his words.

"Yes, I want to talk with you about our collaboration." He leaned toward me and kissed my neck. "I'll be leading the design but I want your help. There's something special I want to show you, too. The formula I told you about that I'd like your input on."

It was mine. He was talking about my formula.

He seemed to realize the change in his tone had affected me. "Raquel." His thumb eased past my lips. "I need you passionate and ready to bring out your seductive side."

"Is that what this was about?"

"It can't hurt, right?" He looked dangerous in that moment.

Pressing my hand to my lips, I swooned at his devastating presence. Even after what Damien had told me, I was still spellbound whenever Astor came near me. This, this was a kind of madness that had taken possession of me.

He buttoned up my blouse. "I have your taste in my mouth and that means I take a part of you with me."

"Astor," I whispered.

"Is it enough?" He eased a strand of hair behind my ear.

"What do you mean?"

His fingers traced my lips. "Do you want to take a step toward something more?"

I lowered my gaze because there was still this undercurrent of mistrust between us.

"Think about it," he said softly. "Let's start with this perfume. Working on it together is a process we can both trust."

"A collaboration born out of passion," I agreed.

Yet I've already created it.

"I'll see you in my office. Let's get to work."

I nodded, sensing our time together was running out.

Astor stepped away and opened the closet door, pausing for a beat then turning around to face me. "It's safe to come out. They're not back yet."

"Just need a second."

"Sure you're okay?" He gave me a gentle smile.

"I'm inspired, Mr. Beauregard. I'm ready to wow you."

His face was marred with confusion. "Raquel, if I admit that you and I—" He turned away for a second and then glanced back. "The last time my life felt this perfect…"

His words roused hope in me. "Before you went to live in Cuba?"

Astor's brows shot up in surprise. "Yes, right before then," he said softly.

"What happened?"

Don't tell me…don't break our spell.

He hesitated. "I made a decision back then…the wrong one. But it was also the only one." He left, closing the door behind him.

I stared at the spot he'd been standing, my heart aching for him and for myself, too, because today could not be undone and words could not be unspoken.

I headed to the restroom and within minutes had freshened up and straightened my clothing. A comb through my hair and a dab of lipstick and I was ready to face the world again, though I felt a little awkward with no underwear on.

This day was beyond extraordinary and I needed time alone to process all I had learned. I also needed time to recover from these blinding orgasms. Astor knew he had the advantage when he rendered me weak like this…and for a second I wondered if that was the point.

I rode the elevator all the way to the executive floor. Stepping out onto the upper level, my gaze took in the luxury design of chrome and glass and the many doors leading off to what looked like private offices. A centrally located reception desk had Taylor sitting behind it.

She threw me a wave. "How's it going?"

I closed the distance between us. "Good." I glanced around for Astor's office. "How are you?"

She lowered her voice to a whisper. "I'm fine. The boss is in a great mood, too, so you're in luck."

"Oh, brilliant." That made me smile.

Following Taylor's gaze, I looked behind me.

Astor was leaning against a doorjamb. "Thank you for coming up, Raquel." He looked thoughtful. "I haven't seen you since…"

I tilted my head, amused by his humor.

"I was just bringing her in to see you," Taylor said.

When I stepped inside his office I was immediately impressed by the blue glass desk in the center of the room, a sleek-looking iMac resting on top of it. Photos of all the exquisitely designed Beauregard bottles created over the years lined the walls.

Astor claimed his swivel chair, leaning back and resting his legs on the desk, an amused look on his face.

"I'm looking forward to collaborating," I said, my heart beating fast.

There was no way I could say anything that would link me to this perfume.

Astor reached for what looked like a small remote and pointed it at the window. It rapidly fogged the glass, concealing us from the outside world.

He pushed to his feet. "This is the incomplete formula I want your help on." He approached the picture frame on the wall behind his desk, lifting it off to reveal a safe.

"A formula?" My throat tightened.

Astor's fingers turned the dial. "We need to add a note."

Peering over his shoulder, I stared into the safe for my ledger but all I saw were a few folders. He withdrew one, stepped back, and placed it on the desk.

He sank into his chair again and swiveled side to side. "I've tried several ingredients and they just don't land."

I couldn't allow myself to view the scientific breakdown of a formula that was meant to belong to this House and then purport it to be my own. My thoughts spiraled, trying to come up with excuses that could get me out of this predicament.

"Have a seat?" he offered.

The door burst open, startling me.

"Am I late?" Penelope hurried in on spiked heels, clouded in the scent of magnolias. She swept toward Astor's desk and sat on the edge of it, her legs dangling casually.

I glared first at her and then at Astor. His expression was calm, but then again he was often difficult to read.

"We can't wait to hear your take, Raquel," cooed Penelope. "We need to get this to market."

Astor got up and rounded the desk, walking over to me. His hand brushed along my arm, sending chills down my spine. "Show her how talented you are."

I swallowed the bitterness of doubt. "I'll try."

Astor's gaze narrowed. "Just look at the ingredients and tell me what you think we can add." He pulled back a little. "Raquel?"

I'd given myself over to him so many times...and all those seductive moments had led to this...

"Give us the missing piece," said Penelope.

No, this isn't what you think it is...

I couldn't help but feel that Astor and his sister had set me up. One word from me and I would lose everything.

"I'm intrigued to hear what you think." Astor reached for the folder and brought it over to me.

"Have her smell it," snapped Penelope.

"It's here?" I swallowed my trepidation. "The bottle is in this room?"

Astor flipped open the folder.

My gaze rose to meet his as my body stiffened in response to his formality. His serious stance told me that whatever we had been—or what I'd thought we were—was now over.

"Ms. Wren," he said quietly, "please share your thoughts on the formula. Let's see it finished."

Chapter
TWENTY-SIX

I LOVED HER.

Quite simply, I had fallen for this woman and I believed now more than ever that I could trust her. The ghosts of my past were dissipating, my hope rising and those old doubts lifting...setting me free.

She set me free.

Raquel strolled into my office, wafting the scent of roses overlaid with my cologne, which had rubbed off on her, and beyond those tones I detected the delectable aroma of our combined chemistry.

Not that long ago I had knelt at her feet and lavished affection between her thighs, worshiping her while savoring her moans. In that moment she had become mine...in that moment nothing else had mattered because she was with me again.

I'd savaged her pussy possessively after seeing Damien in my parking lot. He'd upset her, which meant he still affected her, and that had twisted my jealousy into a quiet rage. Those raw emotions had merged into a desire to comfort her, spoil and soothe her, and—more than anything—fuck her.

Standing on the other side of my desk, Raquel had transformed herself from a passionate lover to a professional chemist. Her lab coat and serious expression reminded me that she was a talented employee and deserved respect.

And yet she was much more than that to me. I could still taste her...this woman was quite literally absorbed into my senses.

"Have a seat?" I gestured to the chair opposite.

Raquel didn't move and our eyes locked on each other, tension bouncing between us. She was complicated but I didn't mind that about her. The woman was an enigma, and I'd felt drawn to her bravery.

Penelope burst through the door in a cloud of fake business acumen and superiority. "Am I late?" She pushed herself up to sit on the edge of my desk.

I ignored her arrogance and once again focused on Raquel.

"We can't wait to hear your take, Raquel," said Penelope. "We need to get this to market."

I pushed to my feet and rounded the desk, approaching Raquel. Maybe it was Penelope's overwhelming presence that had thrown her.

I was just about to warn Raquel my sister was joining us for our meeting when she had burst in unannounced. Still, since Penelope had discovered this scent in its current form, I had honored her right to be here for the completion of the formula.

I found this process stimulating and intriguing, trying to imagine all the possibilities I couldn't yet see. This formula I hadn't been able to crack so far because no matter how much I tweaked or added or removed the ingredients, I couldn't decipher its originality...its destination felt out of reach. Yet something told me Raquel could unravel the elements which evaded me. This mysterious scent in a way reminded me of her.

I ran my palm up Raquel's arm to comfort her. "Show her how talented you are."

Raquel swallowed hard. "I'll try."

I squeezed her arm reassuringly. "Just look at the ingredients and tell me what you think we can add." I pulled back to read her expression. "Raquel?"

"Give us the missing piece," Penelope piped up.

I frowned at Penelope's belligerence. Raquel didn't owe us anything. Yes, she was our employee, but this was inappropriate.

"I'm intrigued to hear what you think." I reached for the folder and brought it over to her, trying to offset Penelope's obnoxious demeanor with an air of professionalism.

"Have her smell it," my sister snapped.

Raquel's gaze widened with concern. "It's here? The bottle is in this room?"

I flipped open the folder.

"Ms. Wren, please share your thoughts on the formula. Let's see it finished."

Raquel stepped back, refusing to look at the folder's contents. "I'm going to go grab something from the lab," she said, staring up at me.

"What do you need?"

Raquel backed toward the door. "I'll just be a few minutes."

"That's fine." I watched her leave in a hurry, feeling puzzled by her behavior.

When I spun around to look at my sister, she was wearing one of those satisfied smiles that told me she was close to getting something she wanted.

What the hell had just happened?

Chapter
TWENTY-SEVEN

Raquel

F INALLY, I COULD EXHALE AS I STEADIED MY NERVES OUTSIDE ASTOR'S office. I took a few seconds to put my game face on so I could face Taylor.

Now it all made sense.

What Penelope had witnessed her brother do at Bridgestone all those years ago had left her bitter and cruel because she couldn't even trust her own sibling. The circumstances of their past had forged them both into who they were today—two ruthless professionals willing to do anything to get what they wanted. It had been hard to read Astor, he was always guarded and secretive, and yet I'd just witnessed their mutual offensive.

With my head held high, I strolled over to Taylor's desk and forced a smile.

"Penelope wants me to grab a folder from her office."

Taylor pushed to her feet. "I can get it."

"No, that's all right. You look busy."

"I'm trying to finish a few things because we're all leaving early. Are you off soon?"

"Yes, right after this."

She pointed to a door on the east side of the building. "Penelope's got that great harbor view."

"I'll be right back." Knowing Astor and Penelope were nearby made my heart do a flip. The fact I was betraying Taylor's trust made me feel nauseated. She'd been kind to me and yet this was a chance I had to take.

You can do this.

That familiar anger welled up inside of me. How had my life come to this? Me snooping around other people's offices, me having to pretend I wanted to work here...

This was all Damien's doing. If he'd just kept it in his pants and been loyal, loved me the way he'd once vowed to, none of this would be happening. Everything I was doing could potentially set me up for a lawsuit I had no money to fight.

Every time I felt like I had a handle on my life, a day like this swept in to fracture the ground beneath my feet. I had no choice but to keep moving.

Inside Penelope's luxurious office, I barely noticed the art deco desk and the prints of glass bottles like the ones on Astor's walls. Quickly, I searched through her filing cabinet, easing each drawer out slowly so it wouldn't make a noise. Finding nothing, I went over to her desk, meaning to search the four drawers on either side.

I inhaled sharply when I saw an unmarked manila envelope hidden beneath a stack of magazines.

When I reached in and felt that familiar shaped ledger I stifled a sob, feeling vindicated, feeling all I had risked and all I had done had been worth it. I had been proven right.

Penelope knew I was the creator of that scent.

Hugging the envelope to my chest, I ran over the plan. I could walk into Astor's office right now with the ledger and accuse them both of stealing.

Penelope would deny it.

They both would.

They had too much to lose to ever admit stealing my formula. My heart ached with the possibility that Astor was an accomplice…that he knew this had been in her office all along.

That he had led me on.

All that time I had slaved away in their lab. All those hours I had given to them despite everything. The realization hit me that the ledger had been easy to find—because it didn't matter now. Seconds ago, I had stood in Astor's office about to view a formula I could be accused of copying into this ledger *after* the fact. The only way to convince Astor I hadn't stolen that formula was to never have seen it.

I started to head out of Penelope's office and jolted to a stop.

Taylor was standing in the doorway.

Chapter
TWENTY-EIGHT

R AQUEL HAD BEEN GONE TOO LONG AND PENELOPE WAS GROWING
more impatient with each passing second.

"Let me call her." I pulled out my phone and dialed
Raquel's number. The call went to voicemail. "Hey, Raquel, where
are you?" I hoped she'd detect the lightness of my tone to lessen the
tension.

I reached for my desk phone.

"Where is she?" snapped Penelope. "I have another appointment."

I shot my sister a warning glare and said into the phone, "Hey,
Arabella, is Ms. Wren down there? Can you send her to my office,
please?" I hung up.

Penelope fisted her hands on her hips. "She lost her store, right?"

"That's why she needs this job."

"How can you be certain she's not a corporate spy?"

"Don't be ridiculous." I hid my doubt from her.

"You're in love with her?"

"She's only been here a few weeks."

"She's up to something."

"Raquel is extremely qualified."

"The way you look at her—"

"Do I look like a man who does insta-love?" Yet even as I spoke those words, I felt the truth deep inside. Raquel had swept into my life like a vision of loveliness, and I'd craved her presence since the first day we'd met at Bridgestone. I was missing her right now.

Where are you, Raquel?

Penelope slid off the desk and came toward me. "We need her to give us the missing piece—" She waved her hand at the folder.

"We have other chemists—"

"She's the best for this."

"And why do you think that?" I studied her.

She threw up her middle finger at me.

I breathed out a frustrated sigh. "You're painfully discourteous this morning."

"Because my gut is warning me not to trust her."

"You know me, Penelope," I said, trying to soothe her. "I don't do relationships."

"So why is she living in your home?"

I flinched. "Who told you?"

She crossed her arms. "So…she's moved in?"

"She needed somewhere to stay."

"Wow, she got you good."

"It's temporary." I didn't even want to think about her leaving.

"What did she say to persuade you?"

"What more do you want?" I leaned back against the desk. "Have I not given you the best of me?"

"Don't go there."

"I mean us, now. With all I do to keep you appearing as my equal here."

"Don't I deserve it?"

No, she fucking well did not because she was never here. "I know what I'm doing."

Her lips trembled. "What if I lose you?"

"You're my sister for God's sake."

She fell into my arms. "Promise me she won't find out about Bridgestone."

"I never think of it." My thoughts dragged me back to that vast house with its sprawling corridors. In my nightmares, I still ran down those halls through a never-ending blackness.

"If we get this scent perfected," Penelope said softly, "I'll have given this company something to make you proud."

I hugged her tight. "I'm already proud of you."

"I love you, Astor."

I kissed the top of her head. "Let's think about a name for it."

She peered up at me. "Okay."

That seemed to calm her, though I knew this scent deserved a unique label. That was why I paid the staff in the marketing department so well.

"Pull back on the partying, okay?" This was my way of saying stay away from the cocaine. It made her jittery and turned her into a raving bitch—and when she got that crazy I was the only one who could talk her off the ledge.

"I do it to forget," she admitted.

My throat tightened with sorrow. "Try not to think about that right now."

Her lips trembled, as though she'd gone there anyway. "We forgive each other, right?"

"Of course. You know that."

"And you got to live in England."

I forced a smile. "Made me the man I am."

She looked like she was going to say something else, but then closed her eyes in defeat.

"What's wrong?"

"My Porsche needs servicing."

I hoped she wasn't lying. "I'll have the money transferred." Keeping my sister on a budget seemed controlling, but this was my way of keeping her out of rehab.

"How was Mom this morning?" she asked.

I shrugged. "Didn't see her, just visited the horses."

"You always were her favorite."

Penelope's words made me want to pull away from her. No, I wasn't Mom's favorite, not even close. I had been the one to be sent to Havana and forbidden to have any contact with my family. Every time Penelope spoke those words I wanted to break something.

Fuck. So much damage created from one reckless decision. Those haunting memories always found me. Penelope had a way of laying them at my feet...

Once, when Cuba became too much and they were threatening to send me to England, I stole a boat and tried to return to Miami. I'd failed to even get out of the harbor, though at fourteen it was a decent try.

The pain I'd felt over that long ago rejection hadn't faded with time and distance. In recent years I'd tried to salvage the time I'd lost with my family, but failed. I'd returned to a mother who hardly knew me and a sister who stared at me with confusion in her gaze. I reminded them of our horror-filled past.

Yet I couldn't find it in me to stop loving them. *Or not forgive them.*

"Go see Mama," I said softly.

"Next week." She raised her gaze to mine. "I'd die without you."

I stepped away and raised the folder. "Let me get this to the lab."

I was glad I had an excuse to leave my office. Penelope's energy made me apprehensive and her impertinence had ruined Raquel's creative focus.

I stopped off at reception to talk with Taylor. "I want all the staff out by two. That gives everyone time to get home."

"I don't think the hurricane's on course to hit us."

"These things can turn."

She pointed at me with insistence. "You leave, too. Go hunker down."

I gave her a kind smile. "Taylor, call me when you get home."

She rolled her eyes.

"I mean it."

"Got it, boss." Her frown narrowed and she swallowed her nervousness.

I turned to follow Taylor's line of sight toward Penelope. "Do you need me for anything else?" I called over to my sister.

She came toward me. "I'll get a percentage?"

"Of the perfume, yes, of course."

She had delivered the notes of our new scent so she deserved a generous commission. But I was ready to send her to an investor who would tie up her money until her taste for Miami's vices had faded.

She swapped a smile with Taylor. "I'm heading out."

Taylor gave a nod. "I'll do a loop of the building before I lock up."

"I appreciate that," I said, following Taylor's conflicted stare toward Penelope's office.

Taylor started to say something.

I gestured for her to hold that thought as I shot off a quick text to my horse trainer, Jacob Nestling, who'd just sent me a message that he was heading over to Bridgestone to secure the horses. He'd volunteered to remain near them during the storm.

"Next time, make sure you're wearing a scent from our collection," snapped Penelope to Taylor.

"It's a gift from my mom," countered Taylor. "Estee Lauder."

"I don't care what it is," said Penelope, "as long as it's ours."

"Seriously?" I gritted my teeth, resisting the urge to berate her in front of Taylor.

"I'll only wear it on the weekends then," said Taylor.

I threw her a grateful smile for tolerating my sister's outburst and headed for the elevator. "Keep me posted on your whereabouts," I told Penelope. "Stay away from the harbor."

She gave me a thin smile.

Yeah, sis, I know your dealer sells his drugs from a boat.

I waved the folder in the air. "Let's get this done."

"Tell Ms. Wren we want it by Monday," she said.

I stepped into the elevator.

I felt protective over Raquel and was prepared to shield her. I'd not seen Penelope quite this suspicious of an employee before. Her radar had picked up on how fond I was of Raquel and I put her errant behavior down to her protectiveness.

We'd always looked after each other. Until *that* day when I had been escorted off Bridgestone's property and hadn't seen the place again for decades. Guilt remained with me for those terror-stricken hours that had unfolded in the dead of night and even now bled into my every decision, every action and every thought.

Wanting to cleanse myself of my sister's toxic energy, I felt the need to wrap my arms around Raquel and bury my face in her hair, drawing in the comfort she brought.

Feeling uneasy when I peered through the glass door into the lab and didn't see her, I walked through the air-controlled door and looked over toward Arabella's office. She was on the phone. The technicians were at their stations. I searched the storeroom—where pleasant memories flooded back—and then the coffee room.

Approaching Raquel's area, my curiosity was piqued when I saw the square cologne bottle on her workstation. Resting against it was an envelope addressed to me.

I called over to my senior chemist, Joseph. "Where's Ms. Wren?"

His gaze floated over her workstation. "I think she left."

"I just came down," I said, pointing to the elevator.

"She used the stairs, sir." He returned his attention to his screen.

Raquel's handbag was gone. That was strange. And I didn't like the idea of a note. Maybe, just maybe, she'd headed back up to my office.

I tore open the envelope.

Dearest Astor,

Forgive me for leaving without saying goodbye. I cannot continue to work here. This has nothing to do with what happened between us and I need you to believe that. I want you to know what we had was what I needed and I thank you for the time we spent together. Every single moment of it.

I've left you a parting gift!
—Raquel

Dread consumed me.

My mind ached from the strain of trying to comprehend what she was saying. My heart twisted with the idea she had walked out without saying goodbye or telling me why she'd left. I shouldn't have pushed her so hard in our meeting. Shouldn't have ruined what was obviously a fragile relationship.

The crushing pressure in my chest verged on unbearable.

My gaze darted to the storeroom and I paled at the thought of what we'd done in there being the cause. Yet her note expressed she'd enjoyed our time together. I laid it down and lifted the bottle.

I removed the stopper and lifted it to my nose…aromas of leather, Frankincense, and black suede. My body shuddered from the other ingredients I couldn't pinpoint because they were blended so well—an alpha scent contained within glass.

She'd captured the fugue…

Thundering hooves of thoroughbreds under the control of their masters as they weaved around each other competing for the win, turf thrown up, the heat of the afternoon sun bearing down and leaving a delicious burn to the skin, the squeeze of a heel to edge the horse left or right to snatch the advantage, the worth of well-worn boots squeezing gently to inspire the stride…and then came after-notes of popping champagne, caviar and kisses, salty sweetness, and the delicious art of the win.

How dare it be left on a workstation in a frigid lab? It deserved an unveiling at a lavish function where it was celebrated as a cologne with a fuck-boy edge.

Raquel, you did it. You pulled it off.

Imagine what she could do with my other formula.

Win her back.

From our first meeting, she'd promised she could deliver a world-class scent and the fact she had and then left like this cut too deep.

What we had was worth fighting for.

Go after her.

I dabbed the liquid onto my wrist and tucked the bottle into my pocket along with the note. Grabbing the mouse, I shook awake her computer and stared at the file on the screen. With a click I read the list for her fuck-boy formula.

She knew you'd look there.

Following the route she'd just taken, I hurried though the fire door, ascending two steps at a time and quickly reaching the first floor. I burst into the foyer and hurried for the door. I braced myself for the stormy weather on the other side.

Chapter
TWENTY-NINE

Raquel

HOLDING BACK TEARS, I WAITED ON THE CURB OUTSIDE THE HOUSE of Beauregard, my gaze snapping over to the front door, my heart racing, hoping Astor didn't try to stop me.

Covered in a sticky sweat from the humidity, I wiped my brow as I doubled-checked to make sure my ledger was still in my handbag.

I'd just had a close brush in Penelope's office with Taylor. She'd walked in as I had finished searching for my ledger. As far as I could tell I hadn't alerted her to what I was trying to accomplish there. Still, if she mentioned the encounter to Penelope, and she probably would, the storm would not just be out here.

Leaves swirled in a frenzy as the wind bent the surrounding trees at torturous angles, whipping my clothes and hair. Relief hit me when I saw Damien's BMW turning the corner. I hated myself for having him pick me up…especially after the poisonous words he'd spewed about Astor.

I have no choice.

I had to make it back to Dunedin and with this hurricane brewing no driver other than my crazy ex would risk it either. He wanted to get back to Embry, so his motivation to help me wasn't unselfish. More than this, he loved to be proven right.

I didn't want to believe Damien's gossip about Astor's past. There was no record of it online when I'd searched for proof that any of it was true. And so much time had passed it made me wonder if people had gotten their facts wrong.

Thoughts of Astor suffering stayed with me all the way to his home on the water. He'd saved my life in there without a second thought from that downed power-line. Surely if there was anything sinister about him he'd have let that cable get me. Then again, maybe he just needed me to deliver those final notes on that perfume.

I had to grab my belongings and then put South Beach behind me.

I was leaving behind a part of me I couldn't define…a part that had started to believe there was someone else out there for me. Perhaps someone I would love even more than Damien.

Say it. Admit you love Astor.

"I wish it was different," I muttered to myself.

"What was that?" asked Damien.

"This is his place." I pointed to the house.

Damien parked the car in the driveway and made a remark about how Astor clearly had too much wealth and time on his hands. He didn't know him like me, didn't know how hard he worked and that he deserved this place more than most people.

I told Damien to wait in the car and then hurried over to the front door. Getting in was easy, since he'd given me access. I merely followed Astor's instructions and pressed my palm to the entry pad of his high-tech system.

We had something special—*had*—I reminded myself, because doing this would end whatever sort of relationship we'd begun. Falling for Astor Beauregard was one situation I'd not accounted for. We were complicated and wonderful and confusing and everything I'd not foreseen. I hoped he would forgive me and never once suspect me of stealing any of his formulas. That level of betrayal would leave lasting damage.

I wondered if Astor had found my parting gift of that unique cologne he'd asked me to create. If nothing else he'd believe hiring me had been worth it if only for these last few weeks of delivering something special in the way of a cologne he could be proud of.

A wave of guilt washed over me as I thought of that bottle of Orris bulb oil in the bottom of my handbag I'd taken from his lab. I placated myself with the fact it could serve as payment for the cologne I'd created for him.

Being back in Astor's home brought fond memories even in the short time I had stayed here, from the meals we'd cooked together to that near tragedy where he had saved my life. And the sex, of course, which was the best I'd ever had.

Don't think of that now. Don't think of all those nights of love-making that made your toes curl and your heart open.

This man wasn't ruthless. He was kind even if he had his own demons to fight. During the days we'd spent together I had seen another side to him, a side he seemed to hide from everyone else.

I had to pack quickly.

Hurrying up the winding staircase and along the hallway, I made my way toward Astor's bedroom and paused for a moment staring at the ruffled bed. So many pleasures beneath those sheets… We'd had a remarkable closeness neither of us could deny.

Forgive me.

Dragging my empty suitcase onto the bed, I flung it open, throwing my clothes inside and then scooping up my shoes. I quickly gathered my toiletries from the bathroom and tossed them into the suitcase, too.

When my phone rang, I rummaged through my handbag ready to tell Damien I needed another five minutes.

"Raquel?"

My heart skipped a beat. "Astor?" I said softly, closing my eyes in response to his voice on the line.

"Tell me you're okay," he said.

"I'm fine."

"Have you left The House of Beauregard permanently?"

I hesitated. "Did you find the cologne?"

"Yes, it's fantastic. Let's talk about it."

"I can't."

"Are you going to sue me for sexual harassment, Raquel?"

"No," I burst out. "Every moment with you was with my consent. I liked it. I liked it a lot."

"Even what we did earlier?"

"Yes."

"I meant in the storeroom."

"I know."

"Did I hurt you? Or scare you?"

"No."

"Are you sure?"

"Yes, this has nothing to do with any of that."

"Tell me how I messed up so I can put it right."

"It's not about us."

"Have you gone back to Damien?"

"No, never." I took a deep breath. "I need his help to get back to Dunedin."

"I'll drive you."

"I'm okay."

"Driving toward a dangerous storm isn't wise."

"I have to go home."

"Look, stay at my place if you want. I'll leave you alone."

"Are you watching me on the cameras?"

"I got an alert on my phone. It's how the security is set. I'm not stalking you if that's what you're suggesting."

"Is there a camera in the bedroom?" My gaze darted to the ceiling.

"No, they cover the outside. The driveway. The garden. Nothing inside."

"What if we'd done it in the pool?"

"I would've told you. Look, I need to see you, Raquel. I need to talk this through because I'm not sure what's happening here."

"I have to finish packing."

"I know he's waiting for you outside."

My mouth went dry with guilt.

He cursed quietly. "He can stay there with you. If it keeps you safe."

"Don't."

"Don't what? Be kind to you?"

"Yes."

"Would it help if I told you—" He let out an exasperated sigh. "I like you a lot, Raquel. A lot more than…"

"And I like you."

"Then tell me what's going on?"

And then I realized Astor was on his way to the house. "I have to go."

"Don't hang up."

"Astor—"

"I need to put this right."

"I'm sorry it ended like this."

"Why does it need to end?"

"It's gotten complicated and I want you to know I didn't expect it to go this way."

"What way?"

"Being with each other…caring about each other."

"Don't drive toward the storm. Promise me, Raquel. Forget the rest and just be safe."

"I have to go." I ended the call and stared at my phone, tears stinging my eyes as I tried to convince myself I was doing the right thing.

With no time to waste I finished packing, sealed my suitcase, and dragged it down the staircase, being careful not to scratch the hardwood panels. I rolled it outside and shut the front door.

Quickly, I made my way to Damien's car idling in the driveway. He was texting on his phone. When I reached the BMW I banged on the window to get his attention.

He lowered the window. "All done?"

"Are you sure it's okay to drive in this?"

Damien smirked. "We have six hours before the hurricane hits, so yes."

"The benefit of knowing a weather girl," I mumbled miserably, throwing my suitcase onto the back seat.

Chivalry really was dead. Though at least Damien was willing to drive me home, I quietly mused, taking one final glance at Astor's beautiful home.

Maybe it had been him who had hidden my ledger in his sister's office safe. There was too much doubt surrounding me and I'd risked so much to get my book back.

I climbed into the passenger seat and pulled the seatbelt around me as a burst of lemon scented air-freshener brought on a wave of nausea. Damien's betrayal was now anchored to that stark citrus smell.

In a flash of inspiration I reached into my handbag and pulled out my ledger. Damien looked at it and then smiled at me. "That your notebook?"

"Yes, would you do me a favor and keep it safe for me. It contains all my formulas."

He reached over and took it from me and then turned to place it on the backseat, right next to Embry's beach bag. "Anything for you," he said. "You know that."

"Just for a day or two."

His gaze swept over Astor's home. "Let's get you out of here."

I nodded in agreement, though it hurt like hell. My time in South Beach, with Astor, had been the happiest days of my life.

Chapter
THIRTY

MAYBE IT WAS RAQUEL'S SCENT LINGERING ON MY SKIN OR THE NEW masterful cologne she'd created that I'd dabbed on my wrist to remind me of her, or maybe it was how she had eased into my life effortlessly that made forgetting *us* impossible.

Raquel had changed my world irrevocably and this was the reason I refused to imagine her no longer in it. *Damn it*, I needed to know what I'd done to have her literally run out of my life.

When a man drives hundreds of miles into the eye of a storm these are the questions he asks himself: Why her? Why now? And how the hell had I lost her so suddenly?

I'd avoided emotional attachments before but Raquel had broken down my barriers and gotten to the core of the man I was. Seeing myself through her eyes had brought me a sense of belonging for the first time.

You should have told her that.

I'd realized too late she was the light that had been missing in my existence; the beauty I'd spent years trying to elicit from creating artificial moods in bottles, formulas to stir the soul and inspire love, the elusive all-consuming affection I'd failed to experience.

Until her.

Raquel was worth fighting for.

And I wasn't going to let that prick worm his way back into her life and hurt her again. She deserved better than that. She deserved the best that life could give her.

All that I can give her.

I pressed a button on my Range Rover's dashboard. "Call Jacob."

A ringtone sang from the speaker phone. "Hey, Boss," came Jacob's upbeat voice.

"How are you?"

"We're doing great. The horses are hunkered down and I'm going to stay in the office attached to the stables. No need to move them but if things change you'll be the first to know."

"I appreciate that," I said. "How's Vedado?" Had I not been on my way to Dunedin I would have been with him now.

"Fine. I'll keep an eye on him."

"Call me if you need anything."

"Where are you?"

"Heading over the water toward Dunedin."

Jacob's silence almost made me think our call had dropped.

His voice came back on. "Isn't Dunedin in the line of the hurricane?"

"I'll be fine."

"What's so important in Dunedin?"

"A friend."

"Okay, well get him out and we'll see you soon."

I didn't correct him. "See you soon, Jacob."

The car jerked as I tried to steady it with an ironclad grip on the steering wheel, fighting one hundred mile an hour winds whipping around me. Having driven this route many times I knew it well, but the sparse traffic proved I was probably insane.

I had to know Raquel was safe. Should she need to escape this part of the city she'd be with someone who had the resources to make that happen. The thought of her stranded with no supplies sent a chill through me. *She's sensible.* She knows Florida and she knows the kind of preparation needed to weather a storm of this magnitude.

When I glanced left I flinched at the surging ocean crashing against the bridge wall and spilling over. This hurricane was already wreaking havoc. Torrential rain splashed my windshield and my wipers strained to clear the constant blur. Straining to keep my focus on the road, I occasionally saw wildlife searching for shelter and kept alert in case any of them got into difficulty and needed rescuing.

By the time I arrived in Dunedin, I was close to feeling like a wreck myself. I left the car parked in front of Perfume Girl.

I ran over to the shop, instantly getting drenched and chilled, and banged my fist on the door.

This was probably the most reckless I'd been in a while, but then again I'd swam with sharks while trying to rescue a canoeist. And facing off with this storm was me pushing my luck.

But Raquel was worth it.

The door opened. Raquel was standing there with red eyes and a weary face. Seeing her like this sent a jolt of guilt through me. Had I caused her pain?

"What are you doing here?" she said.

"I was in the area," I joked, trying to ease the tension.

She gestured frantically for me to enter.

Stepping inside, I shrugged my coat off and threw it in the corner. It would leave a puddle on her hardwood floors, but from the racket outside that was the least of our problems. "Have you secured the windows?"

"Just finished." She looked over toward the front of the store, which was covered in wood to protect the glass.

It flashed through my mind that she couldn't have managed that task alone. "Is Damien here?"

"Of course not."

"Did he offer to help?" I pointed at the window.

"He wanted to be with Embry." She raised her hand defensively. "I didn't want him here."

Those were the words I needed to hear. "What can I do?"

"You shouldn't have driven in this."

"I could say the same about you."

"I live here."

"Raquel, you risked your life to—" I stepped back to give her some room. "I need to know why you left suddenly. I'm assuming it wasn't just the storm?"

She gave me an accusatory look, her expression one of trepidation. "You should have called first." She hugged herself.

"You didn't answer."

She gave a resigned nod. "Let me get you a towel."

Raquel led me toward the back of the store. Taking in the line of bottles and pipettes and all the supplies needed to create a scent, I shot her a look of concern. This was an insane time to be playing chemist.

"I was keeping busy." She forced a thin smile. "Come up."

Following her, I let out a sigh of reassurance seeing she was okay and I would at least be here to sit out the storm with her. "We're looking at a Category Three," I said, "but it feels stronger."

"Because we're so close to the ocean."

Yes, I had noticed. My sodden clothes clung to my flesh. "I'm dripping on your floor," I said apologetically.

"It's fine."

I followed Raquel into what served as her bedroom—though this was probably meant to be the office space or extra storage for the shop downstairs. Using my best stony-faced expression I feigned no interest in her makeshift bed. The mattress had been dragged away from the window. Her roughing it had been the reason I'd rescued her from here, and I felt another twinge of guilt, worried that I may have had a part in all of this.

The windows rattled as the wind whistled and whipped outside. Any damage to the store would affect the value of the building. I started to ask about her insurance, but then decided she didn't need to hear that right now.

I stripped off my pants, relieved to be rid of the soaked trousers, and then pulled off my damp shirt. My boxers had to come off, too, and it wasn't like she hadn't seen me naked before.

I looked over at her ready to ask if she had a robe.

Her gaze swept over my torso and bare thighs. "I'll grab you a towel." She spun around and hurried into the bathroom. She quickly returned with one and handed it to me.

Rubbing the towel over my head to dry my hair, I threw her a grateful smile and then wrapped it around myself. "Do you have a spare robe? I'll put my clothes in the dryer."

"They could shrink."

I shrugged. "A risk I'm willing to take."

"Of course." She hurried over to her wardrobe and brought out a blue silk robe with a Chinese design on the back.

"I can't wear that."

"It's this or nothing."

"Don't you have anything left over from…?" Yeah, from her expression asking that question was a bad idea. "It's fine." I motioned for her to give it to me.

Dragging my arms through the sleeves, I felt like a complete idiot. It was too small and short at the hem and the sleeves hit halfway up my forearms. This summed up my fucking day. I was standing before her looking ridiculous—and the way she was trying to suppress a laugh proved it.

I opened my palms in defeat. "Well, that's the last of my masculinity gone."

"You look cute."

I chuckled. "I'm willing to risk my clothes shrinking so I can hold onto some dignity. Where's the dryer?"

"I'll wash them for you," Raquel said, smiling.

The tension had lifted, and I hoped it might stay this way.

I held her gaze. "Tell me you're okay."

"I'm home, so yes."

Outside came the sound of metal crashing against metal.

"Hope that wasn't my car," I muttered, though in all honesty a car could be fixed. I wasn't so sure we could.

"You shouldn't have risked it," she said, gathering up my sopping wet clothes.

"I'd do it again in a heartbeat. Just tell me what's really going on with you."

"I'm working on something downstairs that will explain everything."

"That's not vague at all."

"Once I complete it I'll be ready to talk more." She nodded as though thinking this was logical.

"Did you come up with a new scent? I mean other than the cologne you left at your workstation? You're concerned I'll want to own it because it was designed under my roof, and on my time?"

She gave me a kind smile. "It preceded my time at The House of Beauregard."

"The new cologne you left with that note…" I shook my head in admiration. "It's fantastic, Raquel. It really is."

"That'll pay for the Orris oil."

"What Orris oil?"

"The bottle I stole from your storeroom."

"Which one?"

"From the Lithuanian collection."

She'd taken one of the ten five-year-old bottles of oil that we'd perfected—the rare irises that cost a small fortune.

"Keep it." I shook my head. "So this has nothing to do with me? It's all about your ambition to create a new scent?" There was no other way to say it. "I know you want to save your store, but I feel like collateral damage."

She let my clothes slip from her arms and fall to the floor. "That's not it at all."

"Then enlighten me."

"During the break-in someone stole my ledger that I write all my notes in. *And* they stole my perfume sample." She was staring at me as though I might have answers.

"I'm sorry to hear that."

"If I can replicate it I can save this place."

"It was the one you hoped to license to Dazzle and Bazaar?"

"Yes."

"License it to me."

She sighed. "It's complicated."

"I get it. If you created this formula under my roof its ownership would be questionable."

"I didn't want you to believe I spent all of my time there simply working for myself."

"I'd have been willing to discuss all of this with you. It's me, Raquel."

She lowered her gaze. "Legally you'd be protected. The formula would belong to you."

"So all you needed was a few weeks' salary and you'd have the funds to see you through to the end of the month?" Is that what we were looking at here?

Her expression looked conflicted. "No."

"Then explain why minutes after leaving a meeting with me and my sister you left?" I gestured, showing my frustration. "Without saying goodbye."

"I couldn't let the meeting continue."

"Why?"

She drew in a sharp breath. "Did Penelope say anything to you before you left work?"

"She's eager to see our new formula resolved." And her passion for once was inspiring.

"How did she seem?"

"No different, why?"

"I'm sorry I left without saying goodbye. I needed the time to resolve an issue."

I shook my head. "I'm trying to understand. I thought you and I were going somewhere."

"I just got divorced, Astor. I'm still picking up the pieces of my life and I'm not sure I could cope with…"

"I thought everything was good between us?"

"You told me you don't do relationships."

"Before you, I didn't."

"I refuse to be the fallout as a result of your reluctance to…"

"Love?"

"You don't strike me as someone who wants that level of commitment."

I let the strike of her blow settle in the silence because that's what her words deserved.

Finally, I broke the quiet. "People change." I gestured around the room. "I'm here aren't I? You told me your leaving had nothing to do with us?"

"It didn't, not really, but it's complicated and right now I'm not ready to tell you everything because the proof of why I'm doing all this is sitting on my workstation waiting for me. That's what I was doing when you arrived."

"Proof of what?"

"I need a few hours." Seeing my frustrated expression, she added, "My formula ended up in someone else's hands."

"How do you know?"

"Trust me, I'm sure."

"Let's get it back."

She gave me a rueful smile. "They believe it belongs to them. That it was developed in-house."

"Can you tell me who has it?"

She held my stare.

"Would Damien do this? Steal and sell your formula on the black market?"

"He's not cutthroat. Anyway, that's why we're selling the store. So he'd have the money to buy a new home with Embry."

"The one in South Beach." I remembered her telling me that.

If Damien was trying to impress Embry and was going for a waterfront property, he'd have the motive to betray Raquel. Those homes went for millions. He'd need more than the money he'd invested in this place. "How about an employee?"

"I had a part-time assistant. Sarah never showed any interest in what I did in the lab."

"When she heard you were selling the store maybe she thought you wouldn't notice?"

"She was in North Carolina with her parents. She wasn't in Florida at the time of the break-in."

Which was actually a great alibi. "That article about your store in *Vogue*?" I tried to say it as kindly as possible.

"You saw that?" She gave a nod. "The publicity was great for the store."

"They hailed you as a talented perfumer. Which you are."

Her shoulders slumped with realization. "I announced to the world I had a lab here."

And she'd already admitted she'd failed to upgrade her security. "I have contacts in the industry. I can help."

"I have to face this alone."

I waved that illogical idea away. "Afterward, will you be willing to explore the possibility of us again?"

"If that's still what you want."

I walked toward her and cupped her face in my hands. "I'm here right now. Doesn't that mean something?"

She peered up at me, her face sweet and trusting.

Being this close to her again was all I wanted, all I needed, and I tried to convey my feelings to her. "I'm good for you. I know this with every part of me. And you've broken through my defenses. You see *me*. And you help me trust what we have."

"Astor, what happened to you to make falling in love so hard?"

I broke her gaze, unwilling to bring all that poison into this special moment. "Just tell me there's a chance for us. If you say there isn't then I promise to never mention it again. I will leave here after the storm and you won't hear from me again."

"Promise you'll have an open mind."

"With you?"

"With how we began."

"I'm more interested in what we can become."

She looked conflicted, but then gazed up at me with hope in her eyes.

"I'm here to chase away your fears. I'm particularly good in storms." I gave her a comforting smile. "I'll keep you safe." I hugged her.

Being under siege from the weather would be the cruelest strike of all if I wasn't going to be able to touch her. Realizing I was probably overwhelming her, I let her go and stepped back. "Do you want me to leave?'"

"It's not safe for you to go."

"And if it was? If there was no storm?"

She gave a resigned nod. "Stay."

"Let me help with your formula?"

"No."

"Okay, I'll find something else to do. Show me the supplies." I needed to get my hands on a flashlight in case the lights went out.

"They're downstairs." She picked up my wet clothes again and walked into a closet, dropping them into a washing machine. She added detergent and started the cycle. I just hoped we'd not have a power outage before she'd dried my clothing or I was destined to wear this silly robe for the duration of my time here.

She shut the closet door.

"Go on then. Work on your perfume. I'll make dinner." I strolled over to the fridge and opened it. "I can't get over how small this thing is."

"It's meant to be temporary." She crossed her arms.

"As far as I'm concerned it is." And being here was going to provide the time we needed to talk.

"Astor, thank you for understanding."

I turned to face her. "I'd do anything for you."

Her expression softened. "I'm glad you're here."

"So am I," I said, walking back over to her. "Let me prepare the emergency supplies in case we need to bolt." If the storm turned we'd need to evacuate and fast. "We'll keep the Weather Channel on."

"Let's avoid the channel with you know who on it."

"I don't know, seeing Embry battered by a merciless storm might be entertaining."

She gave my arm a playful punch. "The good news is I have enough supplies to last for days."

I winked at her. "I always loved hurricanes."

Chapter
THIRTY-ONE

Raquel

I F ASTOR WAS HERE TO LOOK FOR MY LEDGER, HE WAS NEVER GOING TO find it. Yet he seemed sincere. The fact that he'd driven all this way meant everything.

I watched as he knelt in the corner rummaging through the emergency supplies. He found two flashlights and set them aside.

I handed him a mug of tea. "There you are."

He wrapped his hands around it. "Thank you."

I took a sip of mine and the warmth soothed me. "Astor, I want you to know that this isn't about me choosing my profession over us. This is more complicated than that."

He stood. "I thought I was obsessive, but you really are the perfume girl."

Maybe my obsession had caused a chink in my marriage just big enough for Embry to wedge through. I had to make sure I didn't ruin another relationship because of this. "I suppose I can be a little obsessive."

But surely, if he had been the right man for me, Damien would have supported my passion as I had his. After all, that's what people do when they love each other. They care about what makes the other come alive.

Astor stepped forward. "I love that about you, Raquel. I love that you have a passion."

His words made me beam with happiness. "I love that about you, too."

He seemed to mull that over. "I was thinking about the person who stole your scent."

"Oh?"

"Do you know them?"

I swallowed hard, wondering where he was taking this conversation.

"You didn't want to look at the file in my office," he said. "You don't believe I stole it, right?"

"No, I..." All I needed was a few hours and Astor would be right here to see it. "I thought it best not to look at anything you were working on."

"I can't shake the feeling that I'm somehow involved."

I decided to change the subject. "Are you hungry?"

He nodded. "I'll finish preparing the supplies and then cook for us. You do your thing."

"The stove's upstairs."

"How does ravioli sound?"

"Perfect. There are more snacks in the cupboard if you get hungry." I stepped into his arms and hugged him. "I'm glad you're here."

"Me too." He pressed his lips to my forehead. "More than you'll ever know."

He picked up a flashlight and headed upstairs.

I made my way into the lab and set to work. This was my happy place, and even though the world out there seemed chaotic and full of danger, in here, alone, I could lose myself in the process of creating.

While waiting for Damien outside The House of Beauregard, I had used my iPhone to photograph the last page of my ledger to record my formula. I trusted Damien but if I lost that notebook it would take me weeks of work to formulate the ingredients. The day I was going to upload the data to the Cloud, the burglary had happened.

Wait...

Hadn't Damien visited my store the morning of my meeting with Anna at Dazzle and Bazaar? He'd dropped off the papers for me to sign with the realtor—the same forms that still sat in my inbox. I'd set my handbag on the counter and left him alone with it for five minutes to go fetch his Italian cookbook, which had somehow ended up with me. He would have had enough time to take the bottle out of my bag and hide it on the shelf.

Enough time to sabotage my meeting.

No, I was tired and not thinking straight. He wanted the money I was meant to get from Dazzle and Bazaar, so there was no incentive for him to do something like that. I needed a break from all this stress and as soon as I finished this perfume I would be taking one. Right after I set another appointment with Anna Rosenthal at D & B, ready to make licensing this a reality.

After carefully preparing the ingredients, I sat on a barstool with my ear buds in, shuffling songs on iTunes to keep the crashing and wailing outside at bay, and added each one carefully. Then I drew the Orris oil into a pipette.

The work was time-consuming and hypnotic.

I jolted when Astor's arms wrapped around my waist. He pulled me back and I leaned against his chest, relaxing as he hugged me. I looked over my shoulder to see he was dressed in his own clothes again. "What's the time?"

"Eight. How's it going?"

"Almost there." All I had to do was add the Orris. I nudged it aside so he wouldn't see it.

"Let me sniff?" he said.

"I want you to experience the grand finale."

"Sounds enticing." His lips brushed my neck. "Let's eat."

"I just need a few more minutes."

"Come on, the food will get cold. You work too hard."

I slid off the barstool and let him weave his fingers through mine.

This was where I had gone wrong with Damien...I had put my work before my relationship and that couldn't happen again. This was me turning a new leaf and not being so obsessed that those around me were forgotten.

Astor's attention turned to the window. "Things are really kicking up out there."

He led me upstairs where he'd placed two plates on the counter-top, ready for the ravioli bubbling on the stove.

I only had one chair, so we resigned ourselves to sitting on my makeshift bed on the floor, and I marveled at how Astor was willing to rough it for me. The ravioli was delicious. This was soul food and I felt so much better already, my stomach full from the tasty tomato pasta dish.

"Thank you for letting me stay at your place," I said. "I'm going to find somewhere soon."

He looked surprised. "You're always welcome in my home, Raquel."

"Things change so fast. One minute I was living in a home I loved and then suddenly I couldn't stay there anymore. Damien refused to leave and, to be honest, there were too many memories."

"I'm sorry."

"I miss my books. Don't have room for them here. They're in stor-age along with some pieces of furniture I couldn't let go of. Damien kept the rest."

"Don't take this the wrong way," he said. "But can we not talk about him?"

"Sure, of course. I'm sorry."

"I just want to talk about us, Raquel."

I nodded. "I bet you have a great collection of books at Bridgestone."

He looked thoughtful. "When I was a kid I used to hide out in the library. I found this old book with photos of the Sistine Chapel in the Vatican. That was the first time I discovered that life really is full of contradictions."

"Why do you say that?"

"Many of those paintings on the Vatican ceiling are of female Sibyls, who were ancient oracles. Michelangelo revered them for their ability to predict the future. And yet later, women were burned alive as punishment by that same church for supposedly having that same gift."

"How did you discover that so young?"

"Like you said, we had a great selection of books." He looked at me with a smile. "It was the best thing about the house."

"I never thought of how the church turned on itself like that."

"Well, it's a male-dominated society." He gave a shrug. "That's why children are confused. We send mixed messages."

"You don't seem too fond of that house?"

Astor stared at me. "How do you mean?"

"Why did you leave there when you were so young?"

He hesitated. "After my dad died my mom thought it best I live in a country with a culture that ran in my blood."

"Astor," I encouraged softly.

He broke my gaze. "I don't remember much. Not really."

"Have you blocked the memories out?"

His expression was conflicted.

"How did your dad die?"

Astor's somber gaze held mine. "Under tragic circumstances."

"How do you mean?"

He sighed. "My past is my past. I leave it there."

I reached up and cupped his face. "Did he hurt you?"

"He destroyed everything in his wake." Astor looked away. "Can we talk about something else?"

"Okay, um, tell me something about you I don't know." I got up and carried our plates over to the sink.

Astor pushed himself up. "What are you curious about?"

"That's not how it works. Go on, impress me."

"I once went scuba diving in Egypt's blue hole. It's one of the most dangerous places you can choose to dive."

"Are you an adrenaline junkie?"

"I was twenty. I'd just come back from England and was reckless.

I hadn't seen my family in a long time. I was working through a lot. I missed England and yet I wanted to be home. I didn't feel like I fit in anywhere. I bought the place on the beach you stayed in and that helped a lot. I prefer it."

"Why didn't you come home for a visit while you were in England?"

"I was discouraged from doing so."

I frowned at the cruelty of it. "Do you feel like South Beach is your real home now?"

"Yes."

"Are you happy?"

Astor went to speak but couldn't seem to form the words.

"Oh, Astor."

"You lost your mom, too, right?"

"Yes, while I was in my first foster home with Mrs. Clark." I spoke her name fondly, because she had been kind despite me not being her own child. "I was sent to live with her because of the incident that drew attention to how my mum wasn't caring for me properly. I was taken away from her. That was the last time I saw my mother before she died."

"I'm sorry, Raquel." His tone carried sympathy.

I still felt guilty about the incident in our garden shed. I had brought it on myself. Had I stayed quiet and not gone out as my mother had wanted, I would have been with her at the end. Instead, she died alone in that old house because of me.

I gave him a sad smile filled with regret. "I was making perfume in the shed. I was nine years old and not meant to be in there."

"What happened?"

"I was stung by a bee. I'm allergic to them."

"That could have been fatal." He looked concerned. "Do you carry an EpiPen in case you're stung again?"

"Always."

"Someone found you, obviously. I'm guessing it wasn't your mom."

"I was found unconscious and barely hanging onto life by a neighbor who had seen me go in there. They carried me out and called an ambulance. All the while my mum was asleep upstairs."

"Thank goodness for nosy neighbors."

"This one saved my life."

"What was it like growing up in foster care? Did you ever get adopted?"

"No."

"Isn't that how it's meant to happen?"

"Yes. I always hoped that someday someone would come and save me."

"Let me save you," he said softly.

"Not sure I need saving now."

"What about you?" he said. "Tell me something about you I don't know."

"I just did."

He shook his head. "Something that makes you happy."

I rested my hands on my hips. "Would you believe I can salsa dance?"

"Really?"

"Really and truly."

Joy flashed across Astor's face and then he grabbed his phone and scrolled through it.

"What are you doing?" I asked.

The song "Havana" blared out of his iPhone, its beat enough to have me swinging my hips and laughing at what he was suggesting.

Astor was going to dance with me right here in the midst of a storm.

He moved to the tempo with an expert swing. "Ready?"

I laughed. "I was born ready."

All those lessons hadn't gone to waste.

He wrapped his arm around my waist and swung me around and around. Then he suddenly let go and we were mirroring each other with the sexy dance moves, stepping fast, our feet moved in sync with each other. He grabbed me again and swung me around and around as we dodged the mattress, dancing wildly around the room.

"Wow," he called out. "You have rhythm."

"But we already knew that," I shouted over the music.

"Ha! Yes we did, Raquel."

"You're not so bad yourself, Mr. Beauregard."

He showed me some sensual new steps. "Try this."

"I can do that."

Astor danced effortlessly. This was Havana in Astor's blood...its culture, history, and everything that was rich and wonderful about Cuba that ran through his veins. I loved this about him so much because it made him exotic and alluring. He was everything wonderful that my world had been missing.

He was behind me now, moving slowly, seductively, and I let him lead me as the music soaked into my body and we became one.

Astor spun me around and cupped my face, kissing me hard and then staring into my eyes. "Be mine, Raquel, no matter what."

I fell against him and crushed my lips to his.

Astor lifted me and lowered us both onto the mattress while the storm raged outside and the Cuban music flowed around us. It was beautiful and romantic and we hurried to undress—both of us tearing off our clothes. I wanted to feel his skin against mine, wanted to kiss him everywhere, and most of all I wanted to believe that this was pure and real and everything that I had once dreamed a relationship could be. The way he looked at me convinced me he cared, the way he spoke my name as he reached around to unclip my bra and set my breasts free so that his mouth could lavish affection on each nipple, nipping and biting, sending ripples of pleasure through me. I wanted to lick him all over and this made me laugh.

"What?" He stopped to look at me.

"You're just so gorgeous, Astor. I feel so lucky."

"If there's any doubt about how I feel about you. This bed proves I'm willing to go to hell and back."

Then he began speaking Spanish, the words flowing sweetly, sounding romantic and dreamy—even though he was probably just saying how much he hated my bed.

"What did you say?" I asked.

"I told you how I feel about you." He beamed at me. It was another one of those drop-dead gorgeous smiles that would have melted my panties off if I'd been wearing any.

"Are you going to translate for me, please?"

"I'm going to show you."

How had I ever walked away from him? Right now, this second, I couldn't fathom how I had had the strength to place my happiness over his. I loved this man more than life itself—and I had been too blinded by ambition to see it...too stuck in my old ways to understand what he meant to me.

When he thrust into me, I arched my back and shuddered beneath his power, never wanting to be parted—as though it were possible to hold back time, hold on to him forever.

We came together violently, enraptured, and during those minutes of him just looking down at me with his hands on either side of my body, I felt as though love was passing between us.

It seemed that we made love for hours, him waking me and taking me again. And then it was my turn to awaken him, scooting down the mattress to suckle his cock until both he and his erection stirred and we went at it again—two lovers unable to keep our hands off each other.

And in those passing moments, all the pain, all the hurt, all the betrayal and fear slipped away and all I was left with was peace. Even the storm was giving up its fight.

Astor turned his head toward the window, frowning. "Did you hear that?" He pushed himself up onto his elbows.

"What?"

"Howling?"

"The wind?"

"It sounded like an animal." He got up and stared out at the pouring rain.

"Come back to bed." I tapped the mattress.

"No, listen." He started to get dressed.

"What is it?"

I reluctantly got dressed, too, and followed him downstairs.

"Are you going out?" I was surprised that something had gotten him so worried. "Be careful, okay?"

Astor hesitated by the front door. "My coat's still wet? I'll just have to brave it." He stepped out, raising a hand to shield his face against the gusting wind and rain. "It's coming from over there."

"Hold on, I'm coming with you."

"Stay inside." Astor hurried away.

I stood in the doorway and watched him go, reluctant to lose sight of him. Rain battered my face but I didn't care, I just wanted him to be safe out there. Flying debris was a real hazard.

He knelt behind a car and tried to coax something out from beneath it.

I looked back into the store wishing I had brought towels down with us. Astor was getting soaked to the skin again.

He headed back toward me holding the collar of a dog. As they drew closer I could see it was some kind of hound with a long nose and floppy ears. The animal was cowering and kept glancing up at Astor as though aware he was being saved.

Astor pulled him into the store. "Sorry about the mess."

I stepped back and closed the door behind them. "It's fine, of course."

The dog shook his body and water spattered us both, making us laugh.

I knelt to pat the dog. "Hello, boy, what's your name?"

His tail wagged with happiness.

Astor ran his fingers along the collar, at the same time fighting off a lick from the animal. "There's no tag. He might be chipped. He's still a puppy."

"How can you tell?" He looked big to me.

"No plaque on his teeth. They don't get that until they're a year old."

"Did you have a dog once?"

Astor stared up at me. "Yes, I had to leave him behind when I was sent to Cuba."

It made me cringe to think they had done such a thing to him.

"I loved that dog. He was a Labrador."

"What was his name?"

Astor shrugged and focused on the wet hound. "Maybe someone's reported him missing."

I rubbed my hand over the dog's damp head. "His owner must be worried sick."

"Let's get him some water and dry him off."

We led him into the back of the store and Astor found a dish and filled it with water. I grabbed towels and within a few minutes we had a much drier dog.

It was fun to watch Astor playing with him. It was one of the things I loved the most about him—the way he loved animals and the lengths he'd go to in order to save them.

I made us tea and we let the dog run loose to explore the place and give him time to feel safe again. Astor and I sipped our drinks in the front of the store while sitting on the chaise lounge watching him sniff around. Every now and again he'd come over to us for a pat on the head.

"He's adorable," I said.

"I'm going to call him Caine."

I laughed. "As in Hurricane?"

Astor's gaze held mine. "Maybe he'll be our first dog?" He leaned toward me and grabbed my waist, pulling me into him. "Maybe we can give him a forever home."

"Don't get too attached. Someone might claim him."

"I'm already a goner."

He kissed me and I smiled against his lips. "Umm… let me think of what might suit him. He looks like a Pooky-Boo."

"Let him keep some of his pride, at least."

"Wouldn't it be wonderful if he does become ours?" I rested my head against Astor's shoulder. "And the way we found him, too."

He agreed with a nod. "He looks hungry."

"I'll go find something for him to eat."

Astor pressed his lips against my throat, making me tingle, and making me feel reluctant to break away from him. But I hurried up the staircase and found some chicken that would be okay for Caine to eat. It wasn't perfect but it would tide him over until we could buy some proper dog food. I chopped it up into little pieces and carried it downstairs in a cereal bowl.

When I made it back to the front of the store, I placed the dish on the ground and looked around for Astor and the dog.

They were gone.

I looked for them in the lab and when I didn't see them I wondered if Astor had taken Caine outside to use the bathroom. I didn't like the idea of them being out there and hurried into the front of the store to check on them.

Oh, God…

I stared at the open drawer of the corner cabinet and my flesh chilled with the realization, hurrying over to see that the small ampoule of my perfume was missing.

Astor had found it.

I bolted toward the front door and felt a stab of fear when I saw Astor putting Caine in the backseat of his Range Rover.

"Astor!" My heart shattered into a thousand pieces when he looked back at me with a stricken expression.

I ran out not caring about the door being left open. "Where are you going?"

"The worst is over." He gestured around him. "Time for me to get going."

I held his gaze. "You found my bottle, didn't you?"

He dropped his gaze, and when it rose again to meet mine I saw the accusation in his eyes. His look of pain was too much to bear…it was as though his agony was mine.

"Astor. It's the same formula that was stolen from me."

"I let you in."

"I need more time to prove—"

"I wish you all the best." He opened the driver's door.

"Wait, please, give me the chance to prove what I'm saying is true."

Astor shrugged. "You had me there for a while, Raquel. God, you're good at this."

"I need to add the Orris oil."

"From the bottle you stole from me?"

Stunned, I realized I'd just given away the final ingredient of the scent's formula. Astor's expression became unreadable.

He clenched his jaw. "How much did they pay you?"

Unable to bear the thought that he suspected me of betraying him, all I could do was squeeze back tears. After all we'd shared and all we had done together, our passionate lovemaking that still had my body thrumming from his touch...

Yet all this time I had doubted him, too.

I held my hands together as though in prayer. "You think I stole it? I would never..."

He climbed into the Range Rover.

I ran over and rested my palm on his window. "Astor, you must believe me."

The engine roared to life.

"Step back," he mouthed.

I took several steps away from the curb and pressed my hand to my chest to ease the agony I was feeling as I watched him pull away and speed off. Drenched from the rain, I realized for the first time that I didn't care about that scent at all.

Being with Astor had been enough.

All my life I had been trying to replicate that feeling of home...and for the first time I had felt it with *him*.

Once again, I'd let happiness slip through my fingers. I'd lost everything.

Chapter
THIRTY-TWO

I KEPT MY FOCUS ON THE ROAD AHEAD, CHECKING FOR DEBRIS IN THE PATH of my car and looking out for any animals that might need rescuing. The storm had left chaos around me—though this wasteland was nothing to how I felt inside.

I'd become vulnerable, ignored the warning signs that Raquel had another motive. I'd let my guard down and allowed her to get close. I'd welcomed her into my inner circle and she'd taken full advantage of my kindness.

Another hard lesson… *Trust no one.*

I searched for a distraction by listening to a business podcast and speaking to Caine, who was panting away on the backseat with his tail wagging.

An hour into our journey, I stopped off at a pet store to buy a few supplies for him. He needed a leash, food bowls, and a couple of toys to chew on as I drove us to the other side of the state. And we both needed to stretch our legs.

I planned to make inquiries about his ownership once I got home. Right now, this guy was keeping me company because that familiar loneliness had started to seep back into my soul. The same kind of loneliness I used to deny existed.

Before *her*. This betrayal felt like the cruelest strike.

I needed a reminder of how much she had wronged me so that I didn't turn this damn car around. Tapping my coat pocket, I felt the ampoule. One whiff of that formula and the truth had come tumbling out.

Somehow, she'd stolen that perfume from the House of Beauregard.

Raquel's deceit was unbearable because I had gotten closer to her than I had anyone else. She'd used my affection for her own ends... used it to infiltrate The House of Beauregard—and it had been me who had invited her in.

The journey back to South Beach was a blur.

The last place I wanted to be was Bridgestone. The origin of all my nightmares and the place I'd first met *her*. Still, I had responsibilities I couldn't ignore.

I parked my Range Rover in front of the manor and climbed out, gazing toward the stables and wanting to head over to them and check on my horses. I couldn't wait to see how they'd faired, especially Vedado. He was temperamental—any loud noises startled him and I hated the fact I'd not been here with him.

Still, as I looked over at the house, guilt made me a dutiful son. *I should check on Mom.*

I opened the back door and leaned in to attach the lead to Caine's collar. With one light tug he leaped out of the car to join me. With the dog by my side, I took my usual route around the back of the vast manor, soon reaching the windblown garden with its ocean view beneath the dusky sunshine. The affects of the storm were minimal here, though a few larger plants had been pulled up by the roots.

Caine raised his leg and peed on a corner patch of flowers. I glanced up at the house to make sure no one caught it.

Reaching into my pocket, I pulled out the ampoule and again opened the stopper, breathing in the familiar scent and realizing my joy over its magnificence was spoiled. I'd been passionate over all the possibilities of what we could do with it, and now that excitement was tainted. I would have to choose my words carefully when I explained all of this to Penelope. She was so fragile I knew the thought of losing her precious scent would upset her. I had exposed my family to this…

I pulled my phone out of my pocket and made the call.

"Mrs. Beauregard's residence," Arthur answered in his clipped British accent.

He'd served as my mom's butler for over ten years and was now a part of this place.

"It's Astor. Can you have my mother meet me in the garden, please?"

"I'll be right there, sir."

The call dropped and I stared at my phone. Then I saw him at the back door working the lock.

"Hello, sir," he called over. "I'm afraid your mother's feeling a little under the weather." He gave a thin smile. "No pun intended. Are you able to visit her in her room?" From his look of sympathy Arthur knew he was asking no small thing.

Entering that house was a nightmare I wasn't prepared for. Not today anyway… not after the disaster that had left me emotionally spent.

With a tight jaw I turned and stared out at the water. "I should probably check on the horses."

"She'd love a visit, sir. She hasn't been out of bed in days."

Balling my hands into fists, I reassured myself this was nothing I couldn't handle. It was just a house and I shouldn't allow bricks and mortar to have that kind of power over me. With that logic burning up my brain I gave a nod and headed inside.

"You have a new dog?" Arthur stared down at Caine with affection. "Some kind of hound?"

"I found him running loose in the storm." I offered the leash to Arthur. "May I ask you to get him some water?"

"Of course, sir." Arthur beamed as he escorted me to the foot of the sweeping staircase.

"I can find my own way," I said.

He hovered and then leaned down to pat Caine's head. I suspected it was Arthur's way of making sure I was okay to go on alone. He knew I hated this place and at times I suspected he knew why. I waited for him to walk away before I swiped my brow with my sleeve and returned my gaze to the staircase.

On the way up my hand gripped the banister too tight and I had to take a few seconds to calm my racing heart.

This is ridiculous.

It had all happened decades ago. Yet as soon as I made it to the top step and faced in the direction of what was still my mother's bedroom, even after all this time, all that had unfolded in that room came rushing back...

I saw the blurred figure of a boy running along the hallway—me.

Like a ghost heading out of the shadows, I recognized myself at the age of thirteen, bolting down the wide hallway where I stood now...a young boy drenched in terror as he ran towards that room.

I wouldn't have taken another step had it not been for my mother needing to see me and me needing to know she wasn't as sick as Arthur had indicated.

The boy ran into *that* room ahead of me.

Don't go in...

With each step, each breath, I was reminded that I'd not entered this house for decades. Yet I sensed I'd never left, not really...these walls still held me hostage as though the vines clinging to them were choking me, preventing a part of me from ever leaving.

A burst of lemon air freshener hung in the air. The red carpet was hardly worn from the lack of visitors in this enormous house that had never been a home.

Nudging the door open, I peered in, keeping my focus on the large bed that sat in the center of the bedroom, my mother lying in it, not moving. Stepping in, I reasoned if she was asleep I would have a reason to leave.

She slowly turned her head to look at me. "Astor." She raised her hand, gesturing for me to come closer.

"Mama." I closed the gap between us and sat on the edge of the bed beside her. "How are you?"

Her frail hand grasped mine. "One of my headaches."

"Can I get you anything?"

"Arthur's taking good care of me."

"Glad to hear it."

It was impossible not to sweep my gaze around the room, the memories as sharp and cruel as the day they were made. That fucking chair in the corner was the same. Why the hell had she kept it?

"Thank you for coming to see me," she said.

"Sorry, work and everything else. I owed you a visit."

She pulled back a little. "What happened?"

"How do you mean?"

"You look so weary."

"It's nothing."

"Tell me what happened?"

I managed a sad smile. "I met someone I liked but it didn't work out."

"Why didn't I meet her?"

"We weren't together long." Which didn't matter—I'd thrown myself into my first true relationship and I'd been filled with hope, had been soothed in ways I couldn't define.

I'd fallen hard.

"Did she hurt you?" she asked softly.

"It's no big deal," I lied. "Tell me how you're feeling right now. Should I call the doctor?"

"Goodness, no. He won't appreciate being called for a headache."

I brought her hand to my mouth and kissed it. "It's good to see you."

And it was...my sweet mother had made many mistakes, but our bond still felt unbreakable.

"How's Penelope?" she asked.

"Fine. I'm watching over her."

"You're a good brother." Her expression became haunted with

sadness. "You are too good for us all, Astor."

"Don't, Mom."

Her deep brown gaze held mine. "We ruined your childhood."

My thumb caressed her hand to comfort her. "Look how happy I am now."

Was happy, I corrected myself. I had tasted happiness with Raquel and yet fate had torn us apart.

"I shouldn't have let you come in here." My mother's voice snapped me out of my melancholy and threw me headfirst into grief. "I know it upsets you."

"Stop," I said firmly. "That's all forgotten."

"You were too young."

"Mom, please." I sat up straight. "How are the horses?"

"Jacob came to visit. He told me they're fine. Though Vedado didn't do so well."

My mouth went dry. "What happened to him?"

She waved it off. "He's too skittish. Why do you love that horse so much? He's so damaged from what they did to him that he won't trust anyone."

"He trusts me, Mama."

She reached over and ran her hand through my hair. "Yes, yes he does. I think that's why you two connect with each other. You've both been through so much."

I gave her hand a squeeze. "I'm going to check on him."

"Of course." She pushed herself up and rested her back against the headboard. "Thank you for visiting. I feel better now."

"I'm glad." I let go of her hand and stood. "Can I get Arthur to bring you anything?"

"Some tea, perhaps."

I leaned over and kissed her forehead before heading for the door. Before I stepped out of the room, I turned and looked back at her with a smile. Even now it felt good to say it. "Her name was Raquel."

"So pretty. What a shame."

Leaving that bedroom behind, I tried to shake off the feeling of dread that clung to me like it once had all those years ago. As though that room had somehow entered my consciousness and become a part of me.

I walked past my old bedroom and descended the staircase with the memory of that sound—a gunshot—ringing in my head.

The bullet had not only deafened my right ear for hours but had also stolen my world from me. The damage it could do to a human skull was unimaginable.

So much blood...

I made it through the parlor, down the hallway, and into the guest bathroom before the bile rose in my throat. I retched in the sink as the agonizing memories overwhelmed me.

When I was finally done, I washed my mouth out and splashed my face with water.

Staring at my reflection, I told myself that I didn't have to enter this house ever again. Not if I didn't want to. Next time I visited Mom I'd meet her in the garden and the conversation would be about selling this place once and for all. It was too big for her anyway. Surely she'd come around to my way of thinking?

I made my way back toward the foyer, needing to get outside and inhale the fresh air. I sucked in a breath of concern when I saw Caine sniffing in the corner with his leash dragging behind him. My fear was realized when he raised his back leg to pee on the kentia palm sitting in a priceless vase.

Yes, my sentiments exactly.

God, I love that dog already.

Arthur hurried into the foyer, looking around nervously. I threw him an amused smirk when he saw what Caine had done to the vase, as though the old mischievous me had never been suppressed.

"Can you take Mom up some tea, please?" I asked him.

"Yes, sir."

I patted my leg to get Caine's attention. "Come on, boy. Let's go visit the horses."

Chapter
THIRTY-THREE

MY FINGERS GRIPPED THE STEERING WHEEL TIGHTLY AS I TURNED A corner into the elite-looking neighborhood. It was hard to stay focused with this constant ache in my chest.

I no longer cared about the store I'd left behind in Dunedin. It was, after all, just a building. It was the hurt I had caused Astor that crushed me more than anything. I was going to fight for what was right and at the very least prove I had no ill intent.

Another wave of regret hit me over the fact I hadn't completed my formula before he'd walked out on me. Another few minutes and I could have proven to Astor the scent was my creation.

It was one thing to have a perfume bottle in my possession, but to reverse engineer a scent would take a lab that was way more advanced than mine. I wished I'd kept my ledger and that way I could have shown it to him.

All this chaos had me making the wrong decisions.

More than this, I wanted to prove that what Astor and I had was real. Yes, I had accepted his invitation to work at The House of Beauregard, but surely he'd see my motive was pure when I had stayed with him in South Beach.

What we had was too precious to let slip away.

Which was why I was winding my way down Blueberry Lane looking for Damien's address, and gawking at the multi-million dollar properties that surrounded me. Now I realized why he'd needed the money from the store to be able to afford to live here. Or at least to chip in a tenth of what Embry had spent on their new home.

Though I couldn't see it from here, I knew their front lawn would face the water.

Wow, people. Here was my life crumbling around me and everyone else was getting on with theirs in the best possible way.

I rang the doorbell and turned around to admire the street, where there was not even one dropped leaf anywhere from the storm. The cleanup had been quick and efficient. This neighborhood was a world away from what I had known with my ex-husband.

Embry opened the door. "Hey, Raquel, what are you doing here?"

"I've come to see Damien."

"Was he expecting you?" She looked concerned.

"I'm here to collect a ledger I gave to him for safekeeping." I'd actually called his number and left a message, but she didn't need to know that.

"Come in." She stepped back.

"Thank you."

The interior matched the grandness of the outside, with its modern open plan design. Here and there were unpacked boxes proving they'd just moved in. My focus was on the sprawling garden—and beyond it the breathtaking view of the water where I saw luxury yachts floating by. No doubt the guests aboard the tour boats would also be awestruck by this waterfront property, along with the many others running along the bank.

"You have a beautiful home. The view's spectacular." It sounded overly polite but I didn't want to put her off the idea of me having access to Damien's office.

"I love it here. We're still unpacking so excuse our mess."

I wrapped my arms around myself, thinking that if things hadn't gone south in my marriage I might be the one living here. "Goodness, being a meteorologist really pays off. This must be from all the danger money they pay you?" I winked to soften it.

"I wish. Covering those storms is a rush though. I love my job. This is all Damien." She gestured for me to follow. "Want a drink?"

Despite my mouth being dry, I declined. "What did you mean about Damien?"

As she walked down a hallway, she turned to look over her shoulder at me. "Damien found this place and put a bid in as soon as it came on the market. It was an easy *yes*. The guy who owned it before was an architect so there's some unusual features that make the place stand out." She pointed to the sparkling pool of water. "It's actually deeper than the usual swimming pool. He's a diver so it's where he trained his family so they could join him in Jamaica."

I had only been half listening. I was still trying to work out how my ex had afforded this place. "Has Damien been hired at a new restaurant?"

"Right now, he's still at La Traviata." She smiled and stopped in front of his office. "He's relocating next week to a new restaurant in South Beach as head chef."

His visit to The House of Beauregard made more sense now. He really had been in the area for business.

She led me into the office.

I took in the floor-to-ceiling bookshelves, leather furniture, and the window overlooking their enormous garden, trying to imagine where Damien had gotten the funds to afford this sprawling home. I'd Google how much this place had cost him later, but right now my focus was on his desk, my gaze scanning the mess.

The sound of a ringtone came from another room.

"I need to get that," said Embry.

"I'll wait." I gave her a polite smile and watched her leave, then sprang into action, hurrying over to his desk and shuffling through the papers. Glancing up, I checked the doorway to ensure Embry didn't catch me rummaging around and continued my search in the filing cabinet.

Oh, thank God.

I found it lying underneath the files in the bottom drawer, as though he'd gone out of his way to hide it. Maybe he'd not wanted Embry to know he was helping me out by keeping it safe, since it might have set off an argument.

I shoved it into my handbag and walked over to the window just as Embry returned.

"Hey," she said. "That was Damien on the phone. He wasn't expecting you."

"Would you rather I wait until he can be here?" I asked kindly.

"I think it would be best."

"I can come back. I'll be in the area for a while."

"Oh?"

"I'm visiting Astor." She didn't need to know our relationship had crashed and burned last night. I ignored the way she glanced around Damien's office to see if there was anything missing.

We walked back toward the front door.

"I have to get ready for work," she said in way of an excuse.

"Of course. I should have called you. I thought Damien would be home."

Her face became unreadable. "He told me he spoke to you about what my father heard about the Beauregard family."

"I'm taking it all with a grain of salt until I know more."

"You like him a lot, don't you?"

"Yes, I do." And even now after everything we'd been through, I missed him.

Her sigh spoke volumes. "Be careful. He comes across as a bit of a playboy."

"That was my first impression, too." And I'd not forgotten how she'd batted her eyelashes at Astor, either. My ex was no match for him.

"We just don't want you to get hurt," she added.

"Well, first impressions can be wrong," I said. "Take the first time I met you—though *met* isn't really the right word for it. Your ass was in the air and my husband's dick was in your pussy. Understandably, I jumped to the conclusion that you were a whore."

Her back stiffened. "Damien told me you were separated."

"Which you later discovered was a lie, right?"

"You were having problems."

"Another lie, Embry. One which you fell for."

She raised her chin. "The fact you had no idea your marriage was failing—"

"Not a fact, a lie."

She gave me a thin smile. "You're divorced now so it's all in the past."

"It still hurts."

"People fall in love." She shrugged.

Yes, bitch, I was in love with my husband before you swept onto the scene like one of those hurricanes you're so fond of and then decimated my life.

Or maybe, just maybe, she'd set me free…

"Just get to know Astor better, okay?"

"Your concern is touching, but I already have. He's a great man."

"He's good looking, but I'm not so sure you're a good match."

My deep sigh reflected my sadness. "Can't you just be happy for me?"

"If I was you I'd be digging around looking for more answers on him."

"Maybe I could speak with your dad, then?" I gave a shrug to let her know I wasn't letting her ruin my day with her jealousy.

She stepped through the front door to close down my visit. "Apparently Astor's mom was in the room when his dad died. She has all the answers, it seems. Why don't you ask her?"

A car alarm went off and it grated on my nerves.

"Have a safe trip back to Dunedin," she said as she turned and rested her hands on the door, ready to shut it. "I want you to know, Raquel. I've always prided myself on celebrating women's rights. On being a good friend. I never envisioned myself as the other woman."

"What are you trying to say, Embry?"

"I'm sorry."

There was still too much pain in my heart for me to make the leap to forgiveness. "Statistically speaking, it's likely he'll cheat on you, too. You know that, right?" I couldn't help myself.

"Don't come back here," she snapped.

"I don't need to." I tapped my handbag. "Got everything I need right here." I turned and walked away, my hands shaking.

"You better not have stolen anything!" she called after me.

I offered her a warm smile and climbed into my car, started the engine, and drove away from the house, still trembling from finally facing off with her.

With a punch at my dashboard, I had Adele singing about how her ex was a loser and it actually lessened my grief. No, what had changed was Astor Beauregard had come into my life. I allowed myself to think back to our time together. Despite all we'd been through there were enough memories to soothe me.

I wanted that again.

I want him back.

As I drew closer to his offices, my body tingled with an equal measure of anticipation and excitement. This is what he did to me, he made me feel aliveness that until now I'd not experienced.

At three in the afternoon the traffic in South Beach was light and I managed to get to The House of Beauregard quickly. With my ledger clutched to my chest and my mouth dry, I hurried into the reception area bracing myself to see Astor.

I gave a polite smile to the receptionist on the first floor who watched me head up the staircase to the upper level. When Taylor saw me her eyes widened in surprise and she stood up to greet me.

I approached her. "Hey, Taylor, I've come to see Astor."

"Raquel, what happened?" she said, lowering her voice. "Why did you leave so suddenly?"

I hated seeing that conflicted look in her eyes. "It's complicated—"

"What were you doing in Penelope's office? I mean, really?"

"Looking for something that belonged to me."

"Well, look who came back." I heard Penelope's voice behind me.

"I'm surprised you're brave enough to show your face, Ms. Wren. My brother told me what you did. You have some nerve."

I swallowed hard. "Can I speak with Astor?"

"You've done enough damage," she said.

I turned to face Astor's office hoping he'd overhear us and come out to greet me.

"I only need a few minutes with him."

"Please escort Ms. Wren from the building, Taylor." Penelope's expression was triumphant.

I stood my ground. "I know you had something to do with stealing my formula."

She looked defiant. "I have no idea what you're talking about."

"I found this," I said, raising my ledger, "in your office."

Her gaze narrowed. "Sounds like you planted evidence to cover your tracks."

I clenched my jaw as a dull ache of realization hit me—I'd never be able to prove I was the victim.

"Show us evidence that the perfume came from you."

I raised my ledger. "I'm going to show it to Astor."

Penelope sneered. "It's Mr. Beauregard to you. My brother fired you. Get out."

Taylor shot me a worried look. "What did she do?"

"Corporate espionage. Ms. Wren stole a formula."

"I didn't." I spun to face Taylor. "Please, tell Astor I'm here."

Taylor took my arm and whispered, "Walk with me."

I let her guide me away and down the stairs. I didn't want a scene that would make me look like a disgruntled ex-employee. I wanted to stay calm and keep my dignity.

When we made it outside, I eased my arm out of Taylor's grip and walked toward my car. "I'm fine."

"No, you're not." Taylor glanced back up at the building.

I suspected she was looking to see if Penelope was watching from the upper floor window.

"What's going on? I don't understand." Taylor sounded hurt. "Tell me you're not a corporate spy."

"You don't really believe that, do you?"

"I don't know what to believe."

"Well, I'm not. My formula ended up here." I'd wanted answers, but wasn't going to tell her that was why I had accepted the job.

This was my problem to solve and I wasn't in the mood to try to convince her. I hated that our blossoming friendship was tainted with suspicion.

"But you work here," she said. "It's in your contract that anything you create—"

"Before," I told her. "It was stolen before I came here. I found this in Penelope's office."

"I let you in her office. I trusted you."

I chose to ignore that. "I know the new fragrance they're about to roll out is mine."

"Can you prove it?"

"I'm trying."

"You hurt him, you know," she said softly. "Astor really liked you."

"That upsets me more than anything."

"I mean, what is so important that you'd throw away what you guys had?"

"He told you about us?"

"He was giddy over you, Raquel. He's a great guy and I can't get over how you're willing to throw that away." She held my gaze again. "Why is that perfume so important that you'd risk ruining your relationship with him?"

"It took years to create. My heart and soul are in it. If I license it I could save my shop. But I don't care about any of that now. I just want to see Astor and prove my intentions were good."

"Can't you just create a new one?" She cringed as she spoke the words. "I mean, why blow up your job and betray Astor…"

"It represents all that I am," I burst out. "It's the scent of my soul."

"Oh, God," she said. "You really believe that?"

I swiped away a tear. "Tell Astor I never meant any of this to happen. Tell him I love him."

Taylor watched me get in my car, and then tapped on the window.

With a press of a button I lowered it. "I'm sorry if I put you in a tough position, Taylor. I value our friendship."

"I'm fine." She glanced up at the window again. "Look, I didn't tell you this but Astor's at Bridgestone. If you leave now you'll catch him."

Swiping at another rogue tear I gave her a nod of thanks.

"Drive safe," she said. "Promise?"

I nodded, giving her a watery smile.

She'd gifted me with a chance to persuade him I was telling the truth. All I had to do was show him the formula in this ledger and I would be exonerated.

Why hadn't I done that before?

Because you wanted even more evidence than that, I reasoned. A perfume made with him in the store would have been indisputable.

They say hope is a dangerous thing, but it was all I had to hold on to. As I drove up the road leading to Bridgestone Manor, a sense of calm came over me. Maybe it was because I was drawing closer to seeing Astor again, or maybe it was because I knew deep down we'd shared something precious that neither of us could deny, something that would outlast this nightmare.

The remnants of the hurricane could be seen in the scattered leaves and ragged palm trees—though South Beach had been spared the brunt of the damage.

Astor's Range Rover was parked outside the manor. I felt a jolt of excitement when I saw proof he was here. I parked beside his car and headed toward the front door.

After five minutes of waiting for someone to answer the doorbell I went for it and entered. Standing in the foyer I called out, "Hello!"

The entryway was vast and lavish…a true statement of wealth with its tall oriental-style vases holding their lush green plants and the bright touches of color that reflected their Cuban heritage.

I tried to imagine what it would have been like growing up in this big house. My flesh chilled as I thought about Astor spending his childhood here and then being forced to leave it suddenly.

A noise coming from upstairs drew my attention, and I held on to the banister as I ascended, ready to explain why I'd turned up unannounced. Surely Astor felt the same about not giving up on us so easily, that we were worth fighting for. A connection as deep as ours couldn't be thrown away. Surely some part of him believed that, too.

My gaze swept up. To the right of the balcony stood an elegantly dressed older woman, her familiarity to Astor convincing me she was his mother.

"Sorry to bother you," I called up. "I'm looking for Astor."

"Raquel?" Her expression was unreadable.

"Yes, Astor told you about me?"

She gave me a thin smile, then turned and headed away.

I hurried up the staircase and along the balcony, following after her, hoping she'd not consider me rude. "Mrs. Beauregard, may I speak with you?"

I caught her subtle nod as she walked into a room. I followed her, feeling like this encounter might in some way vindicate me. A woman who had endured life's cruelest blows would have empathy for others...an ability to see both sides.

She'd led me into a spacious bedroom. Though the drinks trolley was out of place.

"My son informed me you are no longer together." She walked over to the drinks trolley and poured herself a Scotch. "Want one?"

"No, thank you." Saying it was too early would be rude. "I need to speak with Astor," I said. "I want to explain something."

Her gaze settled on my ledger. "My daughter told me you stole something from them." She took a sip from her glass.

"It's a misunderstanding."

"I see."

"Astor grew up here?" I asked softly.

"Of course."

"You have a beautiful home."

Her expression changed. "Circumstances were not kind to us."

"I'm sorry to hear that." I looked around wondering if this was where it had happened. It wasn't just the chill in the air...it was the way Mrs. Beauregard glanced at me, as though sensing I knew more. She'd stayed in this house, in this room, prolonging the agony.

What happened in here?

"Why was Astor sent away?" The words slipped out in a whisper.

"When you have children, Raquel, you do whatever it takes to protect them. But when one of them falters you are left with a dilemma that will affect you for the rest of your life. Everyone suffers."

"I'm sorry you went through that."

She swallowed, hiding the pain. "I was powerless."

"Astor..."

"My beautiful boy was taken from me. I should have protected him. Should have told them what really happened."

"What do you mean?"

"I failed him. That's why I refused to sell this place all the time he was away. I believed he'd come home and I would make up for his lost childhood. I was forbidden to have any contact with him. With my *own* son." Bitterness weighed heavily in her words. "And I agreed to it for his sake."

My heart ached for her.

"When he did return he was not the boy who had slipped from my arms. He was changed irrevocably." She shook her head. "He refuses to come into this house." Her sadness was reflected in her gaze. "He'll visit his beloved horses and then he always asks me to meet him in the garden."

"What happened in here, Mrs. Beauregard?" I stepped closer.

"When you marry someone you're not thinking of the children you'll have, you're thinking of yourself and how the other person makes you feel."

"That makes sense," I said softly.

"I didn't know he was violent. After we married..."

"Your husband hurt you?"

Her sorrowful gaze rose to meet mine. "I never thought I'd become so lonely."

I looked around her self-imposed prison.

She stared off into space. "My husband was so loud he woke the children. We were arguing. Well, he was. I knew well enough to remain silent. They found me lying on the floor with my jaw broken, barely conscious." She squeezed her eyes shut.

"When one of them falters."

My thoughts scattered as I realized if she was on the floor barely awake then it had been one of the children who had defended her. And it had been Astor who had been sent away. Penelope had been so much younger than him.

I heard the floor creak behind me.

"Raquel?" Astor stood in the doorway.

Guilt made me tongue-tied for a moment. "Astor."

"I see you've met my mother." He gave me a rueful smile. "Why don't we go for a walk?"

With a nod of thanks to Mrs. Beauregard, I turned to go.

"Raquel," she whispered.

I faced her.

"I had a choice," she said softly. "And Astor insisted he make it for me."

I tried to unscramble what she meant.

"Please, Ms. Wren," said Astor.

I followed him out into the hallway. "I was looking for you."

"Well, now you've found me." He gestured toward the stairs. "Shall we?"

Gripping the banister, I descended the steps alongside him, looking over to gauge his reaction, but he was too hard to read.

"I hear you stopped off at my office?" He glanced my way.

"I wanted to talk with you." I followed him to the center of the foyer.

Astor looked over my shoulder. "It's fine, Arthur."

"You know her, sir?" said the middle-aged man dressed like a butler.

I was once again reminded how wealthy they were.

"Yes, I do. Thank you, Arthur." Astor took hold of my wrist and led me down a long hallway.

"Are you okay?" I asked him.

He gave me a humorless smile. "How are you?"

"Not good."

"I'm sorry to hear that."

"Astor, I lo—"

"Don't say it." His hand shot up. "Not now. And not here."

I clutched the ledger to my chest. "How's Caine?"

"He was a stray. He was boarded at a dog rescue and escaped through a hole in the fence."

"It was a good thing you found him."

Astor's expression hardened. "What are you doing here, Raquel?"

"I need to show you something—"

"I heard you threatened my sister?"

"I did no such thing."

"She called me. You upset her."

"Ask Taylor," I said defensively. "She was there." I pressed the ledger against his chest and he took it from me. "Astor, I should have shown you this instead of fussing over the formula when you were at my shop. Bear in mind I never saw your ingredients. You never showed them to me."

His frown deepened. "What is this?"

"It's proof." I forced a smile to reassure him.

He gave a resigned nod, then opened the book and flipped through it.

"The last page." I watched him skim. "The last formula is the one I was working on. Recognize it?"

He looked confused. "What am I meant to be looking at?"

Astor flipped open the book for me to see the last page—only it was not the right formula. It was the previous one.

"Give it to me." My voice faltered as I took it back from him and flipped to the where the formula was meant to be. "I don't understand."

Looking closer, I ran my fingertip along the faint tear in the middle where the page had been ripped out. My thoughts racing, I tried to recall when I had last seen it—before I'd given this to book to Damien for safekeeping.

"He tore out the page," my voice rasped. "Damien…"

"Ah."

"I took a photo with my phone." I went to reach for it.

"Don't." A flash of sympathy showed on Astor's face before his expression morphed once more into hard-edged doubt.

"You have to believe me, Astor."

He came closer, so close his body pressed mine back into the wall. "Raquel, I can't deny that what you and I had was special. But it's over. Whatever you intended it to be—"

"I don't understand." My lips trembled.

"Let's take these memories with us and forget the rest," he whispered. "This is how I want to remember you."

"Remember me how?" I exhaled sharply.

His hands cupped my face and he pressed his lips to my mouth firmly, his tongue darting and dancing with mine, comforting and soothing and promising that somehow, some way we'd survive this…

Until he pulled away from me, his eyes filled with sadness. "Goodbye, Raquel."

"But—"

He turned and headed down the hallway.

There were no more words that could be spoken. I had outstayed my welcome and the air had become suffocating in this old house. The ghosts haunting this place had found me, too.

With my ledger clutched to my chest I bowed my head in shame and hurried out the front door realizing this last piece of evidence had been stolen from me, too.

What hurt me most was the knowledge that Astor's trust in this world had been shattered again…by me. He'd saved his mother all those years ago, but in doing so had ruined his own life. Glancing up at the sprawling manor I realized it was nothing but a prison keeping the past alive and those who dwelled within it forever trapped.

Unwittingly, I had reaffirmed his distrust in the world, tainted his happiness.

As I drove my Alfa Romeo down the long driveway, I refused to glance in my rearview mirror and be reminded of all I had ruined.

Chapter
THIRTY-FOUR

I SLAMMED THE RANGE ROVER'S DOOR SHUT AND STOMPED TOWARD THE strip club. I wiped sweat from my brow. After blasting air-conditioning in my car, I'd been hit by a wave of Florida's sticky heat when I had climbed out.

Usually I didn't care, but lately, small things had bothered me more.

This afternoon, I had walked away from the first woman who had ever gotten to me in a way I didn't know was possible. Raquel had thrown my instincts off and I'd succumbed to her smile, her voice, the way she walked...her body had left me craving more.

I couldn't get her out of my thoughts, couldn't believe what I had with her was over. Our beginning had come to an abrupt end. We had felt perfect together, our bodies and minds melding as one in such a way that I had dared to believe I had at last found *the one*. Our connection was so profound that the inner numbness I'd felt for most of my life had finally lifted, allowing a deep love to touch my heart. We had parted cruelly, ending my long-sought after happiness.

All that was left was that old familiar loneliness.

The sound of rock music grew louder as I headed into the club, a musky aroma immediately assaulting my senses. I could smell the scent of spilled beer and spicy chicken wings. Upon the center stage danced a slim stripper wearing only a thong, her fake breasts jiggling and a faker smile hiding her boredom. Men stood around the stage, now and again sliding dollar bills into her thong. They were rewarded with flirty smiles as she bent over to show off her butt.

The stripper found my gaze on her in the crowd and I politely gave a nod and then focused on finding my sister. Penelope was in a booth with her friend Mirabelle. I slid in and sat opposite them.

"How did you know I was here?" Penelope asked. "Erwin?"

Her driver *had* tipped me off but I wasn't going to let her know that. "Gut feeling."

"Why are you here?" Penelope slurred her words.

"We talked about this," I shouted over the music. "I don't like you coming to these places."

"You need to lighten up," she said. "Wanna drink?"

Fuck it. Actually I did.

I gave a nod.

"What do you want?" Penelope got the attention of a roaming waitress.

"Scotch," I mouthed.

She made sure the waitress got my order. "On the rocks," she told her.

"Macallan," I said.

The waitress threw me a seductive look. "Sure."

I didn't want to be here. I wanted to be hanging out with Raquel at a restaurant or on a boat as we watched the dolphins swim beside us—or better still I'd prefer to be in bed gloriously fucking her.

"How are you?" Mirabelle called over.

"Fine." It was all I could be bothered to say to her. She was a bad influence on my sister and I was exhausted from landing back at square one with that same conversation about her reckless behavior.

My scotch was set before me and Penelope muttered something about putting it on their tab. I threw cash on the table anyway and then gave her an accusing glare.

"No. I don't do that shit anymore."

"Glad to hear it." Though her dilated pupils revealed she'd done a hit of something, and it was probably cocaine. She wasn't just high on booze. Now wasn't the time to threaten her with rehab.

"Is it over?" she asked.

"Is what over?" I leaned forward to hear her better.

"That thing with our ex-employee."

"You mean Raquel?"

"Yes." She looked annoyed because to her it was obvious.

I took a gulp of Scotch and it warmed my throat as it went down. "I couldn't be more excited about our new formula."

"Me too. Glad that other stuff is behind us." Penelope turned to Mirabelle. "Lots of drama at work."

"What?" Mirabelle shouted over the rave.

"Problems at work," repeated Penelope.

"Something came up that I want to talk with you about," I said. "I can't find the formula you wrote for our new scent." I held her gaze. "I need a breakdown."

She swallowed hard and that made my gut twist in doubt.

"I have it in my office," Penelope said. "Can we not talk about work?"

I leaned forward to ask her another question.

Penelope leaped to her feet and beamed at me. "I have a gift for you."

"Can I finish my drink?"

"Bring it."

"Find somewhere we can talk." I pushed myself up and followed her, carrying my drink across the floor and through a doorway. We entered a private booth decorated with plush velvet seats and wispy red veils hanging here and there.

"Sit there," Penelope said, pointing. "I'll be right back."

I threw back my drink and looked around for somewhere to set my glass, assuming she'd gone to the bathroom. Five minutes later, my sister walked back in followed by a stunning brunette.

The woman bit her lip suggestively as she unhooked her bra, revealing natural tits, her nipples beading from the chill.

She idled up to me with a flirtatious look in her eyes.

"Whatever he wants," said Penelope.

"Sure." The brunette sat beside me. "Lap dance?"

I looked up at my sister. "I think we can take it from here."

Penelope flipped a lock of hair over her shoulder and laughed, glancing back at us as she walked out. "Have fun!"

With my sister gone, I turned my focus on the stripper. "What's your name?"

"Tiffany."

"Your real name?" I smiled at her.

"Do you want another drink? I can get you one." She stood for a second to reposition herself on my lap, and then leaned forward to kiss me.

I pressed my hand to her chest to stop her. "I'm seeing someone."

"They don't need to know." She went for my zipper.

I gripped her wrists and my gaze rose to meet hers. "What perfume are you wearing?"

"Nothing."

"You smell great."

She licked her lips suggestively.

"There's something I would like you to do for me." I grinned.

She smiled. "Of course there is."

"Would you mind if I—" I reached into my jacket pocket and lifted out the bottle Penelope had given me. "May I?"

She leaned back suspiciously. "What is it?"

"Sniff." I held it up to her nose.

"Perfume?"

"Yes. It's something special I'm working on. Wear it and you'll double your tips tonight. It's that good."

She leaned back and pushed her breasts up to me in way of an invite.

I wet the end of my finger with the liquid and dabbed it on Tiffany's throat. Then I placed the scent beneath her armpits and streaked it across her belly. She grabbed my hand and made sure my fingertip found her erect nipples.

"That feels so good." She moaned. "God, it smells divine."

Her reaction made me feel a stab of guilt. This was ridiculous—Raquel and I were over and yet I felt this was betrayal in its rawest form.

"What now?" she mouthed.

"I need you to give the best lap dance of your life."

She smiled seductively. "I can do that."

"Good." I eased her off my lap and stood.

"Where are you going?"

"You do women, I take it?"

"Of course."

She accepted the hundred dollar bills I handed her and scrunched them into her palm.

"I'm a perfumer and this is part of my process." *For this, anyway.*

"But…what about you?"

"I'm leaving. Don't mention the perfume to my sister. If she asks its name tell her you can't remember. Tell her you bought it at Walgreens. Then change the subject."

"That's kind of weird."

"Five hundred dollars worth of weird. Are we on?"

"Hell, you've made my job easy."

"Then we're both happy." I gave her a slight bow. "When's your next shift?"

"Tomorrow at noon. Why?"

I turned and walked into the dimly lit hallway.

Within a few minutes I'd left Penelope with Tiffany for a lap dance. Heading out, I gave my sister's driver a wave of thanks as I passed his parked car, reassured he would get the women home safe. Walking over to my Range Rover, I raised my gaze to the horizon.

The evening had brought glorious reds and oranges across a

vanilla sky and I took a few seconds to admire the sunset. Bitterness from the aftertaste of that Scotch lingered, but it was nothing compared to the level of betrayal that surrounded me.

And then, as I opened my palm and stared down at the Lalique bottle I'd found at Raquel's shop, the same one I believed was Penelope's, it dawned on me…if this was my sister's then there shouldn't be another bottle back in my office drawer.

I leaped into my Range Rover and sped off toward The House of Beauregard.

Chapter
THIRTY-FIVE

Raquel

MY HATRED FOR DAMIEN HAD RISEN TO AN ENTIRELY NEW LEVEL.
I drew in a sharp breath and reminded myself that screaming at him wasn't going to get me answers. *No*, a cool and calm demeanor was best with him. Though I had failed at that the last time I had been to his home and faced off with Embry.

She stole my fricking husband. I mean, what did she expect, flowers?

Of all the people I could have entrusted with my ledger, I'd given it to him. The one person I should never have trusted.

It all made sense now.

I drove through the posh South Beach neighborhood once again, knowing now that I had paid for the privilege of Embry and Damien living here. He'd sold my formula to Penelope. Now that I had my ledger back with that page ripped out by him, he would soon find out I knew the truth.

I parked my car in the driveway and rang the doorbell. Hearing footsteps approaching from the other side, I straightened my back ready to face off with the man who had betrayed me twice. He'd been the one to fake a break-in so he could steal my formula.

He probably believed he had stripped my will to fight.

Damien was wrong.

The door opened and he stood there in ripped jeans and a tight T-shirt. I knew that smug expression. Years of marriage gives you the advantage when it comes to reading your man. He wasn't mine anymore, and I almost felt sorry for Embry. I read culpability in him and he probably read my anger.

"Hey." He leaned forward to look out at the street, as though checking to see if there would be any witnesses to what was about to go down.

"I need to talk with you." With a gesture, I indicated I would rather speak inside.

"We're kind of in the middle of something."

"It can wait."

"Great."

"I mean *your* shit can wait." I barged by him and headed into the living room. "Is Embry here?"

He walked toward me. "What do you want?"

"I know what you did, Damien."

"What did I do?"

"I asked you to look after my ledger and you tore the last page out. You tried to destroy evidence of my perfume."

"I have no idea what you're talking about."

"Just so you know I took a snapshot of it on my phone. I still have it."

"Well, that's good." He sighed unconvincingly. "Look, it wasn't me. There's a lot of confusion and this storm—"

"Cut your bullshit."

"Are you jealous?" He gestured around. "We're living like this, and you can't stand it."

"Where did you get the money for all this?"

"Embry's a TV celebrity. Endorsements, that kind of stuff."

"She told me the money came from you."

"Our financial situation has nothing to do with you."

"It does when you're using *my* money."

"Did Astor Beauregard kick you to the curb? Is this why you're so pissy?"

"We're fine."

"No, you're not."

"And how would you know that?" Had he talked with Penelope?

He looked defiant. "He's a successful businessman and he can have anyone. Why settle."

My jaw tightened at his cruelty.

His expression became accusatory. "Embry told me you went through my office. What else did you steal?"

"I only took what's mine...minus the page you ripped out." I folded my arms. "I know you sold my formula to The House of Beauregard."

"Did Astor tell you that?"

"I found my ledger in Penelope's office. Right before I gave it to you. I know you're working with her. How much, Damien? How much did she pay you to betray me?"

"Come on, sweetheart, you've been under a great deal of stress. You just found out your boyfriend is a murderer and—"

"Don't you dare...you don't know what went on in that house."

"And you do?"

"He's a good man."

"If he has it, just ask for it back." He glared at me. "But as your proof of concept is gone you may want to let this one go."

"How could you betray me again? We had some good years together, didn't we?"

"I need you to let me and Embry get on with our lives. No more turning up like this. It's not good for anyone."

"Listen to me. I am *not* letting you get away with this."

"I'm going to make some tea." His smile didn't reach his eyes. "We need to discuss this calmly."

Grinding my teeth in frustration, I glanced around to see the packing boxes were gone. They were settled in. Their new life had officially begun. Damien wanted this behind him and I knew how stubborn he was…how manipulative. It was a trait that had come out a year after we'd been married, but I had tolerated it back then and tried to act like the good wife. I had compromised all I'd held dear.

What a revelation. I was finally over this asshole.

Spending time with Astor had helped me move on. I wasn't willing to let him walk out of my life. Not with the way it had ended, anyway.

Or maybe, just maybe, there was no going back.

Don't think of him now.

Don't weaken your resolve.

I stood my ground. "The cameras didn't record during the theft. Only you knew I'd had them installed."

"I never came back to the store after our last argument."

"You mean the one where you delivered the forms for me to sign for us to sell the business? During that time, I know you reached into my handbag and removed the perfume I was going to take to Dazzle and Bazaar."

"Don't blame me for your failures."

"That time the cameras were working, Damien." I was bluffing, but I hoped it would convince him to tell the truth.

He looked conflicted. "I was looking for a pen."

"In my handbag?"

"I just wanted what was mine. I worked hard to get that place up and running for you."

"And now you're tearing it down."

"Open another store. Create more formulas. I've moved on and you should, too."

"I want justice." My voice trembled. "I'm not letting this go."

He gestured toward the sliding glass door, and I followed him outside to the garden.

"This is what we'll do for you," he said. "We'll talk to Embry's dad about getting more information on the store theft. You need closure…I get that. Though it's not fair of you to point the finger at me. I've done nothing wrong."

In a daze, I stared at the calm blue water in the swimming pool. It looked inviting, and as Embry had told me it was surprisingly deep. A tourist boat floated by filled with several loud, happy partygoers. Some of them waved at us and Damien waved back.

"It's a great location," he said. "Getting this house has taken hard work and sacrifice."

"What are we doing out here?"

"Thought I'd grab some honey for our tea." He stared across the garden.

A shudder of terror slithered up my spine when I saw them—pale wooden slats were stacked into a beehive.

"You didn't," I burst out. "I can't believe…"

"I'll use the honey from the bees in desserts. I'm all about improving the environment and making it a better place. Bees are endangered now, but you already know that."

I rummaged frantically around in my handbag searching for my EpiPen. I pulled it out, praying I'd not have to use it.

"You sold me out," I stuttered bitterly.

"Oh, that's right." Damien ran a hand through his hair. "You're allergic to bees."

"Fuck you."

"So no tea, then?"

I spun around and entered the house, shoving my EpiPen back into my bag. I almost tripped on a rug as I hurried through the living room.

I flew out the front door and stormed toward my car. Shaking, I leaped into the driver's seat and struggled to get my key in the ignition.

It was hard to see straight. I was close to hyperventilating, but I forced myself to focus as I locked my car doors.

I had been married to a man I hadn't known at all. What he'd done was sociopathic. The same man who vowed to love and honor me was prepared to have me die in the worst way. I concentrated on my breathing, trying to calm my heart rate. Passing out wasn't an option. I'd be vulnerable if Damien managed to get a bee inside my car.

Would he try that? I shot myself an angry glare in the rearview mirror.

Yes, he fucking well would.

Reaching for my phone, I inhaled deeply, needing to tell someone what had happened here.

I had missed a text from Astor: *Hey, Raquel, I wanted to check on you.*

I didn't want to alarm him so I went with: *Something just happened. I need to talk to you about it.*

Astor: *I miss you.*

Miss you too. I nearly sobbed in relief that he still felt that way.

Astor: *Sorry for the misunderstanding.*

I let out a sigh. His words meant everything.

I glanced up to make sure Damien hadn't followed me outside. Reassured he was still in the house, I texted Astor back: *I'm sorry if I hurt you. It was never my intention.*

Astor: *Can I see you?*

Yes, oh, yes. I needed to talk about all that had happened and hopefully clear the air, too.

Me: *I know who stole my perfume.*

Astor: *Do you have evidence?*

The question brought on a bout of nausea. All evidence had been destroyed and that photo I had taken of the formula wouldn't be enough. All I had was my word.

Astor: *Still there?*

Me: *I know Damien did this.*

Astor: *Meet me on the Riveting.*

Me: *I can be there in half an hour.*

Astor: *See you soon.*

I threw my phone into my handbag and sped off down the winding road, knowing I would never see this neighborhood again.

Within half an hour, I was boarding the *Riveting*. Astor's impressive yacht had been easy to find in the harbor. I imagine he'd chosen this location because his home was too personal and work wouldn't have given us much privacy. This place would enable us to talk freely.

I couldn't wait to get everything off my chest. I wasn't sure how Astor would react when I told him what Damien had done, but at least he had reassured me in his texts that he missed me. There was still hope for us.

Being near water always soothed me. I stared out at the horizon, looking forward to the day when I could get my life back to some kind of normal routine again.

I made my way to the upper deck and walked into the luxury dining area, stopping in my tracks.

Penelope folded her arms. "Astor sends his regards."

"He's not here?" My voice broke with the realization.

"Something came up."

I turned, wanting to leave, wanting to put distance between us. I didn't want to have a conversation with this woman without witnesses.

"We want to put this behind us, Ms. Wren," she said.

I paused in the doorway. "Put what?"

"Our mutual misunderstanding."

My body went rigid with the gall of this woman. "Penelope, I fully understand what happened. I'm under no illusion. I know my ex-husband sold you my formula and you are hoping to pass it off as yours."

She raised her hand to stop me from saying another word. "We've come up with a compromise. Something you will find more than satisfactory."

I followed her gaze toward a round table, upon which lay an envelope. "What is that?"

She walked over to it. "It's more than you would make from selling anything at your store." She slid out several sheets of paper and a check. "It's made out to you. One hundred thousand dollars."

"What's that for?"

"This will help keep your store open. This is a very generous offer."

My thoughts raced with the possibilities. Yes, that check would help in the short term but that was not the point. My husband had collaborated against me and no amount of money in the world would put that right.

They were paying for my silence.

She held up a form. "Sign this and the check is yours."

"A non-disclosure agreement?"

"It's only fair."

"Fair?" I wrapped my arms around myself, trying to fathom how she or Astor believed this was okay. "You're admitting it's my scent, then?"

She pointed to the check. "This guarantees your compliance."

"I'm not signing it."

"The other form states you will agree to stay away from my brother. It's in lieu of a restraining order. Though if we have to take that route…"

"He doesn't know I'm here?" I realized. "It was you texting me from his phone."

"You're standing on precarious ground, Raquel. I know some very dangerous men who could make your life uncomfortable."

"When Astor hears about you threatening me—"

"Contact him and the deal is off."

I forced a smile to let her know I wasn't the least bit intimidated.

"We were just fine before you came on the scene," she snapped. "Go back to the hole you climbed out of."

"Actually, before my ex sold my formula to you I was well on my way to having a great life. You drew me into your world. And you fucked up because you underestimated me. Now you want me to go away."

"Will you sign it or not?" She raised her chin. "This is non-negotiable and there's a time-limit."

My future hung in the balance.

That check would save my business. Hell, it would pay my salary for a full year or more and I could get my life back.

Perfume Girl would live on.

Penelope was right; I could continue to create endless scents and colognes and go on with my life like nothing bad had happened.

Perhaps I should put all of this behind me, swallow my pride and accept the fact I'd failed to secure my store and protect my formulas.

Letting go was the healthiest choice…the wisest choice. Goodness knows what the stress had done to my body and heart. As for Astor, he would always believe I had used him to get ahead in my career. That right there hurt more than anything.

Penelope offered me a pen. "You'll come out ahead by accepting this amount of money."

All I had to do was reach for that pen, sign my name on those papers and it would be over.

All I had to do was betray myself.

And promise never to see Astor again.

Chapter
THIRTY-SIX

J OGGING ALONG THE WATERFRONT AT DAWN WITH CAINE SPRINTING BESIDE me should have been the happiest start to my day. Yet my life still felt incomplete. I couldn't get Raquel out of my thoughts and couldn't find solace in knowing she was hurting.

I had to forgive myself for falling hard. I wanted to reconcile the memories of us that were etched in my soul like a torment I could no longer endure. She'd swept into my world and helped me see what was truly important instead of obsessing about business and sales and branding. I had felt like I was living a full life when I was spending time with her.

I needed to work through the betrayal of her taking a job at my company under the guise of a chemist. I needed to let that go and forgive her.

Standing on the wooden boardwalk overlooking the water, I admired the reds and oranges of the brilliant sunrise and drew the fresh air into my lungs with gratitude; this was nature's beauty at its finest.

I was getting back on track and settling into my usual routine—the one where there was no woman to wake up to and eat breakfast with, or take a walk with, or watch a movie with, or any of those other fulfilling activities we had shared. I was falling back into the place where loneliness was the norm.

Although Caine's loyal company was helping to soothe my melancholy. It was hard to fall into a depression around his goofy playfulness.

Breathing in the fresh morning air, I admired the lush foliage and the views of the blue-grey ocean. A seagull swooped low and we watched him dive and soar.

I looked down at Caine. "What do you think, boy? Ready for another mile?"

Caine answered with a vigorous wag of his tail and we headed off along the pathway, him pausing briefly to sniff at a scent here and there and me using these moments to look out at the vista.

We paused to admire a sea turtle making his way across the grass toward the water. Going anywhere near it was foolish with the probable threat of alligators lurking just out of sight. I kept an excited Caine tight on his leash until it was time to head home.

With my morning walk done, I drove to my beach house and we ate breakfast.

A few hours later, I showered and shaved and the rest of the morning was spent working in my office. Occasionally I was interrupted by my furry friend, who wanted a pat on the head and a game of tug with the chew toy he'd brought me.

I'd gotten him a large bed and enough toys to keep him occupied for hours. The fact that he was housetrained was an extra bonus. His chip had him now registered to me as his new owner.

The dog I'd had as a boy, the same one I had left behind, had been the one reason I had not gotten another pet until now. This felt like Caine had found me right when I needed him.

He would always remind me of Raquel, the two inextricably connected because of us rescuing him in the storm together. Despite nature doing its worst, I was grateful that it had brought this cute guy into my life.

"We need to get you a bath, boy," I told him.

He wagged his tail in agreement.

"I take that as a *yes*." I rubbed my face into his neck, breathing in the scent of dog that brought so much comfort and was rewarded with his licks and snuggles.

When lunch time neared, I left him to play in the walled garden and drove into town.

My instincts had led me back here—the same strip club I had visited the night before. The bored looking bouncer gave a nod to welcome me in. The music bled out to the street and I questioned whether I really wanted to know the truth. Someone was going to get hurt and I was caught in the middle.

The injustice I had endured as a boy had left me with a deep-seated belief that no one should suffer due to another's wrongdoing, so I went inside.

I had lingered on the edge of this sentiment many times, having built The House of Beauregard from nothing. One wrong step could result in its downfall. And what hung in the balance of truth was the happiness of those I loved.

With each step I took, I knew casualties were inevitable.

Breathing through my mouth, I braved the familiar scent of stale beer and the greasy aromas from the lunch menu. The place was quiet compared to last night and the music level was more tolerable. I recognized Tiffany amongst a group of five other women who were eating salads in one of the far booths.

Their curious gazes turned on me when I approached them.

With a bright smile I greeted Tiffany. "Sorry to interrupt your lunch." The last time I'd seen her she'd been half-naked and I'd been in no mood to party.

"Astor, right?" Her accent was pure New Jersey.

I'd missed it before, but then again she'd been sitting on my lap and flirting. She was pretty and the dragon tattoo curling up her right arm hinted at a rebellious edge.

"Do you have a minute?" I asked her.

She threw an amused look at her friends and then smiled at me.

Chapter
THIRTY-SEVEN

I PULLED THE LAST OF MY CLOTHES OUT OF THE CLOSET AND PACKED THEM into my suitcases. With just a week left here I wanted to be ready when the time came to leave. It wasn't so much that I had given up, I had just let go.

Everything was fine. I was doing great and getting through this and as long as I kept busy, I wouldn't think of him.

Him.

The man who had shined a light in my life made me feel alive again. The very man who had rescued me from the agony of divorce and betrayal, and all I had done in return was bring him pain. When I could no longer keep the memories at bay, my chest tightened and I lay on the mattress, rubbing my hand over my heart as though it could ease the ache.

As a form of self-punishment, I relived everything I had done…going to work at Astor's company, letting us become more than friends, letting him fall for me.

I had been given the ultimate chance to love and be loved again and I had ruined it because I'd been obsessed with my perfume.

I should have been moving forward because that was where my

happiness lay. Should have had faith in the here and now and savored every single second with Astor, because every single breath without him felt like an eternity.

I ran my hand over the duvet covering the mattress. This represented what I was willing to sacrifice—or maybe, just maybe, it had shown me what I was able to endure.

Perfume Girl would always be a part of me. I loved this store and had poured my soul into every corner, believing that losing it would break my heart. But causing Astor pain had hurt me worse.

I would never get over Damien's cruelty and the thought of his betrayal clung to every cell in my body, a toxicity I didn't deserve. He was willing to do anything to get me out of the way because the world he'd built would come tumbling down if the truth came out about how he'd gotten hold of his money. Embry probably wouldn't stay with him if they lost their dream house.

I would find my own way to the truth.

I always do.

My thoughts went around and around trying to imagine how it had gone down. Had Damien reached out to Penelope at The House of Beauregard and led her to believe the scent was his to sell? She'd probably paid well for it. Though the fact she hid my ledger in her office hinted that she knew he'd sold it illegally.

If this scandal came out it would taint The House of Beauregard forever. Someone had to take the fall in all of this and that person was me, apparently.

The meeting on Astor's yacht with Penelope a few days ago had offered me the chance to keep Perfume Girl open.

But I couldn't accept her offer.

No amount of money would put this right and I'd refused to sign the nondisclosure agreement, too. Signing it would have proven to Astor that I had set out to manipulate him, that I hadn't cared at all.

Why couldn't I stop thinking about him?

Astor felt as much a part of me as each breath I inhaled, as though our souls had touched and were irrevocably connected in some way.

With most of my personal belongings packed away, I looked around this scant room that had served as my bedroom. There were lonely memories here but also happy ones…like those hours Astor had spent with me in this quiet room after coming all that way to make sure I was safe in the storm.

We were worth fighting for, but I knew he'd be protective of his sister—she was family, after all. But our relationship had burned brighter than any I'd ever had.

With thoughts of him still clouding my mind, I showered and then dressed in a short silver cocktail dress, the kind that would help me blend into the soirée that I was going to gatecrash tonight. This dress was my favorite Stella McCartney, and I felt feminine and sexy in it—and empowered, too.

After curling my hair into bouncing spirals, I applied make-up, going for a fresh look with light mascara and pink lipstick. I wasn't trying to stand out—I just wanted to feel good about myself.

Taking action had always been my thing. Fighting in my own elegant way for what was right and doing everything in my power to protect my reputation. It was hard to be brave and push on, but I had to keep going because I had a goal worth fighting for.

The ringing of the shop's doorbell interrupted my thoughts. I took the steps down toward the front of the store.

When I saw Damien standing on the other side of the door, I hesitated for a beat before relenting and unlocking it.

The man now standing in my shop with his hair disheveled, looking cute in his own bad boy way, meant nothing to me now. Affection had been replaced by scars, and what had once been love was now indifference.

He looked worn down like he'd just finished a long shift at the restaurant. There was no way he'd be commuting to South Beach each day, and the thought that he could be staying somewhere close by until he started his new job sent a shiver of uneasiness up my spine.

"Hey." He gave a nod of greeting.

"What do you want?" *No,* you don't threaten a person and then expect them to be cordial next time you see them.

"Did you sign the realtor forms?"

So much for an apology…

"Over there." I pointed to the glass-fronted case, now empty because of him.

He walked over to the countertop and picked up the envelope, sliding out the contract. "Thanks for signing these. I'll get them to the realtor."

I gave a shrug.

"Okay then, looks like we're all good, right?" he said.

"That depends on how you define good."

He showed a hint of remorse. "Are you going out?"

"Yes."

"You look pretty."

"Damien, you've already proven what kind of man you are. There's no coming back from that."

He broke my gaze and looked around. "It was fun while it lasted."

I gave him a wry smile. "Hope she's worth it."

"She's every man's dream. And I get to have her."

"Let's hope she doesn't turn into every man's worst nightmare."

"You might want to wear something a little less revealing so you're not mistaken for a whore."

"Damien, Embry may be able to detect a hurricane but I've discovered that I have one inside me. That's the best thing to come out of this."

"What are you going to do?"

"I have somewhere to be."

He shrugged. "It's over."

"Is that a statement or a question?"

"Are you going to let it go?"

"There are many things I am letting go of, yes. And there are some things that are worth fighting for. So for me this is a new beginning. "

And it felt so damn good to say it.

He walked toward the door. "Take care, Raquel."

I watched him leave and locked the door behind him, exhaling with relief that he was gone.

I walked over to the countertop and picked up the empty envelope that had held the documents to this place, wondering who would purchase my store. The sale would mean I'd have enough money to keep me afloat for a few months but it still made my heart ache.

Looking around at this bare space without its bottles and décor, its prints stripped from the walls, made me realize that *I* was Perfume Girl, and I could take my talent with me and begin again.

I headed into the lab and with a few clicks opened my safe. I reached in and removed my precious scent in its delicate bottle...a pretty spare glass container. Not as pretty as those Lalique bottles I had once owned. The fact that Astor had walked off with the second one was almost laughable.

My life was a grim tragedy where nothing went right.

I held the bottle up to the light and admired the liquid's luminosity, and then tucked it safely into the bottom of my handbag.

I turned the lights out, grabbed my coat and handbag and headed out the front of the store, knowing I was locking up for one of the last times.

I climbed into my Alfa Romeo and set off for the long drive to South Beach.

The six hour journey gave me time to think, to strategize, to dig deep and try to find forgiveness. I would need all my emotional strength for the next several hours.

You can do this.

When I finally pulled up to The Setai Hotel in South Beach, I felt relief that what lay ahead would soon be over. I left my coat in the car and handed over my keys to the valet. After a quick visit to the bathroom, I was ready to head to the grand party being hosted on the back patio of the hotel.

The House of Beauregard's HR department hadn't taken me off their email list yet so I'd been notified of this party that Astor was hosting. Apparently, he liked to reveal a new perfume in the grandest style and this one was being held in a lavish setting where guests could enjoy the ocean view. Tables had been set for dinner, and in the center on its own table was the showpiece itself—a square bottle resting on a silver platter.

I turned away from it with a jolt of fear. Were they revealing my fragrance tonight? Was the new scent to be hailed as a product of The House of Beauregard my creation? A wave of nausea hit me.

My gaze roamed over the luxurious table settings and the elegantly clad guests. Many of the faces I recognized from work. There were about one hundred people sipping wine and munching on hors d'oeuvres.

And then I saw her…

Penelope was dressed in a white, expensive suit, looking stunning as she laughed with her friends.

When her gaze caught mine it felt like daggers striking my chest. I spun around and quickly made my way to the other side of the crowd, all the while scanning the faces in hopes of finding Astor.

Penelope's glare burned my back until I reached the other side of the patio. I gripped the short glass wall finding the courage to glance back her way. She was talking with someone from the hotel staff—possibly reporting me as a gatecrasher.

My cover was blown and I'd only just gotten here.

With my head bowed so I didn't make eye contact with anyone else, I made a beeline for the stairs that led to the beach. I would wait it out until I saw Astor from this vantage point and then return to the party. They couldn't kick me off the beach as this was public property and from here I could see the guests and hope to catch a glimpse of *him*.

I had to put this right and the bottle in my handbag was my way of proving the truth. I couldn't wait to have my say. I peeled off my heels and felt the warmth of sand beneath my feet as I headed out for a walk to shake off the uneasiness I felt.

Frothy waves kissed the shoreline and as I let the calming warmth roll over my feet I exhaled a breath of courage.

A flash of movement drew my attention and I turned to see a dog sprinting toward me.

Caine closed the gap between us, leaping up and resting his sandy paws on the front of my dress, his big ears flopping and his goofy sweetness shining through and making me smile. I gave his neck a scratch of affection.

Raising my gaze, I saw Astor walking toward us from farther down the shore.

"He's going to get me in trouble," he said. "He's not allowed on the beach."

"I won't tell anyone." I dusted the dry sand off my dress.

He looked concerned. "Is your dress okay?"

"Of course." He looked weary and it made my heart ache, thinking that it had been me who had done this to him.

Astor grabbed Caine's leash. "Sit. Good boy." His gaze met mine. "I'm glad you're here."

I motioned to the party. "Got an invite from HR. You need to take me off their list of employees."

He smiled ruefully. "How are you, Raquel?"

"Fine. You?" I wanted to run into his arms, press my face against his chest and breathe in his scent.

"I've been doing a lot of thinking."

"Oh?"

He gave a shrug. "I need to send you a check for the time you were with us."

"That's very honorable."

"I'm an honorable man."

My gaze snapped to the guests overlooking the glass banister. "Which scent are you showcasing?"

He went to answer and then hesitated.

"Is it mine?"

"Yes."

I swallowed grief in all its cruel forms. It was done, it was over, and any returning to an *us* was impossible.

"Raquel, we need to do what's best for everyone." He let out a deep sigh as he held my gaze.

"I want you to know, Astor. My feelings for you are genuine. I never meant to hurt you. I saw a chance to get my formula back and took it. Not once did I set out to cause you any pain. You and I—"

"You should have told me, Raquel. Just come out and told me what was going on."

"I wasn't sure if you were in on it." I turned my gaze to the water. "As I got to know you I knew you could never do something like this."

"This is what I propose—"

"This is not about money or opportunity. That perfume means more than all of that. To me it's something special. To me it's the essence of—"

"Love."

A wave crashed over my feet but I hardly noticed it.

Him knowing what this scent meant to me made the agony soul-deep. I had poured years of work into trying to recreate that feeling of a happy childhood...before innocence was lost. Until now, nothing I had created had come close.

My affection for Astor had been the final part of the process in helping me intuitively find the rest of the way to a formula that was right. A love that couldn't be.

Tell him, tell him all of it. Let nothing be left unsaid.

"So, you finished the formula?" I asked.

He glanced back at the party. "Which one?"

"I'm talking about mine. I added the final touch, Astor. Whatever you did with it would never make it as profound as what I've come up with."

He looked surprised, as though I was still betraying him.

Tears stung my eyes. "I wasn't ready to create it until now. This perfume reminds me of the purity and innocence of my childhood. It was my time with you that helped me finish it."

Astor stepped closer. "Let me hold you."

I needed to resist this man's charms, but as he wrapped his arms around me and I rested my cheek against his chest, it felt right and I had to surrender to the comfort of his embrace. We fit together so well, and it distressed me to think of all I'd lost and of all that really mattered… *him.*

"What is she doing here?" Penelope snapped from behind us.

We stepped away from each other.

"Penelope," said Astor, "let's take this somewhere quieter away from the—"

"What does she want?" She teetered a little.

"I invited her." Astor gave me a kind smile. "HR sent her the invite at my request."

"What the fuck?" Penelope glared at him. "Why?"

Astor moved closer and reached for her arm to help steady her.

"No." She shoved away his hand and faced me. "This is a private event."

"Penelope, it's fine," he said.

She looked horrified. "What do you mean?"

He reached for her arm again. "You've had too much to drink—"

"Why are you doing this to me?" she asked, her voice faltering.

"Because this is the cologne she left behind for us," Astor said gently, "and she deserves to see it well received."

I stared at him, realizing this event was showcasing the cologne I had created for him and not my stolen work. All the tension left my shoulders with this revelation.

"Why did you accept the invite?" snapped Penelope. "What do you hope to achieve?"

I reached into my handbag and held up the glass bottle. "I never saw your formula. Here is the proof I created the new scent that you say I stole from you. I could never have reverse-engineered it. You know that, Astor."

Penelope glared at me. "I created it—"

"We both know that's not true." Astor turned to face her. "There were two bottles. I found the other one in my desk drawer."

Penelope's smile dissolved when she realized he was talking to her.

"She's manipulating you."

"Don't do this, Penny," he pleaded with her.

"Don't call me that," she said bitterly. "Are you willing to throw it all away for her?"

"Go inside and I'll join you soon, Penelope," he said firmly.

"No, you don't send me away. This company is as much mine as it is yours." She hurried toward me. "Are you after more money?"

I flinched at her closeness. "I didn't accept your offer, remember?"

Astor looked horrified. "Did you pay her to go away?"

"No amount of money is worth losing my integrity," I said.

"That's no proof." She stared at the bottle. "You stole that from us."

"She never saw the formula," Astor verified.

I offered the bottle to him, but he shook his head and smiled at me. I lowered my arm to my side, feeling unsure.

He faced Penelope. "If you created this why didn't you recognize the scent on Tiffany? A professional would recall the scent they masterminded."

"Who the fuck's Tiffany?" she snapped. "The stripper who gave you a lap dance?"

He looked over at me. "There was no lap dance. We merely talked."

"You enjoyed it so much." Penelope cackled. "You got her to dance for me."

Astor looked calm. "I dabbed her with the perfume. Went back to see Tiffany the next day and she told me you didn't notice it. You didn't ask what she was wearing."

"Because there were so many other scents around us—"

"You didn't notice it," he said, staring at her, "because you didn't create it."

My world spun.

I had been exonerated…this was really happening and Astor was really defending me. They continued to argue, but I hardly heard them—I was too overwhelmed by the truth finally being brought to light.

"So you went back to see that stripper you liked?" Penelope

sneered at him. "That's interesting."

"Yes, I did," he replied calmly. "I suspected you had bought the formula off Damien Silver who had stolen it from Raquel. I needed to see proof before I took action."

She looked shocked. "Damien told you that?"

"Penelope, I know he bought a multi-million dollar house on the waterfront." Astor tilted his head. "On a chef's salary."

She glared at him, aghast. "You don't believe me, your own sister?"

He smiled. "Tell me the components. Right now, the base notes."

"We have guests, Astor. People are waiting."

"I'm waiting," he said firmly.

Her lips trembled.

Astor gave her a sympathetic look. "If I made you feel in any way that you had to come up with a new perfume to impress me, I'm sorry."

She held his gaze, mulling over her answer. "You're jealous I invented something that doesn't have your name on it."

"Don't," he said with tenderness.

"I own half the company."

"So what is the issue here?" he asked.

Her breathing became panicked. She looked lost. "I need to repay this debt."

He looked surprised "What debt? There is none."

"Every day I carry around guilt for what happened to us. Every day I see what it did to you."

"It's behind us, Penelope."

She wagged a finger at him. "No, it's not. I carry the burden of what happened with me every day. You know this and you use it against me."

"I never have."

"You're using *her* against me."

"How?" He raised his hands in frustration.

She glared at him. "She's an interloper. She needs to go. She'll push me out."

"I would never," I said.

Penelope stomped closer. "Everything was fine before you came along."

I flinched when she got too close. "I know what happened that night," I said softly. "What *really* happened at Bridgestone when you were children."

Penelope looked at her brother with a panicked expression. "You told her?"

"I told her nothing," said Astor.

"You carry the guilt for something that wasn't your fault," I told them both, and then turned to her. "You saved your mom's life, Penelope."

Astor was shaking his head telling me not to go there. He was protecting her even now. Even after all she had done to him.

"You were very young and very scared," I kept my voice low. "Neither of you deserve to carry the guilt even one more day."

She pressed a hand to her chest. "Who told you? Did you force the truth out of my mother? I know you went there. I know you broke into our home at Bridgestone and talked with her."

"She didn't break in," said Astor.

"My father was going to kill her," snapped Penelope.

"I know," I whispered.

Her tone softened. "You weren't there. You wouldn't understand."

"Oh, I do." I glanced at Astor. "More than you realize."

She looked broken. "I did what had to be done—"

"Stop!" Astor looked stunned at her confession.

I turned to him. "You told them it was you?"

The waves drowned out my voice.

Astor's gaze was locked on Penelope—the sadness and shock he was feeling reflected in his hazel eyes.

My heart broke all over again for him, thinking of the consequences he'd endured for letting everyone think he had pulled the trigger.

"It was a long time ago." I heard the agony in his voice. "It's all forgotten."

"And forgiven," I said, turning to Penelope.

Our gazes rose to the few guests standing on the glass-front balcony above who had apparently overheard Penelope's confession that it had been her who had picked up that gun and pointed it at her father—and fired the fatal shot.

Astor cringed as he looked up at the people staring down at us in silence. Then he moved close to Penelope and wrapped his arm around her. "Let's get you home."

"I got that formula for you," she said. "I wanted you to forgive me. All that they put you through because of me. I wanted to do something good."

"It's over now," he soothed. "Raquel, will you take Caine for me, please?"

I took the leash from him and watched Astor escort his sister away.

Waiting on the beach with Caine, I stared out at the water.

Though a weight had lifted from me, I couldn't rejoice because Astor was in torment. He would have wanted to believe his sister was innocent of stealing my formula. Choosing me in that moment had to have caused him pain. Yet he had done it anyway.

All I could think of was how he had suffered for all those years because his mother hadn't told the authorities the truth. Her haunting words came back to me: *I should have protected him. Should have told them what really happened.*

She knew it wasn't him. And Astor had carried that burden of guilt all of his life to protect his sister. Penelope's burden had been seeing her brother's childhood stolen on that very day and enduring their terrible separation.

I walked Caine up the beach a little ways to put some distance between me and the noise of the crowd. I sat on the sand with him lying next to me and I tried to draw serenity from the hypnotic rhythm of the ocean. My heart bled for Astor and all he had suffered. I felt for

Penelope, too. She may have saved her mother but she had killed some part of herself in the action she'd taken. Her confession felt like the final piece of the puzzle surrounding Astor and I felt an outpouring of love for him.

This was what my heart had told me all along—he was a good, strong man of principle who had sacrificed his life for those he loved.

A pelican swooped low and my gaze followed it until it disappeared from sight.

"May I join you?"

I looked over my shoulder and saw Astor standing a few feet away. A spark of hope glittered in his eyes and he gave me a kind smile. Caine rolled onto his back for him and Astor walked over and knelt down to give him a belly rub.

I patted the sand beside me. "Sit here."

He joined me. "Penelope's friend is taking her home."

"How is she?"

"My sister will be okay."

"I'm sorry."

"I'm sorry you got caught up in our dysfunction." He reached over and began to rub my back as though I was the one who needed comforting.

I shook my head. "All these years…the things you've had to endure in secrecy."

We sat side by side staring out at the ocean as the waves seemingly tried to soothe this moment and all that had gone before.

Astor broke the silence. "I remember it vividly. Still have nightmares about that house. *That* room. If only I had gotten there before Penelope. Maybe I would have merely threatened Dad with the gun. I don't know."

"You made the ultimate sacrifice for your sister."

"There was no other way. It happened so fast. There was no time to think or strategize. I woke up to the sound of my mother screaming. Then she went quiet. I went to check on her. My dad was drunk and staggering over her. He punched her face and she slid from the chair to the floor and lay still. He'd broken her jaw."

I rested a comforting hand on his arm.

He let out a deep breath and continued. "Penelope was eleven. Her bedroom was next to theirs, which was why she got there before me. Mom had gotten the gun to protect all of us. Dad was still shouting at Mom even though she was clearly not going to fight back." Astor sighed heavily, seemingly reliving the anguish of that night. "Penelope picked up the gun and pointed it at him."

In my head, I heard the gun go off, the bullet finding its mark and changing their lives irrevocably. One cruel consequence leading to another until the entire family had been decimated.

From a little way down the beach, music carried from the party— Kate Bush singing "This Woman's Work" as a devastating backdrop.

"The final straw was my dad kicking my mom in the abdomen. It forced Penelope's hand. She feels guilt over it every day and I carry guilt for not knowing whether I would have had the strength to do it. It was the reason I took the blame."

I imagined the chaos, the horror of that night, and my heart softened for Penelope. She had to cope every day with what she had done and live with the knowledge that her brother had paid the price.

Astor turned to look at me. "It's a day of revelations, it seems."

"It is."

"Can I ask you something?"

"Anything."

"How did you know your perfume had ended up at The House of Beauregard?"

"A customer came into my shop and told me she saw you with the bottle. They are unique. I bought two of them in Paris. Her saying she recognized the scent and the bottle was too much of a coincidence to ignore."

"Who?"

"I think her name was Skye?"

Astor looked thoughtful. "Was she a waitress?"

"Yes, she was your waitress at a restaurant in South Beach."

He looked surprised. "I hope you sold her a decent bottle."

"I did."

"One of mine?"

"No, one of mine, actually."

"Well, at least there's one less person wearing *Play With Me.*"

"True."

"Raquel, I want you to know I wasn't going to give up on us. I found that other bottle in my office and literally stood staring at the wall for half an hour. I couldn't believe my stupidity."

"Don't."

"There was so much damage to undo."

I turned my gaze to his. "I suppose we needed time for the dust to settle."

"No, that wasn't it at all. I needed to find a way to put things right for you. I felt dreadful for walking out on you after the storm. I will never forgive myself."

"I need you to forgive me for accepting a job as a ruse."

He bit his lip, looking guilty. "I might have seduced you into it."

"It's good to talk it out."

"Promise me we always will...talk it out, I mean."

I gave a nod. "How's your new cologne being received tonight?"

"Very well. Who knew a fuck-boy scent could arouse such excitement."

I elbowed his ribs and he burst out laughing.

"You look beautiful," he said.

Peeking into my handbag, I asked, "You don't want to smell my perfume?"

"Well, if you put it that way."

"I'm serious."

"Deep down, I suspected you had created it right from the start."

His words stunned me. "How?"

Astor held my gaze. "It reminded me of you."

A soft breeze blew a strand of hair across my face and he reached out and tucked it behind my ear.

Somehow, someway, we had arrived at a life-affirming truth for both of us—one I hoped would set us free. Resting my head on his shoulder, soothed by the rhythmic sound of the waves kissing the shoreline, I exhaled slowly, feeling the remnants of my heartache fade away.

"Raquel," he said, "please come home."

Chapter
THIRTY-EIGHT

I INSISTED ON DRIVING RAQUEL'S ALFA ROMEO TO MY PLACE IN SOUTH Beach. She didn't argue. She'd already driven so far this evening and I wanted her to relax. We had the roof down and the breeze caressing us as we drove along the waterfront with Caine sleeping in the backseat.

This was all I could ever ask for…

To be able to glance over at the woman beside me who threw smiles my way, each one feeling like a gift.

After everything that had happened we had found each other again…after all we'd been through we were still here, together, and I knew this meant we were destined to be.

For the first time since we had been parted I didn't dread walking into my house. With her hand in mine, I led her into what I hoped would one day become her home, too.

I tapped my leg. "C'mon, Caine." Opening the sliding door to the garden, I let him out to play.

"I'll never get tired of the view."

With a lingering look at Raquel, I said, "Neither will I."

She blushed.

"Let me fix you a drink," I said, inviting her into the kitchen.

I wanted to tear her clothes off and ravish her in the hallway, but after the tumultuous evening we'd both had I wanted her feeling safe. As I uncorked the bottle of wine, she walked over to the dining room table and examined the ten glass bottles that marketing and I had developed for our new cologne—the same one born from Raquel's genius mind.

"Have you come up with a name yet?" She turned one of the glass bottles in her hand.

"You like that one?"

She gave a nod. "It's gorgeous."

"Then that's the bottle." I smiled at the design she was holding.

It was square and had a masculine edge, its stopper adding the style and class we'd talked about.

"Don't let me influence you."

"Raquel, you influence me in all I do." Every inhalation, from the one I took right now back to the day I had first met her. "We have to work on our marketing strategy. I need your input."

"So you're not calling it *Fuck-Boy* cologne, then?"

"Maybe I will." I grinned.

She stared at the bottle in her hand. "I'm thinking something like this for the campaign: A cologne that provides a glimpse into the world of our beloved alphas—the men we adore who play hard but also love hard. The kind of man who isn't afraid to explore new territories. The professional who passionately leads in their chosen field. The scent that attracts The One."

"Impressive."

"Your secret's out, Astor."

I poured the wine into two tall-stemmed glasses. "You've always seen me, Raquel. *Me.*"

"And I love all I see."

"Do you have it?" I glanced at her handbag.

"Mine?" Raquel reached into her bag and removed a small glass bottle, then handed it over to me. "Here."

I took it from her and uncorked the bottle to breathe in the delicate scent. "You added wild roses."

She looked impressed. "From Cornwall. What do you think?"

"Well, a scent is best appreciated on skin."

She held out her arm to me.

"Wrist is too obvious."

"Oh?"

"Yes, for this experiment I'm going to need you naked."

Raquel dragged her bottom lip along her teeth and unzipped her dress, stepping out of it and letting it pool at her feet. She stood there looking stunning in her lacy underwear with her hair curling over her shoulders.

"Where would you like to dab it?" she asked.

"I'm considering. Might need some time to think this through." My gaze drank her in...her beauty, her elegance and her serenity.

She reached around her back and unhooked her bra. It slid off her arms to the floor.

"Seems a reasonable place," I agreed, stepping forward. I dabbed some of the perfume between her breasts. Leaning in, I appreciated her tenderness, her compassion and, as the notes lifted from her skin, her remarkable scent of love.

Carefully, I placed the bottle on the table and then reached for Raquel, cupping her face and leaning in to press my lips to hers, tasting her mouth, kissing her gently, passionately, revering her beauty.

Raquel reached for the new bottle of cologne. "Your turn."

She dabbed some onto her finger and watched me unbutton my shirt before touching the amber liquid to my chest, leaning forward to breathe in the musky leather and spice.

"It's effective." Her fingers reached for my zipper and released me from my pants. "It makes me want to do this." She knelt before me.

"Well, this is market testing at its best."

"Thought you'd like it."

"Oh, God, Raquel, that's..."

She drew me into her mouth, sucking and lapping and sending

shudders of pleasure though me.

I didn't want to be that man anymore, the one who wooed a beautiful woman only to turn away when they wanted more. *This time* it was me wanting more, needing more, and needing her more than the air I breathed. Raquel was the most important woman in my life and I didn't want what we had to ever end. I had to somehow convey what she meant to me.

Lifting her up, I sat her on the edge of the table and nudged her backwards, tearing off her panties. I was hungry for her, desperate to taste her and make her arch her back with pleasure.

I was gone completely, lost in her and never wanting to find my way back. Not even my past could have kept me away from her—this was me claiming my lover and asking for forgiveness for all I had put her through.

I buried my face between her thighs, possessively taking her with my mouth, but lavishing her with all this affection wasn't enough…it would never be enough.

She shivered beneath me. "Slow down."

"This is slow," I teased. "This is me claiming what is mine."

"Oh, God, the things you say." She arched her back. "I want to come with you inside me."

"For you, anything," I whispered. I rose up and stood between her legs, and as she lay back on the table I slid inside her, burying myself deep and feeling her muscles clenching. I leaned forward to hold her hands and weave my fingers through hers.

This was purity, our brilliant connection that was brighter than the sun. This was the song poets chased after, two hearts becoming one. Raquel called out my name and I whispered hers, still awestruck that she was finally mine.

Epilogue

One year later…

I<small>T WAS THE WAY THE GLASS BOTTLES LINING THE SHELVES REFLECTED THE</small> myriad shards of light that mesmerized me, the soft hues glinting off the sunlight that streamed in through the window, the liquids within promising to kiss the soul and then set it free.

Each fragrance delivering an experience that would last until the end of the day, some well into the night.

I adored the décor…the prints on the walls, the glass-fronted display cabinet filled with even more bottles and the red chaise lounge providing a cozy seat for customers as they savored the tranquility around them, listening to classical music playing as a backdrop to a luxurious moment of self-care.

This is what Perfume Girl meant to me—a safe refuge where women brought their girlfriends, their mothers or sisters, or a place they visited alone where they could steal a few moments for themselves.

I turned to look up at the words elegantly painted along the back wall:

Every romance has a scent.

At the end of this blissful business day I marveled at how busy we had been and thanked my lucky stars for this incredible real estate on Espanola Way in South Beach, with its generous foot traffic and endless stream of tourists who enjoyed spoiling themselves in my store.

All this was thanks to one man—the handsome gentleman who was peering through my glass window wearing a generous grin.

Astor mouthed. "I have it!"

Bursting with excitement, I rounded the display cabinet and hurried to the door, meeting him halfway. He stepped inside the store and lifted me up, spinning me around in a hug as I laughed with joy.

"I missed you." He nuzzled my neck.

"Missed you, too." We'd parted at breakfast and though I loved every second of being here I had also counted down the minutes until I saw him again.

He looked around and smiled. "How was today?"

"Busier than I ever was in Dunedin."

"That's great. How's the new staff working out?"

"Fine. Emma's just left. She's a great fit."

"Allow me." He spun the sign on the door to CLOSED and with a click of the lock he sealed us in.

Astor walked me backward until my body hit the countertop and then lifted me onto it, easing between my legs.

"People will see." I pointed to the window.

"Let them watch me worshipping my fiancée."

Resting my head on his shoulder, I brought up my hand and admired my sapphire engagement ring, which brought back happy memories of us in Havana a few months ago. We had danced all night and then he'd gotten down on one knee and proposed with this exquisite stone encased in a gold band.

Saying *yes* had been easy.

All I had gone through, all the loss and all the pain had led me to him. And now, as I looked back, I had no regrets…only gratitude that I had kept my faith in myself and the world, believing everything would work out fine.

This was more than fine. These were my dreams coming true, too wonderful to believe at times. I'd been blessed with a devastatingly charming, funny, kind fiancé whose constant romantic texts throughout the day brought me happiness.

He laughed as he reached into his pocket. "I almost forgot."

He placed the luminous crystal bottle with its clear liquid on the counter and his gaze rose to study me. "What do you think?"

I reached for the cut glass bottle and examined it, blinking in amazement at its shape, the silver base and the way the light caught the perfume within. "It's...."

"You like it?"

"Astor, it's incredible. It's more than I could ever have imagined."

"We need something special for this one," he said. "I brought in a glass designer and he emphasized the way the formula attracts and then deflects light."

Contentment flushed my cheeks.

"It suits it so well." He reached for the bottle and held it up. "I love the name."

"*Lumière.*" As I spoke the word, waves of happiness flooded into me. Another dream was coming true in the most wonderful way.

"More good news," he said. "*Lumière* has been picked up by the major department stores and will go on sale in a matter of months." He reached for my hand. "I thought you might like to attend the advertising meetings so we can come up with an inspiring promotion."

"I would love that."

He kissed my wrist. "All that's left is to celebrate. I booked us a table at Triple. Hungry?"

"Starving."

He reached for the bottle and opened the glass lid, dabbing a drop on his finger. "I want you wearing it."

Tilting my head, I felt his forefinger trailing down my throat and then he leaned in to sniff me. "Heaven on earth," he whispered.

"You're my heaven on earth, Astor Beauregard."

A flash of happiness spread across his face. "Marry me."

"You already asked me, remember?"

"So I did."

"The answer will always be yes, Astor."

"How did I get so lucky?"

"I'm the lucky one." I let my gaze wander around the store. "Thank you for making this happen."

"You made it happen, Raquel. This is all you."

I gave his arm a gentle squeeze. "How's your sister?"

"She's doing great. Mom, too. She's agreed to sell the house."

"Oh, that's wonderful news."

"Mom's excited to find somewhere smaller and she's even decided to take up golf!"

"That will be so good for her."

"Thank you, Raquel, for everything you've done for us."

"I feel the same way." I cupped his face. "This store is perfect."

"My perfume girl is perfect."

I wrapped my arms around him, feeling true peace from the love we had found together.

With the store securely shut and the state-of the-art alarm system set, we drove to Triple, sharing our enthusiasm for the meal ahead—especially the lobster bisque the restaurant was famed for, and its seafood ravioli, ready to be savored with a tall glass of white wine. We were shown to our table and didn't even need to look at the menus. This was one of Astor's favorite restaurants.

We talked as we waited for our server to take our order. Astor told me about all he'd been up to and I gave him the details of my routine, and when he reached over the table to hold my hand, it was a perfect ending to our day.

He flinched when his phone pinged, then pulled it out and stared at the screen.

"What's wrong?" I asked.

"It's happening."

"What?" My heart raced at seeing his conflicted expression.

Then he gave me a wide grin. "The sea turtles are hatching."

I got to my feet in a rush. "What are we waiting for? Let's go!"

He threw an apologetic wave to the concierge, then grabbed hold of my hand and we hurried out onto the curb.

"Every day I'm reminded how perfect you are for me," he said, and then frowned when he noticed the expression on my face. "What's wrong, Raquel?"

I pointed to the bee resting on the windshield of our car. Astor gave a nod, reaching around and gently cupping the bee in his palm.

He walked a few steps and opened his hand to set it free. "There you go, little guy."

We watched it fly away.

When Astor returned to my side, I rested my head against his chest.

"You okay?" he asked.

"With you I am, yes."

"This is my job, Raquel, to protect you from the beasties no matter what size they are."

"And my job is to love you so much that I make up for everything you've been through."

He pulled me into a tighter hug. "You already have, Mrs. Beauregard." He tilted his head. "Just trying it out on you."

"It sounds perfect."

"You're perfect, Raquel, and I'm crazy in love with you."

My sigh was wistful. "I love you so much, Astor. You make me so happy." A few moments later, I gasped and looked up at him. "We have turtles to save."

Within twenty minutes, Astor and I were walking across the sand heading toward the conservation team. The gang waved when they saw us.

Astor beamed at me. "Look at the moon."

My gaze rose, taking in the brightness of the light reflecting off it and the way it beckoned to us so brilliantly.

"Lumière," he whispered. *"*A light that leads the way to freedom.*"*

This was wisdom…to live in the present moment and be the best version of myself, showing gratitude for all I had been blessed with.

With our fingers entwined, Astor led me farther down the golden sandy beach. I knew the light I had been searching for all my life was *him.*

And I wanted to share this great love with the whole world in every conceivable way.

Acknowledgments

Dearest Aunty Marg, this one's for you. Thank you for sharing stories of Nan and Mom and keeping their memories alive.

I'm the luckiest girl in the world to have such a wonderful group of friends who support my love of writing. I never take this for granted. It means I can throw myself into my passion whole-heartedly.

Thank you to my rock star agent Kimberly Whalen. Your wisdom and strength are a gift I value deeply. Look at what we have on its way!

To my dear friends Bob Lange and Marko Kuo, the best entertainment lawyers a girl could have, thank you for all you do!

Peter Katz, I'm eternally grateful for your support and generosity. You go above and beyond, and I can't thank you enough.

To Debra Presley and Drue Hoffman at Buoni Amici Press PR who represent me in all things when it comes to social media and are constantly offering the best advice. I couldn't do this without you both. From the quality of what you do as publicists to your generosity of spirit, you are the best team an author could have.

Najla Qamber, you blew me away with the cover art for *Perfume Girl*. I am a fan for life. I can't wait to see what else you come up with! Stacey Blake, you again made my book look so pretty with the formatting. I am always wowed with what you do.

Thank you to my incredible P.A. Karen Hulseman who kindly joined me with this book release to share news of *Perfume Girl*. Your expertise and drive are inspiring.

My beloved editor Debbie Kuhn, thank you for lending your talent and skill to ensure my readers enjoy a lovely read. And thank you for loving my characters as much as I do.

Lauren Luman, you give your time and support generously to me and so many other authors. You're a bright light in our romance community. Thank you for all you do. You welcome new readers and make others feel at home in our online groups.

To my dear friends Hazel Godwin and Heather Amber Pollock, I count myself lucky to know you both and can't wait for the day when I get to give you two a hug of thanks. Thank you to for Pam Stack, my dynamic producer on The Romance Show podcast and giving me the opportunity to reach out to authors and share their love of storytelling with the world! A shout out to the amazing Lydia Rella. Thank you for all you do for me and other authors!

To Melissa Saneholtz and Tracey Suppo over at Book + Main. Your site is everything we romance readers have been waiting for. Thank you for supporting us the way you do and sharing your platform. Thank you for all you have done for *Perfume Girl!*

My deepest gratitude as always to the generosity of all the bloggers and reviewers who continue to share news of my books. It's because of all of you that our stories find readers. For that I am forever grateful.

I'm waving at you my darling Romance Lounge members on Facebook who cheer me on and are always there with a kind word or a crazy cute GIF. I love the way you support each other. The words I write are always for you.

Thank you to my parents and my beloved sisters Liz and Mand. Having a family who believe in me is priceless.

Brad, thank you for always being there and sharing my dream and allowing me to be part of yours. This journey would not be what it is without you. You encourage me to give my best and inspire me creatively.

And to my readers, you give your time and trust when you read one of my novels and for that I am eternally grateful.

Also from
VANESSA FEWINGS

Available now

THE ENTHRALL SESSIONS:

ENTHRALL
ENTHRALL HER
ENTHRALL HIM
CAMERON'S CONTROL
CAMERON'S CONTRACT
RICHARD'S REIGN
ENTHRALL SECRETS
ENTHRALL CLIMAX

And

THE ICON TRILOGY from Harlequin:

THE CHASE
THE GAME
THE PRIZE

NEW

Coming in 2019
from bestselling author Vanessa Fewings

PERVADE LONDON

A dark, edgy romance series about true power and everyone it
touches.

for more info

vanessafewings.com

*Vanessa is also on Instagram, Twitter, Facebook, BookBub, and Pinterest
@vanessafewings*

*For those wanting to chat more with Vanessa,
visit the Romance Lounge on Facebook.*

CPSIA information can be obtained
at www.ICGtesting.com
Printed in the USA
LVHW042104121218
600231LV00002B/196/P